Joyce Carol Oates is the author of twenty novels and many volumes of short stories, poems, essays and plays. She has been honoured by awards from the Guggenheim Foundation, the National Institute of Arts and Letters, the Lotus Club, and by a National Book Award for Fiction. She is a three-time winner of the Continuing Achievement Award in the O. Henry Award Prize Stories series. Ms Oates is a member of the American Academy and Institute of Arts and Letters. She lives in Princeton, New Jersey, where she is The Roger S. Berlind Distinguished Professor in the Humanities at Princeton University.

JOYCE CAROL OATES

Because It Is Bitter, and Because It Is My Heart

PICADOR

PUBLISHED BY PAN BOOKS

First published in Great Britain in 1991 by Macmillan London Limited
This Picador edition published 1992 by Pan Books Ltd,
a division of Pan Macmillan Publishers Limited
Cavaye Place London SW10 9PG
and Basingstoke

Associated companies throughout the world

ISBN 0 330 31730 X

3 5 7 9 8 6 4 2

A CIP catalogue record for this book is available from the British Library

Printed in England by Cox & Wyman Ltd, Reading, Berkshire

In Memoriam
R.C.

CONTENTS

PART ONE

The Body

1

"Little Red" Garlock, sixteen years old, skull smashed soft as a rotted pumpkin and body dumped into the Cassadaga River near the foot of Pitt Street, must not have sunk as he'd been intended to sink, or floated as far. As the morning mist begins to lift from the river a solitary fisherman sights him, or the body he has become, trapped and bobbing frantically in pilings about thirty feet offshore. It's the buglelike cries of gulls that alert the fisherman—gulls with wide gunmetal-gray wings, dazzling snowy heads and tail feathers, dangling pink legs like something incompletely hatched. The kind you think might be a beautiful bird until you get up close.

Hammond, New York, Waukesha County, sixty miles south of Lake Ontario, is a city of thirty-five thousand inhabitants, a place of Ice Age terrain, saw-notched ridges, hills steep as attic steps. As it approaches the river valley the land gives a sense of hunching down, preparing for a drop. There are hills in Hammond where drivers are obliged to park their vehicles with the front wheels turned sharp against the curb and the emergency brake on full force and other hills where no one in his right mind would park at all. Fog and mists appear to ooze upward out of the earth, concentrating in the low-lying areas. This morning, April 3, 1956, 8 A.M., the mist above the river is chill and clammy as the interior of another's mouth.

The fisherman, elderly, stands with his gear on a six-foot concrete abutment above the choppy water, staring, as the shreds of mist shift and eddy and coil about, teasing the eye.

A bundle of rags, maybe.

Dead dog or sheep carcass. He's seen them before.

A freighter passes out in the ship channel bound for the lakes and there's a damp yeasty-tasting wind from the factories upriver and the chalk-colored chimneys of Diamond Chemicals & Plastics on the farther shore and a part of the fisherman's brain is rehearsing what he will be telling others for the remainder of his life . . . how he'd come out to fish, he hadn't come for trouble. Fishing this stretch of the Cassadaga below the railroad yards and close by the colored section of town, fishing to fill the long hours of the morning, small enough pleasure, God knows. And now this morning this terrible thing. This thing floating in the water amid the river debris and froth with a look delicate as lace, and the goddamned gulls, the garbage birds, flapping and struggling above it. Even before he understands what it is, the head, the human head, the upside-down face, a hand, outstretched fingers, arm caught in a snarl of rusted cables, even before the sight of it is unmistakable, his bowels begin to clench, he feels the first stabs of panic. For like calls out to like, in the extremity of terror.

He snatches up a loose chunk of concrete and pitches it at the gulls. "Get out of there! Get! *Get!*" he shouts. "Filthy bastard *things!*"

It could be his own son there, he's thinking. Though his own son is a grown man living five hundred miles away and would bear no resemblance to that body at all.

* * *

4

In Neeley's Diner the proprietor Al Neeley calls police headquarters to report the body in the river, reading off the emergency numbers from a grimy card affixed to the wall and dialing as if this is the sort of thing he does all the time. But his deep voice quivers a little: "Hello? Police? We need some help down here, there's a dead body in the river off Pitt Street." This time of morning, the diner is crowded with customers. All the stools at the counter are taken. Most of the customers are men in work clothes but some are older men, white-haired, solitary, like the fisherman, time on their hands. Two young nurses from Hammond General are having coffee together. The fisherman is being asked questions: stammering as he tells them what he saw, first time in his life he'd seen a *human being* in the Cassadaga, he can't seem to catch his breath from hurrying here and there's a roaring in his ears and Neeley's voice rises impatiently: "White, or colored? The dead man."

The fisherman blinks dazedly, as if for an instant he doesn't know the answer. But of course he does.

"White."

By 8:30 A.M. the sky above the river is blue as washed glass, rippled with vertical wisps of cloud. At the foot of Pitt Street a small crowd has gathered to watch a police rescue squad lift the body from the river. It's a delicate procedure, involving a hook; not raw flesh but something neutral like clothing must be snagged. If a body has been in the water for some time the hook sinks into flesh like soft bread dough packed onto bone.

A human body being pried out of a knot of fraying cables and river filth is a powerful sight. All vision is narrowed to a tunnel. You can't look anywhere else.

"This isn't any show!" Patrolmen are warning people off.

In the water, rocked by the waves, are three police officers in an outboard motorboat marked HAMMOND POLICE DEPT. At the end of the concrete abutment another officer stands calling instructions through a bullhorn no one on shore can hear clearly.

There's an ambulance waiting, motor running.

There's a vehicle from the Hammond Fire Department.

A growing crowd, even children. Teenagers on their way to school. Fifty yards off, in a weedy lot just below the Northern Pacific railroad yard, a half dozen Negroes stand contemplating the scene . . . but don't come any closer.

A police photographer stands on the abutment, one foot on a post, taking photographs.

"Who is it?"

"What happened?"

"Jesus—is that a *body?*"

"Somebody drowned?"

There is a collective sigh as the body is lifted toward the boat—but then it snags on something and falls back. Little Red was a husky boy with a heavy head and thighs like hams, and his lips in the rigor of death are stretched in a leering smile. He gives the impression of resisting these many hands without being able to see them.

Then he's in the boat. The body's in the boat.

Then on shore. A dead weight leaking filthy river water.

Then it's being lowered onto a stretcher by three grim-faced uniformed men and covered with a khaki-colored blanket.

To shield it from so many eyes.

A Dixie cup, very white, is blown across a stretch of pebbly ground. Up on the access road, a car radio is playing a snatch of bright brassy music—somebody shouts for it to be turned off. A photographer for the Hammond *Chronicle,* hair slicked back against the curve of his skull, plastic raincoat flapping around his legs, is taking pictures one after another after another . . . as if the fact of a body, a body where no body is supposed to be, has made the day special.

Underfoot is coarse large-grained sand that has blotted up all color. Chips of mica glint in it like millions of tiny eyes.

"Oh, my God—who *is* it?"

There are two Garlocks waiting to make the identification and to ride off sobbing with the corpse.

Not Little Red's mother, who is known to be sickly and erratic in her behavior—"not right in her head"—and not Little Red's father, who isn't living with the family on Gowanda Street though he is known to be in Hammond somewhere. Instead it's Little Red's older brother Morton, married, with small children of his own, and a nineteen-year-old woman named Edith, one of Little Red's young aunts or cousins—the Garlock household, or households, contains many relatives.

It's that kind of family: the father, Vernon, brought some of them up from West Virginia to do defense work in Hammond, back in the early forties, and other Garlocks followed. And they've had babies since—lots of babies.

Little Red: must have been five feet eleven, one hundred eighty-five pounds, thick neck and thick arms and shoulders, fatty muscle, small glittery slate-colored eyes and a sly moist smile learned from the movies . . . and his hair wasn't red, not since he'd been a baby. He wasn't retarded, but slow-seeming as if on purpose, to antagonize, to tease and worry.

His real name is Patrick Wesley. This name he'll be identified by, properly, beneath an old photograph of him that will appear on the front page of the next edition of the *Chronicle*.

Morton Garlock and Edith Garlock are crouched over the dead boy. The crowd is very still, listening to their sounds: the words are impossible to make out, but the sounds are unmistakable.

Out in the ship channel, a freighter passes slowly, immense washes of water behind, rocking and shuddering against the pilings.

The gulls keep their distance.

The night before, Little Red hadn't shown up at the house on Gowanda. No one reported him missing because no one had thought of him as missing exactly . . . he stayed out sometimes all night; he was hard to manage . . . and it's that kind of household, the Garlocks, nine children, different-age children, and other relatives, and their wives or husbands or lovers, spilling over into two or three rented places so no one is ever certain of another's whereabouts unless they are together in the same room. Poor Mrs. Garlock has been beaten so often . . . the police don't trouble to go down there any more; it's risking your life, to set foot in that door . . . she's a vacant-eyed worn-out woman of forty whom neighbors sometimes find sleeping in their cars parked at the curb or, wrapped in a blanket, in their garages or back yards. She wouldn't know that Little Red was missing, Morton Garlock is telling police, she'd be thinking . . . if she was thinking . . . he was in school, this time of day.

Though Little Red had quit school on the day he'd turned sixteen.

The newspaper photographer continues to clamber about taking pictures. In the next edition half the front page will be given over to the local murder: sixteen-year-old boy, corpse in the water between six and nine hours, probable cause of death multiple blows to the head by a blunt instrument or a rock. A photograph of the stricken Garlocks and a photograph of the crowd of spectators . . . like clumsy mourners at a funeral, not knowing exactly who is being mourned or why they are there.

By the time the body is borne away in one of the official vehicles, the Negroes watching up in the railroad yard have vanished.

There remains nothing to be seen. But people stand around, vague and waiting. For as the wind picks up, and the sunshine is chill and veiled and gritty-tasting, there is a slow realization that this will be an ordinary day after all . . . an ordinary weekday.

Tuesday. A long long stretch ahead.

There's Officer Furlong, Eddy Furlong, from upper Pitt Street himself, talking with some neighborhood men. Haugen, Lukacs, McDermott . . . they all know Vernon Garlock, he's the kind of guy you shake your head over, a hard drinker, hot-tempered, always in some sort of trouble or other . . . and his kids, his older boys especially, everyone knows what they're like.

("White trash," some Hammond residents might say, but not these: these are neighborhood people whose judgments are more subtly calibrated.)

"Better not speak ill of the dead."

8

"Yah. Any damn dead."

They're working their way toward mirthful grimaces. But they keep their voices low, lowered.

Furlong clears his throat, tries not to sound official, merely curious. "Any of you guys know anything? I mean this . . . that happened . . . any idea what's behind it? Who?"

The men shake their heads.

Somberly, not quickly, they shake their heads.

There's a smell here like rotting fish. A shiver walks over them. When they leave here, the waterfront at the foot of Pitt Street, when they go off to work, and later back home, how will they be able to explain *what it's like* to someone not here?

Haugen shudders. "Hell of a thing. Some people . . ."

". . . the most shitty luck."

"Poor Vernon."

"Poor *her*."

"Who's gonna tell her? The police find the right people for that?"

And a shiver walks over them another time.

As they break up to leave, Eddy Furlong feels a shy touch at his wrist, so light, so tentative, he'd almost not need to notice.

It's one of the high school girls. Or maybe she's younger.

About fourteen years old, with a delicately boned face, large eyes, a squinty slitted look to them like minnows darting in shallow water. Furlong almost recognizes her . . . almost has the name. He could not say is she pretty, that fair pale lightly freckled skin with a waxy sheen, a look cold and stricken as if, so close to death, she's lost her creaturely warmth.

A scared little girl. Telling him something so faint and rushed Furlong can hardly hear.

"Hon? Speak up, please." Furlong is twenty-nine years old, not tall but broad in the shoulders, sandy wavy hair, married, a father, thinks well of himself . . . he knows this girl, or knows the parents, just can't say the name.

The girl's hair is whipping in the wind. She glances over her

9

shoulder to where, up on the access road, her girlfriend is talking with some boys, dawdling, lighting cigarettes and tossing the matches in the air . . . it's a school morning and aren't those kids almost late for school? Or don't they give a damn? This being a special event, seeing some poor bastard hauled from the river, his face mashed like raw meat and bloody sockets where there'd been eyes. Furlong is waiting for those kids to laugh and clown around so he can tell them get on away from here, and fast.

He's prepared. He's a quick, angry man when it's needed.

"About what happened . . . I think I know . . . I mean, I have an idea . . . how it might have . . ."

"Yah? What? Speak up, hon."

He stares at her and sees those deep shadow crescents under her eyes. A look that's adult and sad.

Anyone who can't sleep has time for a lot of thinking.

Officer Furlong is observed talking at the edge of the cordoned-off area with a girl who hugs her schoolbooks to her flat chest as if they're giving her warmth. She's telling him something earnest he has to stoop to hear, though he isn't writing anything down—just listening.

The girl has a head of bushy frizzy hair—her best feature, the women say—that's so fair a brown it looks silver, ablaze in the sun, shot with atoms of fiery light. Her eyes are a strange green-gray, pellucid as glass marbles, with a look of transparency; she knows to stand tall and look an adult candidly in the face. As she speaks, her forehead is crisscrossed with tiny lines. She is wearing a thin cloth coat, navy blue, nothing on her head, no gloves, and her shoulders are high and narrow and taut as she hugs her books and a plastic purse against her chest. Furlong leans close, nodding, as she tells him what she knows: that the Garlock boy was in trouble with motorcyclists from out of town . . . those bikers who race on the dirt track at Oldwick and come into Hammond weekends, drinking, getting into fights in the east end, riding their big Harley-Davidsons up and down the hilly streets . . . of course the Hammond police know these troublemakers well, and Furlong is grim and brisk and absorbed, nodding as the girl speaks. "I didn't know him and I don't know anyone in the family, it's just something I heard . . . he threw a rock at a motorcycle and almost caused an accident and ran off but they found out who he was and came back looking for him," she says. Her voice is shy and halting and comes to a stop altogether. Furlong asks when did this happen and she shakes her head; she doesn't know.

"I . . . I'd be happy if you didn't tell anyone I was the one who told you this," she says.

"Right," says Furlong. "What's your name, miss?"

"Iris."

"Iris what?"

"Courtney."

"You related to Duke Courtney, maybe? Persia?"

"They're . . . my parents."

At this, Furlong smiles. Deep and wide. A smile so quick, like sun piercing cloud, you feel the force of being that engenders it—absence palpable as any presence.

From this, the girl backs off.

Furlong longs to ask her more questions but decides against it, she looks so frightened. He calls after her, "Tell your father and mother Eddy Furlong says hello, will you?" and she nods yes, she will.

He stands, hands on his hips, right hand resting lightly on the polished wooden grip of his pistol, and watches the girl hurry away to catch up with her friends. If they are her friends. As she climbs to the road she stumbles . . . or maybe she's overcome with a sudden spell of faint-headedness . . . but she recovers almost at once and keeps on. And doesn't look back.

By late morning the waterfront area at the foot of Pitt Street is deserted. Police have cordoned off a thirty-foot stretch of shore: DO NOT CROSS. BY ORDER OF HAMMOND POLICE DEPT.

There are scattered fishermen on the far side of the river, most

11

of them Negroes, sitting on their customary rocks, girders, slabs of concrete. But none on this side, within the range of all that's visible from the foot of Pitt Street.

The wide-winged gulls have returned, circling in the gusty air, dipping, dropping, picking in the debris, emitting their high-pitched bugle cries. Out in the ship channel a barge with the smudged white letters UNION PACIFIC ORE moves slowly from east to west. The morning shifts to midday, and the ridge-rippled sky turns opaque, the color of lard. Against the pilings and the crumbling abutment and the ravaged shore the waves slap, slap, slap . . . like the pulse of a dream that belongs to no one, no consciousness, thus can never yield its secrets.

2

"Miss? Please, miss? Ma'am, help me."

Persia Courtney hasn't seen the woman cowering in the drugstore doorway at the corner of East Avenue and Holland until with no warning the woman steps out blindly into her path and there's the shock of a collision. And Persia is the one to cry, "Oh—I'm sorry!" and the one to feel, in her confusion, a moment's teeth-jarring pain.

But the woman hardly notices. She has her fingers closed tight around Persia's wrist. A hand like a chicken claw, or that's the way it feels; Persia stares and sees it's a normal hand, or nearly: a thin film of dirt, a scattering of scabs and sores, but a worn-smooth gold wedding band on the proper finger and bright crimson nail polish just beginning to chip. The woman's hair is stiff broom sage and she is wearing a soiled cotton housedress. "Please, miss, don't scorn me . . . please help me," she begs. Her voice is a low hoarse scraping

13

sound like steel wool scouring a pan, but Persia can recognize the accent: hillbilly.

It is Vernon Garlock's wife. Persia can't think of her name for a moment, then remembers: Vesta. "Vesta Garlock?"

"There's one of them following me, miss. I can't get home."

"What?"

"A nigra. Following me. I can't get home."

"A what?"

"*Nigra.*"

The word is an exasperated half scream in Persia's ear.

Vesta Garlock is in her mid or late thirties so far as Persia knows, but the poor woman looks twenty years older. Her skin is tallow-colored, bruised and blotched. There's a fang-sized gap where one of her front teeth is missing—from a blow, as neighborhood rumor has it, of her hot-tempered husband's. And her eyes. Those eyes. Wild as a horse's eyes that's snorting and pawing in his stall so that the groom is obliged to bring out the blindfold. I was scared to look into those eyes! Persia will say.

The woman is pleading, whining. "You're so beautiful, miss . . . *you* go first. Please. *You* walk with me, huh? Then they won't pay no attention to *me*. Won't go after *me*, then."

"I don't see any 'nigra' that's following you," Persia says, looking up and down the street. "Maybe you're imagining things."

"Ma'am, just don't leave me!"

"I see some *Negroes* . . . who are not looking at us. I see that brown-skinned lady up ahead, with the baby stroller . . . *she* surely isn't looking at us." Persia speaks sharply, impatiently; she isn't the kind of person to suffer fools gladly. Nor is she the kind of person who feels much sympathy for crazy folk like Vernon Garlock's wife, whose people shouldn't let her wander around loose; Persia thinks maybe these crazy folk bring it all on themselves, their hard luck, even the way they look, blotched skin and missing teeth.

She'd walk off, polite but stiff, but the woman's damp wild eyes are showing a rim of white above the iris, and she's gripping Persia's arm. "Please, ma'am, for Jesus' sake, then—*don't leave me to the nigras.*"

14

Wouldn't it be comical if it wasn't so sad: this beat-up hag imagining any man in his right mind, black or white or whatever, would look with lust upon *her*.

Persia says with a sigh, "Oh, all right! Where do you want to go? Oh, I guess I know where you live: a ways down Gowanda Street? By the Loblaw's?"

Mrs. Garlock grunts an eager assent. She doesn't seem to know the name of her street; like the neighborhood dogs she makes her way around by unerring instinct. But Loblaw's Groceries is a landmark.

So they set off in that direction, no more than three blocks out of Persia's way, Persia conscious of people on the street staring at them. Staring at Vesta Garlock, and staring at *her*. Persia Courtney with her gorgeous red-blond hair, "strawberry" blond as it's called, her black and white polka-dot silk dress, her spike-heeled black patent leather pumps . . . the pretty outfit she wears in her position (Persia does not refer to it as a "job") as hostess at Lambert's Tea Room downtown. Persia Courtney, wife of Duke Courtney, and the hillbilly Garlock woman, who is ranting in her ear about nigras: their animal ways, the "mark of Satan" on their foreheads. Why the other day, Mrs. Garlock says, this big black buck poked her toes in the park where she'd fallen asleep on the grass . . . another time, right upstairs in her bedroom, changing Dolly's baby's diaper, she looks up and sees in the mirror a wicked black face like the devil himself. And the way they send their thoughts to you . . . so it's impossible you can't know what they're thinking. And what they'd like to do to you.

"Down home we don't hardly have them at all," Mrs. Garlock says excitedly, "or if we do, they keep to themselves. You can go for miles and miles, I swear, all the way across the state . . . never see a nigra face. *Not a one*."

Persia says, "Me, I'm crazy for Billy Eckstine. I'd drive across the state, to hear *him* sing."

Mrs. Garlock isn't listening. She's hanging on to Persia like a child both scared and willful.

Persia sniffs and sighs. She is good-hearted enough to see the

15

humor in all this. Such episodes can be transformed into one of her stories, to be told to Duke and their little girl that evening. You won't believe what happened to me, on the way home! You won't be*lieve*, you two, how come I'm late!

And Duke Courtney will gaze at her with that look of . . . that melting prideful this-beautiful-girl-is-my-wife look of his.

Summer 1953. Persia hasn't yet asked Duke Courtney to move out of their Holland Street flat ("Just so I can *think*, not always just *feel*, like some sixteen-year-old girl doesn't know which end is up"); she has just begun her brief tenure at Lambert's Tea Room, that elegant place with its black marble floor like a glimmering pool and its Irish-crystal chandeliers aglow at all times in its churchly interior and its beautifully dressed and impeccably polite lady customers who smile so sweetly and pay Persia such compliments and leave behind such meager tips.

This summer, Duke Courtney is "in sales" (in the home appliances department at Montgomery Ward, that store's top department) and doing very well, though his work is several notches downward from his connection with Jacky Barrow, now ex-mayor of Hammond . . . who kept Duke Courtney on his payroll as speechwriter, political and budgetary consultant, friend and aide, jack-of-all-trades . . . until it all came to an end. (The less said of that end, the better. As Persia observed, at least Duke's name appeared only a few times in the newspaper, in the most lengthy fact-filled articles.) And now Duke complements his income with speculation, as he calls it: shrewd bets at the racetrack, carefully plotted poker games. "Speculation" is not the same as "gambling"; gambling is for fools.

Over the years, Duke has developed a complex theory of luck based upon laws (of averages) and factors (specific and concrete): for instance, a simple harness race can be broken down into a set of mathematical figures, arranged in columns, having to do with the horse's former performances of course but also with the quality of the driver, the condition of the track, the weather, and other miscellaneous factors, which in themselves are constantly being altered.

On the most basic level, if one always bets on the favorite, doubling the size of the bet with each subsequent race (regardless of whether any, all, or no bets have been won), the possibility of walking away with a sizable purse is considerable. One day in Cleveland, arriving with $40 in his pocket, he'd walked away with $6,000; another time, when Persia first visited a track with Duke, at Batavia Downs, he began with $50 and walked away with $8,300. It's the point at which laws and material factors come together, Duke says, that the human will can seize control of its destiny.

Persia's handsome, ambitious husband is also contemplating becoming part owner of a Standardbred (harness-racing) horse . . . though perhaps it would be better for him to go into partnership with a friendly acquaintance who owns a Hammond supper club where he and Persia might work together . . . might, in fact, perform: they are superb ballroom dancers, in the mode of the Castles, the legendary dance team of Vernon and Irene Castle who earned, at the peak of their fame decades ago, as much as $30,000 a week. "The Incomparable Courtneys," they call themselves, Duke with his patrician features, Persia with her beautiful face and naturally wavy naturally red-gold hair and tireless ebullient manner. For why not?

This being the United States of America, and the Courtneys so talented, so gifted, so attractive, so eager to please, why not? Like Fred Astaire, Duke Courtney is clearly the sort of long-legged lean limber man who cannot fail to age gracefully; and Persia, though now a bit past thirty (Persia's birth date is a family secret but after her death Iris, her daughter, will discover it was March 4, 1922; thus on this midsummer day of 1953 she is thirty-one years old): *why not?*

Persia says uncertainly, "I guess . . . I guess we're here."

The Garlocks' eyesore of a house on Gowanda Street, which Persia enters that day for the first and only time in her life, is in Lowertown (as the poor section of Hammond is obliquely called); up the block from a storefront church SECOND CALVARY ZION BAPTIST,

17

around the corner from the notorious juice joint POPPA D's. The house has been built flush with the sidewalk, not an inch of grass, children's toys and household trash spilling out into the gutter.

"Mrs. Garlock? Vesta? What is *wrong?*"

Mrs. Garlock is babbling of something else now, no longer "nigras." She appears frightened of her own house . . . but that can't be possible, can it?

Persia helps the whimpering woman up the steps, through the rusty screen door, trying to comfort her but not knowing what to say. Inside, it's the millennial present tense of poverty. A wash of debris to Persia's ankles, an assault of smells: greasy, syrupy, baby formula, baby vomit, baby excrement, the Garlock odor grimed into wood, wallpaper, the very foundations of the house. Persia is appalled. Persia tries not to feel melting with pity. "Hello? Anybody home? Your momma's back!" Her voice is weaker than she'd like.

The front room has been made into a bedroom of sorts. There's a sofa with bedclothes on it, a mattress on the floor, a filthy pillow . . . no pillowcase. Towels, dirty undergarments, children's clothes, children's toys, a baby's playpen into which yet more household debris seems to have drifted . . . no, Persia squints and discovers an actual baby in there. Napping in all the mess, sprawled on its back like a drunken man. A baby of about nine months.

An eye-watering stink of urine and ammonia lifts from that airless corner of the room.

Persia calls, "Hello? Please—is anybody home?"

What Mrs. Garlock is frightened of now, clinging to her as she is, Persia can't guess. Not a word of this hillbilly woman's makes sense.

Two towheaded children with the Garlock look in their faces poke their heads through a filmy curtain strung up between the rooms, stare mutely at Persia, back off. A husky boy of about twelve, barefoot, in filthy overalls, with a raw blemished skin and small gleaming-red Garlock eyes, appears . . . and stares rudely at Persia as if he has never before seen anyone or anything like her. Then asks, suspiciously, "Whatcha doin' with Momma? Howcome *you're* here? This here's *our* house." His stare is long and hard and assessing, a grown man's. Persia says, quickly, "Your mother doesn't feel too well . . . she asked me to walk home with her. Someone should call a doctor, maybe." The boy snarls at Mrs. Garlock, "Momma, for shit sake whatcha doin'! Actin' like you're crazy or somethin'!" Within seconds mother and son are fighting, and Mrs. Garlock, inches shorter than the boy and twenty pounds lighter, manages a windmill assault upon him, cuffing his head and shoulders, cursing like a man, until the boy gives her a violent shove and slams out the front door, and Mrs. Garlock is sitting on the floorboards sobbing angrily, weeping. "Devil, damn devil . . . don't know who they are . . . devils."

Persia wants to leave the Garlock household quick as she can (she hears heavy footsteps upstairs) but something holds her. Her eyes dart quickly about as if she means to memorize details, nuggets of fact, to bring back to Duke for his amusement; if, this evening, he's in a mood to be amused. *You won't believe this. Oh, it was . . . squalid.*

Gently she says, "Mrs. Garlock? Are you all right? Did he hurt you? Maybe I should help you somewhere, get you calm. Would you like an aspirin?" She's staring down at the woman's head, at the thin frazzled colorless hair, hoping she won't see any signs of lice. More than once since their move to Curry from the "nice" place on Java poor Iris came home from school infected; it's no laughing matter. She notes too how extraordinarily thin Mrs. Garlock's legs are in the calf, a sickly dead-white, covered with coarse brown hairs.

Suddenly Mrs. Garlock opens her eyes wide and says meanly, "Don't look! Don't judge! You're too young! You're too pretty! *You can't know!*"

Then she shuts her eyes tight. Hugs herself, begins to rock energetically from side to side, lips drawn back to expose truly ghastly teeth. Persia loses all patience. "Oh, you *are* crazy!"

Vesta Garlock is past hearing.

Persia goes over to check the baby in the playpen; her conscience wouldn't allow her not to. "Poor sweet innocent thing in all this mess," she murmurs, leaning over the railing. But the baby

19

sleeps on unperturbed, drooling, diaper reeking, face blank and bland and round as a saucer . . . not, thank God, sickly looking.

Persia contemplates the Garlock baby for some minutes, dangerous minutes maybe, for what if it's Vernon Garlock upstairs and he's about to come down, what if that nasty-eyed boy comes back; she's heard plenty of things about the Garlocks and other hillbilly families and how the men treat the women, including sometimes their own daughters . . . but the baby sleeping, just lying there sleeping, holds her transfixed.

She's thinking how her little girl Iris is growing up so fast, she'd dearly love to have another baby . . . oh, God, how she'd love to have another baby. The happiness of feeling it inside her, coming to life slowly, then not so slowly; then, after it's born, the countless hours of hugging, rocking, whispering . . . giving baths where each movement of her hands is special, privileged . . . napping together in the afternoons when Duke is gone . . . a darling little blue-eyed baby looking at Persia, at her, fixing its wondering stare on *her*, alone of all the world. *D'ya love me, honey? Mommy loves you too.*

Except: if Persia Courtney has another baby she'll have to feed it formula this time, not nurse. Because Duke Courtney doesn't want his wife's lovely breasts to get all saggy and broken-veined and the nipples ruined, like some women's . . . and neither does Persia. And if she nurses, as she did with little Iris, she wouldn't be able to drink with Duke, wouldn't be able to go out drinking with him, share his good times with him; God, how Persia and Duke need their good times!

Persia wonders, suddenly inspired, would she have time to change that poor baby's diaper, before one or another Garlock came in and discovered her? If she could find a clean diaper, that is, in all this mess.

3

"Don't stare, Iris. Haven't I told you that's rude?"

She wonders if their blood too, like their skin, is darker than the blood of Caucasians. Of "whites." She has heard the mysterious words "black blood," "Negro blood."

Aunt Madelyn murmuring with a fierce shake of her head, "That's black blood for you!"

At the racetrack one day, a gentleman friend of Duke's slyly observing of another not immediately within earshot, he wouldn't be surprised if the fellow wasn't trying to "pass . . . pass for *white*." And the scandalized laughter in response.

Persia scolding prettily: "Oh, what a thing to say! Oh—what a thing to *say!*"

"Look at his lips: the size of them! And his hair."

Staring after them in the street, on the trolley car, on the city bus, where, as if by a natural tug of gravity others cannot register, they drift to the rear, polite, courteous, silent; choosing to stand hanging from hand straps back there where the ride is bumpier, where exhaust fumes accumulate, rather than take empty seats nearer the front where "whites" are sitting. The dividing line, sharp-eyed little Iris observes, shifts from day to day, from bus ride to bus ride. It's fluid and unpredictable, depending upon the numerical proportion of "whites" to "blacks."

"Why don't they sit with us?—there's room," Iris whispers in Persia's ear. The two of them are together in one of those odd open seats flush with the side of the bus and there is plenty of room beside Persia for a young black mother and her two-year-old, but the woman, hanging from a hand strap, gazes sightlessly beyond them and Persia nudges Iris into silence: "Just *hush*."

As Hammond eases downward toward the river, as Uptown shifts to Lowertown and the buildings and houses and even the trees become shabbier, there is an increase of dark faces, an ebbing of white faces; and Persia sighs, runs a hand through her hair, says, "You can tell we're getting near home, can't you. Uh-huh."

They've moved again. From Java Street to Curry, from Curry to Holland. Each time the moves are sudden and rapidly expedited— "expedited" is Duke's word, one of his favorites.

Now they live on the very edge of Lowertown. (You would not want to say Niggertown; the only people Iris has heard say that have been drunk.)

The Courtneys don't go to church, but around them many others go to church. Sunday mornings on East Avenue are amazing: the streams of churchgoing Negroes. . . . The gorgeous colors of the women, their hats, dresses, like peonies, big luscious plump-hearted flowers. Men with their slicked-down pomaded hair. (And how it strikes Iris's eye, the strangeness of Negroes with gray or silver or white hair.) The boys in suits, white shirts, neckties. *Are these the sloe-eyed boys Iris sees in the park, the boys she knows she should be wary of and avoid?* And the pretty little girls Iris's age in starched cotton dresses, sashes tied in bows and bows in their hair . . . like dolls. Walking self-consciously in their dressy shoes. Little white anklet socks.

Iris stares greedily. These skins like cocoa . . . milk chocolate . . . bittersweet chocolate. A darkish purple sheen like the sheen of fat Concord grapes. And shoe polish: the rich black oily polish Daddy allows her to dab on his good shoes with a rag, then rub, rub, rub until the leather "shines like a mirror . . . can you see your own face?"

Dark dark eyes flashing slantwise to her.

Strange nappy woolly hair.

"*Don't* stare, I said," Persia whispers, giving her a poke.

Iris starts to ask, "Why—" and Persia says, "Just *don't.*"

But the question Iris wants to ask is too abstruse for the few words in her vocabulary. Why are they . . . the way they are? Different from us? The same, but different?

Iris wonders why, if the Negro children stare frankly at her, at her pale drained-looking skin, her pale greenish-gray eyes, her hair that isn't brown or blond or any precise color at all, she can't stare right back?

Persia says, "They don't know any better, some of them. *But we do.*"

Iris has been taught that "Negro" is the proper word, in two equally stressed syllables: "*Ne-gro.*" Say it too fast, or carelessly, and you get words you don't want: "nigra," "nigger."

"Colored" is acceptable too, sometimes; it's the word Aunt Madelyn prefers. (Madelyn Daiches, whom Iris loves, isn't Iris's aunt, really, but a cousin-twice-removed of Persia's.) Aunt Madelyn has many "colored" friends, she says, women friends, and fine people they are too, but the race as a whole . . . "the-race-as-a-whole" . . . can't be trusted.

And there is Iris's Uncle Leslie (Duke Courtney's older, bachelor brother), who speaks uncomfortably of "minority populations," of "African-American people," sometimes, even more uncomfortably, of "African-American peoples" . . . as if, though he knows what he wants to say, he is at a loss to find the words to express it.

Thus Leslie Courtney hesitates to say even "Ne-gro." Will never say "colored." Or "black." (Says Leslie vehemently, "They are

23

no more *black* than I am *white*.") When he is robbed of his camera, his wallet, and his wristwatch one summer evening in Cassadaga Park, Leslie is pained to describe his assailants to the police in terms of the pigmentation of their skin. It becomes a family joke, or one of Duke's family jokes: "Did y'all hear about the time my brother was mugged by three 'African-American' jigs?"

"Jig" is one of the words Iris has been told she must not say, ever. Like "nigger," "coon," "spade," "spook," "shine." Yet when Duke uses the word everyone laughs, it's so . . . unexpected.

Not that Duke would say such things in his elder brother's presence; he wouldn't. To Leslie, racial and ethnic slurs, as he calls them, are an insult to all.

Leslie Courtney is a photographer with a meager income. He lives alone at the rear of a cavelike little shop at the derelict end of Main Street . . . a soft touch, as Duke observes, for every deadbeat who wants his or his children's pictures taken but can't afford to pay. Leslie has been taking photographs of Iris . . . sometimes Iris and Persia, if Persia will consent . . . for many years. His weakness is for children generally; he has hundreds of photographs of Negro children, singly or in groups, since he lives in a Negro neighborhood (a "mixed" neighborhood is the slightly disapproving term Aunt Madelyn uses), of no commercial value; these, he sometimes displays in his shop window as if he were proud of them.

It has become a familiar issue, whether Leslie Courtney with his gifts should become known in Hammond as a "Negro photographer"—that is, a photographer with a predominantly Negro clientele—or whether, as Duke thinks, he is damaging his reputation irrevocably. If Leslie drops by for a visit and stays late, Duke will shift to this subject, painful as it is to him, for, as he sees it, his reputation too is involved. The brothers "discuss" the issue, don't exactly "quarrel," sipping Duke's whiskey . . . for both Courtneys like to drink and give evidence, as even a small child can observe, of liking each other, and themselves, just perceptibly more when they are drinking. Leslie says he takes photographs of human subjects with no particular reference to their race; an artist must seize beauty in what's close at hand, and certainly there is beauty in children,

children of any "color," and in any case, as a so-called Caucasian, he shares in the unspeakable burden of guilt Caucasians must feel for their exploitation, over the centuries, of the African-American peoples. "Slavery," says Leslie, "is the great abomination of our country," staring and blinking as if this abomination were before him, palpable, terrible, incontestable, and Duke cannot resist—for Duke Courtney, sometimes against the grain of his own best interests, is a man who *cannot resist*—saying slyly, "Y'know, Les, the Caucasians didn't invent slavery, in fact: *the black Africans did.*"

Leslie's eyes shift their focus behind the round lenses of his eyeglasses framed in thin, bright gold. He says in a trembling voice, "Yes. All right. But one abomination does not excuse, or even mitigate, another. The chain of evil must be broken at some point."

"And so it has been, and so it remains," Duke says soothingly. "Lincoln signed the Emancipation Proclamation on New Year's Day, 1863."

Says Leslie, "De facto, there remain slaves."

Says Duke, "De facto, they have put themselves in that category."

The crashing sound of ice cubes being dislodged from a freezer tray.

Another time, after Leslie has gone home sullen and muttering, Persia asks Duke why on earth his brother is so emotional about Negroes; is it some sort of Christian sentiment? And Duke sighs in annoyance and says, "No. Worse. The poor bastard identifies with them . . . 'niggers.'"

But what *is* "black blood"?

Everyone in Hammond is talking about the custody case in which a local justice took away the two children, aged nine and four, of a woman who, divorced from her "white" husband, married a "mulatto" and took up residence in a "colored neighborhood," the judge's decision being based on the premise that such a marriage was detrimental to the children's well-being. Says Aunt Madelyn, "It's a sad thing for a woman to lose her children, but you have to draw the line somewhere."

Says Persia, "They'd have to kill me before they'd take *my* children away."

Iris, staring at the newspaper photographs of scared-looking people, asks, "What is a 'mulatto'?"—pronouncing the word with a strong "u," as in "mule," a word she knows. "Is this him? Here?"

Persia tells her it isn't anything *she* has to worry about.

Duke tells her it's a white person with Negro blood or a Negro with white blood—"mixed blood."

Iris asks gravely, How does that happen?

Duke says, "Sweetheart, all kinds of things happen when people get careless!"

Blood, Iris Courtney learns, is everything.

Blood. Bloodlines. Pedigree. "Purity."

At the Batavia Downs racetrack Duke Courtney explains patiently (to a woman: but not to Persia, who scarcely needs to be told) how, in champion horses, power descends through bloodlines exclusively: "In predicting the performances of horses," he says, "bloodlines are everything. Nature favors the aristocrat! These beautiful creatures, in the flesh, are but the embodiment of an idea."

Grizzled-gray-haired Mr. Jacky Barrow, mayor of Hammond on the Republican ticket, high-ranking "secret" officer in the local Masonic Lodge (which, at last, Duke Courtney is invited to join), explains his private views on race to a gathering of friends . . . as they are being borne choppily eastward on his yacht *Erin Maid,* on the Cassadaga River, to the New York State Fair in Albany, a gay noisy rowdy group of adults with here and there a wide-eyed child in tow, like nine-year-old Iris Courtney. "We must keep this a White Man's country, whatever we do. These are difficult years, and this is our trust. This is the sacred foundation laid by our forefathers. The Republic was founded by White Men . . . it was established by White Men. Look: nobody, least of all me, wants to deprive the colored population of their rights, but it is a proven law on this earth. The opposite of purity is mongrelization."

The *pop!* of a fresh champagne bottle being uncorked.

This dazzling-bright Sunday afternoon on the river, Persia and

Duke Courtney, the most striking couple in the mayor's circle, demonstrate their dreamy stylized foxtrot as "My Foolish Heart" blares from the radio, followed by a snappy syncopated "Buttons and Bows" as everyone applauds. Then Mr. Barrow, yachting cap on his head, stubby legs swaying, dances with tall lovely Mrs. Courtney, grips her so sweatily tight his fingers permanently crease her peach-colored chiffon dress. Iris is staring as if memorizing but unaccountably falls asleep in the overhead sun, wedged between rubberized cushions as Duke Courtney's long limber legs in white linen trousers cavort across the deck . . . and when she's wakened, her tender skin smarting as if, in sleep, she'd been soundly slapped, it's to the identical voices, shrieks of laughter, happy music she had heard hours before.

Her mommy and daddy's friends, having a good time together.

A *party*. On the *Erin Maid*.

And that night in Albany, in the plush-carpeted hotel room where the Courtneys are guests ("All expenses paid!" gloats Duke), Persia trundles her feverish little girl off for a bath, rubs cold cream—yes, deliciously *cold*—on her sunburnt face and shoulders.

Persia has done up her heavy red-gold hair in quick pincurls smelling of setting gel, and there's a mask of cold cream too on her beautiful face . . . gives her a queenly haughty look. She says, "There's nothing so nice, baby, as being *clean*, is there. *Clean* outside and in." Pronouncing her words with care, not wanting to slur syllables, eyes eating up her drowsy little girl in the tub as if— though Duke is waiting impatiently for her, there's a party in full swing in Jacky Barrow's suite, *Where the hell are the Courtneys?*— she'd love to throw off her clothes and slip into the sudsy bubbly bathwater tart as lemon juice, herself. "Wish I had time to be clean as my little darling, always," Persia whispers, leaning dizzily to kiss Iris on her snubbed-button nose, "outside and in. *Always.*"

Another episode the adults talk about, for a while, is how John Ritchie died.

John Elmore Ritchie, thirty-eight years old at the time of his death at Hammond City jail, August 1952, Negro, U.S. Army veteran of World War II, wounded in the Philippines and walked with a drag to his left foot . . . married, six children, one grandchild . . . worked for the Orleans County Sanitation Department, a frozen-faced black man with some mental worry he might provoke violence or harm to others if he spoke too loudly; thus he rarely raised his voice above a whisper outside of his home or church (he sang in the men's chorus at Second Calvary Zion Baptist), nor did he make abrupt unpremeditated movements with his body or look too directly at people whether black or white, and especially white. So John Ritchie is coming home on East Avenue about 6 P.M. this late-summer day and a Hammond City police car pulls over and two policemen get out yelling to him to "stop and identify yourself," their billy clubs out and their voices raised, as if there was already some trouble, some threat.

On account of this poor sad-faced Ritchie wears eyeglasses with thick lenses, and eyeglasses on a six-foot burly Negro with a scar or a birthmark on his forehead like a fossil imprinted in rock is an extreme look close to answering the description a white woman gave police earlier that day of a coal-black Negro who threatened to assault her . . . stopped her car turning off the Oldwick Road yelling and cursing at her pounding the hood of her car with his fist . . . tried to smash the windshield with that same bare fist . . . a "stone-blind drunk" nigger with coal-black greasy oily skin and hair in tufts like "greasy black soap" . . . a "raving" madman . . . and he's wearing dark sunglasses. And it's John Elmore Ritchie's bad luck he resembles this Negro, or anyway it seems so: the size of him, and the glasses, and the "suspicious behavior" the white cops are alerted to, just spying him there on the street walking along dragging his leg like he didn't want to call any attention to himself.

So they stop him. Ask him what's his name where's his identification where's he going where's he coming from is he drunk? high on weed? what're you doing, boy, with that knife? "concealed weapon" on your person?

Not that John Ritchie has got any knife, concealed or other-

28

wise, nor ever did, not being that kind. It's just cops' jive talk and shit like that.

So John Ritchie's too scared to answer, or too frozen . . . frozen-faced. Like already he'd been slammed over the head, stunned like a steer going to slaughter.

They said, the Ritchies, when he came back from wherever he'd been, in the Pacific, from the army hospital there, he wasn't the same man who'd been shipped out . . . didn't even look the same, entirely. And he'd be fearful of doing injury to his children by touching them or even looking too direct at them, looking anybody too direct in the eye out of terror a wicked thought could leap from one mind to another; and sometimes too, when he was sleeping, or singing in the chorus, his hands would move and wriggle on their own like something out of the deep sea you'd expect to have claws, capable of quick darting movements and lethal attacks. So these hands he kept down at his sides when he was conscious of the need to do so, and when the white cops yelled at him he went stony still in the street like at attention in the army and seemed almost not to hear them, the things they said to him, nor even, at first, to feel their billy clubs prodding and poking and tapping . . . until finally his glasses flew off and they had him spread-eagled leaning against a wall using their billy clubs some more, for maybe it seemed in their eyes this weird nigger was stubborn or sullen or "resisting" police officers in some special sly fashion of his own, judging from the scrunched-up look of his ugly black face, that look like something hacked in stone, a terror so deep it has turned into something else, too subtle and elusive to be named.

Now John Elmore Ritchie is bleeding from the nose and mouth and some neighborhood people have stopped to watch . . . from across the street. This is the unpaved end of East Avenue, Lowertown as it shifts into Niggertown; neighborhood folks know not to get too close, in such circumstances, and to keep their mouths shut. The cops are striking John Ritchie, asking him questions the man can't or won't answer . . . never says a word except grunting when he's hit . . . then suddenly he covers his face

29

with his hands and turns and butts with his head lowered like some maddened bull or something, hits one of the cops in the chest and sends him six feet backward and now there's sure hell to pay.

A second patrol car pulls up. A police van pulls up. There's sirens, walkie-talkies, men with pistols. And they have John Ritchie on the ground in the dirt and the man is fighting, he's fighting like some crazy old bull, so they wallop him over the head and kick him till he stops . . . drag him into the rear of the van . . . the cops yelling to the black people watching, "You want trouble? Which one of you wants trouble?" with their pistols leveled and primed to use, and John Ritchie they claimed died in the Hammond City jail early in the morning of the following day—banged his head against the bars of his cell they said and this was corroborated by police witnesses and two or three inmates—and after John Ritchie's funeral at Zion Church and for two nights following black people gather in the street on East Avenue and Pitt, and word goes through Hammond there's going to be trouble . . . *going to be a black uprising* . . . and there's a small army of city cops and New York State troopers . . . police barricades set up in the street and traffic rerouted and a 9 P.M. curfew in effect all weekend . . . young black men mainly are the disturbers-of-the-peace the cops are alert to, and disperse. And they disperse them, and others. And there are no arrests. And that's how John Elmore Ritchie dies and gets buried in Peach Tree Cemetery.

This episode they talk about, the adults. For a while.

The Peter B. Porter Elementary School on Chautauqua Street to which Iris Courtney transfers eight weeks into the school term— the tearful consequence of a weekend move, Curry Street to the fourth-floor flat on Holland—is an aging brown-brick building with an asphalt playground crumbling at its edges, fenced off at the rear from hillocks of ashy chemical-stinking landfill. *You are not to play there. You are not to scale the fence and play there. You are to play only on the playground.* At recess the younger children surge shouting and screaming amid the swings, the rusted teeter-totters, the wicked monkey bars—where the nastiest accidents happen, or are caused to

30

happen. They are white and Negro . . . but mainly white. The older children, fifth- and sixth-graders, stand about in good weather, eat their lunches out of paper bags on gouged picnic tables bolted to the asphalt paving, whites and Negroes at separate tables; and there one day is Iris Courtney the new sixth-grader, pale, freckled, shy, watchful, in the pretty red plaid jumper Momma bought her as compensation for the pain, as if there could be any compensation for such pain, of the sudden humiliating change of address, the new and utterly friendless terrain.

Daddy has said you must learn to roll with the punches . . . everyone must learn. And better young than old.

Iris learns. Iris is shy but Iris learns.

Fairly quickly she makes friends with one or two girls who are accessible . . . then with a few more . . . and even a boy or two, the less pushy, less aggressive, less dirty-mouthed boys . . . none of them are Negro, of course, or, as it's said here, "colored"; the two groups keep to themselves most of the time, eating lunch in separate groups, playing together, talking, wisecracking, scuffling, fighting . . . and drifting homeward from school, since the colored children live generally to the north in the section of Lowertown near the river and the white children live elsewhere.

Though there are exceptions, of course.

Iris Courtney learns. Perhaps she is too watchful, a little coldhearted. Dropping one friend as she acquires another, willing to walk several blocks out of her way, after school, to accompany the popular girls in her class, the girls she knows instinctively to court and who appear to like her: "Iris, c'mon with *us!*" In any case there is the excuse, should an excuse be required, of returning to the flat on Holland Street along a commercial stretch of East Avenue, browsing in store windows, buying herself a soft drink, skimming through magazines and paperback books in the drugstore until her head aches and her eyes begin to lose their focus . . . for when she gets home, to this new "home," neither Persia nor Duke will be there.

Iris's father has a succession of jobs, in sales, management, "public relations." He is a brilliant salesman, naturally gifted, he has superior skills as a manager, and his experience with ex-mayor Barrow has given him considerable insight, as he says, into the workings, the mechanism, of certain not-entirely-public aspects of the public sector . . . but his heart is elsewhere. Yes and his brain too: he's a speculative man by temperament, not a gambler but a speculator, a thinker, philosopher, analyst. He is setting enough by for a stake, as he calls it, a stake in the future, for he hopes to invest in—but it's bad luck to talk of such things prematurely.

Bad luck, good luck. "Luck."

But a wise man makes his own luck. Says Duke Courtney.

Persia is selling ladies' lingerie at Freeman Brothers, the largest, best department store in Hammond.

In Mrs. Rudiger's sixth-grade class at Peter B. Porter Elementary School there is a tradition of many years: boys and girls under her instruction are seated not in alphabetical order exclusively but according to a highly convoluted system of private classification, and a student's position in the classroom is subject at all times to abrupt and unexplained changes. Good grades, though not necessarily intelligence; good "citizenship"; cleanliness and clean habits; size, height, sex, race . . . these are factors in Mrs. Rudiger's kingdom, which the seating chart with its slots for handily movable names authenticates. The half-dozen Negro boys are wisely separated, but their seats are inevitably toward the rear; the nicest, most docile, best-groomed Negro girls are seated as close to the front, in several instances, as the third row; the rest, girls, boys, all of them "white" but not reliably "white," are arranged so that, seated at the desk from which she rises only sporadically, massive doughy-skinned Mrs. Rudiger—she must weigh two hundred twenty pounds, veers around on a metal-tipped cane like a listing elephant—can gaze out most directly, most immediately and agreeably, at the attractive faces of her favorites while keeping an instinctive scrutiny of the others, the potential troublemakers in particular. Like a mill worker in whom decades of labor have reduced the singularity of days to but one buzzing anesthetized sensation, Mrs. Rudiger inhabits a cosmology in which only now and then, and always unexpectedly, individual faces, voices, beings, souls emerge.

Iris Courtney, for instance.

The child is a puzzle to Mrs. Rudiger, and Mrs. Rudiger does not like puzzles. Clearly, she is a superior student; clearly a decently brought up, perhaps even well-bred girl in this motley mix; she gets perfect scores on most of the tests, hands in carefully prepared homework and special assignments, answers her teacher's questions in a bell-like voice . . . but rarely volunteers to answer; nor does she volunteer to assist Mrs. Rudiger in the subtle and indefinable ways in which certain of the other girls assist her, in the daily struggle to maintain discipline amid incipient chaos. In such classrooms in such schools there is a ceaseless drama of wills, as in meteorological crises between contending fronts of atmospheric pressure, and only the benevolent cooperation of the majority of the students allows order to be maintained . . . some species of order, however harsh and whimsical.

In this, Iris Courtney is not one of the "good" girls.

Suspicious Mrs. Rudiger understands that the girl only pretends to be shy and well-behaved. It is a pose, a ruse, a game, an artful befuddlement. In spirit, Iris Courtney sides with the outlaws. Her polite classroom smile is wickedly elastic and capable of shifting—with a quick sidelong glance at a classmate, whether girl or boy, white or colored, in the seat beside hers—into the subtlest of smirks. Her neat clean clothes, her decent shoes, her well-brushed fair brown hair, her posture, her outward deportment, the calm, composed, cool gaze of her pebble-colored eyes, all mask a wayward and mutinous spirit that reveals itself in unguarded moments: a shoulder's shrug, a rolling of the eyes, a stare of flat disdain as Mrs. Rudiger speaks or, with a creaking of the floorboards, heaves herself to her feet to write something on the blackboard. She would catch little Iris Courtney whispering or passing wadded notes or yawning into a cupped hand or doodling in the margin of her textbook, except the shrewd girl does not allow herself to be caught.

One of Mrs. Rudiger's English grammar exercises involves sending students to the blackboard to write out sentences and diagram them; then calling upon other students to come forward and "correct" these sentences. But she quickly becomes wary of allowing Iris Courtney, despite the girl's talent for grammar, to stand at the blackboard where Mrs. Rudiger can't see her face at every instant . . . for she is convinced that the girl casts satirical glances out at her classmates, judging from stifled giggles here and there, downcast smiles, undercurrents of shivery amusement that ripple to the very bottom of the room . . . to those coal-black slouching boys—Hector, Rathbone, Rollins, "Mule"—who are Mrs. Rudiger's natural enemies and who, had she the power, she would erase from the surface of the earth.

Ah, had she the power!

Of course, Mrs. Rudiger, whose eyesight is uncertain and whose hearing is not so keen as it once was, isn't altogether certain that Iris Courtney *is* rebellious. Maybe the poor drained-looking child is just nervous? Self-conscious and twitchy? Maybe the class, rousing itself from lethargy, laughs not with her but at her? For there are days in succession when Iris is, to the outward eye, as *good* a girl as Mrs. Rudiger's favorites; thus, gets moved toward the front of the room: third row, center. White children on either side.

Like the other teachers at Peter B. Porter, all Caucasians, Mrs. Rudiger believes in a formal division of whites and colored whenever possible. Her prejudices reveal themselves in only the most discreet of ways. When, for instance, the public school doctor makes one of his dreaded "surprise" visits to the school, it is primarily the colored students whom Mrs. Rudiger sends down to the gymnasium; her special favorites she spares the ordeal of a public health examination on the assumption that their parents can afford doctors of their own. At such times Iris Courtney finds herself herded along with the others—colored, poor-white, frightened and humiliated—worrying her feet will not be clean, her underwear grimy. She is hot with shame submitting to the scalp-lice check like the most slovenly of the Negroes . . . some of whom invariably do have lice. I hate, I hate, I hate, she thinks, not knowing what it is, apart from Mrs. Rudiger, she hates.

Among the Negro girls it is Lucille Weaver who arouses her

covert admiration. Lucille is quick-witted, funny, a natural adversary of Mrs. Rudiger's: with a droll pug face, very dark; a derisive laugh; thick black hair plaited and twined in braids heavy as rope. In gym class, Lucille is a terror: the white girls learn to step quickly out of her way. Iris would befriend her if only to placate her . . . except, how?

Just before Christmas recess Mrs. Rudiger singles out both Iris and Lucille for embarrassment. It is a stratagem of some ingenuity. Perhaps it is even innocent. On one of her whims she shifts Iris's seat to the fourth row, beside the clanking overheated radiators; Lucille Weaver's desk is beside hers. When Mrs. Rudiger gives an impromptu arithmetic quiz, it happens that both Iris and Lucille have the same answer, the correct one, to a problem involving fractions which no one in sixth grade is really expected to know; the coincidence is too much, and Mrs. Rudiger accuses Lucille of having copied Iris's paper. Stony-faced Lucille is called to the teacher's desk to explain herself and stands mute and appalled as the class stares and Iris Courtney writhes in her seat. Mrs. Rudiger says, "Lucille, how do you explain . . . ? How do you account for . . . ?" and long minutes pass. The room is silent except for the radiators. Lucille shakes her head; Lucille has nothing to say; it's impossible to tell if she is guilty or sullen or stricken to the heart, or simply confused. Perhaps she did copy the white girl's answer, without knowing what she did? Her usual arithmetic scores are barely passing.

"Lucille," says Mrs. Rudiger, "*did* you copy the answer? If you tell the truth, dear, it will be all right."

She regards the black girl, ugly as sin, from beneath compassionate eyebrows. It is part of Mrs. Rudiger's teacherly strategy at such times to suggest how authority is tempered with mercy.

Lucille Weaver, staring at her feet, mumbles something inaudible.

"Lucille, please don't lie," Mrs. Rudiger says calmly. "Of all things in heaven and earth *do not lie.*"

Lucille stands as if paralyzed. No one wants to look at her, yet there is nowhere else to look. Mrs. Rudiger is shaking Lucille's test paper as if the very paper gives offense. She says in a voice of fair-mindedness, "If you insist you did not cheat, will you demonstrate your mathematical ability? On the blackboard? Right now? I will read off the problem to you, and—"

Lucille begins suddenly to cry. It is not an admission of having cheated but, being larger and more shameful, seems to contain an admission. The class shifts in their seats; there is a collective misery and relief: now it is over, now Lucille can sit down. Mrs. Rudiger scolds them for many minutes as Lucille sits hunched and weeping at her desk . . . no one even wants to look at her, especially not the good colored girls who are Mrs. Rudiger's favorites and who stare at their white lady teacher with terrified unblinking eyes.

By the clanking steaming radiators Iris Courtney feels pure cold. Doesn't look at Lucille either. Thinking if she'd been brave she'd have said *she* cheated . . . but she isn't brave. Just sits there, shivering.

And that afternoon on the way home from school Lucille and two of her friends shove Iris Courtney off a curb, knock her into a gutter of filthy rushing water, her saddle shoes soaked, knee scraped raw and bleeding, the palms of both hands; they shriek "white bitch, white asshole bitch" and cuff and kick and then they're gone, running down the street laughing, and Iris picks herself up, biting her lip not to cry, not to give them that satisfaction. "Dirty nigger bitches! *Dirty!*"

And she says nothing to her mother, not a word.

And next time she sees Lucille Weaver and her friends she surprises them with the ferocity of her attack, her sudden wild anger. You'd think the skinny white girl would be fearful but, no, she's mad as hell, has Persia's hot quick temper, and though it's surely a mistake to cross the playground to start a fight Iris rushes straight at Lucille and strikes her with her schoolbooks, and the girls scream, and scuffle, and punch, and kick, and another time Iris is knocked to the ground hard on her bottom stunned and breathless and her nose bleeding, but she sees that the black girl's nose too is rimmed in blood.

And bright red blood it is, sweet to behold. Just like her own.

36

Letters in official-looking enve-
lopes, sometimes stamped REGISTERED MAIL: RETURN RECEIPT
REQUESTED, come for "Cornelius Courtney, Jr." Follow him from
one address to another, one season to another. Bills . . . or the second
notices of bills . . . or Internal Revenue, Washington, D.C.

Duke cringes, seeing that name. That name!

But snatches up the envelope, rips it open with a jaunty
thumbnail, walks out of the room humming. Quickly, before Persia
appears.

Atop the bureau in Persia and Duke's bedroom is a photograph of
Private First Class Duke Courtney, aged twenty, framed in silver,
brown-toned, taken by Duke's brother, Leslie. In it, Duke has an
angel's face . . . a truly beautiful face. A mere boy. The fact of this
photograph of Iris Courtney's father *before he was Iris Courtney's father*
might terrify Iris if she allows herself to consider it.

Like bones, bones, blood, pulsing muscle-hearts, walking erect in envelopes of skin like sausage.

In a gay mood, her boogie-woogie mood as she sometimes calls it, Persia covers the glass, the boy's face, with damp luscious kisses.

"My old honey," she says. "Yummy-honey. Better-looking any damn day than Errol Flynn."

Duke runs an embarrassed hand through his thinning wavy hair.

"Jesus! *Wasn't* he!"

Names. Like the wavy bluish glass, its perfect transparency marred by secret knots and curls, in the vestibule fanlight of the old house on Java Street: altering your vision unawares.

"Can you imagine me as 'Cornelius Courtney, Jr.' for my entire life?"

As if the insult to his integrity were fresh and not thirty-odd years old, Duke can work himself up to actual anger. His eyes drain to the color of ice and his nostrils look like black holes punched in his face.

Iris laughs but quickly sobers, seeing that her father is in one of his serious moods.

He tells her he changed his name as soon as he'd come of age; which is to say, left home. Joined the army, joined the war. "Thank God for the war!" says Duke. Though he was wounded in action— has not one but two Purple Hearts to prove it—he looks back, he says, upon his youth with real nostalgia. For one thing, the world was younger then.

"Did you change your name in court, with a judge and all?" Iris asks.

"I changed it in here," Duke says. He makes a gentlemanly fist and strikes it against his heart.

Iris was told as a small child that she has no grandfather on her father's side of the family . . . no grandmother either. Duke Courtney and "his people" don't see eye to eye on life, thus why beat a dead horse?

It's the kind of question, appalling to envision, even a child knows isn't meant to be answered.

Persia tells Iris *she* is named for something special: the iris of the eye.

"I thought I was named for a flower," Iris says, disappointed.

"An iris *is* a flower, of course," Persia says, smiling, "but it's this other too. Our secret. 'The iris of the eye.' "

"The eye?"

" 'The iris of the eye.' The eye. The eyeball, silly!"

Persia snaps her fingers in Iris's eyes. The gesture is so rude and unexpected, Iris will remember it all her life.

After this disclosure, Iris doesn't know whether she likes her name. Her favorite name at the time is Rose-of-Sharon, that of a pretty brown-skinned girl at school.

Persia's name really is "Persia." Her mother named her; it's her authentic Christian name, in black and white right on her birth certificate.

Over the years so many people . . . especially, Iris gathers, male admirers . . . have asked Persia about her exotic name, she has perfected a little story to explain. Each time Iris hears the story she feels an absurd thrill of apprehension, as if fearing the story will go wrong; each time Iris hears the story it is precisely the same.

"My parents had some perfectly normal, ordinary name picked out for me," Persia says, her vanity unconscious as a child's, "like Margaret, or Betty, or Barbara. . . . Then in the hospital my mother was glancing through a magazine and she saw pictures of this beautiful country—in Africa, I guess—but not, you know, black Africa. The people there are white. Or, at any rate, light-skinned. There were mountains in these pictures, and a sea like an emerald, and some strange kind of temple—a 'mosque'—and my mother said she knew she had to call me 'Persia.' No one could talk her out of it, though they tried. 'Persia' she wanted, and 'Persia' it is."

Gazing at her watery-seeming reflection in Persia's dressing table mirror, when Persia isn't home, Iris wets her lips with the pink tip of her tongue.

" 'Persia' she wanted, and 'Persia' it is."

Someday, she will have her own story to tell.

After the move to Holland Street, to the mustard-colored brick-and-stucco building from whose tarpaper roof Iris Courtney can see the Cassadaga River drifting in a long slow curve from east to west, motionless at this distance as a strip of wallpaper, the earth begins to shift on its axis.

Always at such times you wait for balance to be restored, for things to "right" themselves. Until the act of waiting itself becomes the "rightness."

Duke has a new job as a "manufacturer's representative," and this new job requires traveling by car . . . and odd hours. There are midnight telephone calls; there is Persia's voice raised sleepily, then angrily. For sometimes Duke Courtney is, Iris gathers, not out of town at all but involved in marathon poker or euchre games right here in Hammond; sometimes, flushed with winning, he cannot resist calling home. Or, stricken with losing, drunk-sick, repentant, he is calling for "my bride" to come fetch him in a taxi.

In their Java Street house, in the attractively wallpapered living room with several windows, the sofa the Courtneys chose on one of their extravagant shopping trips—featuring four outsized pillows and two giant seat cushions, made of impractical crushed velvet in lavender and green splotches—looked dramatic as an item of furniture in a Hollywood musical; in this new cramped, low-ceilinged place, jammed against the end wall and taking up nearly every inch, it looks monstrous and sad. Mornings, Iris steels herself to seeing it made up hastily as a bed.

If it is Persia who has slept there, Persia is likely to be up; if Duke, Duke will still be sleeping . . . sleeping and sleeping. A "hero's hangover," he calls such fugues. He sleeps in boxer shorts and thin grayish T-shirt, snoring in erratic gasps and surges, like drowning; disheveled silver-glinting hair on a makeshift pillow is all Iris will see of his head. He lies hunched beneath a blanket, in any weather, as if he were cold, face turned toward the wall.

Persia and Iris prepare for the day, for going out, careful not to disturb him. Duke can be mean in the morning before the memory of his guilt washes over him, bringing color to his cheeks.

Iris whispers, "Momma, what's wrong?" Persia lights a cigarette and says, "Who wants to know?" Regarding her daughter with brown bemused eyes as if she has never seen her before.

Who wants to know?

The sort of puzzle, a heart riddle, a twelve-year-old can almost grasp.

When Iris trails home from school—she has friends, she goes to friends' houses, hangs out sometimes on the street—Duke will be gone. Persia won't be home, and Duke will be gone. But the glamour sofa will still have the look of an emergency bed, big pillows heaped on the floor, blanket lying where it fell.

And that smell, that unmistakable smell, of a body in sleep: alcoholic headachy rancid sleep.

Now Persia is a waitress, now she gets decent tips; returning late from her job, seeing that Duke is still out, she sometimes turns around and hurries back out herself, high heels clattering an alarm on the stairs. Iris calls after her, "Mom? Mommy?" and Persia's voice lifts out of the dark, "I won't be long, hon!" Persia knows where to find her husband . . . some nights. There is the Cassadaga House, there is Rick Butterfield's, there is the Four Leaf Clover Club, there is Vincenzo's. . . . Some nights, though, she doesn't come home until two or three in the morning, escorted to her very door, without him.

In bed but rarely asleep at such times, Iris waits to hear a stumbling on the stairs, voices. Who are the men who bring her mother home? she wonders. And does her father know?

She's very frightened but believes her interest to be merely clinical.

* * *

Gently pulls her Girl Scout uniform off its wire hanger, eases it out of the stuffed beaverboard wardrobe at the foot of her bed, pads barefoot into the other bedroom where there is a floor-length mirror as well as the heart-shaped mirror over Persia's dressing table. Stands holding the dress against the front of her body, gazing at her reflection, admiring the color of the fabric, its texture and substantiability, the several fine-stitched badges she has earned, *Iris* embroidered in shiny greenish-gold thread above her left breast. She'd wanted more than life itself to belong to the Girl Scouts, to the troupe at school; to be a part of that circle of girls, the most popular girls; to wear this dress, this beautiful dress, *as casually as the others* . . . She'd pleaded with Persia: Please; oh, please, please, I will never ask for anything else again.

Now she stares, her eyes damp with emotion. Holding the dress, the long perfect sleeves, against her body, her arm folded over it like a lover.

Persia stares at Duke Courtney, who is unshaven, tieless, a soiled look to his best white shirt, a cheapness to the gold flash of cuff links. He's home at the wrong hour of the day.

A gusty whitely glowing November day. She'll remember.

He has just informed her that they are in debt. He has borrowed money not only from the loan company that financed their 1953 four-door Mercury sedan but from a second loan company . . . has borrowed money from his brother Leslie . . . and from friends of whom, in several instances, Persia has never before heard. Duke has been forced to confess since, today, embarrassingly, before noon, he is obliged to drive their car, the very car he requires for his job as a salesman, to the loan company headquarters uptown. Such words as "repossession," "default," "in lieu of," resound like drunken song lyrics in her head.

My God. Duke has even borrowed money from Madelyn.

"But the poor woman works in that terrible beauty salon . . . she doesn't have any money!"

"Maddy wanted to go in with me on a bet at the Downs," Duke says evasively, running a hand through his hair. "It wasn't exactly a loan. Only seventy-five dollars."

He smiles one of his reflex smiles. His nostrils are wider and darker than Persia recalls. In his fair, thin-skinned, handsome face, the narrow-bridged nose is becoming swollen and venous.

"Strictly speaking, we both lost. The bet." He smiles again. "But I repaid the loan."

"You repaid it? You did?"

"I said I did."

"How much do you owe? I mean . . . in all." Persia is frightened but tries to keep her voice level. Though their daughter is at school she has a perilous sense that there is a third party in the flat with them, listening.

"Why does it matter, Persia, how much? A sum."

They are standing in the kitchen, a formal space between them. Persia in her pink quilted bathrobe, a surprise gift, and a luxury gift too, from Duke, on a Valentine's Day long past. Going grimy at the cuffs, frayed at the hem. Persia is barefoot and almost naked beneath the robe. Begins to feel the linoleum-tiled floor tilt under her feet . . . like the teakwood deck of that gleaming white yacht *Erin Maid*.

Since confiscated, among other items, by the Hammond City Council.

Duke is trying to joke. "*We* owe, darling. Not just me. You've spent most of it yourself, in fact—groceries, clothes. Things Iris 'simply has to have.' "

"But how much?"

"Not all that much."

"Duke, honey, please"—Persia's voice begins to falter—"how much?"

Duke sighs; rummages through a drawer for a pencil and a note pad; scribbles down the figure to show Persia as if the numeral is too shameful, or too intimate, to be disclosed orally. Persia whispers, "Oh, God." She yanks out a chair, sits blindly at the kitchen table, her hair, having endured elaborate pin curls through the night, now suddenly limp, straggling in her face. She hasn't put on any makeup yet this morning, so her skin is ivory pale, glazed. Without lipstick her lips look unnatural.

"And all this went for cards? At the racetrack?"

"And in a business investment. I tried to explain." Duke fetches a bottle of Jack Daniel's from the cupboard, pours each of them a drink in a whiskey glass. His manner is edgy but controlled. "Also, honey, as I said, household expenses. Life isn't cheap these days."

"But your job—"

"Never mind about my job."

"Your commissions. Didn't you tell me—"

"Persia, the money went. Money *goes.*"

He pauses, smiling at her. He is standing, Persia is sitting. His is the advantage of the natural actor who inhabits, not only his own body, with consummate ease, but the larger, invisible, indefinable body of the space about him. Watching Duke Courtney, though they have been married nearly fourteen years, have been joined together in lovemaking more times than Persia could wish to calculate, she feels her hair stir at the nape of her neck as if it were being caressed.

Duke says, "Hey. Love. My love. You know we love each other." He touches her as if shyly. Touches her breasts, loose inside the quilted robe. "That's the main thing, Persia."

"Is it?"

"Isn't it?"

"The main thing?"

Duke picks up his glass and drinks, nudges Persia to join him. It is a lover's gesture: wordless, yet edged with reproach. More urgent than Persia wants to acknowledge.

But Persia doesn't drink. Not just yet. She is thinking—or, rather, the thought is forcing itself upon her—that the figure Duke scribbled on the notepaper is probably a lie.

45

Her eyes veer wildly, she makes an abrupt rising movement, for an instant Duke thinks she is going to hit him . . . but instead she embraces him, arms tight and crushing around his waist, warm face pressed against his chest. Her smell is that of something being crushed in a moist fist.

6

Early summer. But hot. Heat like a quivering wall you could press your hand against.

Upright as a sinewy black-glittery snake, Sugar Baby Fairchild jumps cannonball fashion from the topmost girder of the Peach Tree Bridge, screaming, *"Bombs away!"*

And here's his fifteen-year-old brother, Jinx Fairchild, running off the girder as easily as another boy might run on a flat surface, thrashing his long legs, screaming, *"Look out below!,"* a comical squarish grimace opening up the lower part of his face.

Cavorting and preening, performing flawless dives when they wish, for the benefit of the admiring white girls.

They all know that Peach Tree Creek, emptying into the Cassadaga River by way of the trashy ravine edge of the railroad yard, meandering through the scrubbiest of the back lots of Lower-town, is a dirty creek—picking up sludge from factories in its passing and bottles, tin cans, old tires, bones, yes, and raw garbage and used condoms and sewage from drains—not a decent creek for swimming but it's close by, and fast-running in its approach to the river so the scum doesn't accumulate, and deep, as deep as twelve feet beneath the bridge, and dark, deliciously dark, a cool glossy serpentine feel to the current, reflections under the bridge dancing and darting like shreds of dream pulled out into daylight.

Unlike the open river where the shoreline is rocks and broken concrete, or the public pool at Cassadaga Park where, under the watchful eyes of white supervisors and the white lifeguard, playful black boys like the Fairchild brothers aren't made to feel welcome.

Here, they can do any damned crazy stunt they want to do.

The white girls Iris Courtney and Nancy Dorsey shouldn't be swimming in Peach Tree Creek . . . probably. They are not the only girls swimming here this afternoon but they seem to be the only white girls, and they know they're noticed.

But who's to know or care? Who would inform their families?

The Fairchild brothers haul themselves up out of the water, streaming water like seals. The sun strikes sparks on their dark skin: Sugar Baby first, then Jinx. Sugar Baby is always first. Slapping their thighs, dancing on the balls of their feet. Whoops of elation, yodels and yells. Someone in the water below calls up to them and Sugar Baby, pretending outrage, cups his hands to his mouth and yells back, "*You* the peckerhead! *You* gonna split you head like *guts!*"

The Fairchild brothers are not twins but it's easy to mistake one for the other unless, like now, they are standing together, with a look of boys contemplating themselves in the mirror and liking what they see. Sugar Baby is seventeen, taller than Jinx by an inch or two, must be six feet tall in his bare feet, ten pounds heavier, and very mature . . . *very* mature in his tight-fitting trunks like black elastic molded to his genitals and buttocks. His hair is springy and matted, his grin all curvy teeth. Girls stare at him and forget to look away blushing.

Sugar Baby cups his hands to his mouth again and calls over to the white girls, whom he knows from the neighborhood, "Gimme the high sign, honeys! You gonna gimme the high sign? Hnnnnnn?"

The girls have no idea what he's talking about; his Negro dialect is laid on so heavy, so rich, they can barely decipher a word.

Nancy Dorsey ducks her head as if fearful of looking up too directly at Sugar Baby, locking eyes with his. It has happened more than once between them . . . it has happened frequently. She murmurs a warning to Iris Courtney to ignore the Fairchilds, both leaning on the bridge railing overhead. The water casts a shivering reflection upward onto her face, giving it a dissolving look.

Iris Courtney laughs, the notion is so fanciful. Ignore *them?*

Iris, swimming in four feet of water, in and out of the sheltering shadow of the bridge, looks up and sees Sugar Baby and Jinx looking down. Two smiles, all white curvy teeth.

Sugar Baby teases, impudent, hooded-eyed. "Don't gonna gimme no high sign, hnnnnn? Don't *know* no high sign, hnnnnn?"

It's a relief when the brothers resume their diving and swimming, clambering up the sides of the rusted girders.

In the shadow of the bridge Nancy Dorsey cuts her eyes at Iris and presses a fist against the tight-swelling bosom of her swimsuit. "Oh, God, my heart's beating like crazy."

Iris doesn't say a word.

Peach Tree Creek at this spot is a lovely cavernous region, sounds echoing from the cobwebbed underside of the bridge, the farther creek bank tangled and clotted with vegetation. There's a brackish smell, though, the girls don't want to get in their hair; they're swimming with their heads lifted out of the water, a little stiffly, self-consciously. Iris Courtney's hair is in a bunchy ponytail, Nancy's loose to her shoulders. The girls have little in common really except that both their mothers are working and they have no sisters or brothers (at least at home: Nancy does have an older brother somewhere) and their fathers are not living with them . . . on a regular basis.

Balanced atop a high girder, lanky arms outstretched and hands flopping loose at the wrist as if broken, Sugar Baby goes into his Little Richard act: high-pitched jabbering screech—"*Tutti Frutti, Tutti Frutti Tutti Frutti*"—as calmly he steps into empty air to fall like a dead weight into the creek.

49

Jinx, not missing a beat, executes a perfect somersault dive, hardly raising a splash.

Nancy Dorsey whispers shivering in Iris's ear some words Iris acknowledges with a sharp startled laugh.

The white girls stretch out languidly in the sun, on a flat bleached rock like the palm of an uplifted hand. A familiar old rock; they've lain here before.

It's a humming sort of day . . . time dragging backward. No purpose to going home.

There are some Negro girls swimming with the Fairchilds, some other Negro boys who glance their way from time to time, two or three white boys, small children splashing near shore . . . no purpose to going home. Iris says suddenly to Nancy, "My mother told my father he's mean-hearted, the other night: chunk of ice where his heart should be. Now I'm worried I might be the same."

Nancy says vaguely, her eyes on the bridge, "*I* wouldn't worry. Shit."

Iris Courtney is wearing a single-piece jersey swimsuit the color of dried blood; Nancy Dorsey is wearing a two-piece suit with a tight ribbed bodice, bright green parrots splashing in a maze of gold. Nancy is the more physically developed of the two: breasts, hips, thighs, dimpled smile. Iris is leggy, long-armed, narrow boyish hips and small hard breasts. Glancing uneasily down at herself she sees flesh white and vulnerable as something pried out of a shell.

When Persia accused Duke of being mean-hearted, he'd flared up angry and incredulous. Icy eyes in a hot, slapped-looking face. Now Iris is thinking it's surely a sign of mean-heartedness . . . you can't know.

And if you can't know, how can you change?

She watches Jinx Fairchild scale a sharp-angled girder to get to the top of the bridge, as easily as if he's been doing it all his life. Her toes twitch and cringe in sympathy. As if somehow it's Iris Courtney up there too. . . . Nancy complains of Sugar Baby, he's got a *mouth* on him, that guy, he'd better watch that *mouth* of his. "A colored boy could get into trouble saying the wrong thing to a white girl. I do mean trouble."

50

On the bridge's topmost girder Jinx Fairchild stands cautiously, straightening his long lanky legs. Iris has seen him play basketball in the neighborhood park and at school: those long legs, long arms, playful deadpan smirk. Jinx is darker-skinned than Sugar Baby, as if the sun has baked him deep and hard. His woolly hair is cropped short, his rib cage shows fleet and rippling inside his skin. Clowning pop eyes rimmed in white in a dark dark face.

Iris knows that Jinx's true name is Verlyn: Verlyn Rayburn Fairchild. She has seen it in official lists at school; Jinx has just graduated from ninth grade, two years ahead of her. And she knows where he lives, in a small wood-frame house with a porch and a side garden in the "good" section of black Lowertown, East Avenue as it shifts from white Lowertown, a quarter mile, maybe less, from her own building . . . a short distance across weedy back lots and the old canning factory property and an open drainage ditch. Beyond the Fairchilds' short block East Avenue is unpaved and the neighborhood changes abruptly: tarpaper shanties, yards heaped with trash, small children spilling over into the road, wandering dogs, that smell of garbagey overripeness and things burning, a place where human distinctions are overrun. But the Fairchilds don't live there.

Sugar Baby's true name is Woodrow: Woodrow William Fairchild, Jr. Last season he was a star basketball player at the high school, the best colored player on the team. But he isn't returning in the fall, says he's got better things to do. Nobody ever needed a diploma for carpentry or bricklaying or construction or hotel or railroad work: nigger-boy vocational-school shit like that. Says Sugar Baby in that voice you can't tell is it quavering with hurt or anger or jivey good humor, *he's* got better things to do.

Anyway, Sugar Baby says, Jinx is the real thing. You watch . . . *him* coming along.

Iris watches: Jinx Fairchild atop the Peach Tree Bridge, executing a backward dive even as his friends try to distract him: a single astonishing fluid motion, arms and legs outstretched, unhesitating, flawless, slicing the dark water fast and clean and sharp as a knife.

51

August 20, 1955: Leslie Courtney's fortieth birthday.

Which is not going to be celebrated, as Leslie Courtney's
birthdays have frequently been celebrated, in the Holland Street flat
... since things there, as Persia Courtney says, are still unsettled.

"Unsettled."

This word, neutral, fastidiously chosen, evokes in Leslie
Courtney's mind's eye a vision of a small boat being tossed in stormy
water.

Leslie telephones his sister-in-law Persia two or three times a
week, to see how things are. If Duke is home, he speaks with Duke.
Duke is not often home.

It's one of those summer days when the sky is banked with rain
clouds like plum-colored bruises. Heat lightning flashing soundless
above the river.

How, on such an afternoon, did they both forget the umbrella?

Persia doesn't think of it until, getting off the bus, a sulfurous-tasting wind rises in her face. She says, "Oh, damn." Then, "You know, I can't be expected to remember every damn thing."

She and Iris are carrying Leslie's two wrapped birthday presents, plus the cake, which is probably why they forgot the umbrella.

Iris has learned that the most innocent remark—though few of Iris's remarks to her mother are in fact innocent—can trigger a quarrel. So it's with caution she points out that they can always borrow an umbrella from Uncle Leslie if it's raining when they leave.

Persia says with her helpless-sounding laugh, the new laugh that means hurt, anger, befuddlement, "It's the principle of the thing. The forgetfulness. Like an old sweater unraveling."

She's on the street with a cigarette slanting from her lips, wavy hair streaming, mouth very red. Iris recalls, a few years back, Persia nudging her to observe a woman smoking on the street: *cheap*. No matter how good-looking the woman, Persia warned: *cheap*.

Iris says, "Well, I hope the cake turned out."

Persia says, "Any idiot can make a cake out of a mix. That's the entire point of mixes."

COURTNEY'S PHOTOGRAPHY STUDIO—"Portraits of Distinction"—is located at 591 North Main Street. It's a small shop with a single display window, squeezed between a shoe store that sells mainly to Negroes, though owned and staffed by whites, and a seafood store that emits a powerful briny odor in all weathers. When Iris thinks of her uncle's photography studio she thinks of the doomed lobsters, black, spidery, giant-clawed, groping about in the bubbly water tank in the neighboring front window.

Staring in the window of Leslie's shop, mother and daughter are silenced for a moment, seeing their likenesses on display . . . amid many other portraits. The glass is flyspecked, many of the older photographs are discolored. What a jumble! It's like a common graveyard: photographs of unknown men, women, and chil-

dren . . . black faces beside white . . . landscapes of the city of
Hammond . . . the riverfront . . . "artistic" studies that yield their
designs only after a long minute's scrutiny. It seems that Leslie
never takes anything out of his display case, only adds: like the
interior of the shop, where the walls are covered with framed prints.
"There we are," Iris murmurs to Persia, feeling a stab of emotion,
sheer emotion, nameless inchoate emotion sharp as tears, "and
there. And *there*."

"Oh, spare me!" Persia says. But she looks.

For as long as Iris can remember her parents have joked and
complained and worried aloud about her uncle Leslie: his lack of
"normal" ambition . . . the "squalor" of his little shop . . . the
mystery of how he makes a living. And he's a brilliant man, a true
original, Duke insists extravagantly: "My superior in every way."
For as long too as Iris can remember Persia has been bringing her to
sit for double portraits in Leslie's studio—"Persia-and-Iris portraits," Leslie calls them—though the sessions leave Persia increasingly restless. Her vanity has long since been sated.

It offends Persia too that Leslie does nothing with the finished
products, beautiful though they are, except to give prints to the
Courtneys and display others in the studio, rudely mixed with the
likenesses of strangers.

"Why doesn't he take the old ones out?" Persia says, annoyed.
"They're so *old*."

Iris wipes roughly at her eyes. "If that's actually me—that
baby—I wish I could remember. Momma, I don't remember any
of it!"

Persia says, "I remember."

Mother and daughter stand staring through grimy glass seeing
mother-and-daughter gazing placidly out, each pair of photographed likenesses inhabiting their inviolate time beyond the
breath of perishable things.

Again Persia says, sighing, "I remember."

On their way into the shop Persia warns Iris, "Don't let on, for
God's sake, that we really don't want to be here. You know how
Leslie is."

"What do you mean?" Iris says, surprised, rather hurt. "*I* want to be here. *I* don't have anything else I'd rather do."

Persia says quietly, "Well, I do."

"My God, what *is* this . . . ? Persia, Iris . . . you shouldn't have."

There's a crinkling electric sheen to the fancy red wrapping paper on the presents as, a bit clumsily, Leslie Courtney unwraps them . . . careful not to tear the paper. He's smiling so deeply, his eyes behind the gold-rimmed glasses so misted over, it almost seems he might have forgotten that today is his birthday. He'd planned a photography session—has everything, including a vase of white roses, in readiness—but a birthday?

He *is* agitated . . . funny man. Thanking them repeatedly. Hugging and kissing Persia on the cheek, hugging Iris. Hard.

There's a handsome cowhide wallet from Persia, a dappled blue silk necktie from Iris: both presents acquired by Persia by way of a friend who manages the "best" men's clothing store in Hammond, a poker buddy of Duke's. And there's the angel food cake, vanilla frosting in tiny crests, like waves, and four pink candles, and HAPPY BIRTHDAY L.C. spelled out in tiny red cinnamon candies. In a giddy mood—such moods, lately, Persia and Iris find themselves sharing—they'd placed the candies on together that morning, giggling like children. *The absurdity of it!* Persia sniffed. *Frosting a cake! Birthdays! When our lives are . . . what they are!*

But she'd laughed, her happy laugh, lifting her hair from the nape of her neck with both hands and letting it fall, that mannerism of hers that means a kind of abandon: What the hell!

"It's your fortieth birthday, Leslie," she tells him, lighting a cigarette, "a one-and-only occasion."

Leslie is pouring wine for Persia and himself, dark red wine in long-stemmed crystal glasses . . . that probably aren't too clean. Persia is resolved not to notice. He has given Iris a glass of lemonade so sugary it hurts her mouth.

He says, laughing, to indicate his words are to be taken lightly, "Isn't every occasion 'one and only'?"

* * *

Once, years ago, in Leslie Courtney's studio with its backstage theatrical look, its air of drama and expectancy, when Persia and her little daughter Iris were posing for his camera—on the white wicker love seat, that piece of furniture graceful as the s in calligraphy, a favorite prop of the photographer's—Leslie said in an outburst of candor that his vision as an artist was to photograph every man, woman, and child living in Hammond, New York: "every soul sharing a single instant of time."

He'd spoken passionately. His pale eyes had a yellowish flare. A shaving nick on the underside of his jaw glistened red.

Persia Courtney cut her eyes at him and laughed.

"God, Les. *Why?*"

Leslie's scratchy old phonograph is playing bright music from *The Marriage of Figaro*. Still, Iris can hear their voices.

"*He* said . . ."

"Yes, he would. That's . . . his version."

". . . were the one to ask him to leave. And now . . ."

"*Did* he pay you back? Or is that another of his lies?"

"Yes, I'm sure he did . . . sure he did."

"Ah, now *you're* lying!"

Iris lets the book fall closed, photographs of H. Cartier-Bresson. Wanders out of the room. Long-legged as a yearling horse, and restless. They aren't going to miss her.

There's a lot to look at in Uncle Leslie's "bachelor's quarters": on virtually every square inch of wall space he has hung framed photographs, his own and others', prints, antiquated maps. The interior of a skull crammed with too many thoughts.

A sly stink of wet sand, brine, fish penetrating the walls. But after a while you don't notice.

Leslie Courtney has rented the store and the three-room apartment to the rear at 591 North Main Street, Hammond, New York, for the past twelve years, since moving to Hammond from his family hometown in the southern part of the state. First his brother Duke, newly married, moved to Hammond . . . then Leslie. You would conclude the brothers are close.

The photography studio itself is small and perpetually cluttered with equipment. Leslie is always buying new cameras, or new camera attachments, or props for his portraits . . . and not throwing anything out. It's a room lit with a single muted light except when a blaze of lights is turned on. Thus to Iris, who has seen it since a time when, in the most literal terms, she was incapable of comprehending, let alone remembering, incapable even of comprehending herself as a being of consciousness and identity, the studio has an air familiar as a dream she has visited numberless times yet, awake, has not the power to recall. But there is the sharp razorish odor of chemicals from the darkroom, that odor fierce and familiar.

A low platform like a child's idea of a stage . . . the heavy dark velvet drape hung over a plywood partition . . . the tripod . . . the props . . . the work counter and shelves crowded with equipment. Above the work counter a dozen negatives are clipped to a wire: ghost figures that resolve themselves into human shapes, faces, pairs of eyes, trusting smiles. At what do we smile when we smile into the lens of a camera? Why this trust, this instant's elation? Iris peers at the negatives without touching them—she knows better than to touch them—sees that the subjects, a hand-holding young couple in Sunday clothes, are no one she knows. They have luridly black faces and arms . . . meaning they are "white" people.

Iris's uncle once remarked to her that he never took self-portraits as so many other photographers did (Iris had been looking at a portfolio of moody self-portraits in an issue of *Camera Arts*) because he was always embodied in the photographs he took of other people . . . even of landscapes, whatever. You couldn't see him, but he was there.

An absence, he said, but there.

Iris said she didn't understand . . . but then, no one understood Leslie Courtney when he talked "serious." Leslie said he didn't understand either, exactly. But that's how it was.

Leslie Courtney's most representative photographs, accumulated over a period of nearly thirty years, are on permanent, dusty display at the front of the store. Here too things are continually being added, nothing removed: baby pictures, family pictures, brides and grooms in their wedding finery . . . graduation classes in academic gowns and mortarboards . . . uniformed American Legionnaires, parading . . . sports teams, Rotary clubs, Sunday school classes, Chambers of Commerce, Flag Day ceremonies, office picnics . . . Hammond street scenes, views of the Cassadaga River, factories and slag heaps and smokestacks . . . scenes of the winter countryside . . . montages of babies and children in which constellations of faces are crowded together, as in a human hive—and in their midst, in no evident relationship to anything else, are photographs of the Courtneys: Iris's father as a dashing young man in his twenties, in a straw hat, a cigarette in a holder jutting FDR-style from his mouth; Duke and Persia as "The Incomparable Courtneys," in elegant formal attire, poised in what appears to be a foxtrot position, arms upraised, legs gracefully stretched, each pair of eyes gaily locking with the camera lens; Persia, very young, a beautiful dreamy full-faced girl, with her infant daughter wrapped in a lacy shawl . . . and with her year-old daughter . . . and with her two-year-old daughter . . . so, it might seem, to infinity. The camera's gaze is waist-high, a technical trick to make the subjects appear taller than the viewer, more exalted. Iris never wants to seek out these photographs but always does. As soon as she walks into the shop.

Feeling that stab of visceral horror: *You are going to die, here's proof.*

She's on the street in front of her uncle's store, drawing deep hard breaths, fresh charged rain-smelling air. Though there are shafts of bright sunshine piercing the clouds it has begun to rain . . . fat breathless drops. And there's a roiling kind of light. And a rainbow, the palest glimmer of a rainbow, above the spires of the big bridge.

Iris breathes deep into the lungs the way Duke and Persia inhale their cigarettes, as if drawing life from them. Iris too has begun to smoke, some . . . though never in the presence of adults.

She hears thunder that turns out to be, a minute later, not thunder but the roaring of motorcycles, the revving, gunning, uphill climbing of a dozen Harley-Davidsons on a street below

Main, along the river. Punks and hoodlums, Iris's father has said of the youngish leather-jacketed unshaven men who drive these motorcycles; just steer clear of them, he has warned. Iris looks but cannot see them from where she stands.

For this afternoon's photography session, Iris is wearing a pale yellow summer dress, eyelet collar and cuffs, and flat-heeled black patent leather "ballerina" shoes, and her snarly hair has been shampooed, vigorously brushed, fixed neatly in place with gold barrettes. Her delicately boned almost-beautiful face gives no suggestion of her thoughts, the crude mean forbidden filthy thoughts that so often assail her, even at dreamy moments.

Though now it's another sort of thought entirely, sudden as a flash of summer lightning: He's going to show up here, today! Of course! His brother's fortieth birthday!

Persia slices wedges of birthday cake for the three of them, Persia holds the knife out commandingly for Leslie Courtney to lick. "Is the frosting good?" she asks. There's a bright aggressive edge to her voice; the wine has brought a flush to her face.

Leslie grins like a boy and says, "Yes, yes, *very.*"

The scratchy old phonograph is playing orchestral music from *Carmen,* turned low.

Persia smiles and jokes with Leslie, and then for some reason she's staring . . . and not smiling. She is possibly thinking, This isn't the one, this is the brother. Then the crystal face of her wristwatch catches her eye. "Oh, damn! I have to make a telephone call, Les. Do you mind?"

Certainly Les doesn't mind.

He's curious about whom Persia might be calling but he doesn't mind. And he's too much of a gentleman to ask.

Persia makes the call at the front of the shop, as if not wanting to be overheard. And Leslie and Iris are left alone together . . . slightly uncomfortable together . . . for Leslie is thinking that he should say something to Iris about Duke Courtney's behavior, his inexplicable behavior these past several months, for which Leslie feels a confused sort of guilt; and Iris, stuffing her mouth with cake, is hoping Leslie won't say anything about Duke except that he will be coming over this afternoon, he's late but he means to help us celebrate, he wanted you and your mother to be surprised.

Leslie says awkwardly, "Your angel food cake is certainly a success, Iris."

Iris shrugs as if embarrassed, or annoyed. "Oh, they made us learn, Uncle Leslie, in school. All the girls have to take home economics class starting in seventh grade." Suddenly she's laughing, an angry sort of laugh. "Making beds, learning to cook, sewing skirts, aprons, pot holders. My God, pot holders!"

Leslie says reprovingly, "But the cake *is* delicious. Much better than bakery cake."

"Is it?"

It seems rude, Persia gone so long.

In Leslie Courtney, Duke's handsome patrician features have been smudged as if by a mischievous giant thumb. His eyes are beautiful and gold-flecked and shy and squinty. His hair is the color of damp sandpaper, shading to gray. His prim, boyish glasses give him an air of perpetual expectation, like a man always on tiptoe. Iris has overheard her father joking that her uncle Leslie has been in love with Persia for twelve years . . . but why is that a joke?

Above Leslie's head, on the wall, is a large framed photomontage, one of the "constellations" he used to make out of numberless miniature photographs of children. In it, hundreds of children's faces are squeezed together in a vertiginous crush, multiplied by mirroring and repetition techniques in the shape of a Christmas tree: MERRY CHRISTMAS 1949! the caption reads in silver lettering. Both white and Negro children are in the composition. Iris recalls that her own face, at the age of seven, is somewhere in the design, in fact several times, but she has forgotten where.

The effect of the Christmas tree constellation is less one of celebration, which Iris's uncle had intended, than that of a smothering cascade of humanity. Staring at it, you feel your breath start to quicken.

But since Leslie sees her staring at the composition Iris is led to say, not altogether sincerely, that it's too bad he doesn't do the constellations any longer, and Leslie says, "Yes," with an air of perplexed hurt, "I think so too. I never understood why the people you'd expect to be most enthusiastic, the children's parents, didn't support them . . . some were even unpleasant. I was even accused of being 'eccentric' by a columnist for the *Chronicle,* a self-styled critic." Considering the composition on the wall, Leslie appears, in profile, brooding and almost angry, like Duke Courtney recalling an old injustice. He says, "I was applying a law of nature to art, as I always do in my noncommercial work. I don't remember the precise principle now, but it was a sort of mathematical formula . . . the same faces repeated, some in mirror reversals. The symmetry of faces, the symmetry of the Christmas tree. . . . You know, Iris, you're in the tree somewhere."

Iris says, "Maybe the faces are too small. For the parents' taste, I mean." She speaks hurriedly, before Leslie can get to his feet to look for her miniature face. She feels a sickish dread of seeing it.

Leslie says stubbornly, "But that was the idea of the constellation as a form. And theme, too—individual faces *are* small, in the tree of life. Obviously!"

Iris says, "And Uncle Leslie, you know, whites and colored mixed . . . that offends some people. Some parents."

Leslie shrugs. This might be a revelation to him, but he isn't in a mood to pursue it. Instead, he refills his wineglass. Though Persia's glass is two thirds full, he refills it too. To the very brim. Quivering.

By five o'clock, when they are in the photography studio, the storm begins in earnest, pelting rain. The wind shifts to several winds, rocking the building. There is genuine lightning now, and loud cracking thunder, the waning light soft as cinders and a taste as of burning in the air . . . but in the studio they feel themselves sheltered. Safe.

Posing in the blaze of lights, Persia says, "I've heard that savage people won't allow their pictures to be taken because they think their souls will be stolen from them . . . but it's not that way with me. Whenever I see a picture of myself I think, There's proof: I really am here."

Her telephone call seems to have raised her spirits. Made her into a prism in which ordinary light becomes radiant. And she has deftly freshened up her face for the camera: Revlon powder with a fruity scent and bright red lipstick curving to her lips in a smile more natural than her own.

And there's the wine. Wine helps.

In the photography studio, Leslie Courtney is all business. He's quick, deft, unerring. Bending over Persia and Iris, adjusting lights on poles, checking the degree of light as it bounces off skin, contemplating his subjects as a single subject: a problem in composition. Strange, he can look at them, now, without love.

In a juvenile murmur Iris says, "If you aren't here, Mum, where *are* you?" But Persia lets the taunt slide by, doesn't even hear.

Mother and daughter are posed sitting together on the white wicker love seat—whose paint has begun to flake off—and at Persia's elbow there is a white vase containing one dozen white-stemmed roses. Persia is wearing a gauzy summer dress with an iridescent-greenish sheen, pearls around her neck, pearls screwed into her ears. The boat-necked bodice of the dress fits her full breasts snugly, and she has crossed one restless leg over the other: the kind of woman who is clearly not the age she seems but years older. Though she and the girl beside her don't in fact resemble each other very much, it's obvious that they are related.

Sisters, perhaps.

Iris says, irritated, "Don't, Momma, that *tickles.*"

Persia says, "I'm just trying to wet down this little curl or whatever . . . you don't want it to stick out, do you? *You're* the one who never can stand to see how you look."

"Uncle Leslie can retouch it."

"Uncle Leslie can't work miracles."

Iris squirms, uncomfortably warm under the lights. And the lights always make her uneasy, resentful, put her in mind of the tonsillectomy she'd had at the age of five, Momma and Daddy assuring her it was nothing, wouldn't hurt, just "going to sleep," and there was the astonishing, unbelievable *ether mask* so calmly fastened to her face as she struggled and screamed . . . the adults, surgeon, nurses, attendants, calmly observing as she pitched forward and died.

Though the storm has broken the air is still humid, close. Iris feels sweat prickling at all her pores. She blames Persia for making her wear this damned dress, the collar, the cuffs. . . . She says, in an undertone, "A true artist can work miracles. A true artist can do any damn thing."

"Don't say 'damn.' "

"*You* say 'damn' all the time. *You* say a lot worse."

"That's my privilege, Miss Smartie," Persia says. She laughs, belches, disguises it as a hiccup. "The privilege of the damned."

Iris scratches at an armpit, she's so suddenly miserable.

Where is he? Why is he making them wait so long?

Iris says meanly, but somehow it turns out pleading, "Oh, Momma, you say such extravagant *things.*"

Leslie Courtney is hunched under the black cloth, behind his camera on its tripod: the beautiful expensive Kodak that is the grand gesture of his professional life up until now. Sometimes he's wakened in the night as by a stabbing toothache, wondering how he dared buy himself such a camera, how his income, his "prospects for the future," justify such an expenditure.

Each time he studies that woman under the lights, through the viewer, through the camera's clinical eye, he is amazed . . . reduced to an intimidated silence. It's an uncanny power Persia Courtney possesses, to light up her face at will—shining eyes, seemingly radiant smile—forehead smooth and unlined as if she were still nineteen years old, all adult strife, all marital heartbreak, yet to come, not even imagined.

Beside her, Iris appears to disadvantage. It is as if Persia has stolen all light from her daughter: she's an old-young child with sallow skin, dents beneath her eyes, tension in her jaw. Leslie feels a pang of guilt. He flinches from seeing, in a thirteen-year-old child, that small hard skull pushing through the flesh.

So he teases her, as he has done, here, behind the camera atop the tripod, for years: "Iris—can't you give us a *smile?*" He says, "When you were a little girl I'd bribe you with peppermint lollipops. Remember?"

She remembers. She smiles. Tries to smile. That quick happy-seeming smile, like Persia's.

Tucked close beside her, Persia maintains her radiant pose. Her mind clearly elsewhere, Persia, beneath the lights, is perfect.

"Some people"—Leslie sighs—"have to be bribed even into *happiness.*"

He begins to click the shutter. At last.

Until, a half hour later, the lights suddenly go out.

Persia and Iris cry out in unison; Leslie stares transfixed into darkness, utter pitch-blackness—where there'd been, an instant before, such light.

The storm has shut off their power. He should have expected it. He says, "Stay where you are, Persia! Iris! I'll get candles . . . just stay where you are. You might hurt yourself in the dark."

It's going to be all right, he tells himself. He has enough shots, he has some heart-stopping shots, he won't be cheated.

It's one of those mean gusty late-summer storms, blowing down from Lake Ontario: rain drumming against the windows, forks of lightning above the river, peals of thunder. Like *wartime,* Persia observes, in the movies.

They light candles, the three of them, shivering and excited as children, and grope their way to the front of Leslie's shop, to stand for some entranced minutes watching the storm—rain on the pavement like the tracery of machine-gun fire, veined flashes of lightning—then the thunder, which is deafening. Persia says as if thinking aloud, "This decides it: I'd be crazy to go out tonight!"

At the back, in Leslie's snug bachelor's quarters, they wait out the storm. There's an air of shelter here, secrecy, coziness. With a flourish, as if he'd long been waiting for this moment, Leslie lights a kerosene lamp; like most Hammond residents he's prepared for

64

power failures. Persia says luxuriously, *"This* is unexpected." Leslie empties the bottle of wine into her glass and into his; in a murmur Persia adds, *"Fun."*

Iris is too restless to sit with the adults. She moves from window to window, watching the storm. The air is fresh, edged with chill, smelling of rain, something sulfurous—a smell like the river, too—mixed with the briny odor from the fish store adjacent and the garbage cans in the alley. Where rain pelts, hammers, drums, slams like drunken revelers. Is this what she has been waiting for, these hours?

She thinks, I hate you all. I don't need you, not a one of you. She thinks, I'm happy.

By the gauzy halo of light from the kerosene lamp they finish the bottle of wine, then begin a bottle of Leslie's favorite bourbon.

Leslie Courtney is thinking, The woman is a prism in which ordinary light, refracted, reimagined, becomes radiant.

Persia says, "In a flash of lightning it's as if your skull is pried open, isn't it? And you're spilled out, somehow? Not you-who-you-are but you-inside-of-you. As if the world is ending and you see how . . . silly you've been, and petty, and small-minded, and stupid, thinking the wrong things mattered, all along. Does that make sense?" She laughs nervously, yet is pleased with her words. She is a woman whom men have so often flattered with their attentiveness to her words, such pleasure comes as a reflex.

Leslie has been staring at her. "What? Does what make sense?"

"I must be drunk."

"No, you're not."

"I'm *not,* I can't be. I've only had . . . I haven't had much." She watches Iris passing through a room, two doorways away, a long-legged child, headstrong, secretive, with a look of deep hurt. . . . Why hadn't Persia had a second baby, before it was too late? She says carefully, "This rain! It's like we're inside Niagara Falls. Washing everything away . . . all the dirt." There is a long pause. A lightning flash, and a beat of several seconds, and resounding thunder . . . the electrical storm at the heart of the rainstorm is moving to

65

the east. She says in a lowered voice, suddenly urgent, "It's true, what he told you. I was the one who asked him to leave. So that I could think. So that I wouldn't always just . . . feel." She adds bitterly, "Duke has that effect upon women. He counts on it."

"Does he!" Leslie murmurs.

Persia says, "When I found out he'd betrayed me, gone outside the marriage—"

"Betrayed you? How do you mean?" Leslie asks. "Not with other women?"

"In different ways," Persia says quickly. "I don't want to go into details. If you love and trust someone he can betray you with a word . . . an expression on his face. You know. Or maybe," she says carelessly, "you don't know."

"Well," says Leslie, smiling at his long bony fingers, "that's possible."

"When I first found out, I was almost happy . . . the way you are when something has been decided for you. Because when you love another person there is something off-center in you, like, you know, your soul is partly inside that person; it's been drawn out of you and it's in someone else? and might be injured? And you can't know, you really can't know, if it won't be? My parents are just farm people I guess you would say—I mean, Duke *did* say—simple people I suppose, they're Methodists, and they believe in Jesus Christ as their redeemer, and that sort of thing, but if you asked them to explain or to analyze, the way Duke analyzes things, to shed a little light on the subject, as Duke says, they'd clam up . . . they'd be embarrassed and resentful. Because there are things you don't talk about. Because there aren't the words. And falling in love with someone so different from yourself and anyone you know—getting married, having a baby, starting a family, living, you know, an adult life, living what you believe to be an adult life, a real life—nobody talks about these things, nobody seems to know the words. Like dancing, and suddenly the old steps aren't there for you, or the beat is wrong, so you have to improvise." She speaks quickly, half angrily, lifting her hair from the nape of her neck and fanning it out and letting it fall several times, not knowing what she does.

66

"But you love him," Leslie says softly.

"But I can't live with him," Persia says. She smiles, she's triumphant. "*I won't.*"

So they talk together, Leslie and Persia. It *is* as if they're beneath a waterfall, sheltered there, snug and secretive and conspiratorial. They talk in lowered voices . . . drift into silence . . . resume talking again . . . following the natural drift, Leslie Courtney is thinking, of whatever happens.

There is the conviction in him, lodged in his breast like a heartbeat, that an understanding of a profound sort is passing between him and Persia Courtney . . . if only Persia will remember in the morning.

Says Duke Courtney reverently, "Is there anywhere on earth more . . . unearthly . . . than a race-track on the day of a big race?"

At Schoharie Downs, this first Saturday in October, the air has a brittle whitish cast. The sky is a perfect blue like washed glass.

It's the afternoon of the Eastern States Sires harness-racing competition for two-year-old trotters, and the stands, which will seat approximately nine thousand people, are quickly filling. Voices sound and resound like windblown strips of confetti; a giant American flag whips raglike above the green-shingled clubhouse roof. When the Courtneys enter the Downs, several drivers are doing warm-up exercises with their horses on the track. The horses are Standardbred trotters, uniformly dark, sleek, high-headed, with the breed's broad strong chest and powerful legs. Behind them their drivers in brightly colored silks appear child-sized; the two-wheel sulkies, "bikes," appear scarcely larger than toys, wheels spinning dreamlike above the dirt track. Iris stares as if she has never seen racing horses before, never felt the visceral shock of such beauty, such animal grace, strength, power.

Like Persia, Iris has cultivated a hardness of heart, a cuticle to protect her heart, against such places: the mysterious places to which Duke Courtney is drawn. Yet here, like Persia herself, she is suddenly weakened. *Is there anywhere on earth more . . . unearthly?*

PRIVATE—MEMBERS AND THEIR GUESTS ONLY hangs in commanding slick-white letters outside the tinted glass doors of the clubhouse cocktail lounge. But Duke Courtney is a guest of course. Duke Courtney, guiding his wife and daughter, pushes on happily through.

A good deal of money is going to change hands here today.

Duke Courtney's host Mr. Yard, Duke Courtney's new friend, millionaire Standardbred breeder and owner from Pennsylvania, the gentleman with the clubhouse privileges and the wide wet porcelain-white smile, nearly bald, shiny-headed, in a striped lemon-and-gold blazer with brass buttons and a red carnation in his lapel, this nerved-up gregarious man paces about rubbing his hands briskly together as if in anticipation of the fact that it will be those hands . . . *those very hands* . . . into which some of the money will fall. With a happy sigh he says, "That's the one sure thing! The one absolutely incontestable and unavoidable sure thing! *A good deal of money is going to change hands here today.*"

Duke has explained to Persia and Iris that Mr. Yard is the owner of several horses, the most promising a two-year-old trotter named Lodestar, entered in the Eastern Sires race, for which the first-prize purse is $45,000. Naturally, Duke has bet on Lodestar, a combination bet—in which, should the horse win, place, or show, Duke stands to win—"a reasonable bet, a friendly bet, not at all excessive," as he assures Persia. Though Lodestar isn't the favorite, though the odds are 4 to 1 against his beating out the favorite, he's clearly one of the most promising horses, since his track time has averaged 1.59 and has been steadily improving. In the car driving to Schoharie, Duke and Persia spoke together quietly, carefully,

69

gently, of numerous things, things of the sort Iris might be allowed to hear, felt herself in fact meant to hear, and only when Duke parked their car in the massive parking lot behind Schoharie Downs did Persia ask how much he'd bet. Duke said, "Only one hundred dollars. Cross my heart."

And he'd turned to wink at Iris.

Mr. Yard, Mr. Calvin Yard, whom Duke has described as warm and unpretentious and "wholly democratic" despite his wealth, is with a party of some fifteen people, drinking and talking and laughing together in the cocktail lounge, when the Courtneys appear. It's flattering: he does seem to be genuinely happy to see Duke Courtney, to shake hands with him as if they were old friends, as if Duke were a younger brother perhaps, and to meet Duke's wife and daughter. "Here they are, Cal—my girls! My Persia, and my Iris!" Iris feels her father's hand at the small of her back, nudging. With Iris, Mr. Yard is warm and courteous; with Persia, Mr. Yard is warm and exuberant, grasping her hand, staring at her, murmuring, "Persia Courtney—at last! My dear, I've heard so much about you." Mr. Yard is in his mid-sixties, thick-necked, with small pink-rimmed eyes, a kindly mouth, no wife or immediate family in attendance; and Persia Courtney, though not entirely relaxed, far from her usual party self, manages to smile prettily, if a bit archly. "Ah—I'd better not ask *what*."

Mr. Yard throws his head back and bawls with laughter. It's the kind of happy human sound others just naturally echo.

October 6, 1955: a week to the day since Duke Courtney has moved back to the Holland Street flat. Not all his things are there yet—his things are scattered throughout Hammond, it seems— but *he's* there . . . in his rightful place, as he says. Where his heart has been all along. As he says.

A black waiter neatly uniformed in white brings drinks to Mr. Yard's party; not long afterward, he returns with more drinks . . . that same waiter or another. There are several black waiters and it's easy to confuse them in their uniforms; a uniform has the effect of making individuals look alike but with these clubhouse waiters it's their manner too, their coolness inside their friendly smiles, *Yes, sir,*

No, sir, Right, sir! Iris notes that all the clubhouse patrons are white, all the waiters black. If Schoharie Downs is like other tracks Duke has taken her to there will be few black faces in the stands, no black drivers.

Iris once asked Duke why, and Duke's answer came quick and glib: They'd be out of place, sweetie.

Iris notes too that, of the men in the cocktail lounge, her father is surely the most attractive . . . as Persia, even in her subdued mood, is surely the most attractive woman. Energy seems to shimmer from Duke like heat waves above a summer highway; an interior radiance glitters in his eyes, not icy now. Duke Courtney is the man in any group who shakes hands most vigorously and happily . . . a man who is most himself when shaking hands or causing hands to be shaken in his presence.

And laughter: there's always laughter in Duke Courtney's presence.

Now Duke sees Iris watching him, winks, and flashes her the high sign . . . thumb and forefinger forming a little O.

To Iris's surprise her father comes over to join her where she's standing alone, lonely seeming, by a plate glass window overlooking the track.

"Been missing my little girl, all this time," Duke says, "those months. Like a piece of my heart was bitten out, y'know?"

Though Duke doesn't sound sad: sounds very cheerful, in fact.

It's the racetrack high. Iris has heard Duke speak of it, even philosophize about it: a definite sensation, in the chest, guts, groin. Oh, yes.

In the car, as they'd left Hammond and approached Schoharie, Duke had begun to hum under his breath, hum and sing a bit as, around the house, in good moods and bad, Persia so often sings. ". . . *my heart is aglow!*"

Duke repeats he's missed his little girl so much but Iris can't think of a single word to say in response, her brain seems to be struck blank: here's Daddy squeezing her against him with an arm slung around her shoulders so her heart quickens with pleasure sharp as dread, Daddy's big gold Masonic ring prominent amid the

71

gold-glinting hairs of his knuckles, and she's tongue-tied; he's a little hurt but teasing. "It sure doesn't sound as if my best baby missed *me*."

Iris mumbles yes of course she did, yes Daddy of course.

Duke doesn't hear, so she has to repeat it. "Yes, Daddy. Of course."

The past several months have been "knotty" times, Duke says. As Iris knows. Working his ass off, driving that car—on commission, no salary—in the hick regions of the state. But he's determined to get that load of debt off his shoulders and begin again; he'll make it up to Iris, to Iris and Iris's mother, she knows that, doesn't she?

Iris says yes she knows it.

Duke says, lowering his voice as if imparting a secret, "Sometimes, honey, it's the hardest thing on earth, I'd say it was the most courageous thing, to keep your distance from the very people you love more than your own life. Because you can love too much and you can do injury with your love, lose sight of proportion, perspective. Someday when you're older you'll understand." They are standing at the window; Duke's attention is being drawn down to the track where, in their colorful silks, more drivers are warming up their horses. The grandstand is nearly filled, there's movement everywhere. A sky lightly feathered with clouds. Even through the plate glass the tension of the racetrack can be felt like the quickening before an electrical storm.

Iris is startled by the sudden shift in her father's voice: "Can't you at least look at me? Here I am for Christ's sake baring my heart to you and . . . you can't even look at me?" Laughing, annoyed. "Bad as your mother."

Iris says, "I *am* looking at you, Daddy."

It's true, however, that Duke Courtney's daughter's eyes are narrowed and cold beneath those straight pale eyebrows: icy seagreen-gray so like his own.

It's possible that both father and daughter are remembering the identical episode: one vague morning in Duke Courtney's life about a year ago when he came to consciousness on the living room

72

sofa aware of a presence in the room silent and watchful . . . watching him . . . and only after a confused period of time (minutes? an hour?) did he realize that this presence was his own daughter, his little girl Iris: standing some feet away staring at him, wordless and detached with an almost clinical absorption in the struggle of a badly hung-over man to come to his senses, and he'd mumbled, *Iris? Honey? Can you give your old man just a . . . just a hand?* because it seemed to him he needed only to be sitting up, his full strength and rationality would flood back if he were only sitting up, but Iris hadn't responded, she stood her ground just watching, wordless and terrible in her detachment, and when he finally managed to get his eyes open and sit up it was a long time afterward and the room was empty, the apartment empty, both Iris and Persia were gone . . . his little girl gone.

Slipped away from him in his hour of need, without a sound.

Duke Courtney stares at his thin-faced pretty daughter wondering if she has begun to menstruate yet. Has Persia informed him? Should he know? Or has he forgotten much that he should know?

With his subtle seductive reproachful air Duke glances over at Persia, says, "Your mother at least seems to be enjoying herself," and then, when Iris merely nods, Iris can't think of any response so she merely nods, Duke says, "This might be a special day, honey. A day to remember. Might just be that Daddy has a nice little surprise up his sleeve." Now Iris's interest is quickened; he presses a forefinger against his lips and against hers. "But I don't want your mother to suspect. I want to watch her face . . . *so don't breathe a word.*"

Iris asks, "What is it? What surprise?"

"Uh-uh, sweetie. Mum's the word."

"Daddy, tell me."

Duke hugs her and turns her away from the crowd, saying, as if this were the true subject of their conversation, "You know I love you, Iris, don't you? You and your mother both?"

"Yes, Daddy."

"No matter the knotty times we've gone through, the three of us? No matter the . . . bad things your mother might have told you, about me?"

73

Iris's eyes are downcast, shy.

"Guess she's told you some things about me, huh? No need to go into details."

Iris says nothing.

Duke is talking, talking with passion yet in a way vaguely, as if, even as he speaks, he is thinking of other things; his attention is on other things. Turning his nearly empty glass of Scotch so that the melting ice cubes shift and tinkle like dice. "Law of nature, Darwinian evolution . . . the family, genetic unit. And a law of human morality. Blood. Bloodlines. Connections between people . . . their actual physical selves . . . bodies. . . ."

Iris wants to ask what the surprise is, the surprise that's a secret, but she knows better than to interrupt.

Down on the sunny track one of the horses suddenly breaks stride; he'd been pacing and now he's cantering, he's veering and plunging but his driver is strong-wristed and brings him back into control.

As Duke Courtney has said about races and horses and breeding, that's all it's about: control.

"You understand, don't you? My love for my family has always come first. I'd kill any man who tried to interfere with my family, any man that ever . . . it's just that life sometimes fights life."

This peculiar remark hovers in the air; Iris Courtney will remember it forever—*life sometimes fights life*—even as Duke Courtney's voice lifts, evaporates. In the midst of his urgency he's staring out the window—who can blame him?—those beautiful trotters and pacers, the drivers in their bright silks, the impending races. And the crowd in the grandstand: thousands of excited men and women, strangers, shimmering and winking particles of light, a hive of featureless faces, souls, *It's just the world,* Duke Courtney seems to be telling his daughter, *the world's infinite richness, and you a single heartbeat among so many.*

Iris says smartly, on the edge of insolence but not quite, "Of course I understand, I'm not a total fool."

* * *

74

Their seats for the afternoon of racing are in a specially reserved area of the clubhouse section, courtesy of Mr. Calvin Yard. Directly above the finish line, the blinding autumn sun comfortably at their backs. The best seats at Schoharie Downs.

"Great, huh? These seats? So aren't you glad you came, hon, instead of . . . moping around at home?"

Privilege gives a harsh tawny flare to Duke Courtney's eyes. He's a gentleman who takes no favors for granted and never forgets a friend . . . or an enemy.

Persia says, "Yes. I suppose."

Persia has always feared the racetrack atmosphere, it goes so swiftly to her head. Like a Bloody Mary before noon: that innocent tarty tomato taste, the terrible thrumming kick beneath. Before you know it every old vexation in your blood has turned to mere bubbles that *pop! pop! pop!*

But Persia laughs; Persia is beginning to enjoy herself.

Iris sits beside her gnawing at a thumbnail as the preliminary races pass loosed and uncontrolled as dreams. The speed of horses' bodies is always a sobering sight: the thudding hooves, the straining heads and necks. In the second race, at the half-mile point, a horse in the midst of the thunderous pack wobbles sideways and in an instant there's a tangle of horses, bikes, drivers . . . the stands ripple with little screams . . . Iris hides her eyes. The spill involves three horses; there are injuries, a medical team in attendance.

In a gesture both grandiloquent and resigned, Duke Courtney tears up his ticket for that race, lets the green pieces flutter away in the wind.

Persia casually inquires, "How much did you lose?"

In a navy blue sheath with a wide-shouldered little jacket, in a hat with a graceful scalloped brim and a single cloth gardenia, warm skin, red mouth, something stark and scared about the eyes, Persia Courtney is going to be tactful with her husband, and she is going to be careful with her husband . . . knowing now that she loves him, loves him more than life itself.

75

Plunging his life into her, tearing open her body between the legs. *We're fated*.

These are small pari-mutuel bets, Duke assures her. Token bets of $35, $50. His only true interest of the afternoon is the Eastern States Sires race . . . that is, his interest conjoining with Mr. Yard's: Lodestar. Lodestar and what he might, he just might, do this afternoon on the track. A colt who broke two minutes at his first qualifying heat, whose sire is a Hambletonian winner and whose dam is . . . how many thousands of dollars, hundreds of thousands, perhaps even millions, might a horse of such quality earn for his owners? Duke stabs at his upper lip with a forefinger. "If only I had the money to invest, if only I'd acted in time. . . ."

"How long have you known Cal Yard?" Persia asks.

"Oh, not long," Duke says. Then, shifting his shoulders inside his linen blazer, "Long enough."

Persia's thoughts, loosened by alcohol, are adrift: there's the October rent to be paid . . . there's last month's utility bill . . . payment on the new car (1953 Mercury bought secondhand from a man Persia knows at work) . . . payments on the old debt . . . life insurance, hospital insurance, dental work for all three of them . . . a new winter coat for Iris since the old is shabby and humiliating . . . and the water heater is always breaking down and if their landlord won't pay to have it repaired . . . Persia sighs. "Oh, shit."

A silver flask, initials C.T.Y., is in her hand; a lipstick-smudged paper cup, her own, is in her other hand.

Before the races began Mr. Yard had taken them off to the paddock to see his colt. So many handsome horses in so many stalls, so many grooms, drivers, owners, guests of owners, so much excitement, expectation, hope—at such moments, though happy social celebratory moments, you feel the true chill of human futility: *we are too many, too many, too many*. At Lodestar's stall, Mr. Yard made a point of drawing Persia forward, Persia who is shy of horses, saying, "Come meet my beauty," saying gaily, "Beauty—meet beauty!" Persia found herself staring eye to eye with the young trotter, surprised to see him still so coltish in his bones, so subdued, with a look almost of animal melancholy . . . secured in his stall, a light-cotton horse blanket draping his neck, back, hindquarters like a shroud. Lodestar is a bay with a lovely white blaze on his forehead and four uneven white "socks," not inordinately tall, rather slender, with a moderately broad chest. "He *is* beautiful," Persia said. Thinking that all expensive horses are beautiful, their expense is the point of the beauty.

Everyone crowded around, murmuring praise. Lodestar held his ground, blinking steadily, twitching his nostrils. The stalls were so clean in the paddock, there wasn't a fly to be seen. . . . In the stalls beside Lodestar were horses, rivals, seemingly more spirited than he: taller, broader-chested, more assured. Iris murmured in her mother's ear, "He seems so *sad*."

Now Persia says, "I thought Mr. Yard's horse looked a little . . . well, quiet. And sort of small-boned too, compared with—"

Duke says, "He isn't a giant. But he's very fast, and he's very smart." The mobile starting gate is moving down the track, a parade of horses close behind. Skeins of braided light move across the track like part-formed thoughts. "He's conserving his strength. Biding his time. You'll see. You have a surprise in store. *I've* seen that horse in action, don't forget."

"Yes," says Persia. "I know."

"And Cal Yard is my friend."

"Yes."

"He wouldn't mislead me."

"No."

Persia feels mildly dazed as if Duke has suddenly begun to speed their car . . . inching them toward 100 miles an hour.

Persia and Duke aren't quarreling and are not going to quarrel. Not now that they are together again, more in love than ever before.

But Duke persists. "Cal's impressed with you. I knew he would be."

Persia says, "He doesn't know me."

Duke says, "He knows what he sees."

Persia has no idea what they are talking about.

Beside her, Iris is listening, though pretending otherwise.

Persia knows very well that her daughter is keenly aware of what's being said, sly child, smarter than she lets on, knows more than she should know. In the past year or so Persia has sometimes heard Iris crying in the bathroom or in her bed, a muffled coughing sound, and it worries her (as she complains to Madelyn) that Iris won't cry in Persia's arms . . . refuses to cry with her. In fact, seeing Persia in tears, she's impatient, jeering, stamps out of the room, *Oh, Mother, will you for God's sake stop that!*

Madelyn says, Now that Duke is back there won't be any need for crying.

How they stare, these thousands of spectators, as the horses run the mile track, each race a miracle of concentration, building to almost unbearable suspense in the home stretch.

Iris too is caught up in the collective excitement, the horses' straining necks, the colorful head numbers . . . legs, manes, tails . . . drivers and bikes plunging in a single straining motion. For the approximate two minutes of each hard-run race, a gigantic happiness.

A happiness she'd like to swallow, swallow, swallow.

"But it seems such a pity to disqualify that horse if he could continue with the race. Why is it so important to keep the gait?" Persia asks. Duke exclaims softly, "Darling, is that a serious question?" And Mr. Yard, two seats down, leans over to say, "But Mrs. Courtney, that's the point of the sport: the discipline, the training, the gait. You are either a *pacer* or you are a *trotter.*"

"Yes," says Persia, laughing, rummaging in her purse for her pack of cigarettes, "but *why?*" Failing to find her cigarettes she slips a hand into Duke's inside coat pocket and extracts, like an expert pickpocket, his pack of Camels. It is a half-hour break before the Eastern States Sires race and everyone is tense, no one more tense than Duke Courtney . . . though, as he's said, he has bet only $100 on his friend's horse.

They talk about harness racing: the history, the tradition. Mr. Yard says, "Chariot racing is the oldest form of racing and the most noble. It doesn't defile the horse's figure by putting some stunted little monkey of a man on his back." Persia says, "But why are Standardbreds trained to run so"—she searches for the word she wants—"artificially? You force an animal to run against the grain of his nature, then he's penalized if—" Mr. Yard laughs in protest, saying, "But Persia, dear, that's the beauty of it, don't you see? It's like poetry, or music, or . . . whatever. The way the horse *runs*." Persia persists. "But it's so artificial. The pacers especially, swinging along like that. If I were four-legged, I'd go mad having to run that way." She shivers and laughs and exhales smoke from both nostrils, as if the vision of herself, down on all fours, naked, right arm and right leg in tandem, left leg and left arm in tandem, has gripped her imagination. The men are laughing at her, but their laughter has the ring of affection. She says, "An animal should be allowed its own nature!"

Duke says, "All sports are artificial, Persia. Sports and games. That's how we tell them from life. They have beginnings and endings; they have rules . . . boundaries . . . absolute winners and absolute losers, most of the time." He's speaking rapidly, aware of the time monitored on the payoff board; he's starting to sweat inside his clothes, thinking of the upcoming race. He forces himself to smile at his wife; he squeezes her fingers in his . . . these many fingers surprisingly cool, considering the heat of the discussion. "As far as that goes, sweetheart, who isn't an animal? On two legs or four? Aren't *you*? Inside your clothes? Inside your makeup? Inside *you*?"

Less than ten minutes before the start of the Eastern States Sires competition, Duke Courtney groans aloud as if in sexual frustration: God, how he'd like to up his ante on this race: to $300! to $500!

Persia, mistaking his tone, says, "Are you crazy?"

Duke laughs angrily. "To try to please you, *yes*."

Just before the race begins Iris glances over, sees that her father's eyes are mad-gleaming yellow, like the reflection of fire in glass.

79

Lodestar and his blue-silked driver begin in an outside, disadvantageous position . . . but the colt is fast and his driver shrewd and he advances quickly, until by the half-mile point he appears to be in fourth or fifth place out of the pack of fourteen . . . by the three-quarters point he is in third place . . . until, at the finish line, amid a confusion of plunging hooves and bright colors and gaudy spinning wheels—and deafening screams—he ends the race in second place, six tenths of a second behind the winner.

Second place!

Amid the handshakes and embraces and ecstatic congratulations Persia Courtney remains in her seat, stunned . . . realizing that, had it not been for her cowardice, Duke would have made far more money on the race than he has.

But he seems forgiving. Hauls her to her feet. Seizes her around the waist like a hungry young lover. Laughs, kisses her—even as she protests, "Oh, God, Duke, I'm so sorry"—and the others are looking on, wide happy smiles. What is it? Persia loses her balance and nearly falls. She and Duke like a drunken couple on the dance floor. *What is it?*

"We're rich!" Duke cries. "Going to be rich!"

It requires some minutes for poor Persia to comprehend the significance of the document Duke has drawn out of his pocket with a flourish to present to her: a legal form of some kind? a contract, sealed, signed, notarized? *Cornelius Courtney, Jr., in partnership with Belvedere Farms, Inc., of Lancaster, Pennsylvania. . . .*

Duke has bought a one fifth interest in Lodestar, he tells her. Cal Yard was generous enough—bighearted enough—to allow him, a small fry like him, to invest . . . just a few thousand dollars . . . in a potential champion, and already, today, in Lodestar's first big race, they've struck it rich: *the second-place purse is $25,000, and one fifth of $25,000 is . . . ?*

Staring at the document, Persia Courtney bursts into tears.

Suddenly, they're everywhere.

She's running. No, she's walking . . . not fast, not slow.

Mmmmmmmmmm sugar. Lookit that.

Oh, man, man . . . hey!

Sheeeee-it!

Hey girl . . . ?

Every sun-splotched space she crosses—sidewalk, street, trashy alley behind the apartment building, following the dirt path across the weedy lot by school, drifting just to be alone in the railroad yard, staring wet-eyed at the river—*hey girl! mmmmmmmm girl!* The boys, the boys' faces, the boys' bodies leap right into her head.

She laughs aloud, she's crazy with it. A fever driving the blood up, up. Chubby Checker bawling from car radios, Fats Domino bawling "Ain't That A Shame!"

This is the season it begins. Like climbing into the roller

coaster at Crystal Beach and no way out until the ride is over . . . *no way out*. She wonders, Will it be for the rest of my life?

It's as if, thinking of other things—and Iris Courtney has many things to think about—she blunders blind into bright empty patches of sunshine where forbidden thoughts are waiting.

Delicious thoughts.

The thoughts sliding in the boys' eyes. *Mmmmmmmm honey where're you goin' so fast? Hey girl where you headed?* Sweet saxophone whistles wet and sliding you have to listen hard to hear . . . have to know what to listen for, to hear.

Friday evening at the Rialto Theater, the shabbier of Hammond's two movie houses, upper East Avenue a short two blocks from the river. Whispers Nancy Dorsey into Iris Courtney's ear, "Oh, God, look. You think . . . ? *Don't look.*"

Nancy Dorsey's hot damp Spearmint breath. Iris Courtney's hot damp ear.

On screen, Ava Gardner's face immense as the side of a freight car leans above Robert Taylor's ashy face on its deathbed; at the top of the carpeted aisle, easing into the shadows, there's Jinx Fairchild and his friend Bobo Ritchie. Why would anyone come in now, ten minutes before the end of the main attraction . . . tall skinny long-limbed black boys with walks swooping as if they're on stilts, eyes greased as ball bearings scanning the dark?

Iris Courtney squints back to see it *is* Jinx Fairchild.

That's the neighborhood boy who makes her think, each time she happens to see him, of the jackknife a boy had, years ago . . . a white boy boastful of his wicked little knife where secret blades and even a corkscrew opened out like parts of the body you'd never guess were there.

Iris Courtney, Nancy Dorsey, Jeannette McNamara—ninth-graders at Hayden Belknap Junior High—sweater sleeves uniformly pushed up their forearms, mildly tarnished identification bracelets on their wrists, skin glimmering ghostly white in the dark. They stare unblinking at the screen as, seemingly by chance, the black boys veer in their direction . . . whispering, giggling, shoving each other . . . stumbling over legs into the row of seats just in front of the row in which the girls are sitting . . . uncoiling the stained seats and throwing themselves down as if, though not really trying, they wouldn't mind breaking the seats or dislodging the entire row.

Immediately their white-glaring sneakers, ankle-tops, Jinx Fairfield's size 12A, swing up to press against the backs of the seats in front of them. And that row of seats rocks too, like a subtle shifting of the earth.

Both boys tear open cellophane candy wrappers with their teeth.

Both boys chew fast and hard as if they haven't been fed for days.

Of course, the boys aren't sitting directly in front of the white girls. Just to the side, so it's easy to talk. What's going on in the movie, they ask, why's that dude dying, who's *she*, anybody like some M&Ms? The girls ignore them, staring at the screen as if transfixed. At first. Ghost images washing over their prim pale faces, reflected in their eyes. Then they begin whispering too. Can't resist. Can't stop laughing. The M&Ms are passed back, sticks of Spearmint are passed forward. There are spasms of mirth, and adults in nearby seats begin to glance back annoyed—murmuring *Shhhh!* or *Quiet please!* or *Shut up!*—which only intensifies the joke, whatever the joke is.

There's the *News of the World,* bomber pilots in formation, an obese maharajah being weighed on a scale, President Eisenhower gaunt as death . . . everything hilarious . . . the boys hunched and rocking in their seats and the girls spilling tears out of their eyes. Then an usher comes and shines his flashlight into the boys' faces and tells them to quiet down, which they do for a while; then the usher returns and shines his flashlight again and Bobo Ritchie growls, "Get outta my face, man," like it almost isn't a joke, though the girls break into peals of shocked laughter; then the usher returns with the manager, a heavyset white man in a business suit, no nonsense about *him,* and he orders Jinx and Bobo out of the theater: an order the boys obey sullenly, lazily . . . rising and stretching and yawning . . . preening for the three white girls and for anyone else who's watching.

Everyone in the Rialto, white and Negro, *is* watching.

"Out you go, boys. Out! . . . Out you go!" the manager says, loud and nervous.

"OK, man, cool it," says one of the boys. "Yeah, man, we be *goin'*," says the other, tall outlaw figures blocking the Technicolor screen, the Fairchild boy zipping up his sheepskin jacket like it's a razor he's wielding, the Ritchie boy, mean as the ace of spades in profile, tugging his wool knit cap low on his forehead like Joe Louis in an old photograph. Jive-talking and loud-laughing, the boys amble up the aisle, followed by the blustery white manager and the young white usher with his flashlight, and when they're gone there's a collective wave of relief in the audience. The Technicolor figures on the screen flood back in.

But Iris Courtney whispers to her friends, "Come on! Let's go!"

She's fierce, she's angry, snatching up her coat as the other girls stare at her astonished. "Come *on*," she says, and Nancy Dorsey hesitates, saying, "I don't know . . ." and Jeannette hesitates, "Oh, Iris . . . we'd better not."

Iris is on her feet pushing out into the aisle, as determined as her friends have ever seen her. "The hell with you, then," she says, running blind up the aisle . . . into the bright-lit foyer smelling of stale popcorn and sugary soft drinks . . . out into the street where a light snow is falling and the sky beyond the streetlights is invisible. The resolve with which Iris Courtney runs out of the Rialto, the strangeness in her pale face and pale eyes, you'd think someone had called her by name or was waiting for her, in the street, in the damp light-falling snow.

But there's no one: the black boys are gone.

I want to do good.

God, if there is a God . . . help me to be good.

At the rear of the fourth-floor walk-up at 372 Holland Street, Iris Courtney's room is a cramped twilit space even on bright days, a cave where light enters only obliquely, as if grudgingly, and is soaked up immediately by the density of the air inside; it has only a single, square window and this window is permanently shaded by an outdoor stairway that slants past it like the edge of a hand shading one's eyes.

Recalling this room, the strangeness of its architecture, the accidental nature of its being "hers," the injustice—to be forced to live for years in a room into which sunshine came so meagerly! with such an air of being unnatural, unearned!—Iris will wonder, as an adult, why her adolescent self did not protest, why she was not resentful or embittered. But only rarely, those years, does she complain to Persia about this room, or perhaps it is the flat itself she complains of, or the building with its rundown façade and ill-smelling stairways and "problem" tenants, or Holland Street, or the neighborhood: Lowertown. When she enters high school at Hammond Central, which is Uptown and miles away, she feels keenly the disadvantage of her address, a social embarrassment that might after all be remedied . . . if things were otherwise.

But in truth this room is the room of her imaginings, her memory, her plottings, calculations, hopes; she spends a good deal of time squatting at the window, head lowered as if meekly, watching the alley, the backs of the apartment buildings across the alley; at night she studies the lighted windows, those windows hidden by shades and those windows exposed; she knows the names of some of the tenants, especially those with children her approximate age, and it gives her comfort of a kind to see them in their homes—eating meals together, watching television together, preparing for bed—in their homes where they are meant to be.

Her uncle Leslie has a series of photographs taken years ago: office buildings, apartment buildings, private homes photographed at night, compositions of dark spaces and illuminated spaces, the camera's eye ground level and distant. You feel the uncrossable distance from *here* to *there*.

Sometimes Iris gets out of bed to crouch at her window, in her pajamas, watching lights across the alley as one by one they go out; if she crouches low, craning her neck, pressing her cheek against the splintery windowsill and looking up, she can see a patch of night-time sky . . . sometimes even the moon.

The moon: that fierce face with its look of interior radiance.

The moon: that evidence of a celestial distance truly uncrossable. A space where human preoccupations have no dominance, not even any language.

God, help me to be good.

God, if there is God . . . I know I am icy-hearted.

God, is there God? And who is "Iris," and why?

Until, in an uncharted instant, the approach of sleep makes a single body of sensation of the awkwardness of her posture at the window, the feel of the splintery wood against her cheek, the voiceless query of which, by day, Iris Courtney would be ashamed.

"I'm just talking in a normal voice—"
    "Oh, for Christ's sake—"
    "Don't interrupt! You accused me of—"
    "Who accused who?"
    "Wrong. Flat out wrong. You're inventing—"
    "Then where *were* you? And Friday too."
    "I told you."
    "And how much, this time?"
    "Honey, I told you."
    ". . . can't stand you lying!"
    "Keep your voice down, will you? You'll wake—"
    "Will *you?* . . . What did you do with the cigarettes?"
    ". . . accusing me. Anyone who knows me, these past few months—"
    "There's a laugh! Precious friends . . . 'buddies' . . . you'd have to think I'm crazy if I . . . where's your lighter? Mine's—"
    "You want some more ice? I'm going in."
    ". . . should both go in."
    "If you were . . . reasonable. . . ."
    "Well, you're not sleeping here tonight, so—"
    "If I wanted to, I—"
    ". . . outrage, the more I think of it. As though I can help it if somebody looks at me. If I didn't have to—"
    "Since when? You love it there: showing off your ass, your tits . . . fancy silky *tits*. You think I don't—"
    "Bastard. You'll wake her."
    ". . . in a normal voice, goddamn it."
    "You going in? I need some ice."
    "Matches?"
    "Uh. On the counter. No, wait—"
    "Honey, if we . . ."
    "Yes, but you're not sleeping in that bed."

". . . just agreed on some principles—"

"That bed you defiled—"

"Jesus, can't you get off that? Broken record . . ."

"It's just that you *lie.*"

". . . fucking broken record."

"Yes, and then you accuse me! Your own friend Jimmy French thought *that* was—"

"Leave that asshole out of it."

"He *is* an asshole; boy, you said it; for once, Mr. Smart Mouth, you said it: lending *you* money."

"Will you keep it down? Her room's right there."

"Ice?"

"Your glass?"

"Need some more."

"*Was* some more. I thought . . ."

"Tomorrow? Or . . ."

"Only be reasonable—"

". . . *not sleeping under this roof. Not.*"

"Damned broken record, aren't you? You telling Iris this kind of shit? You telling my brother?"

". . . worth twice of you. Liar. Bastard."

"You're drunk. Watch out, those cigarettes—"

"*You're* drunk. Last night, and tonight, and—"

"Keep it down, I said."

"Hit me, you bastard, and I'll . . ."

"Just keep it—"

". . . outrage. Saying you love me, then in the next breath—"

"I do love you."

"And your own daughter."

"I *do* love you . . . love you both."

"Don't *touch.*"

"If there wasn't this willful misunderstanding—"

" 'Life is serious,' he says, 'deadly serious, 'cause our lives are running out,' he says. Mr. Fancy Mouth says. 'But life is also—' "

"—also play. Yes, it is! It's self-evident!"

"Mr. High-on-His-Horse. Mr. Horse's Ass. Mr. Fancy Shit."

"Life is serious and life is play if you—"

"Fancy Shitmouth."

". . . willful distortion, reduced to your level . . . stupid-ity . . ."

"Mmmmmmmmmm, listen to him."

". . . hysterical cunt."

"Sunny side of the street. Life can be so sweet."

"Oh, for Christ's sake, Persia. Will you—"

". . . *coat an' get your hat. . . . Leave your worries on.* . . ."

"Nothing worse than a female drunk."

"Mmmmmmmmmm, Mr. Fancy Shitmouth. *Now* he's—"

". . . wake Iris? The neighborhood?"

"That hurts, damn you. Let go."

"Is that what you want? Humiliate yourself, and me, and—"

"Let *go.*"

". . . hysterical, every fucking—"

"Rather see her dead. Like my father said: he'd rather be dead than bankrupt, unable to support—"

"Your father! Don't make me laugh! That . . ."

"You think so? You don't think so?"

". . . his ass from a hole in the ground."

"I'd cut the child's throat and then I'd cut my own, to spare her! You don't believe me?"

". . . deliberate misunderstanding, distortion, everything re-duced to the level of the cunt."

". . . believe me?"

"I'm leaving, then."

"Yes, leave! Go to hell."

"Unreasonable. Every fucking time."

"*Leave.* Go on."

"Humiliate yourself, and me, and—"

"You're not taking that bottle: you leave that. Right where it is, mister."

"I brought it, and I'm—"

"Gonna call the police. That's what. Any provocation, threats, they said—"

"Just keep it down, will you? Jesus!"

"*I'm speaking in a normal voice.*"

"Only listen to . . ."

"More ice? If you're . . ."

"Your glass?"

In that room by the outdoor stairway there's a dressing table Duke built Iris for her tenth birthday out of an orange crate, strips of plywood, two mirrors from Woolworth's: a rectangular mirror for the top of the table and an oval mirror for the back. The pink cotton ruffled skirt was made by Aunt Madelyn on her Singer sewing machine.

Iris's dressing table is a smaller version of Persia's glittering dressing table but she has no cosmetics on it of course, no bottles of perfume, nail polish, moisturizer, only a few dusty glass animals and a little ivory box filled with bobby pins, a child's hairbrush, comb, and mirror set Persia bought for her, and these things Iris pushes neatly to one side as, more and more frequently during her final year at Hayden Belknap Junior High School, Iris hides away in her room to do her homework instead of doing it, as she'd done for years, at the kitchen table; the effort of writing, calculating math, thinking becomes irrevocably bound up in Iris's memory with the distracting presence not only of mirrors mirroring her face but of mirror images overlapping, mocking, challenging one another as in a fun house.

Sometimes Persia raps sharply on the door, pokes her head inside, asks why Iris doesn't come out and join her . . . or, if Duke's home, join them. Why's she hiding away here by herself? Little Miss Antisocial?

Iris says, "It's hard to concentrate out there."

Sometimes, her homework done, Iris reads the Bible here too.

During the brief but passionate period of time when, caught up by the religious enthusiasm of one of the prettier, more popular girls at school, or pretending to be caught up, Iris Courtney attended church services at the Presbyterian church on Attica Street—went to church, in fact, with the girl and the girl's family, all of them true Christians who befriended Iris with an eye to bringing all the Courtneys into the church in time.

The Bravermans. Caroline Braverman is Iris's friend's name.

And Iris hopes to join the young people's choir to which Caroline belongs; she knows she'd be happy forever if only she could be a part of that group of boys and girls singing with such conviction "A Mighty Fortress Is Our God," "Jesu, Lamb of God," "Come, Thou Redeemer!"

("Ridiculous," Duke Courtney says, and he isn't joking. "No kid of mine is going to fall for such crap," and Persia replies irritably, "Oh, leave her alone: it's just a phase she's going through.")

But it isn't a phase, Iris thinks, it's forever.

Please God help me to be good.

Please God help Jesus to come into my heart.

Mostly, Iris is hidden away in her room in dread of Persia and Duke.

Now the weather has turned, now it's freezing cold almost overnight, they can't sit outside on the stairway drinking and smoking and "discussing" their problems. Unless they go out for that purpose, or Duke is away, her parents are together in the small flat, trapped like animals in a zoo enclosure, and the slightest thing can set off a quarrel: a match struck recklessly close to a flammable fabric and there it goes!

Lately, Duke has been getting rough. Striking a wall with his fist, threatening to strike Persia, maybe giving her an open-handed slap, shoving her back against a door frame.

And Persia: what a temper! Suddenly there's glassware being broken, something thrown to the floor, a slamming door.

If someone leaves the apartment, however, it's always Duke.

Male prerogative.

Which leaves Persia behind, shouting and sobbing, "Liar! Bastard! How dare you! I hate you!" Unless there's deathly silence, and when Iris finally comes out of her room she'll discover Persia standing frozen, face wet with tears and mouth silently working.

Sometimes, seeing her, Iris retreats; she's frightened, and she's a coward, and she hates Persia when Persia looks like that, so she retreats back into her room, stares at her pale floating face in the oval mirror, knowing that love between men and women, the love of all the popular songs, is a hunger that mere possession can never quench.

Still, Iris dreams of bodies.

Male bodies. Female bodies.

Mmmmmmmmmmmm the things that happen between them, oh sweetie you don't want to know, that's not for little girls to know and *don't walk swinging your hips, hide your breasts if you can, there are words like "tits" "ass" "boobs" "cunt" "prick" you're not supposed to know, never call attention to yourself never lock eyes with any boy or man* but they seem to be everywhere suddenly, boys who stare crudely at her, boys who merely glance at her, boys who seem hardly to see her at all. White boys. Black boys. Boys at school. Older boys. Men. Two sailors, white duffel bags on their shoulders, striding out of the Greyhound bus terminal, long low wet-sounding whistles, in unison.

The black boys. The neighborhood boys.

Little Red Garlock urinating in the alley, standing spread-legged and deliberate, where Iris couldn't fail to see him . . . the pig.

That strange man who identified himself only as Al, knocked on the door where Iris was babysitting up the street for a friend of Persia's a few weeks ago, and Iris unthinkingly opened the door, and there was "Al," who'd come he said to see Persia's friend's husband: Iris's father's age—boiled-looking skin, eyes the color of quarters, in his shirt sleeves and the temperature must have been 25 degrees Fahrenheit—staring at Iris for just too long a beat before he turned away *yet there is something about the man, the slow smile like an insinuating drawl, the working of his mouth,* something that lodges, poisonous and sweet, in Iris Courtney for weeks.

Duke says, "These colored kids, you know . . . don't get too friendly with them. And don't ever be alone with them. The things a black man would like to do to a white girl . . . Christ, you wouldn't even want to think."

Duke says, "They'd peel the skin off us if they could, they hate us so. But they can't. So they're courteous to our faces when they have to be and we're courteous to them, but don't ever confuse it, Iris, for anything else."

The neighborhood boys. The black boys. Black men. Hanging in the doorway of the Gowanda Street barbershop, screechy-laughing in the doorway of the fish fry place, the barbecue place, Leo's Bar & Grill, Poppa D's, the Cleveland Social Club with its windowless façade painted electric blue. *Don't walk too fast* the white girls caution one another, *don't walk too slow:* scared, tremulous, eyes straight ahead, a tingling in the pit of the belly like minnows darting in shadowy water.

Sometimes the girls overhear snatches of what these men say to one another; sometimes they have to imagine.

Young black man, good-looking, a rolling gait like he's actually cruising in his car—headed south on Pitt Street as Iris is headed north—eats her up with his eyes, makes a smile of his teeth like tusks, discards her like a spat-out rind the very moment they pass each other . . . *and all deliberate, and all stylized.* Like a new loud popular song Iris hasn't yet heard.

She'd thought the young man was Sugar Baby Fairchild, decided no, probably not. She remembers Sugar Baby skinnier, friendlier.

Iris confides in one of her girlfriends, brash, not thinking how it might get repeated at school, "If I was colored . . . I'd know who I was!"

93

11

Saturday afternoon, a day in March 1956 on the verge of melting, and here's Little Red Garlock in green canvas windbreaker and baseball cap worn reversed on his head, knees out, haunches busy, pedaling a bicycle that's too small for him, in and out of traffic on lower Railroad Street . . . and every girl he sights between the approximate ages of twelve and twenty who's close enough to the curb to hear, he's got his special message for: delivered with a wide wet grin, a stretch of his worm-skinned lips, heavy-lidded eyes like killers in the movies. Some of the girls Little Red knows by name, some just by their faces; a few will shout back at him, but most just stare in surprise or disbelief or, strangely, a kind of shrinking shame. It's this shame that excites him . . . fun too to see how the same girl responds differently on different days, depending if she sights him in time. Little Red doesn't give a shit for getting into neighborhood trouble—unless it's trouble with the police, 'cause that's going to be trouble with his daddy too—but his instinct seems to guide him; he seems to know which girls are the right ones, enjoys his weird power of being able to sing out his message to a girl walking on the sidewalk and she'll hear it for sure while others close by, sometimes her own momma or kid sister with her, won't hear a thing, and even if the girl keeps on walking not looking at him doing her damnedest to pretend she hasn't heard, *Little Red knows she has heard*. That's his instinct too.

So sighting the Courtney girl crossing the street Little Red swerves coasting in her direction and croons out, "Hey girlie! hey Iiiii-ris!"—in that sly sliding way he's perfected as if it's a song he's singing to himself, no special meanness to it, or nastiness—"hey titties wanna suck my cock?" and as he hurtles by he gives this white-faced little cunt his best toothy grin and locks eyes with her; she's too surprised to look away in time: "Yummmmmmmmmmmm-mmmm!"

It's said that Little Red Garlock is a retard but he isn't, maybe just acts that way sometimes for his own reasons.

Like now. This bright-thawing March day. Flying on one of his brothers' bicycles, singing out his message to this girl, and this girl, and this girl, delicious as a sticky handful of Little Red's favorite candy, candy corn, he's the kind of tough-jawed hillbilly kid who when his bicycle's front wheel hits a pothole he hardly feels the jolt and kick in his teeth, just flying along so fast and happy and right-feeling he doesn't need to think where he's going, or why, until he gets there.

Little Red Garlock has discovered that, if you haul your ass where it's expected, people will tell you what comes next.

It's the Mayflower Movers warehouse by the river he's headed for . . . yes, where he has a job, started after Christmas. Loading and unloading cartons of furniture with his cousin Carly Boback, $1.20 an hour, best fucking job Little Red Garlock has had ever in his life.

It's said that Little Red Garlock got the way he is, mean and crazy-cunning, by being knocked upside the head one too many times by his daddy Vernon Garlock. Which is maybe true or maybe half true.

Yes, there are eyewitness accounts of Vernon whupping the boy with his belt, chasing him half naked in the street, even in bad weather: Vernon roaring and drunk, the boy whimpering like an animal. Maybe that *was* Little Red, or maybe another boy; there's a changeable number of children in the Garlock household, and they're all the kind that need to be whupped now and then.

By now, when the seventh precinct Hammond police get called by neighbors of the Garlocks—and of other troublesome families like the Feneys, the McAleers, the Winnicks—half the time they don't bother to send a squad car over. It's domestic trouble, it's not their jurisdiction. A husband beating his wife, a father beating his kids—unless somebody kills somebody else it's not their jurisdiction. Vernon Garlock has been jailed several times, his longest stretch thirty days (assault, drunk-and-disorderly), Little Red too has been hauled into the station and slapped around by police and frightened into docility, but in general the seventh precinct is bored with these calls; they have more serious crimes to deal with: murders, armed robbery, nigger punks. When Nancy Dorsey's mother telephoned the precinct to complain that the Garlock boy was "touching" and "doing things to" and "threatening" her daughter, then aged eleven, the desk sergeant told her maybe she'd better move out of the neighborhood or keep her little girl in the house; he ended by saying, "Could be worse: could be a nigger."

They say that Little Red was born dirty.

Not just dirty-minded and dirty-mouthed—he didn't grow into that until aged eight or so—but truly dirty: a patina like the grime of years covered him even as a newborn infant rosy-slick and shining out of his momma's womb.

And he had a full head of carrot-colored hair. A fat husky bawling infant weighing eleven pounds three ounces.

Not just sucking and tugging at his momma's breast but biting, gnawing, bruising: kicking and crying for more milk even as milk dribbled out of his mouth.

As a young child Little Red was forever filthy. Soiled himself

96

and anyone reckless enough to hold him. Soiled every item of his clothing, soiled the bedsheets and blankets, soiled the carpets and floors and walls of the Garlock house, even soiled things the family swore he hadn't been anywhere near! Mrs. Garlock was determined to love him above any of her children because before he was born she'd been granted a vision: the angel Gabriel appeared to her holding aloft in his hand a "bright-shining" baby with flame-colored hair that skipped back a generation to Vesta Garlock's grandfather, who'd been gassed to death in the Great War and buried in some common grave in a place called Normandy, France, of which no one had ever heard—this poor man who'd never had a chance to live out his own life wanted now to return to earth again. The baby was baptized in his name, Patrick Wesley, and Mrs. Garlock tried not to despair of his dirt and his dirty ways, his habit of peeing where he stood or doing worse, and sometimes playing with it, smearing it on the walls: baby shit caked in the poor woman's hair and wedged permanently under her fingernails, streaks of it on everything she cherished, her hand-embroidered sheets, pillowcases, doilies brought north from home.

Years on end Mrs. Garlock did her best with the child. Tried to scrub him clean, teach him the ways of cleanliness. Fighting him down into the tub until her fingers were worn and scabby and Little Red began to get too strong for her, strong and mean. By the age of five Little Red had muscles in tight little bunches, made people stare and laugh, asking was he an adult midget; and that oversized head of orangey-red hair, that head the boy learned to use for butting, even against his daddy sometimes. Vernon Garlock disciplined the boy as he'd done all his children and as his daddy had done him, but a man's arm wearies . . . a man can lose interest even in whipping. Little Red's brothers and sisters soon learned to keep their distance. Thus it fell to Vesta Garlock solely to perceive of herself as the means by which one "Patrick Wesley" was redeemed in the flesh of a second "Patrick Wesley," not knowing where the first left off and the second began—or if the first *was* the second, whole and complete, even in his dirty ways.

Mrs. Garlock prayed to God to show her guidance, then to the angel Gabriel. But where there had been a vision of radiance and certainty now there was nothing.

Little Red was six, that Christmas when Mrs. Garlock made her final effort to scrub him decent and clean: she boiled a five-gallon pail of water on the stove, and this water she poured into the tub, and open-eyed in a dream she tried to force her son into the scalding water . . . but Little Red was too smart for her, and too strong.

Naked as an animal in just his skin Little Red ran off yelping and hid away for three days in the bitter cold, probably under a neighbor's house, feeding himself out of garbage cans and the dumpsters behind Loblaw's Groceries, and when he came back home nobody took special notice of him at first since the household was upset with Mrs. Garlock's raving and lunacy . . . this poor woman was never to be the same again.

There was Vernon Garlock at the kitchen table, a bottle of Genesee 12-Horse Ale in his hand, when Little Red appeared naked and battered and sick-looking in the doorway, and Vernon Garlock stared at the boy as if he'd never seen him before, or never seen such a disgusting sight. "You little shit," Vernon said, "where you *been?*"

Adding, before the boy could reply, in words like the pronouncement of death, *"You broke your momma's heart."*

Nobody's home. It's almost 10 P.M. So Iris Courtney slips on her mother's midnight-blue raincoat and runs out thinking she'll buy some cigarettes . . . like an adult woman.

Like Persia: "Chesterfields, please."

Nobody's home—Iris doesn't count herself—and she has no idea when they will be home or whether one will come home without the other, so she runs over to Cheney's Variety a few blocks away.

It's an April evening tasting of something sweet as peaches, a smell too of rain, that shimmering feel to the streets and the streetlamps and the headlights of cars that make familiar landscapes look unfamiliar.

Iris is going to Cheney's instead of the late-night Rexall's though it's farther away. And not on a block of Gowanda Street that Persia or Duke would like to see their daughter in, nighttime or day.

Iris thinks, The hell with them.

Iris tightens the belt of Persia's raincoat, which is a size or two too large for her. Casting her gaze downward at the coat's sleek blue sheen she feels a rush of excitement.

Thinking, The hell with *her.*

The words of a popular song by a singing group called the Platters are running repeatedly in Iris's head; she can't seem to dislodge them. *0 yes! I'm the Great Pretender!* Iris resists anything jammed in her head but it isn't easy to unjam such things; they seem to float about in the very air—*lonely but no one can tell 0 yes*—like the tinkly mind-numbing tune of a commercial or a movie cartoon, its very rhythms primitive and hypnotic. The human will is a weak muscle, Duke Courtney says, unless it is brought under strict discipline. Sometimes Iris becomes conscious she's been humming a song without knowing it, even singing the words under her breath. Breathy as a prayer.

The brain is what? a radio with a million million tubes, wires, connections? You can't know they're there until something goes wrong and the static starts, every station blasting at once. What you think you *are,* then . . . where is it?

Still, Iris believes in the will. Intends to exercise and discipline and control it like a muscle of her very body.

In Cheney's Variety, the talk is loud and hilarious and punctuated by hoots, howls, laughter: laughter like donkeys braying, like monkeys screeching at the zoo, like that lunatic high-pitched cicada of late summer that Persia calls, hands pressed over her ears, the "razor-bug." The air's adrift in cigarette smoke.

Iris Courtney stands breathless in the doorway. It's as if she has run a long distance through the rain . . . though it isn't raining. A light like candle flame lifts in her eyes, her smile is quick and hopeful, what can be sweeter than the chorus of "H'lo, Iris" and "Hiya, Iris" and "Hey girl!" But her head is buzzing so she can't sort out which one is Jinx Fairchild, or if he has even said a word.

Though he's smiling toward her, eyes hooded, just slightly shy; she guesses, yes, he has.

Iris hasn't been in Cheney's for maybe a week but it seems, now, she'd been here only the night before.

Her quick-darting eyes take in with relief the fact that there is another white girl in Cheney's tonight: Bonnie Haugen with her (white) boyfriend Steve, sitting at the counter. Five black boys and Bonnie and Steve, all of them classmates at the high school, talking about something that has them convulsed with a prurient sort of laughter . . . drinking soft drinks, smoking cigarettes, killing time. Cheney's is the neighborhood place for killing time; it's as if, inside Cheney's, there *is* no actual time.

Though an illuminated wall clock advertising Sealtest Ice Cream is conspicuous on the rear wall, glowing like a moon.

Only Jinx Fairchild has any purpose to being here; he's lazily mopping part of the linoleum floor with a big wooden-handled mop. Jinx works in the variety store after school and much of Saturday. Iris believes that Cheney's, a rundown shabby little place but a cheery little place, is one of the few Negro-owned businesses in the neighborhood; she has reason to think that the owner, a fat good-natured older man, might be a relative of Jinx's, but she has never asked. She doesn't know Jinx Fairchild quite that way, to ask such a question.

Careful as if stepping on patches of thin ice Iris steps over the damp, shining spots in the linoleum. Jinx hasn't been able to get the filthy floor very clean but it's surely cleaner where he has mopped than where he has not.

Iris gets a soft drink from the cooler, selects a pack of Chesterfields from the cigarette display. There is a New York State law forbidding the sale of cigarettes to minors, but the law isn't invariably enforced. When Jinx rings up the sale he says, teasing, "Them cigarettes for your momma, Iris, like last time, or for somebody else?" Iris says, "My momma. You know that." Jinx says, "Yah, your momma ain't seen many of them cigarettes, I guess, last time. Or's gonna, this." Iris says happily, "Oh, she won't mind me opening the pack just to test out one or two . . . she's an understanding kind of momma." Jinx makes a smile of his big white damp-looking teeth and says, "Poor lady ain't got much say in it, any case." These words

101

are so honeyed and melodic they could be anything, even obscenities. It's the music Iris hears, not the sense. Staring up at Jinx Fairchild—such a tall gangling boy the vertebrae at the back of her neck feel the strain—she couldn't say what *is* the sense.

His long fingers, stained brown, but a lighter brown, almost a pale rosy-pink, on the insides . . . when he scoops change out of the cash register, he presses it into her hand like they're shaking hands, black-boy style, the way she sees them do in school.

Blond pony-tailed Bonnie Haugen calls out, as if Iris Courtney were a close friend, not a younger neighborhood girl she'd ordinarily snub, "*You're* out kinda late, Iris—you alone?"

Iris says, coloring faintly, "Oh, I don't mind." She feels the subtle insult, a puddle of awkwardness as they all look at her.

Though perhaps Bonnie, aglow with her boyfriend's attention, shiny-faced, crimson-lipsticked, basking too in the nerved-up company of the several black boys, means no insult at all. She clutches at Iris's arm and says with a snort, "Wait'll you hear the weird stuff these guys been telling us. I mean . . . *weird*." Bobo Ritchie protests, "It's all in the newspaper, man! Ain't no secret!" And Roosevelt Shields says, cutting his eyes at Iris, "Hell, I bet Iris know all about it—*she* the kind don't keep her head in no sand."

Thus Iris feels encouraged to stay in Cheney's. For a while. Though it *is* late.

Though Persia will be worried about her, if Persia comes home before she does. It had not occurred to Iris to leave a note.

They're talking about the lurid case of a Buffalo doctor named Pilcher who was arrested the previous day for "trafficking" in human body parts and organs. For fifteen years, according to police, Pilcher had sold heads, brains, genitals, hands and feet, ears, hearts, kidneys, livers, intestines to medical research laboratories as far away as Tennessee, Florida, Colorado . . . sending them through the mail SPECIAL DELIVERY: FRAGILE. Iris read of the case in the local newspaper, turned on the six o'clock television news to learn a little more. A white man, clerical in appearance, with earnest eyes and a mild stammer, Pilcher was accused of bribing morgue workers at various Buffalo hospitals to provide him with body parts and organs "indiscriminately" from white and Negro corpses . . . though naturally, indigent corpses being predominantly Negro, the body parts and organs were predominantly from Negroes.

On television, Dr. Pilcher denied acting out of profit. His reasons were "purely altruistic . . . in the service of medical science."

In his loud braying voice Bobo Ritchie says, "How they found 'em, some heads wrapped loose in some box, startin' to *leak*. Man, this is the post office! Some cat hadda open that box an' see what's inside!"

Blond Bonnie, coarse-skinned but good-looking Bonnie, sucks in smoke from her cigarette and exhales it contemplatively. She says, shivering, "Jesus, is that weird! I mean . . . sick! You got to wonder," she says vehemently, "what kinda doctor's *that*."

Something about Bonnie's remark, delivered in such innocence, sets them all laughing. It's a moment of high hilarity.

Jinx Fairchild observes, face suddenly crinkled as if this is a thought that hurts, "Man, your head you give so much thought to . . . your eyes you been studyin' in the mirror . . . winding up like *that*. And then all kinds of people don't know you and don't give no damn about you, smart-asses, making *jokes*."

Jinx's voice is an adult voice suddenly, shading off into an aggrieved silence.

The red minute hand of the Sealtest clock continues round and round. Amid the talking and laughing—the white boy, Steve, is doing an imitation of something he's seen in a movie—Iris's gaze is drawn to it repeatedly, yet unseeingly. The clock face is bright-lit, and Cheney's is bright-lit, like a Christmas tree; which is why Iris Courtney is here.

Iris has been clutching her package of Chesterfields; she's forgotten to open it. Now, as if expertly, she tears the cellophane with her thumbnail.

She says, "Jinx, are there matches?"

Bobo Ritchie steps up, says, "*I* got some, honey, you wanna find 'em." Bobo makes them all laugh by flopping his arms out,

103

comically inviting Iris to go through his pockets, frisk him, and in the high spirits of the moment Iris hesitates, comes close to doing so. Bobo Ritchie is sixteen years old, built like a baby bull, saddle-hued skin and nose that looks as if someone flattened it with the palm of a hand, wearing a stained white T-shirt that fits his big muscles snug as a fist in a tight glove. Iris knows that Bobo Ritchie's father was killed by police but she doesn't know why, exactly; he'd been beaten up and killed out of white-cop meanness—or had *he* beaten up some white woman and brought his trouble on himself? Of Jinx Fairchild's friends Bobo is the loudest and the brawliest, and Iris has always shied away from something derisory in his manner. "C'mon, girl," Bobo says, grinning, crowding Iris back against one of the stools, "*I* got lots of matches."

Jinx tosses Iris a matchbook. Says, "Why're *you* smoking, anyway? Just gets a habit."

Roosevelt leans in, smirking. "Jinx, he in trainin'. He a *good* boy."

"Yah," says Bobo, "he one of the best."

Iris lights her cigarette, her hands not quite steady. Out on the street there's the sound of a car backfiring, loud as gunfire.

Jivey Bobo clamps his arm around Jinx's neck as if in a wrestling hold and bawls, with a sniggering grin and a wink at Iris, "Yah, this nigger's one of the best. Gonna get him a basketball schol'ship someday—go to *college!* Like he a *white boy!* Shittin' in a gold-plate *bucket!*"

Jinx wrestles him away, angry, laughing. "Fuck you."

Steve, whose last name Iris doesn't know, draws his comb out of his jeans pocket and in one fluid motion sifts it through his hair: dark-blond, oiled, serrated as a rooster's comb. He's a quiet boy a little older than the others, and for a moment Iris envies Bonnie that he's *hers*. However rough and loud the black boys get . . . flaring up like black boys seem to do.

As if she's only now noticed, Bonnie Haugen says to Iris, "Hey, I like your coat—that's *cool*. Is it new?"

Iris stares down at the midnight blue, the stiff waterproofed fabric, the cheap plastic buttons. She neither recognizes the coat nor knows what Bonnie has asked.

It must be the cigarette; she's beginning to cough. "I don't know," she says softly. Each word is a mysterious effort . . . as if sound and sense have cracked apart. "I guess so."

Bonnie looks at Iris strangely, doesn't ask anything more.

The bright moon clock with the perpetual-motion minute hand is showing 10:47 when Iris Courtney leaves Cheney's for home.

She walks quickly, head lowered. The air is cool, the wind from the river chill as March. In Hammond it's always wintry-feeling except in the deeps of summer when it's *too* hot . . . the fault of living too near the Great Lakes. Snow piled seven feet high bordering the streets in January. Snowstorms blinding the sun. Iris thinks, I'll go live somewhere else; I'll be a photographer who travels.

The stores on Gowanda Street are darkened of course except for a tavern or two and a bright-lit Negro diner with a homemade sign RIBS . . . a few cars, some of them teenagers' with noisy mufflers, blasting radios . . . a city bus marked EAST AVENUE, only a few passengers aboard. But there are people on the street, young Negroes, couples, some children running loose: Negro children of the kind Iris instinctively shrinks from when they charge in her direction, as they are now, yipping and squealing at one another in a little pack, oblivious of others on the sidewalk. Not that they mean harm, they're just oblivious.

Though sometimes they snatch purses. Aunt Madelyn's, once. *Where was I? Oh, I was just . . . out. With some friends. . . . Well, I just didn't think to. You didn't leave a note, yourself.*

Iris has been sucking at her cigarette out of stubbornness; now she tosses it into a gutter. She feels mildly sick. A few days before she'd overheard Persia speaking to Duke on the telephone, Duke at one of the downstate racetracks, Persia speaking with unaccustomed hesitation, sadness. "Not angry at all, honey, just broken-hearted. . . . Oh, Jesus, he *is* so beautiful. . . . But if Mr. Clay

105

and the trainer think—if that's how things are, an injury like that—oh, honey, look: just don't tell me any details, please? Don't tell me or Iris, please?"

And after a pause, "Probably won't ask, after a while. She's like that. Picks up on things . . . doesn't have to be told."

And after another pause, "Truly I don't blame you, honey; like I said, that's water under the bridge . . . just feel so *sad*. He's so beautiful, or was."

Now Iris recalls this conversation, the half she'd heard and the half she hadn't needed to hear, and she swallows hard, thinks, *He's so beautiful, or was.*

In the unnamed weed-bordered alley behind the North Bridge Machine Works, which runs parallel with Gowanda Street to the west and Holland Street to the east, Iris can see fairly well by moonlight . . . isn't afraid to be walking here . . . though she walks quickly, half running, eyes scanning the shadows. She hears the *ping!* of a fat raindrop atop the brick wall beside her . . . another *ping!* . . . the sound of rain in grass . . . but is it raining?

She stops, puzzled. Not quite alarmed, but puzzled. Holds out her hands, glances up at the sky, where there's a filmy half-moon, a scattering of stars.

Iris has turned up the alley because she knows it by heart, the crumbling brick wall behind the North Bridge Machine Works, the acre of untended and seemingly unowned land strewn with trash and garbage where children play, the fire-damaged warehouse with its NO TRESPASSING signs—this is an alley that becomes, in another two blocks, the very alley behind 372 Holland Street. It's a shortcut home, a dark place but seemingly deserted, and she'd wanted to avoid the busy intersection of East Avenue and Holland where at this hour the local hillbilly tavern the Horseshoe Bar & Grill will be in full swing.

But she's stopped, now. Beginning to worry. That sinking sickening sensation that she has made a mistake: in the interstices of the brick wall, which stretches on and on and on, there are mysterious doorways and crevices, she knows; she has explored them herself.

It comes to her: Bobo Ritchie has run up to the next street, which is Girard, and he's doubled back down the alley to cut her off. Iris has seen Bobo and his friends run when they want to run and she knows they are fast. But how would Bobo have known where Iris was going, for certain? She'd looked back several times leaving Cheney's and she hadn't seen anyone going in or coming out . . . or looking after her from the doorway.

Her legs are strong too, if it comes to that.

Iris will run, run, run . . . until her heart bursts.

She's been standing motionless, head cocked shrewd as a listening animal's, and just when she decides there *is* nothing, no danger, another *ping!* sounds against the wall only a few feet away, beside her.

She takes a quick step backward. "Is someone there?"

Muffled laughter, laughter of crude childish glee . . . something familiar about it.

Not Bobo Ritchie. That isn't Bobo.

No black boy: the cadences are wrong.

Not far ahead are the rears, most of them lighted, of several row houses fronting on Holland Street, but Iris's way to them is cut off . . . assuming she'd want to pound against someone's back door and scream for help.

Now a handful of gravel strikes Iris in the face and chest; she cries out more in surprise than pain.

There's a rustling ahead, in an overgrown stretch of scrub trees, bushes, weeds. Then the low, nearly inaudible croon: "Iiiiiiiii-ris!"

Little Red Garlock.

It's known in the neighborhood that Little Red prowls the back alleys, peers in windows where he can, trespasses in back yards, the hallways of apartment and office buildings, sometimes walks off with things for which he has no need, or breaks things, no purpose to it except malicious pleasure. Once the janitor of the

107

Courtneys' building discovered him sleeping in the basement; another time Little Red pushed his way into a woman's house, saying he wanted to use her bathroom, and urinated on her kitchen floor; he delights in behaving as he does and in eluding all attempts to guide or reform or punish him . . . this, Iris has thought, out of a deep animal spite for who he is and to what and whom he belongs.

Little Red has emerged out of the bushes, loose-limbed, grinning.

"Hiya, Iiiiiii-ris! Where ya going!"

He's advancing toward Iris as Iris retreats, stepping backward —she doesn't want to turn and run—clowning around as if this is a game and Iris really wants to play it; she's just pretending to be frightened and angry.

Iris says, "I see *you* too. I know who you are."

Iris says, trembling with hatred, "I'm going to tell my father . . . he'll call the police on you."

Little Red laughs, jogging amiably forward. He's crooning obscene words in a singsong Iris doesn't want to hear and making ugly twisting gestures at his crotch she doesn't want to see.

In this awkward but seemingly coordinated fashion, the one in retreat, the other coming forward, Iris Courtney and Little Red Garlock emerge from the alley onto East Avenue at approximately 11 P.M. of April 2, 1956. Evidently no one sees them. Or will remember seeing them, afterward.

At East Avenue, Iris begins to run.

Little Red sings out, behind her, "Gonna hurt ya titties!"

Iris isn't panicked exactly; she's thinking he can't get her here, on the street: there are cars, there are people close by, she can scream. She's frightened but not panicked, reasoning that she'll be safest running back to Cheney's; she can hide there, Little Red would never dare follow her inside; there's a pay phone, she can call home—and maybe by now someone *is* home—she can telephone the police.

Iris is a good runner, she's good at school sports, basketball, volleyball, elementary gymnastics, she knows how to run without sucking air through her mouth, lifting her knees, keeping to a gait—but she's running clumsily now, her elbows against her sides as, behind her, running too, that pig Little Red Garlock shouts out for anyone to hear who's within earshot, "Titties! titties! hey, titties!"

Persia's glamour raincoat isn't good for running in. Half sobbing, Iris thinks, I hate hate hate you all.

At Cheney's, it looks as if Jinx Fairchild is just closing up: no one else is in the store, only a single light is burning above the cash register, Jinx is pulling a green sweatshirt down over his head . . . dark green, boastful white letter H. It's one of Jinx's basketball letters, awards for outstanding performance.

Uptown at Hammond Central High, the word is that Jinx Fairchild, Sugar Baby's younger brother, is even better than Sugar Baby . . . whom all but the youngest students remember not for himself, not as a presence at school, but as a great basketball player: best Negro player ever at Hammond.

Pulling the sweatshirt down over his head, running his big hands through his frizzy hair, Jinx Fairchild is maybe thinking of this, or of some of this, smiling that smile Iris knows . . . one side of his mouth dented in, as if something is sucking his smile back.

When Iris Courtney pushes through the door with its tinkly little bell, wild-eyed, white as death, Jinx Fairchild stares at her in utter astonishment as if he has never seen her before.

Iris won't remember, afterward—the name that comes to her first isn't Jinx but Verlyn.

But it's Jinx she says, telling him in a breathless spill of words about Little Red Garlock: how he has frightened her, pursued her, she can't get past him to get home, she doesn't know what to do.

"*Him?* That peckerhead asshole?" Jinx says, incensed.

Jinx goes out onto the sidewalk to investigate and, yes, sure enough, there's Little Red Garlock up the block, poised at the curb, watching. Jinx calls out, "Hey, you—go on outta here, asshole! You gonna get in trouble!" Little Red calls back something mocking and unintelligible. Doesn't budge from where he's standing.

This continues for a few minutes: Jinx Fairchild shaking his fist and shouting for Little Red Garlock to get on home, Little Red Garlock laughing and hooting in reply.

Iris stands in the doorway, shivering, not knowing if she should be angry or worried or deeply embarrassed; it seems to her that Jinx Fairchild is disgusted at her too. It strikes her for the first time in her life that, to a black person, two whites might have more in common—more that's deep-cored, familial, ineluctable—than any white might have with him.

Iris says quickly, "I'll call home. My father can come get me." Why is she lying? she wonders. She knows Duke won't be home. "Maybe I can call the police."

Jinx turns back to her, hardly hearing. "What he done to you, that shithead? He touch you? He *done* anything?"

Iris says, "No. He didn't get that close."

Jinx says, outraged, "That asshole, somebody should break his head for him. Everybody knows he's crazy, gonna hurt somebody one of these days; then it's too late. *I'm* gonna hurt him serious, he don't go away."

Iris says, "Can I use the telephone?"

"Yah," says Jinx, hardly listening. He struts up the sidewalk a few yards, waving his fist at Little Red, who laughs and waves a fist back.

Iris drops a nickel into the pay phone and dials her home number with a forefinger so chilled and clammy her skin sticks against the plastic surface of the telephone. There's a ringing, ringing, ringing at the other end; through it, Iris can see the lighted living room as she'd left it, seemingly so long ago, on so whimsical an impulse. There is the sadly glamorous sofa with its many pillows, there are the twin lavender-ceramic table lamps with their glossy purple shades always slightly askew, there is the coffee table, its cigarette-scorched surface hidden, heaped with Persia's fashion magazines and paperback books, bright lurid covers, and Duke's unread back issues of *Time, Life, Fortune, Racing News, Standardbred Illustrated*. . . . Atop one of the tables is the handsome silver-framed photograph of Lodestar taken by Leslie Courtney the previous autumn.

This room, and the other rooms, empty.

Iris hangs up, and her nickel is promptly returned.

Jinx has come back inside, furious. She asks him hesitantly, "Should I call the police? Or . . . you think they'd just laugh at me?"

Jinx stares at her as if she's crazy. His eyes are large, white-rimmed, intelligent and glistening, slightly protuberant; his sharp-boned face looks warmly suffused with blood. "Nobody needs no cops down here! Christ sake! *I'm* not afraid of that redneck bastard. *I* ain't no helpless girl!" He snatches the receiver out of her fingers and slams it back into the cradle. Iris has never heard him speak with so pronounced a Negro accent before.

Jinx locks up the little store. Leaves that single light burning above the cash register.

Outside, Jinx is naturally headed in Little Red's direction. Iris tugs at his arm, pleads with him; why don't they walk the other way, why don't they avoid him, all she wants is to get home. "Please don't get into a fight," Iris says.

Jinx says angrily, "You live up this way, don't you? Why you want to walk any other way, just 'cause of that asshole?" He's incensed, excited, ready for a fight; Iris can feel the heat coming off him. Again Jinx says, as if in contempt, "*I* ain't no helpless girl some shithead can push around."

Little Red is waiting . . . appears to be waiting.

Iris pulls on Jinx's arm harder, pulls at him with both hands, her voice rising to a little scream. "Jinx, *please!*"

So Jinx relents. All right, they can walk the other way. It's clear Jinx Fairchild is the kind of boy you have to scream at and beg and tussle with before he'll surrender to what he knows is good sense.

They're walking north on Gowanda Street out of the district of little shops and tenement buildings, in the direction of the river—an area of warehouses primarily, deserted at this hour—making an effort not to hear Little Red Garlock hooting and crooning after them. It's a place of sharp echoes, sharp fishy smells mixed with the odor of diesel oil. Jinx has Iris by the arm, pulling her along, walking her fast, but he seems oblivious of her, he's so angry: cursing Little Red Garlock and muttering to himself. Iris is thinking that she'd seen Jinx Fairchild angry like this one other time, up at Cassadaga Park, the summer before, when she and her uncle Leslie were wandering through the park looking for portrait subjects (Iris accompanies her uncle sometimes; there's an old family notion that she is his "assistant," his "apprentice," though in fact he rarely requires her; he's the kind of person who prefers to work alone), photographing people, with their permission of course, whose faces or manner or quality of being Leslie felt drawn to; and they'd stood for a while rapt in fascination watching a group of black boys playing basketball, one of them Jinx Fairchild, struck by the boys' skill, the quicksilver shifts and feints of their play, the shots from odd angles and distances that nonetheless sank through the raggedy-netted rim with such precision . . . then the game ended abruptly when a boy elbowed Jinx Fairchild, and an ugly exchange followed, and Leslie Courtney and Iris walked hurriedly away. And that vision of Jinx Fairchild yelling and pushing at another boy, and being pushed in return, Iris hasn't considered until now.

Behind them at a distance of about a half block Little Red Garlock trots in the middle of the street, hands cupped to his mouth. A happy lunacy shines in his eyes. His snarled and grease-stiffened hair, darkened to brown over the years, sits upon his head like a military helmet. What a game it is! How he loves it! Convinced too (for how can it be otherwise?) that the objects of his attention love it as he does.

Little Red Garlock has gone about for days on end seeing the world out of Jack Palance's slitted steely eyes: Jack Palance as the sleek black-clad killer in *Shane*. He has been Jerry Lewis, the quintessential retard. But he's happiest as Lou Costello, following his craziness where it leads like a trail of gasoline to which a match is touched, a Costello who does the kicking and pummeling and

112

hurting himself instead of merely absorbing it, pop-eyed, like a fat two-legged cushion.

Trotting in the street crooning, over and over, "White titties sucks nigger cock—*hey!* White titties sucks nigger cock—*hey!* Big juicy-black nigger cock!" Little Red doesn't weary; it's like riding a bicycle, pedal up, pedal down, round and round, the rhythm, the beat, once you get going you never want to stop.

For all his buffoonery Little Red knows precisely where Iris and the nigger boy are headed. He knows. Iris lives on Holland Street just below Girard (though "Holland" and "Girard" are not meaningful words to him, nor is "Iris," nor even in fact "Little Red"); thus they mean to cut over to Pitt Street at the river, or maybe over to Holland itself, and come up that way and elude him.

But he's too smart for them.

He knows every street and alley and path and shortcut in Lowertown—except maybe for the part of Lowertown, stretching off beyond Peach Tree Creek, that's all colored. He knows ways to climb roofs the people who own the very buildings don't know; he knows cellars, back yards, the geography of virtually every vacant lot, trails through the junglelike woods above Peach Tree Creek, trails through the city dump, every twist and turn and hillock and rocky inch of the trail along the river used by fishermen. His strategy now is simply to let the two of them think he's given up . . . while he cuts over to Pitt Street to wait for them.

Trotting sure as a dog through the alley behind the warehouses, Little Red could navigate this route with his eyes shut, but there's moonlight guiding him, washing around him and on him, luminescent in his eyes. Now Pitt Street: that steep hill. That good feeling plunging downhill like someone is pushing you, a hand at the small of the back.

He's humming to himself, a song without words.

Seeing Neeley's Diner shut and darkened, a giant sardine can, and the vision comes to him: Little Red and his cousin eating pancakes soaked in maple syrup and catsup, his mouth suddenly watering so hard it hurts.

Like his cock stiff with blood, pounding and tingling at the tip, it hurts; somebody's got to pay.

Now he's waiting for them, not even remembering for a moment or two who he's waiting for, just waiting—you haul your ass to wherever and when you get there it will come to you, why—and sure enough he sights them, those two: the nigger so tall he's freaky, the little girl's hair bouncing like silver, and Little Red hunched and grinning is an Indian scout in the mountains spying on his prey. He's got a bow and arrow in hand; he picks up a handful of gravel and lets fly . . . Little Red Garlock is so strong, has been blessed with such an aim, the buckshotlike gravel hits its target at a distance of many feet.

And hurts: hear them cry out?

"White titties sucks nigger cock!" he yells.

He sees in their faces how they hate him and how they're scared of him, knowing they are never *never* going to escape him; he's standing there hands on his hips grinning and happy as Little Red can be happy at such times, glorying in the pain and humiliation and confusion of others he understands are superior to him; yes, he well knows that and the happiness is in knowing it, that fact. For he isn't going to run off like his enemies; *he* isn't any coward. Standing his ground wriggling his hips pretending he's got big balloon breasts wriggling and bouncing too, singing his crooning song *White titties, nigger cock*, and this time the black boy isn't going to run away, you can see in his face he's trapped he's got to fight, so he comes walking quick and sure, not running but walking, up to where Little Red is waiting, and Little Red *is* waiting, and the black boy's so desperate he doesn't understand that Little Red Garlock outweighs him by thirty pounds or if he understands he's too desperate to care, just comes at him and Little Red gives a little scream in delight like Lou Costello might do, a mean-hearted Costello, no coward: "You gonna show me, coon?"

So the boys rush at each other, using their fists, wild swings, clumsy blows, at the foot of Pitt Street in a debris-littered lot beside Ace Trucking, Inc.

Jinx Fairchild is tall and vulnerable-seeming, not used to fighting, or anyway not used to fighting with such deadly seriousness, trading punches with a single opponent, none of his buddies watching, or his brother, and Little Red Garlock is a cunning opponent; his instinct is to bend at the knees, go lower, butt with his head.

Why don't these blows hurt? There's blood flying from someone's nose but no pain, only the sharp surprise and weight of it or maybe the pain is floating in the air and won't catch up until afterward. One of the boys is panting, almost sobbing, the other is just grunting, lips drawn back from his teeth in a grin; he's used to fighting and he's used to fighting dirty, Little Red's style is using his knee, using his head that's wicked if it catches you in the forehead, how can you protect yourself against it . . . you *can't*.

So then they're on the ground. Jinx goes to his knees and Little Red falls on him with a weird, happy yodel, all this time he's aware of someone watching, *someone watching Little Red Garlock,* so she'll tell the tale far and wide, or maybe it's the moon or maybe it's God up in the sky watching and smiling 'cause He's got to be on the side of who's winning, and if Iris Courtney wants to run for help where can she go? What can she do? No cars on Pitt Street or River Road, no houses close by, the closest place is a tavern a mile away on the river but she isn't thinking of that, she's too confused, upset, fearful, circling the struggling boys not knowing what to do, silent herself, wordless, in wonderment seeing that Jinx Fairchild is being hurt, his flailing blows aren't strong enough to hurt Little Red Garlock or even to stun or surprise him; what can she do? How can she help? She tries to pull at them as if to separate them but of course they ignore her, they're fierce as dogs struggling together intent to do harm but clumsy, grunting, cursing . . . she isn't there for them, doesn't exist, pleading, "Don't!" and "Stop!" and, to Little Red, "Leave him alone!"

She's thinking she must get help: she'll run to get help.

At the foot of Pitt Street, the vacant lot beside Ace Trucking, Inc.

A wet gauzy light from the moon. A dull-eyed streetlight at the corner.

Across the Cassadaga River—so wide in the darkness, so evil-smelling, choppy—there are lights glittering on shore, the lights of houses lifting into the hills. Atop the Hammond water tower a ring of lights, faint. And the winking red lights of the Hammond radio station, WHMM.

She'll get help but she doesn't move, she's transfixed watching Jinx Fairchild and Little Red Garlock scrambling about on the ground; they're ravenous to get at each other, grunting like lovers now they're stuck together, the burning flesh of one stuck to the flesh of the other; Jinx's nose is bleeding badly, there's a slash on his forehead that's bleeding badly, and the blood is on Little Red Garlock too. . . . Jinx's sweatshirt with the white *H* has been rudely yanked up to his shoulders, his gleaming dark back is exposed, and Iris wishes she could pull the sweatshirt back down, shield him. . . . *Jinx, kill him. Jinx, don't let him live.*

The fight isn't going the way Little Red Garlock expected, he's been hurt though he doesn't yet feel it, yes, but he does feel something, the inside of his mouth is bleeding, he's in a frenzy suddenly . . . wet blubbery lips . . . cursing . . . picks up a chunk of concrete and slams it against Jinx Fairchild's back and Jinx screams in pain like a wounded animal, managing to roll free—crazed with pain he rolls free—there's something in *his* hand wedge-shaped and heavy, something his fingers close upon in desperation, and he's bringing it down on Little Red's head . . . again, and again, again . . . his breath in a whistling sob.

Iris Courtney, watching Little Red Garlock die, stands transfixed.

I've got to get help, she thinks.

She watches. Can't look away.

PART TWO

Torsion

1

The day of her son's funeral, and the day following the funeral, and the next day, Vesta Garlock's absence is noted in the neighborhood.

On Gowanda Street, on Girard, on Chautauqua . . . in the alley behind the East Avenue stores where it's her custom to rummage through trash cans . . . in the park facing Precious Blood Church where she eats crackers and drinks Royal Crown Cola in all but the nastiest weather . . . in Woolworth's, in Rexall's, in the Mohigan Market & Butcher Shop, in French's Bakery, in Angelo's Diner, in Lulu's House of Beauty where she browses or prowls, makes unexpected visits . . . even as far away uptown as Montgomery Ward's on Main Street and Norban's Discount Clothing . . . in the cavernous vaulted lobby of the uptown post office . . . in the First Bank of Hammond with its regal marble-floored foyer from which, always courteously, the strange unkempt seemingly harmless woman is ejected on an average of twice weekly.

You wouldn't think anyone outside the Gowanda Street neighborhood would know who Vesta Garlock is, yet when Little Red's death is reported in the newspaper, given such extensive coverage, most people accustomed to seeing her guessed she must be the boy's mother.

That one? That crazy woman?

But she isn't crazy exactly, is she? Poor thing!

People familiar with hulking Little Red Garlock, though, find it hard to think of him as "Patrick Wesley." Surely Little Red was no Patrick Wesley! It's as if Death has altered him, so great is Death's power; look at the photograph of him the newspaper prints, years old, an earnest smiling seemingly normal boy of about twelve, only oversized ears and teeth to suggest something that's Garlock, special.

Then one day Mrs. Garlock is back on the street. Making her rounds.

It's strange, the woman looks like a drifter or a somnambulist but in fact she keeps to a well-defined schedule and itinerary: leaves home at sunrise, returns at sundown (if she returns at all; sometimes in warm weather she sleeps out); visits stores in no pattern but never skips Precious Blood Square, where there's a park bench that's *hers;* always rummages through the same trash cans in the alley behind East Avenue. A visit uptown, taking a city bus, is in the nature of a gift to herself, she'll be sure to go to Montgomery Ward's; "Monkey Wards" is Mrs. Garlock's favorite store in all of Hammond, she's almost smiling contemplating the wide aisles, the warehouse size, counters and counters of merchandise, and a certain smell over all, and she can use the ladies' room in the basement, sometimes sleep there; the floor manager isn't vigilant enough to have her ejected.

This morning Mrs. Garlock looks *different:* it's clear that someone has fixed her up in honor of her son's death and funeral.

Instead of her old shabby black coat stiff with dirt she's wearing a green-plaid coat, not new but almost new, a spring "topper," and she's wearing a black straw hat for mourning, and a black dress of some synthetic material that clings to her thin legs. Her hair, frazzled for years, has been washed and brushed and braided around her head by a deft, kindly hand, and her face has a scrubbed, shiny, almost fresh look. In Vesta Garlock too it seems that Death has worked a mysterious alteration.

This morning, passing by Lulu's House of Beauty, Mrs. Garlock arouses a flurry of sympathetic interest where usually there's only pity, dismay, or outright scorn: both operators and both their customers stand at the window to observe, noting in amazement the change in the woman's appearance, and Madelyn Daiches who's so good-hearted hurries out to tell Mrs. Garlock how sorry she was to hear the bad news, the shocking news, she hopes the police find whoever did it soon, but Mrs. Garlock isn't interested in her, not a bit, just crinkles her face up in distaste and turns away, walks away, the fastest Madelyn has ever seen her walk.

"And that's the thanks I get! I was only trying to be kind."

One April morning Hammond city police bring Mrs. Garlock and several other Garlocks to the seventh precinct station; it's the lineup they are asked to see, suspects in Patrick Wesley's murder.

Six men between the ages of twenty-three and thirty-five, arranged on a platform, in a lighted space, as in a burlesque show except everything is scaled down small; everyone is too close together.

All the men are white, all are casually dressed.

Since the killing, police making inquiries everywhere, along Gowanda Street door to door, have met with responses that aren't surprising (since they know the Garlocks) but haven't been helpful. Told that Little Red was a thief, a vandal, a trespasser, a pervert . . . not right in the head . . . damned little bastard that if anybody ever deserved to get killed *he* did. The kinds of remarks that can't be printed in the newspaper or aired over WHMM radio. They've determined that Little Red was killed in a vacant lot about fifty yards from the river, that his body was dumped off a wharf and into the river, but they haven't located the murder weapon . . . clearly it's in the river too, sunk to the bottom, and will never be recovered. They've determined that he'd been seen hours earlier on the street, on various streets, not in the company of the other, younger boys with whom he sometimes hung out, but no one seems to have noticed him later in the evening, or to have admitted seeing him.

The only tip police have had thus far—oddly, this tip has come to them from several apparently unrelated sources—is that Little Red Garlock antagonized a gang of motorcyclists recently and that they'd vowed to take revenge on him.

The other night there was a call from the Cassadaga House where some bikers from Buffalo and Rochester were drinking, and police went and arrested two men, charging them with drunk-and-disorderly conduct; in the precinct station, questioned rigorously and at some length about the Garlock murder, the men had incriminated two other men, who, they claimed, had boasted of stomping somebody the other night in Hammond and dumping his body in the river. "Why'd you do it?" these men were asked. Their reply: "We didn't like his looks."

So S.L. and R.T., two Hell's Angels from Buffalo brought to Hammond for interrogation, are in the lineup at the seventh precinct this morning: unshaven, dazed, pasty-faced, youngish fattish men in black leather vests, soiled T-shirts, oily jeans, and leather boots. With their bikers' costumes and their greasy Elvis Presley haircuts and the fright evident in the very set of their backbones it seems self-evident that, amid the lineup of local derelicts and a single plainclothes policeman, these two are the guilty parties . . . if anyone is guilty of having killed Little Red Garlock on the night of April 2. S.L.'s and R.T.'s alibis for that night too are highly suspicious.

But the Garlocks can't agree. One of them points to one of the suspects, another to another, still another to a third; they're quarrelsome, short-tempered; Vernon Garlock, who hates all policemen, sits sullen and bleary-eyed and won't even speak. And suddenly there's Vesta Garlock's vague wandering incantatory voice, as if she's been speaking all along but without the volume turned up, ". . . his allotment of time on earth, and if it's your time there's nothing to be done. Praise the Lord. In His bosom. I saw the angel Gabriel set his foot upon a cloud, bearing my boy homeward. There is nothing to be done. It is writ, 'Rejoice, and be exceedingly glad, for great is your reward in Heaven.' "

Following this, there's an awkward silence.

So there is no positive identification of the suspects, and the Hell's Angels from Buffalo must be released.

The Garlocks are deeply ashamed of Vesta, want to take her home with them, but the woman's too cunning . . . slips away. Has a request for the police sergeant: "Can you take me up to Monkey Wards? Now?"

The man stares at her. "Montgomery Ward's, ma'am?"

Mrs. Garlock is buttoning up her coat; she's impatient to be gone. "Yes. I said. *Monkey Wards.*"

2

A day and a night of rain, and now the Peach Tree Creek is overflowing its banks. Doesn't look like the same creek.

There's a dizzy angry-seeming rush of water toward and beneath and past the bridge but it's really many waters—snaky churning coils of waters of varying thicknesses—with a stink to it like two white-hot wires going up your nostrils into your brain.

After so much rain, the morning is mud. And glittering puddles. Dripping. Everywhere, the sound of dripping.

And the knife-sharp sunshine that hurts the eyes right through the lids . . . like the human skin is transparent.

Jinx Fairchild is standing on the Peach Tree Creek bridge thinking how the creek isn't any creek he knows, it's a place of perished things come alive again—like that part-submerged tree trunk he sights, a tangle of mean-looking roots still attached, could tear a swimmer's legs off if he was fool enough to mess with it . . .

corpse of a red-furred dog . . . corpse of something resembling a rat
. . . more tree limbs, loose boards, part of somebody's rowboat—all
these things alive, noisy, smelly, splashing white water and frothy
foam like laughter. Weird wild laughter! The kind, when you hear
it, everything in you wants to join in but you can't, somehow.

It's a morning following one of his bad nights. He's leaning on
the railing looking into the creek that's a familiar creek, known to
him as anything is known to him, except it isn't. He's letting that
dreamy sensation come over him—seems to start up from the
legs—they'd noticed when they were boys, he and Sugar Baby:
when you're standing on the bridge, which is solid and unmoving,
watching water rush beneath your feet, holding your eyes open and
unblinking, there's a mysterious moment (when *is* that moment? is
it always the same moment? and why?) when the water becomes still
and you're the one who is moving.

Jesus, must be ten years ago. Jinx and Sugar Baby and some
other children playing in the creek, messing around—except it was
hot then, late summer, that airless dead time, and you could see the
water's skin starting to form in the shallow places and you could
sure smell it though they hadn't thought the smell was actually bad,
only that it was the smell of Peach Tree Creek as natural as any
smell, building a little stronger and ranker day by day—and there's
a shout, there's Momma calling *Woodrow! Verlyn!* in that way she
had when they were little that lifted their heads like she already had
hold of their hair at the crown of their heads, jerking them around,
and they looked up to see Minnie Fairchild furious and disgusted
striding in their direction in her white uniform, whitish shiny
stockings on this steamy summer day, and her face, thinner then,
seemed black with rage—"You two! Damn you! Where's your
sense! I told you never play here, didn't I? Get your asses out of that
shit and get 'em out right now!"—and she'd chased them home so
angry she hadn't time to pause and scold the other children, neighbor's kids, as if it didn't matter, much, that they were playing in
shit too.

At home she'd scrubbed them. That was the worst. Their
heads, and inside their ears, even their fingernails and toenails—

which were dirty, but was it from Peach Tree Creek, or just any old harmless dirt? Made the two of them gargle with that evil-smelling mouthwash she brought home from the white doctor's, and no diluting it with water either, the way, if she was feeling kindly, she'd dilute their teaspoonfuls of cod-liver oil with orange juice. Sugar Baby giggled in Jinx's ear, "Now this stuff *is* horse piss, I bet you"—and Jinx started to gag.

But they'd outfoxed their smart momma. Smartest momma of any they knew but they'd outfoxed her 'cause naturally they came back to Peach Tree Creek to play, year following year . . . wasn't any other place.

Shit or no shit, thinks Jinx Fairchild, it's ours.

Mr. Hannah, tenth grade math, is gently chiding Jinx Fairchild for messing up his geometry test. Was he daydreaming? during the actual test? like his brain didn't know what his hand was doing?

Jinx Fairchild mumbles no.

Jinx Fairchild mumbles no, sir: tricky little courtesy his momma has instilled in him so now it's habit, almost.

How then, Mr. Hannah asks, can Jinx account for the fact that he worked problem number eight flawlessly but made the same glaringly obvious error on number three that every dumbbell in the class made?

Jinx Fairchild mumbles he doesn't know, takes the red-inked test paper in his fingers, and stares at it uncomprehending: 84 percent isn't a low grade but, yes, it's low in this case; ordinarily he'd be puzzled and embarrassed but not today; he's thinking how he did the test last Friday in a haze like a dream, blacked out, and didn't remember a thing of it afterward.

Mr. Hannah has favored Jinx Fairchild all year above even the majority of the white students in his class. He's a white man, Jinx has thought, who favors certain selected Negroes—Negroes easy to like—as a means of demonstrating it isn't anything racial, certainly can't be racist, the way he dislikes the others.

Hates fears loathes the others.

Says Mr. Hannah as Jinx turns to leave, "A mistake like that isn't *like* Jinx Fairchild, was the thought passed through my head," and he means it half teasing, like most of the teachers at the high school he takes himself very seriously, so Jinx nods, backing off; his eyes too hooded and achey to meet his teacher's, he says in parting, "Guess if I did it, Mr. Hannah, it *is* me." Just the slightest edge of defiance in his voice.

Which Mr. Hannah, who favors Jinx Fairchild, doesn't exactly hear.

Everywhere he goes, through every hour and day, he's carrying these hands of his . . . there's a shyness in the glance he gives them, like he's in the presence of something with its own thoughts and its own unknowable consciousness of *him*.

Jinx Fairchild's hands. That have administered Death.

Long skinny fingers he'd thought he knew and owned. Like his penis that isn't always his exactly . . . charged with blood, flexing like a fist . . . and that blood too not his. The most important part of that blood not his.

I have dealt Death. With these hands.

In school, at work, riding the city bus, drifting off to be by himself, Jinx Fairchild steals these quick shy glances at his hands. It's as if he has never really looked at them before. The dark brown skin with its faint oily-red sheen, the pinkish palms, light nails. Such moments, he's fascinated to realize that being brown-skinned is an ambiguous thing, as if his skin's color could fade or wear out. He's a long way from *black*.

Jinx Fairchild's finger span is such that from the tip of the smallest finger to the reach of the thumb he can grip a basketball in his right hand; can't quite manage it with the left. Ten fingers holding a ball as it flies from him, chest level, seemingly without effort, all nerve endings, quick as a cat's eye. Since sixth or seventh grade Jinx has had a strange fantasy of being on the basketball court blind, stone blind, but outplaying the other boys, his fast hands and fast feet doing it all for him. And the bleachers erupting in cheers, the gym a solid vibrating wall of applause.

This past season, when he'd played so well, much of the

cheering in fact for him, it hadn't seemed altogether real. Not heart-pumping real like the fantasy. There Jinx Fairchild is standing tall and loose-muscled and relaxed-seeming behind the foul line in his sweat-soaked green and white Hammond T-shirt and shorts, and his eyes are on the basket and the ball's moving in his hands like a dreamy spinning globe while the pretty white girls in their cheerleaders' jumpers toss themselves crazy—

> *Gimme a J!*
> *Gimme an I!*
> *Gimme an N!*
> *Gimme an X!*

—and a part of his mind detaches itself from him, taking up residence with certain of the older black boys leaning against the wall, boys who aren't at Hammond any longer, never did graduate; it's clear from that angle of vision that if Jinx Fairchild sinks the foul shot the crowd's going to love him and if he misses they're going to see him for what he is: just another nigger-boy.

Most of the time, Jinx Fairchild doesn't miss.

And every basket he sinks, all the points he racks up for the team, the sensation gets stronger . . . everything more unreal. All he's doing is forestalling the time when the cheering stops and they see him harsh and clear as he sees himself.

Yes, it's true: Jinx Fairchild's brain didn't know what his hands intended.

Picking up a piece of concrete—or was it a rock, twice the size of his fist—bringing it down against the other's head . . . not once, to stun him, but again, again, again . . . to kill.

Sure, Jinx Fairchild knows the brittle softness of the human skull, like a sheet of ice that feels hard but, once it shatters, shatters. Yet somehow he'd been a party to smashing it. Administering Death in one! two! three! four! *five!* frenzied hammer blows.

After that, he doesn't remember.

Remembers the girl. The white girl. That floating white-petal face.

Remembers the weight, the heft, of the body . . . remembers the water slapping against the shore.

Remembers, much later, burning his bloodstained sweatshirt in the dump off Peach Tree Street, trying to wash the stains out of his jeans and off his hands.

These things he remembers like flashes of dream that don't connect, but he doesn't remember the person who links them, can't call back any continuous Jinx Fairchild except to know it's him and was him all along. *Run on home,* he'd told the girl, *get on out of here,* and she'd hesitated stunned and blank-faced as if Jinx Fairchild had struck her too; she was about to speak and he advanced upon her grinning wild like a Halloween pumpkin the little kids have carved out but carved out crooked: *Go on, run! Get the fuck away! You got no business here, bitch!*

If that was Jinx Fairchild speaking, Minnie Fairchild's younger boy, her heart, her hope, her light-of-my-life, it was no Jinx Fairchild anyone had ever heard before.

In New York State it's the electric chair. Jinx has learned that electricity flows in circuits: if the circuit isn't looped electricity can't flow. When they electrocute you the circuit is looped by the human body. *It's Death that flows through you.*

They say, in the electric chair, all that voltage crashing through you, you're dancing around like you're being whipped. Raw flesh is being cooked so there's that smell, and a steamy smoke rising out of your head. Jinx knows from the movies there's a hood over the condemned man's head but in his wide-eyed dreaming, these nights, he sees Jinx Fairchild in the chair with the clamps and straps and electrodes, bare head exposed.

As Sugar Baby observed, a few months ago, when headlines were of the "rapist murderer" Tyrone Tilley who was electrocuted at Sing Sing—this weak-minded Negro from only sixty miles away in Buffalo the defense attorneys claimed couldn't remember what he'd done back beyond a day or so, let alone what he hadn't done—"Sure do like to fry niggers in this U.S. of A.! *Hot diggety!*"

* * *

129

"You sick? Verlyn?"

Minnie Fairchild is looking at her son, her sixteen-year-old, slouch-shouldered in the kitchen doorway as if he'd just wandered in from some other world. His mouth is working like he's chewing the inside of his lips, his hands are half hidden at his thighs but peeking out . . . and it almost seems he's peeking down through his eyelashes at *them*.

Quick as the flash of Minnie Fairchild's Singer sewing machine needle comes the unwanted thought that her beloved Verlyn is going to take after his father after all, not after her: *her* brains, *her* common sense, *her* decency, *her* dignity, *her* ambition. But quick too as a flash the thought is gone. "Been acting so sad-hearted these past few days, Verlyn, it just don't seem like *you*," Minnie says, half tender and half accusing. She's easing in the direction of what her sons call Momma-talk: *don't* instead of *doesn't,* old honey inflections the woman can summon back at will like Eartha Kitt purring baby talk to seduce her man.

Minnie Fairchild's four children know that the Momma-talk is just what comes first; if it fails to get results, and fairly immediate results, Minnie-talk will resume.

So Jinx rouses himself, makes an effort to straighten his backbone, smiles at his mother, and tries to speak and can't think of a word . . . just stands there staring.

Minnie is cleaning fish at the sink. Large-mouthed bass Mr. Fairchild caught that day, fishing on the Cassadaga. *Chop!* go the heads. *Chop!* the tails. With a rubber-gloved hand Minnie reaches in expertly to drag out the guts. The kitchen is rife with fish smells; it's the river lapping right up into the house. Jinx is maybe thinking of this or maybe he's thinking of nothing at all, stymied by his mother's energy, which almost crackles off her though she's come home late from the white doctor's far away uptown where she works and hasn't changed out of her nylon uniform and shiny-pale stockings . . . but she's taken off her white shoes with the firm Cuban-style heels and put on her old comfortable around-the-house corduroy bedroom slippers with the toes cut out. Still girdled up tight, though, tidy and seamless as a sausage. Minnie Fairchild is forty-four years old, an exact two decades younger than her husband Woodrow, short, plump, good-looking, with a rich warm brown skin of the hue and luster of horse chestnuts and fastidiously straightened hair that resembles a black-lacquered cap. She has a smallish bulldog face, a full nose, white teeth without a single flash of gold, and she wears bright maroon lipstick day and night.

At her sink Minnie always runs the water loud and hard, so she has to raise her voice to be heard over it, as she does now. "So slow-acting, I just hope you aren't comin' down with some nasty old spring flu," she complains. It's the honey inflection. Jinx feels his heart being fingered.

Jinx means to say, "No, Momma, I'm not sick," but he hears himself say, quiet and frightened, "No, Momma, it's not the flu."

Chopping fish heads and tails, brisk, no-nonsense, squinching up her face as if she hates the smell but showing by her posture and the pistonlike motions of her chopping arm, that, yes, there's a pleasure in this, *chop! chop! chop!* against the old weathered blood-stained breadboard, Minnie doesn't quite hear. She says two things so rapid-fire Jinx might almost not know which comes first: "Well, it better *not* be," and, "Make yourself useful, boy, get some news-paper and wrap up this offal and haul it out back; if there's one thing I can't stand more'n the stink of fish and scales all over everything it's the fish-eye starin' up at me like I'm the one to blame." Minnie's high delighted laughter crackles like twigs burning.

So Jinx Fairchild, prodded into action. does exactly as he's told.

Grateful for something to do with his big skinny bony-knuckled murderer's hands.

At such times Minnie Fairchild bustles around her kitchen making slamming, thudding, scraping noises . . . *tsk*ing at the time, which is always later than she'd like. You'd think, hearing her, the woman resents preparing meals, preparing these good nutritious vitamin-rich meals—her idle old husband Woodrow at the bottom of the garden playing checkers with himself won't come for supper till somebody yells for him and then he's ponderous-slow, deaf in one ear and can't hear in the other, as Minnie complains with her high harsh laugh—but in fact Minnie loves this hour of the day. She loves working in this kitchen (four-burner gas stove and oven, full-sized Kelvinator refrigerator, decent sink, faucets) because she recalls with painful vividness the first kitchens of her married life, let alone the kitchens in which her mother prepared meals for her entire life; she loves her house, which is one of the three or four nicest houses at this end of East Avenue—a wood-frame bungalow, painted brown, with five rooms, an attic beneath the roof's peak, a front porch, a half-acre lot so that, in summer, she can have a garden—though in truth Woodrow is the one who plants and tends the garden; he's got the time for it, and the slow patience and faith. Minnie Fairchild's pleasure in her property is a fierce matter her children have learned to respect, if not share, not even Verlyn, who's the most sensitive, not even Bea, who's old enough (Bea is twenty-five) to remember how things were back in Pittsburgh and to recall the fresh tales of how things were in South Carolina where Woodrow Fairchild was born.

You have to know where you've come from to know how far you've come, Minnie says.

And Minnie says, You don't get a house like this by sitting on your rear.

And Minnie says, You don't *keep* a house like this by sitting on your rear.

And Minnie says, Coloreds crybabyin' about they skin don't get no sympathy from me . . . mock-drawling to make sure the import of her message is clear.

For the past eleven years Minnie Fairchild has had steady, good-paying employment with Dr. M. R. O'Shaughnessy, a general practitioner of some reputation in Hammond, who has his office in his home in the shabby-genteel neighborhood of Franklin Square. Two city buses are required to get Minnie to work and home again. At first Minnie did ordinary housework and cooked occasional meals; then, following the death of Dr. O'Shaughnessy's wife, there came a period of what the doctor called "retrenchment," and Minnie was assigned more and more household responsibilities and even, in time, replaced Dr. O'Shaughnessy's office nurse . . . though Minnie is untrained as a nurse, or even as a nurse's aide. ("Nothing to it," Minnie boasts to her friends. "The main thing is the uniform: you *look* the part, folks think that's what you *are!*") For years Minnie has been bringing home all sorts of things for her family given to her by Dr. O'Shaughnessy or appropriated from his office: samples from pharmaceutical companies of mouthwash, deodorants, muscle relaxants, pills to aid digestion, pills to combat constipation, pills to combat diarrhea, headache pills, sleeping pills, stay-awake pills . . . tins of Band-Aids, sanitary napkins, cotton batting . . . bottles of eyewash and dandruff shampoo . . . bars of complexion soap made with an oatmeal base. The drawers of the house are chock-full of such things, and the medicine cabinet in the bathroom is a true cornucopia. "Momma, what's *these?*" Bea would cry, snatching up the latest item. If it wasn't the case that the Fairchild children were the healthiest in the neighborhood, they were at least the best equipped for sickness.

In addition to helping Dr. O'Shaughnessy with his patients, most of whom are older women, and overseeing the household, Minnie Fairchild also does bookkeeping for the doctor, whose financial records are in a muddle; she pays most of the household bills and arranges for repairs to the house. Dr. O'Shaughnessy lives in a beautiful old 1890s brick house, over-large for a widower whose children are all scattered and indifferent, and this house is in constant need of repairs and renovations. "What would I do without you, Minnie?" Dr. O'Shaughnessy often asks with a sigh, and Minnie laughs modestly and says, "Reckon you'd get along, doctor!" though she doesn't believe this for a minute. O'Shaughnessy is a good-hearted but vague man in his mid-sixties, white-haired, dignified, patrician in his manner and appearance; and, weekdays at least, never less than stone cold sober until evening. Minnie shares his secret: he drinks steadily from six o'clock until midnight each weekday night, and on Saturdays and Sundays the drinking hour shifts to noon; and, sometimes, on Sundays, he will inject himself with a mild shot of morphine in order to endure the sabbath. But, as Minnie says, she doesn't judge white folks: leastways not *this* class of white folks.

Increasingly, these past years, Dr. O'Shaughnessy has spoken of "remembering" Minnie in his will.

("Not that I believe it for one minute," Minnie says.)

Nothing has given Minnie quite so much pleasure in her adult life as telling tales of Dr. M. R. O'Shaughnessy to her women friends, her tone sometimes comical and derisive, sometimes defensive, more often reverential. "How's the doctor, Minnie?" a woman friend will ask, grinning in anticipation, and Minnie will throw up her hands and say laughingly, "No worse!" and the friend will ask, "That man still got patients, the way he behave?" and Minnie will say, "Got *lots*. These rich old white ladies, they'd never go to anyone else; they figure Dr. O'Shaughnessy's seen everything they got and seen it bloat and sag and collapse and go gray, or bald, year after year. Also he takes care not to hurt them any with his instruments—*I* got to warm them—and won't ever tell them anything they'd be fearful of hearing. What better kind of M.D. would you want? Lord, this sad old creature that came in today, all diamonds and furs on the outside, and her swanky chocolate-cream chauffeur had to help her up the steps." And Minnie makes her listener explode into peals of laughter with a graphic description of a patient whom Minnie in her nurse's function had to undress, and then dress, a nightmare of fallen flabby flesh like collapsed bread dough, hundreds of hooks and eyes to latch up in the woman's whalebone corset and brassiere. "If I ever get that bad off, I pray my children will put me out of my misery!" Minnie says, wiping tears of laughter from her cheeks.

Minnie Fairchild isn't religious, or even superstitious. Not a bit. Not since leaving her mother's house. She has a weakness for gospel singing on the radio, Mahalia Jackson and the Caravans her favorites, but all the rest of it, Jesus Christ and that crew, it's white folks' foolishness or outright trickery. The only earth the "meek" ever inherited was earth nobody else gave a damn for . . . says Minnie.

As a small boy, Jinx Fairchild was in the presence of his mother's legendary employer several times; once, the portly smiling white man pressed a silver dollar into the palm of Jinx's hand, and another time he stooped to confide in him, "Your mother's the salt of the earth!" Even then, Jinx took offense at the man's very praise of his mother. Earth, he thought, earth's *dirt*.

Jinx knows there has been, for years, malicious speculation in the neighborhood regarding the relationship between Minnie and her white employer, even scurrilous talk of Ceci being O'Shaughnessy's child and not Woodrow Fairchild Senior's—the girl has a smooth, light, buttery-colored skin—but beyond that he doesn't know and doesn't want to know. The very thought of it fills him with a choking, voiceless rage. Like Bea mooning over some lemony-skinned bastard who treated her like shit. Or Dorothy Dandridge in the movies all the silly Negro girls would die to look like. If there's white blood in *him,* he thinks, it's a long way back and many times diluted.

When Jinx comes back into the kitchen Minnie is frying fish at the stove in her heavy iron skillet and singing huskily under her breath. It's a Johnny Mathis tune . . . or is it Frank Sinatra? Jinx folds his fingers up behind his back and stands staring at the headless gutted bass in the skillet aswim in butter and chopped onions. Hears his cracked voice say, "This body they found? Last week? In the river?" and Minnie says offhandedly, not missing a beat in her singing, "Going to say who did it, huh, Mr. Man-About-Town?" cutting her eyes at him as if they're sharing a joke. Jinx stares and blinks. He knows his eyes are bloodshot and there's the reflection of a dead man's face in them . . . blurred as it sinks into water. Minnie says briskly, "Make yourself useful, boy, don't just stand there in my way—set the table," so Jinx sets the table, watches his quick deft hands set the table; then Minnie says, "See where your sister's at," so Jinx locates Ceci playing with friends out on the porch; then Minnie says, "Pour yourself and her two glasses of milk," so Jinx pours himself and Ceci two glasses of milk; then Minnie says, "About time to call your father," and Jinx's head is ringing, his fingers and toes have gone icy cold as if every eye in a vast, vast gymnasium is upon him, so he says, quick, "Got something on my mind, Momma," and Minnie shoots back as quick, "Some girl? Girl trouble? *That* it? You tell me you been messing around with cheap little pigs and sluts like your brother and I'll warm your precious ass!"—suddenly incensed, indignant, as if this is indeed what Jinx has told her, not waiting for his reply. "Any of them girls would die to catch a boy like you, good clean decent-minded boy like Verlyn Fairchild, a star athlete, damn good student, going to college and all, going to be a teacher or a doctor or a lawyer, and living in *this house,* not some shameful falling-down tarpaper shanty out by the dump!"

Jinx tries not to become confused. He says, "Momma, *listen:* this thing that happened last week, this body they found—"

Minnie, seeing the look in her son's face, slams a pot of boiled potatoes down on a counter and snorts, disgusted. "Taking it all so serious! So grave! Everybody talking about it, even Dr. O'Shaughnessy's patients, like it wasn't some worthless peckerhead hillbilly. *Garlock,* for the Lord's sweet sake! And if it'd been a Negro boy, huh? What then? *Don't tell me, what then!"*

So suddenly is Minnie furious, her pug face tightened like a fist, Jinx stands silenced, a little dazed. His head is ringing worse than ever. But he says, "Momma, before Pa and Ceci come in, can I talk to you? I guess I made a mistake and I—I don't know what to—"

Minnie is fuming. "*Garlock!* Everybody knows what *Garlock* means in this town! Just trash! Dirt! Lowest of the low! It's enough to make you sick to your stomach, all the fuss in the newspaper, the police asking questions! Hadn't better ask *me* any questions, I'd tell 'em some answers! Those hillbilly trash beatin' and killin' their own wives and children . . . worst kind of white folks exceptin' actual Nazis. And if it'd been a Negro boy instead, nobody'd give a good goddamn!"

And Jinx, seeing the glisten in his mother's eyes, feeling the fear that's radiating from her, gives up.

Thinking, afterward, What was I going to ask her, anyway? Whether I should turn myself in to the police . . . or not? Set myself up for the electric chair . . . or not?

These days, Jinx Fairchild is forced to recall how proud he'd been of his "new" name: not Verlyn any longer but Jinx. The name was given him by one of his mother's brothers when he was four years old: "*Here's* the boy gon' cause you trouble, Minnie! He a real devil—a *jinx!*" The joke of it being, partly, that the child was quiet, sober, watchful, the shyest of the pack of children at the family gathering in Pittsburgh; showing no sign of growing tall as a weed as he would some years later, but skinny, and quick-clumsy, as if his lightning reflexes took him a split second or so ahead of where he wanted to be. Every meal, he was the one to spill something at the table; he was the only child to track dirt on a carpet; if the gang of children was fooling around, and his aunt's new lamp, won at Bingo, crashed over, it was Verlyn who was probably responsible . . . while being at the same time clearly innocent, tears of regret, pain, and humiliation brimming in his eyes.

Ain't he somethin'! That boy! Little devil! Little Jinx! Womens, keep clear!—the adults hovering over him, laughing, stooping to hug, to kiss, Minnie herself in high spirits, too riled up by her loud-laughing brothers to scold, or object, though she disliked the name intensely and would never use it. A nigger name, Minnie sniffs. Some deadbeat boxer or racehorse. Just plain common.

Minnie refuses to call Sugar Baby "Sugar Baby" either—*his* rightful name is Woodrow Fairchild, Jr.—though the name Sugar Baby seems to have been with him always, from the crib on up.

With the nightmare concentration of a man reading of his own fate, but reading of it in code, Jinx Fairchild studies reports of the Garlock case in the *Chronicle,* listens to every news broadcast from WHMM he can without arousing suspicion, but never, never, does he make any inquiries about the murder, nor does he, if he can discreetly avoid it, participate in conversations at school or elsewhere in which the "mystery killing" is the subject.

He knows that police are combing the area for witnesses.

Is he a witness?

Is Iris Courtney?

When he thinks of Iris Courtney his mind blanks out . . . like staring into the sun.

The first time the police come into Cheney's Variety to ask

137

questions it's a Friday morning, and Jinx Fairchild isn't there; the second time it's Saturday afternoon and Jinx is there, but so is Cheney . . . a wheezy-voiced black man whom the police officers appear to know and to like. They speak with Jinx perhaps three minutes, asking does he know anything about the murder, did he know the murdered boy, has he heard any street talk, that sort of thing, and there's Jinx Fairchild, this good-looking soft-spoken Negro boy with the lanky colt-legged grace of a natural athlete and an air of racial deference that doesn't seem feigned but bred deep in the bone, answering politely "No, sir," and "No, sir, I guess not," and "Afraid not." Smooth as honey, Jinx Fairchild is swallowed down by the white police, who only think to ask on their way out who was in the store the night of the killing, and when Jinx says he was they say, "But you didn't see or hear of anything, huh?" and Jinx says again, "No, sir, guess not."

He's folded and twined his fingers together inside his belt, to keep them from trembling. If there is danger of their trembling.

The street talk Jinx does hear, in and out of Cheney's and at the high school, is that a gang of Hell's Angels did the killing. White men. As Cheney says, his face screwed up in disgust, "Them leather-jacket assholes on their motorcycles." Jinx blinks and stares and smiles vague as a simpleton. Hell's Angels? White men? Like whirlpools of air bringing up dust, countless whirlpools that combine to a single spiral, rumors of Hell's Angels, motorcyclists, white men combine to a virtual certainty as day follows day.

Then, on April 16, the news is of two arrests: two Hell's Angels in their mid-twenties, from Buffalo. For a full day and more, it's believed in Hammond that the murderers of the Garlock boy have been found and the case is over.

Jinx's first thought is elation. Not me! Not me! Somebody else!

His second thought is pure shame. But I'm the one!

He doesn't go to church the way his father does, but he maybe believes in God . . . maybe. He believes, if there's a God, God will send a sign.

'Cause you know you're the one.

'Cause can't anyone else take your place.

Jinx's father is a religious man—he'd be a preacher if he could speak above a hoarse cracked whisper—but Jinx Fairchild isn't religious out of an old childhood dread of sinking right into Jesus Christ the way his father did, his father and too many others, howling and screaming and weeping on the gospel hours, the sound of it like snakes in a frenzy. *Jesus Christ the Redeemer. God the Holy Father.*

In a panic Jinx thinks, Not me! Please God—somebody else!

He's in terror of a sign that will be unmistakable, but he can't stop himself one day from drifting up Gowanda Street to the block where the Garlocks live, across the street from Loblaw's, where Minnie shops and where, back in high school, Sugar Baby had a job bagging—pissy little job he walked off of, just like that, snapped his fingers and told whoever it was who was hassling him to go fuck.

There's the Garlock house. Ramshackle and rotten-looking, like any nigger house except for the size. But niggers wouldn't be allowed to rent in this block.

This here a white folks' block. Lily-white.

Any niggers try to rent here, they get their heads broke.

A rundown, shabby neighborhood. Row houses, and a brownstone tenement, and some little shops, and the Loblaw's set back in a lot that needs repaving, and the Garlock house with windows open and curtains or strips of plastic trailing out, trash on the front porch, children's toys on the sidewalk. Jinx stands across the street as if transfixed, arms crossed on his chest and hands gripped tight under his armpits, staring, fearful of seeing here in the unsparing overhead sunshine what he suddenly realizes he has been seeing in dreams: Little Red Garlock living as big and brash as he'd ever been, pushing through that ratty screen door, pedaling past on a bicycle too small for his ham-sized legs and haunches. He'd catch sight of Jinx Fairchild over here and smile that slow lewd delighted smile of his. *Hey, nigger! Black nigger cock!*

Jinx's eyes go heavy, hooded, almost sleepy. But he can't move his legs to carry him away.

139

There's a small child playing by himself in the gutter in front of the Garlock house, a little boy maybe three years old, fair-haired but pudgy, the Garlock look in his face; Jinx can make out that look, even from across the street. He's playing with a red rubber ball and suddenly the ball bounces and rolls out into the street and Jinx runs out, swoops down to retrieve it; a single smooth motion and he's tossing it back to the little boy, who's gaping at him dull-witted, astonished, then breaks out into a smile. Big beautiful smile.

Jinx trots on away not looking back. Knows that hillbillies hate Negroes so their children must hate them too.

On his long shaky legs Jinx Fairchild is three blocks away before it occurs to him, yes, he's had his sign.

God trying to tell you something but ain't going to tell you what.

These days, his eyes bloodshot and his lips chewed at, Jinx is fearful of his father. He has the idea that Woodrow Fairchild Senior is possessed of the ability to see right into Jinx's soul . . . through his eyes and into his soul. And Pa would tell him to confess his crime: Go to the police and confess; get down on your knees, boy, and pray Jesus Christ to save you; cast all sin out of your heart and be whole again.

Pa, I can't.

Pa, don't make me.

Can't sleep and can't eat and can't concentrate in school so he skips classes but not to run with his pals; these days, Jinx Fairchild is avoiding his pals too. Even Sugar Baby, who might take one cool appraising look at him and know. *Hey, man, what the hell? You mixed up in that Garlock shit?*

The fear is like a clot of phlegm he can't swallow but can't cough up either.

Mostly, Jinx fears his father. Knows Minnie isn't going to ask him one more question about is he sick-feeling or what's on his mind; no danger from *her*.

Woodrow Fairchild Senior spends his retired days fishing for bass and catfish in the river with his friends; in summer, tending his garden, a familiar sight on East Avenue with its wall of sunflowers at the rear and its big blazing clumps of marigolds and zinnias and black-eyed susans amid the vegetables; and drifting around town to take in the sights and hire himself out for odd jobs, though at sixty-four, a crippled sort of dwarf hunch to his back and his head askew on his shoulders with a look of perpetual surprise, there aren't many handyman tasks he can do. His days of loading and unloading white men's trucks, shoveling coal into white men's furnaces, are about over. He has a small monthly disability pension from the U.S. Government since he was injured in an army training camp, years ago, but this pension, Minnie says scornfully, is as close to nothing as you can get without its being nothing: half of it goes for the sickly sweet Mogen David wine Mr. Fairchild drinks in secret (or seemingly in secret; everyone knows) and half to the Second Coming African Church of Christ the Redeemer where he's a church deacon.

Minnie Fairchild scorns her oldish absent-headed husband for most of his ways, but his churchgoing ways infuriate her. "What's that mean, 'church deacon'?" Minnie has asked, and Woodrow has said, in his hoarse, whispery voice, his voice that's like the wind in dried corn husks, "Means I help out," and Minnie says, " 'Help out'? 'Help out' how?" and Woodrow says, mumbling, "Jes' help out, Rev'nd Goomer depend on me," and Minnie says, "Yes, but how? You tell me how? Where's the money go you give to him? 'Depend on you'—on *you!*—*you tell me how!*" Surely there's a place for that old-timey shoutin' and howlin' and stampin'-around kind of religion, Minnie says, her nostrils flaring in derision, like there's a place for lots of things from down South, conjure ladies and voodoo mumbo-jumbo, *but this place ain't it.* Minnie's scorn for Woodrow rose to a fury some years ago when he'd been fired from his janitor job at Precious Blood Elementary School: a little girl said she had dreams of him, his black face and the way he carried himself, sort of scuttling like a crab, things he said, threatened—and it wasn't clear whether these dreams might not be somehow real, based upon actual events, the Negro janitor at Precious Blood whispering nasty words to this little white girl, reaching up into her panties—and the girl's parents were naturally upset, and the Catholic sister who was principal of Precious Blood was naturally upset, and poor Woodrow Fairchild with his broken voice and skewed head and paralyzing shyness in the company of whites made no effort to defend himself . . . just gave up, came back home. Ever after he's been "retired."

That Woodrow Fairchild—he a sly one.

Pokin' in some little white girl's drawers—and got away with it, almost.

He did? That dried-up hunched old thing?

Wasn't always dried up—noner them are.

Still, he lucky to be walkin' around. Head on his shoulders even if it ain't right.

It was in 1920, as a young man of twenty-eight from South Carolina, that Woodrow Fairchild enlisted in the U.S. Army, and in training camp in northern Texas he suffered the accident that partly disabled him for life . . . details of which he never remembered afterward. The "accident" took place not on the training field but just outside the barracks to which he'd been assigned, a fall from some steps, a confusion of bodies, and next thing he knew he woke in the army hospital with injuries to the upper back and shoulders and neck, his larynx crushed as if someone had set his booted foot upon it and stepped down hard . . . and harder still. But in the hospital, Woodrow Fairchild didn't remember a thing, never did remember, speaks even now of the accident as if it had fallen from the sky upon him, wholly unpremeditated, as inaccessible to interpretation as any act of God falling from the sky or ripping up out of the bowels of the earth, praise the Lord. Minnie Fairchild says to her boys, Verlyn and Woodrow, Junior, "You see what happens, you join up with the U.S. Army? Some poor ignorant good-intentioned Negro boy, in there with all them crackers?" As if Verlyn and Woodrow needed to be told.

Now Jinx has grown so tall, his father looks short to him—not wizened, because Woodrow Fairchild does have muscles, and a large head, gray-grizzled hair like wires—but wrongly short, like it's showing disrespect to him for his sons to stand in his presence. So

Jinx avoids his presence. Or slouches, or sits. Or squats. Looking up at him as he's looking up at him now, this warm-drizzly day at the end of April, Jinx has trotted down to where Pa is sitting on a stump at the bottom of the garden thinking *Now I will tell him* thinking *I won't need to tell him: he will see it in my face* and he sees his father is playing checkers with himself, checkerboard on his knees, red pieces to the left, black to the right; it looks as if, with three kings, red is winning . . . a peace to the wettish air like the hush of fresh bread cooling.

Woodrow Sr. has a dark much-creased skin like the leather of an old valise, a flattened veiny nose, kindly eyes, badly decayed yellow teeth . . . so much older than his wife that people always think he must be his children's grandfather; and Jinx tends to think of him as grandfatherly, affectionate as Minnie isn't always affectionate any longer, but not so shrewdly watchful as Minnie, not so judging. Jinx knows enough not to interrupt his father's checker game, squats beside him watching its progress. Left hand against right hand, what does it mean? To what purpose, such a game? Jinx waits patiently, growing more and more frightened yet at the same time becoming more and more calm; he's thinking he has surrendered himself to his father like the sinners in the old gospel hymn "He's Got the Whole World in His Hands": *Now I am here, I am here.* When the game is over Jinx's father asks him how's he been, voice hoarse and worse-cracked than Jinx has heard it in some time, and Jinx says, after hesitating a moment, "Not so good," and his father murmurs something vague and consoling and mildly inquisitive, laying a hand on Jinx's head as if conferring a blessing. It's a big warm hand, finger span from temple to temple. Jinx peers up at him like a small child hot with guilt. *Don't you see it in my face? Don't you know?*

In a blind rush of words Jinx says, "Pa, I made this mistake I guess. About three weeks ago. Was in Cheney's just closing up and this girl came running in." Jinx hesitates. Should he say the girl was white? Is that part of the story? "White girl," he says weakly. "I don't know her real well but I know her some. A nice girl. Couple years younger than me. And she was scared . . . said there was this guy, this nasty-mouth guy from the neighborhood, after her. And . . ." Jinx pauses again. He's beginning to sweat. His father's big hand is on his shoulder now and his father's eyes have a look of retreating, contracting. Jinx senses that after hearing the words "white girl" his father stopped listening.

Once Jinx says the name Garlock he won't be able to unsay it.

Jinx is squatting on his heels in the soft earth; his thighs and knees have begun to ache. It's a long dread moment that he and Woodrow Fairchild Senior stare at each other as if they've never seen each other before. Jinx is thinking, He knows. Jinx is thinking, He doesn't—he doesn't know. "Got into a fight," Jinx whispers. But there is no way to continue and no way to retreat, unless Pa forces it from him, which, it seems, Pa is not going to do. The elder man's eyes are narrowed nearly to closing.

Jinx finds himself crouched with his cheek against his father's knee, sobbing.

God, he hadn't meant this! Hadn't meant anything like this!

Like a baby he gives himself up to hot shameful sobbing as he hasn't done in years. And Pa hugs him—hugs him hard. Pa lets him cry, Pa's praying over him, directly addressing the Lord Jesus Christ as if Jinx Fairchild isn't even there.

In this awkward position they remain, Woodrow Fairchild Senior and his son Jinx, for many minutes.

Does he believe in God? In the Lord Jesus Christ?

Does he believe in the devil?

That night, the thought comes to him, light as the gossamer of milkweed seed, *If that white girl wasn't living, wouldn't anybody know.*

3

Says Virgil Starling, arm slung around Persia Courtney's rib cage as he walks her, staggering-steady, hips banging, into the kitchen, "Know what you need, baby? Some good solid food in you."

Persia protests. "Oh, honey—I don't think I could manage." Leaning on him, hiding her face in his neck.

She'd almost said *keep it down*. Don't think I could keep it down. Thank God she hadn't.

Persia Courtney's sweet caramel-skinned lover, beautiful Virgil Starling, like no man she's known. Just the look of that man . . . the look *from* him . . . Persia melts like honey.

Would you believe it, after all she's been through?

She wouldn't.

He's laughing that wet clicking laugh deep in his throat. Walking his lady around the linoleum floor to clear her head a little. Humming Chuck Berry's "Maybelline," he swings her, hard-gripping under the armpits so she squeals, winces, hugs him to keep from falling. Says Virgil Starling with certitude, "*I* can manage. *I* say, you better get some good solid food in you."

So Virgil Starling slips on his shirt, puts on his shoes and socks, trots over to Loblaw's, then to the seafood market, then to the Italian bakery—with Persia's wallet snug at his hip—trots back to the apartment and prepares a delicious meal for the two of them: Galveston Gumbo, he calls it.

"Just some messin' around my momma does, it ain't no recipe or anything, just you gettin' it how you want it: thick or thin, real spicy or not, whatever."

While Persia, face washed now and lightly powdered, reddish-gold hair piled atop her head like Rita Hayworth, sits on the edge of the kitchen table, a cigarette burning in her unsteady fingers. She's wearing the champagne-colored ruffled negligee Duke gave her— oh, Christ, how long ago but it still looks good; she's fighting a small tide of nausea but isn't showing it in her face. And thinking she should telephone the club manager to explain about last night—Sonny, it won't happen again I promise—but she isn't showing that in her face either. Nor the worry about Iris, the worry these weeks, and where the hell is the girl right now: like slivers of broken glass on the floor you can cut your bare feet on, not seeing them in time. No, she's watching her honey man showing off for her in her own kitchen, taking over like it's his; she's eating him up with her eyes: the high-assed strut, the bulge at the crotch of the red-russet trousers, the filmy shirt open on his warm near-hairless chest, the loving looks he's casting her. And he dips on over to kiss her, and she kisses him, long wet laughing tongue-kisses, Persia's arms around his neck and the cigarette burning high over his head, but better not get me started again says Virgil, and Persia releases him. And talking, talking, talking all the while: like music you don't even have to listen to, to know it's there, and steady, and you like it, and it's good.

Persia Courtney's mulatto lover, people are saying . . . and so what? Doing it to spite *me*, Duke Courtney is saying . . . and so what, even if that were true?

146

Persia says, surprised her voice sounds so sleepy, "Lover, you're too much for me sometimes. I mean it."

Virgil says, almost modestly, "No man too much for you, Persia, only just half enough."

The sound of that word "Persia" in his mouth goes through her like an electric current; he doesn't say it often.

Persia laughs almost harshly. "You jivin' me, baby?" she drawls.

It takes Virgil Starling a while to prepare the gumbo so they start in drinking beer. Beck's, straight out of the bottle.

Duke didn't like to see Persia drink this way, but Duke isn't here to criticize.

Duke's things are mostly cleared out of the closets and this time it's permanent; he isn't coming back.

Best way of clearing the head: cold bitter Beck's out of the bottle.

"No butter?" says Virgil, frowning. "OK, then, margarine . . . ain't the best for cookin' okra pods but it'll do . . . gotta chop it all up good, and a big strong-smellin' onion, and some nice fresh green peppers like these—mmmmmmm! don't this smel! good in the skillet!—then you pour the stuff in the tomatoes nere; nice fresh tomatoes is best of course but canned ain't bad, maybe a little too sweet. OK, now you get it simmerin' like this on a low flame, then you put in the oysters, then the shrimp . . . only drawback to shrimp is you gotta clean 'em, and that takes time."

Persia says, "I'll clean the shrimp."

Virgil says, "Naw, honey, you sit still."

Persia says, "Why can't I help?"

Virgil says, " 'Cause you ain't in the mood for it."

Persia says, "Sure I am!"

Virgil says, waving his hand at her, "Naw, honey, sit still, you're pretty there just like that."

Persia says, "You think I'm drunk, Mr. Boss Man? Is that it? I'd cut myself with the knife or something . . . cut *you?*"

Virgil laughs and pays Persia no more mind.

He's fast with the shrimp though, fast and efficient, and when he's through there's a scattering of tiny heads, tails, transparent shells on the cupboard counter and in the sink and on the floor. . . . Persia will be stepping on those scraps, crunching them underfoot, for days.

Gumbo's ready! Virgil Starling and his glamour-lady kiss again, and sit at the kitchen table, knees nudging knees beneath it, and eat. There's crusty Italian bread and two cold Beck's right out of the refrigerator, and the gumbo is thick and rich and delicious but Persia isn't hungry—Persia is never hungry any longer, fearful she'll be sick to her stomach, in fact—but with each shaky spoonful her appetite increases . . . what is happening? . . . *is* she hungry? In the end she's eating almost ravenously and Virgil pushes his bowl over to her so she can finish his, lights up a cigarette, watches her eat.

"You like it, huh? My momma's gumbo?"

Persia says, "Oh, yes."

"Good, huh?"

Persia says, wiping her mouth with a paper napkin, sighing, "It's good."

"We're fated, us two"—it's Duke's voice in a murmur—"you know that, Persia . . . can't not know that." And Persia's voice lifts. "What about Iris, then, your daughter? Is she fated too?" And there's a long pause, as if Duke Courtney has forgotten he has a daughter. Then: "She's fated too. She's ours. She's the bond between us that can't ever be broken."

Iris isn't eavesdropping but Iris overhears. These voices penetrating the walls of any room she can hide in.

This is the last clear memory she will have of Duke Courtney in the Holland Street flat and of herself in her old room, fist jammed against her mouth.

In a single feverish weekend, the last weekend in June, Persia Courtney with her friend Virgil Starling's assistance moves herself and Iris and all their furnishings, clothing, possessions—*not* Duke Courtney's: his things Persia leaves behind heaped together in a carton for the building's janitor to store—fourteen blocks south to the upstairs of a two-story wood-frame house on Jewett Street. The house is old, solid, with a high-peaked plunging roof, pewter-gray paint peeling in terse strips from its sides. It is flanked on both sides by similar houses, built almost flush to the sidewalk, no room for grassy front yards. At the rear, the yard is wild, untended, a jungle that lifts to a railroad embankment about forty feet behind the house.

The locomotive's high-pitched whistle and the rattling of freight cars will penetrate Iris Courtney's dreams for the next three years but she has here, at last, a room with a true window and true daylight . . . won't have to crouch and squint up to see the sky.

No outdoor stairway slanting past.

Just this view—Iris stands at the curtainless window, pressing her forehead against the fly-specked glass—the tangled back yard that's new to her vision, the scrub trees and bushes and the railroad tracks elevated about six feet above the natural curve of the earth. Beyond the tracks is a block of row houses, clotheslines strung across their back yards in a discontinuous pattern. She feels a thrill of hope tinged only faintly with dread.

The new residence at 927 Jewett isn't much different from the old residence at 372 Holland except it's smaller by one room, nor is the new neighborhood much different from the old. Jewett is a residential-commercial street skirting the shabby edge of an Italian neighborhood, and though the street is quieter than Holland—"less dangerous," as Persia says—now they must walk two blocks to a bus stop and nearly that far for groceries.

Though Persia plans on buying a car soon. And Persia has the use of friends' cars: she's that kind of woman, never lacking for friends with cars.

And there's Virgil Starling. Virgil Starling who is often around.

Persia says, "He's the sweetest man I've ever met."

Persia says, "He's a good man . . . he's *good* to me."

Persia says, fiercely, "Do you think I care what anyone says? Do you think I'll let anyone interfere with my life? I need to be happy too sometimes!"

Iris notes without comment how, the many hours they're moving into the new apartment—and at one point, helping with the heavier pieces of furniture, Virgil Starling works with a friend, darker-skinned than he—the downstairs tenants of the house and the neighbors on both sides observe them covertly, coldly. Not a hand lifted in greeting, not a smile. No offer of help, of course.

White woman and her daughter and a light-skinned nigger . . . what the hell?

Knowing themselves watched gives them an air of reckless gaiety amid the uprooted battered-looking furniture, the boxes of ill-packed dishware, rumpled clothing, shoes, books. There's sloe-eyed Virgil Starling tramping up the stairs, comically staggering under the weight of one of these boxes with Persia's glamorous wide-brimmed hat on his head, cloth gardenia flopping . . . seeing him, both Persia and Iris burst into screams of laughter.

Virgil Starling plays it cool, feigns puzzlement, hurt. "Hey, man, what's so funny, man? This boy's back damn near broke over you women."

Iris Courtney is shy of her mother's lover up close; his smooth buttery skin is too bright.

And his dark-brown mirthful eyes, his eyes raking her up and down. And the rippled-processed dark-brown hair that lies on his head like a cap, oily and gleaming, its rich scent lingering in Iris's nostrils for hours. His clarinet-sliding voice, "Mmmmmmmmmm! There's a gal looks good enough to eat!"

He *is* a jazz clarinetist, plays sometimes at one or another of the local clubs. To make a living—at least temporarily—he works at Louis the Hatter's, the best Negro clothing store for men in Hammond: which accounts for his stylish wardrobe, his dozens of colorful shirts, hand-tooled leather boots, boxy double-breasted sports coats, snug-fitting trousers. He wears a wide stretch-band wristwatch; he has rings on several fingers. It's possible that he has a wife and children in another city, but who wants to question Virgil Starling on so intimate a subject? Not Persia Courtney, who melts like honey in his presence, throws back her head and laughs uproariously in his presence, as Iris has not heard her laugh in years.

Through an upended mirror of Persia's dressing table propped against a doorway Iris sees slantwise, unknown to her mother and her mother's buttery-skinned lover, how, imagining herself unobserved, Persia snatches up Virgil Starling's hand and kisses the fingers . . . maybe sucks in the tips, bites a little. And Virgil Starling mauls her like a big jungle cat.

Iris Courtney looks away, stricken.

The pang of it sweet and sharp between her legs.

"There's some men don't need to be pure *black* to make a woman feel pure *white,*" Persia Courtney has said.

Laughing over the telephone to one of her woman friends.

"And it's a delicious feeling."

Iris wonders how much younger than her mother Virgil Starling is. And whether that makes any difference in what they do together.

One night in the Holland Street apartment the telephone rang and it was Duke Courtney asking to speak with Persia, but since Persia wasn't there he spoke with Iris—sober-sounding, trying to control his hurt—asking, "Is your mother doing this to humiliate me? Sleeping with this . . . mulatto?"

Iris did not know how to reply. It seemed a deeply shameful thing, to be so addressed by one's father.

"Whose side are you on, Iris? Hers, or mine?"

Iris murmured, "Oh, Daddy. . . ."

"That whore's, or mine?"

The telephone receiver slipped from Iris's fingers, and when she picked it up again the line was dead.

At the present time it's believed that Duke Courtney is living in the old Niagara Hotel, uptown on Main Street. When he learns Persia's new address on Jewett Street he will send a dozen red roses *To my beloved wife Persia and my beloved daughter Iris from "one who loved not wisely but too well."*

How many nights in the new apartment as on this, the very first night, does Persia Courtney on her way out for the evening (or the night) frame her daughter's face in her slender hands, kiss her on the

152

forehead, or, funnily, on the tip of the nose, say with an air of pleading, "Don't wait up for me, honey, all right?—and don't worry?"

Meaning, I don't know when I'll be home.

Meaning, It's my business when I'll be home.

And how many times does Iris Courtney stiffly hug her mother in return, brush her lips against her mother's rouged cheek. "No, I won't wait up," she says. "No, I won't worry."

How many times, these next several years?

Tonight, with Virgil Starling waiting for her downstairs in his car, tonight Persia Courtney looks gorgeous . . . or almost. In an apricot summer knit dress with a tight bodice, hair brushed and gleaming, smelling of a dark fruity perfume that's new to Iris's nostrils; in high-heeled white sandals that emphasize the shapely swell of her calves. By the time they'd finished moving that afternoon Persia was faint with exhaustion so she soaked for an hour in a hot bath, in a luxury of fragrant fizzing bubbles, cold cream smeared on her face, eyes blissfully shut, a glass resting on the tub's rim . . . just to sip from.

An inch or two of Southern Comfort splashed in a glass, without ceremony, hardly counts as a drink.

Persia waves a kiss at Iris from the doorway. "Love ya, honey!"

Iris murmurs, "Love *you*."

That night, Iris is wakened in her new, unfamiliar surroundings by a heart-stopping noise; she's terrified for several seconds before realizing what it is: a locomotive whistle, an endless line of freight trains, a thunderous *vroooooom* as of the sound of Death sweeping over the world.

And does she think of it, of Death; of the pool of blood darkening under her enemy's head or of his body hauled battered and eyeless from the river?

No. She occupies her mind with other things.

Yes. There is, after all, nothing else to think of.

"So quiet these days," Persia comments, brushing a strand of hair out of her daughter's eye in passing, as if it is her privilege to touch, to caress, to prod, at whim. "Where are those friends of yours? Nancy? Jeannette? I kind of *liked* them . . . and that boy who was calling you, what's happened to *him?*"

Iris says with a coolness that makes her mother laugh, "I've outgrown them."

The days are not difficult; it's the nights, and Iris's memory of Jinx Fairchild scrambling across Little Red Garlock's legs, picking up a rock, bringing it down on the other's head again, again, again . . . cursing, sobbing, screaming out words that weren't words, only sounds.

Then Little Red Garlock stopped struggling, stopped *his* noise . . . then he was dead, so quick.

His legs twitching and that's all. And then that stopped too. So quick.

And Jinx got to his feet, and Iris came closer, and they'd stood over the body staring . . . thinking, Was it a trick of his, lying there like a slaughtered hog? in the weeds, in the sandy gravel? hoping they'd bend over him, touch him? then he'd have an advantage?

Surely Jinx Fairchild knew this was Death, the seeping blood, the wide-open sightless eyes, but he was whispering for Little Red to get up, damn you, get up, peckerhead motherfucker get *up*, clearly knowing he'd smashed in the boy's skull as with the edge of a shovel you'd smash ice that's in your way, but still he was dazed, pleading, wiping blood from his own dripping face, whispering, Hey man get *up*.

Then finally he turned to Iris Courtney, saying almost calmly except his teeth were chattering, "*You* . . . get on home. Nothing here for *you*."

She had not wanted to leave him; she'd stood there dumb, leaden-limbed, not knowing what to do until he began speaking more harshly, until his face shifted to show a look of his she hadn't believed she would see in that face and she began to back off in animal fright, knowing he was wild enough and despairing enough to kill her too but he'd be content with driving her off the way you'd drive off a dog, if she obeyed.

154

So she turned, she ran.

Running until her heart burst.

Once it was a matter of days since Little Red Garlock died in the vacant lot at the foot of Pitt Street, then it became weeks . . . now months. The numbness that settled upon Iris Courtney hasn't lifted entirely; it's as if she moves, still, in a suspension of being, a giant's withheld breath.

And what of Jinx Fairchild?

She has had no communication with him, has no idea what he is thinking, feeling, whether he blames her, whether he hates her bitterly as she gauges she should be hated. *I'm the one. I'm to blame. Not you.* Glancing down at the whiteness of her skin she feels a sensation of vertigo, a physical sickness, as if this whiteness were the outward symptom of her spirit's etiolation, a profound and unspeakable not-thereness. For she'd failed him, really, in not running for help and protecting him from his own instinct for self-survival. If he'd wanted to kill his enemy it had been simply to stop his enemy from killing him. In this, Iris Courtney knows herself to blame.

At first, she'd thought she might tell her mother, confess it all to her mother, and Persia would know what to do—keep it a secret, probably—though Persia is emotional and unpredictable; she might have wanted Iris to tell her story to the police, to go to them directly before they came to her. But days passed, and Iris couldn't speak, and Iris wouldn't speak, dazed and sick with dread. The infantile notion consoled her that if police did come to the Holland Street apartment to arrest her, Persia would keep them from her.

In certain school districts in Hammond it isn't uncommon for uniformed police officers, as frequently female as male, to appear in classrooms with papers issued by juvenile court judges and to take away a boy or a girl; not long before, in March, in Iris Courtney's ninth-grade home room, a Negro girl named Chloe was led away terrified and sobbing, the consequence of her foster mother having accused her foster father of having sexually abused the girl—thus Iris imagined herself led away before the eyes of her staring classmates. Excitement and apprehension churn the air in the wake of such drama, each child sitting rigid in his seat thinking, Not me, not me, please never me. Rarely does the distinction seem to be made in juvenile court between "victim" and "criminal," nor does the "victim" feel any less guilty than the "criminal": perhaps more guilty, having provoked the "criminal" to crime. Iris thought, More than Jinx Fairchild, I'm guilty.

And the whiteness of her skin has something to do with it . . . but what?

For months following the discovery of Little Red Garlock's body in the Cassadaga River it is generally believed that the case is continuing to be investigated by Hammond police detectives, but no arrests are made except the mistaken arrests of the two Hell's Angels motorcyclists from Buffalo . . . and there appear to be no suspects. The lie Iris Courtney invented in desperation and terror to save Jinx Fairchild and herself seems miraculously to have passed from her, will never be traced back to her, out of a young police officer's kindness or negligence; with the passing of time it's almost as if "lie" becomes "truth," worn smooth and plausible by the handling, as of a coin, by so many. Thus Iris Courtney, who fears with a part of her mind that she is still in danger of being arrested, comes to appreciate the extraordinary power of duplicity: duplicity given a seemingly artless utterance at just the right time and the right place.

As the police investigation subsides, as, day following day and week following week, there are no "new developments," the name Garlock disappears from the pages of the *Chronicle;* never is it heard any longer over the local radio station WHMM; when people discuss the case, speaking of the murder, the body in the river, "the kid killed by motorcyclists," it becomes increasingly rare that they recall the kid's name. It is the mystery alone that engages their interest, the publicity given to a single unexplained event out of a galaxy of unexplained events, lacking distinction. Little Red is beginning to be forgotten.

Death makes of us abstractions.

156

Remorse cannot be extracted from us.

These somber and illuminating truths Iris Courtney will recall through her life.

Her guilt? She turns it slowly in her fingers, in awe, in fascination, in pride; it's like one of those stones of uncommon beauty found now and then along the shore of Lake Ontario. (Persia and Iris have a glass jar filled to the very brim with such "jewel stones": souvenirs of family excursions to the lake now long forgotten, kept atop a windowsill in the kitchen.) She believes that, should the police ever hunt down Jinx Fairchild and arrest him, he'll be obliged to speak her name; yet it does not seem possible to her, still less probable, that the police will ever discover any link between Jinx Fairchild and the dead boy . . . apart from Iris Courtney, who *is* the link.

Suddenly happy, Iris thinks, We'll never be caught, then.

Iris Courtney and Jinx Fairchild.

It's late August, and one evening, after the movies, Iris finds herself in Cheney's Variety, where she hasn't been since the night of Little Red Garlock's death; she's in the protective company of friends: girls, boys, white like herself, all of them older than Iris, noisy and seemingly self-assured amid the Negroes in the cramped little store. Iris sees Jinx Fairchild at the rear of the store and her excitement is almost unbearable. A raw-boned black boy with a baseball cap jauntily reversed on his head, stooping behind a counter—Iris pushes away from her friends, approaching him blindly, waiting, heart pounding, for him to see *her*—then she realizes that the boy isn't Jinx Fairchild at all; he's approximately Jinx's age and height, skin just slightly darker than Jinx's, but his features heavier and coarser. How is it possible Iris has mistaken, even for a moment, this boy for the other? Jinx Fairchild's features are more familiar to her than her own.

The black boy is staring at her. Iris says apologetically, "I thought you were Jinx Fairchild . . . for a moment."

The black boy lifts his lip in a sort of sneering but appreciative smile. "Huh! Sure makin' me wish I *was!*"

157

Fool.

A killer, and a bad man, and deserving every harm . . . and a nigger fool beside.

This is what happens: Sunday before Labor Day, early in Cassadaga Park before church lets out and the playing areas are aswarm with children, Jinx Fairchild is methodically shooting baskets by himself—the familiar old basket just a netless rim loose against the battered backboard, the concrete rough underfoot—when a Villanova College student comes by, a forward on the Villanova basketball team, and the two play a fierce one-on-one game for hours. It's the most arduous game of basketball Jinx Fairchild has ever played; he's never felt so clumsy, so outclassed.

The college student is white, taller than Jinx, lean and tight-muscled and remarkably fast on his feet, the fastest white boy Jinx has ever seen in person. Introduces himself simply as Neil.

Midway in the game there's a shift of a sort; it's as if Jinx

Fairchild is learning from his opponent the way a leech sucks blood. By degrees the black boy takes on the white boy's style, his technique and his tricks, a certain twisting of the shoulders, a feinting of the head, dribbling in weird varying rhythms, and this style Jinx adapts to his own until at last, nearing noon and the September sun hot and spellbinding overhead, Jinx Fairchild begins to score.

When the game's over, Neil shakes Jinx's hand, grins, and shrugs as if mildly embarrassed. "You're good, fella"—looking at Jinx almost quizzically—"you're the real thing." Neil gives Jinx a pencil and a scrap of paper to write down his telephone number; Neil would like to call Jinx next time he comes home so maybe they can get together, but in the nervous excitement of the moment Jinx's mind seems to go blank: asshole can't remember his own telephone number.

But Jinx is too embarrassed to let on; he just scribbles down some numbers, hands the paper back to his new friend, this fair-skinned sandy-haired smiling white boy telling him he's the real thing, Jinx Fairchild's new friend from whom of course he never hears again.

Jinx Fairchild has taken a human life, but no one knows.
Except the white girl: Iris Courtney.
He thinks of her, and of that fact, a good deal.

All summer Jinx considers confessing his crime . . . but can't comprehend its nature. Can't rehearse the words. I'm the one, he must begin, I'm the one who . . . Yet a part of him, childlike, spiteful, is arguing that Little Red Garlock deserved to die *and you had the right to kill him.*

To whom should Jinx confess: the police? the precinct station up on East Avenue? He sees himself climbing the steps, going inside, panicked white-rimmed eyes darting from face to face and what next? What does he say, to whom does he speak, *what next?*

He's thinking, he hates white people.

White men, especially. Just hates them, as if the color of *their* skin is their fault 'cause it's their choice while the color of *his* skin isn't.

He'll go to the police, even if they're the white police . . . white fuckers. Tell them the truth of all that happened, even if he doesn't really remember. And if he is tried as a murderer, and if he is sentenced to die in the electric chair . . . must be, it's only what God commands.

But Jinx Fairchild isn't certain there is any God. *He* talks to God a whole lot, but *God* sure doesn't talk back.

Whole lot of silence, Jinx Fairchild thinks.

Like shouting in a tunnel, and all you hear, fool, is your own voice echoing back.

The strangest thing is, Jinx doesn't really remember all that happened that night. Remembers the start of it in Cheney's and the end of it—burning his sweatshirt in the woods and sobbing and talking to himself—but the middle part is blurred, hazy. As if he'd only been told it, secondhand. As if the killing of the white boy, Garlock, with that white girl a witness, isn't anything more than a story Jinx Fairchild has heard, in fragments.

One of those neighborhood stories told and retold so many times, when they return to their source they're unrecognizable . . . lumpy and disfigured and covered in dirt like a snowball you keep rolling in the yard till it's the size of a bushel basket and too heavy to budge. Not a snowball any longer, and not recognizable.

In any case, Jinx Fairchild doesn't go to the police. And the police don't come to him.

He's drawn, though, to the foot of Pitt Street.

Just to look. To contemplate.

That trashy vacant corner lot: tall weeds, pieces of concrete, rocks, debris, faded newspaper. Where Little Red Garlock is said to have died, head broken. The way you'd break a pumpkin. And whoever killed him was strong enough to drag the body down to the river . . . out across the wharf . . . strong enough to dump the body into the water.

Where it might have sunk, but didn't. Or floated downstream to empty into Lake Ontario. But didn't.

Jinx Fairchild stands on the sidewalk staring. An observer would wonder what it is the worried-faced black boy is staring at.

He tastes cold, and that blackish bile at the back of his mouth. How am I going to live my life out like this? Is this what God wants of me? Or is it just what happened, and no sense to it?

Jinx shuts his hands up into fists, trembling fists, hides them behind his back. Once there's blood on your hands blood cries out for blood . . . maybe.

How am I going to live out my life?

One day, Jinx Fairchild can scarcely believe his eyes, there at the foot of Pitt Street the little white girl Iris Courtney is standing just across the street, shy, hesitant, watching him. Whether she came along first and waited, or he'd been first and she has just now come along, he doesn't know. For a long moment the two of them simply stare at each other. Only Iris Courtney makes a move, finally . . . a frightened smile, a lifting of her hand in greeting.

Jinx Fairchild just stares. Stands frozen.

Then Iris Courtney hurries across the street to him; he sees yes it *is* her and no mistake . . . exactly as he remembers her except today, in the quiet of the afternoon, only gulls squawking and the sounds of traffic in the distance, Iris Courtney isn't distraught and she isn't fearful and her eyes seem to blaze up in certainty.

She comes right up to Jinx Fairchild, seizes his hand, raises it to her lips . . . kisses it.

Whispers, "You were never to blame. I'm the one."

Three thirty Sunday morning, and Virgil Starling and Persia Courtney are returning to Hammond from a party in Rochester when a state highway patrol car speeds past them on the left, splashing Virgil's midnight-blue Mercury coupe with snow and slush, then purposefully slows so that Virgil, continuing at his own speed, just below the speed limit, is forced to pull up alongside the patrol car . . . and endure a powerful beacon shone rudely into his face.

Into his face, and into Persia Courtney's.

The highway patrolmen flag Virgil down. He obeys immediately, braking his car on the shoulder of the Thruway. Whispering to himself low panicked pleading words that sound like, "Oh, Christ, oh, Christ, oh, my man," and Persia, squeezed in sleepily beside him, her head on his shoulder, sits up confused and frightened, saying, "What? What is it? Police? You haven't done anything wrong," and she's running her hands quickly through her tangled hair as if she's been surprised in sleep, in bed, and Virgil says, "No matter what I done or didn't do, it's who I am." He shuts off the ignition as two state troopers approach their car, pistols drawn. He says, despairing, "And there's you."

Both Virgil Starling and Persia Courtney have been drinking. For hours. But they aren't seriously drunk. Virgil's driving has been cautious, he's kept to one lane and more or less one speed, showing no signs of being impaired; he's a damned good driver could handle this smooth-running car in his sleep so why have the police flagged him down?

Two big-bodied white men, pistols drawn.

A sight you don't readily forget.

Nor is Persia Courtney likely to forget how Virgil Starling scrambles out of his car when he's ordered to, how meekly he turns over his license to the troopers, hunched in his fawn-colored suede coat with the fox fur collar, his slick-oiled hair going white with damp snowflakes, ashy-faced, eyelids rapidly blinking as if with a nervous tremor: shaking his head *no, nosir,* nodding his head *yes, yessir,* in reply to the troopers' loud staccato questions.

Why was he driving so fast?—Is he drunk?—Is this his car?—Where's the registration?—Is he carrying a weapon?—Is there a weapon in the car?—Where was he coming from, and where is he going?—Why in such a hurry?—*Is* that car his?—Where's his gun?—Does he have a police record?—Who's his girlfriend?

Shining the light into the passenger's seat, into Persia Courtney's pale face.

Then Virgil Starling is forced to lean forward against the hood of his car, legs spread, so the troopers can each frisk him, playing rough now, slapping his head down when he raises it, calling him *boy, nigger, coon,* and Persia Courtney, chilled and sober, shouts out the window at them, "He wasn't doing anything wrong, he wasn't speeding, I'm a witness," and one of the troopers shines the light into her face again so that Persia has to shield her eyes, frightened, but angry too, half sobbing, "I'm a witness, I'm a witness, he didn't do anything wrong, not a thing."

The military regalia of gleaming leather straps, holsters,

boots, billy clubs, drawn pistols. Mock-serious white faces, jeering eyes, those loud voices like barking laughter and who dares to resist? Not Virgil Starling, who removes his suede coat and allows the troopers to turn the pockets inside out, tear the bright silk lining (are they looking for dope? is that the pretext?) . . . who tugs off his high-heeled calfskin boots and stands in his stocking feet in the snow while the troopers examine, or pretend to examine, the boots . . . who unlocks the glove compartment, unlocks the trunk, pries off with a tire iron all four of his fancy chrome hubcaps under the white cops' supervision. *Nosir. Yessir.* By this time Persia Courtney too is standing on the shoulder of the Thruway, hunched and shivering in her steely-colored coat made of brushed fake fur that looks so glamorous, surely the cops believe it *is* fur, and they're noting too Persia's spike-heeled pointed-toed shoes, so impractical in this upstate New York weather but so attractive, and her shoulder-length glossy hair that's red-gold, hair in limp lazy strands but still striking to the eye, to any man's eye, and though her face is slightly puffy as if she's been awake for too long, yet not sufficiently awake, she *is* a good-looking woman—good-looking white woman—fucking a nigger.

Persia has been asking them what law Virgil broke, why are they doing this to him, she's going to report them, she says, she knows politicians in Hammond and she's going to report them for this outrage, she says, and one of the cops says to the other, "You smell something? You smelling it?" and the other says, grinning, "Yeah, real ripe," and the first one says, "Ain't ripe, it's *rotten*," but grinning at Persia too, running his eyes up and down her as if it's a joke, why doesn't she laugh, and Virgil Starling too exhausted and sick-faced . . . why's he taking it all so *grim?*

As if only now thinking of it, one of the cops makes a suggestion to the other, a suggestion about what the white cunt could do, she's so hot to get her nigger boyfriend off, and the other cop replies it sounds like a damned good idea, and they laugh companionably together, the two of them, crude but affable, or there's the impression they're affable . . . except for the drawn pistols, the barrels pointed in Virgil Starling's direction.

There's silence except for the noise of a big diesel truck passing on the Thruway, spewing slush across two lanes of pavement.

But traffic at this hour is sparse; there are few headlights in sight.

Persia Courtney shivering in her wet high-heeled shoes is trying to think where they are, how many miles from Hammond, from home. The giddy swirling of snowflakes like frenzied insects confuses her.

Neither Persia Courtney nor Virgil Starling seems to have heard the cop's bantering suggestion so there's silence, and then the cop says it again, and the other cop murmurs something in reply or affirmation, and suddenly Persia is crying, Persia is whispering, "Let us alone, we didn't do anything, we didn't break any law," and her appeal is so raw and childlike, so frightened, the cops take pity on her and within a few minutes the ordeal is over, Virgil Starling is issued a ticket for speeding and sent on his way, driving on to Hammond in absolute silence, sweaty inside his torn stylish clothes and his face that's the warm ripe shade of bananas at the point of disintegration is covered in a film of glittery sweat too . . . and in this silence that has the air of the end of things, of a finality profound yet wordless as death, Persia Courtney slides her arm around Virgil Starling's neck and leans close against him, like before, as if nothing between them has changed—and she's trying not to cry, trying to choke back the ugly sounds that threaten to push from her like spurts of vomiting—for the remainder of the drive back to Hammond and to the house on Jewett Street where her daughter has left a light burning for her in the stairway vestibule and in the kitchen into which she staggers, alone, exhausted, hair disheveled, savage little ladder runs in her stockings, mascara like her very life's blood streaking her face.

She staggers into Iris's room, wakes Iris from a deep sleep, sits on the edge of the bed, weeps in Iris's arms, frightening the girl with her own fear and rage and rambling drunken-sounding despair. Saying, "So awful . . . seeing a man crawl . . . seeing a man crawl and he can't not know you've seen . . . and the two of you aren't ever going to *not know* . . . what it is you've seen."

165

Pass!

Hey boy, hey jig . . . right here!

Mothafucker . . . what you gonna do with that ball?

Stars are winking in the night sky like the lights of distant cities but Jinx Fairchild, shooting baskets in Cassadaga Park, alone, nine o'clock to midnight, never glances up. His concentration is so fierce, he wouldn't know a sky is there.

Hey asshole . . . here!

Ain't goin nowhere, mothafucker!

It isn't another high school boy who is guarding Jinx tonight, no player for Hammond or for any team he knows: an adult man, six-foot-five-inch bastard on top of him every minute, blocking and stiff-arming and breathing into his face, keeping him from every clear shot so Jinx is forced to play it cool and oblique, "Iceman" style, feinting and driving the ball at quick unexpected angles . . . dribbling the ball in tricky different rhythms . . . stopping short,

166

turning on his heel, going for a jump shot . . . checking the impulse to do the obvious.

Nigger, where you think you're goin'!

Sometimes Jinx's guard is white and the weight of the crowd is on his side like gravity, but a white guard is easy to slip; it's the black guard that knows Jinx Fairchild's game . . . almost. If he knew it every inch of the way Jinx would be crippled, paralyzed, he'd be dead, but fortunately no guard knows his game that intimately; thus it doesn't matter if the fucker is bigger and stronger and crueler than Jinx, using his elbow (and the referee doesn't see), stepping on Jinx's foot (and the referee doesn't see), taunting and jeering and panting his hot meaty breath in Jinx's face . . . if Jinx pushes himself to the limit of his ingenuity and endurance and desperation Jinx can outmaneuver the man, break suddenly free, run to the basket, leap and toss and score.

Shit, ain't nobody gonna stop him.

Ain't nobody!

These solitary practice games in Cassadaga Park exhaust Jinx Fairchild as no other games do. These imagined guards.

But on the court, he's safe.

He's safe, on the court. Most of the time.

Feeling the grain of the ball against his fingertips. The perfect weight of the basketball. Snapping the ball outward from his chest, hard; seeing the ball sink through the basket *because Jinx "Iceman" Fairchild's eyes have willed it there.* Sometimes it rolls drunkenly on the rim, as if to tease the opposing team and their supporters; sometimes it drops straight through the basket with only the faintest brushing of the net.

Oh, man. Man, you the best.

Shit, man . . . nobody gonna touch you.

"Iceman," they start to call him, his senior year. 'Cause he's so cool and controlled and deadpan no matter what he's thinking or feeling or the voices inside his head. *Hey, Jinx! Iceman! Baby, you beau-ti-ful!* The college scouts from Syracuse, Cornell, Seton Hall, Villanova, Penn State, Ohio State: Iceman's name and photograph in the local papers from the start of basketball season to the close.

Ain't nobody gonna touch that boy. Yah, he the man.

Dribbling the ball right-handed, then switching to left. Trying a lefty hook shot, getting it on the rebound if it misses. Nobody can come near Iceman when he's got the beat. In motion, he's safe.

Except: sometimes at the foul line, breathing in slow and deep, steadying himself for a free shot, there's too much space for him to think in and he might miss. And everybody watching. And the hush and expectancy of the crowd, twenty rows of bleachers rising against the walls. White faces, black faces, so many eyes. And the white girl's among them . . . staring at him.

At such moments Iceman breaks out into a sweat. In his armpits and in the small of his back.

So many willing Jinx Fairchild to sink the shot as the ball snaps spinning from him to arc through the air . . . and so many willing Jinx Fairchild to miss. *Hey, nigger-boy! Hey, coon!* The Negroes roll their eyes white shrieking *Ohhhhhhh, Iceman!* He's known in Hammond for his professional style, his deadpan cool. Eye always on the ball and on the other players. Concentration only for the game. Not acknowledging the crowd or the applause wild as torrents of rain drumming against the roof and the walls and the barred windows of the brightly lit gym. Even the cheerleaders' parrot cries are not for Jinx Fairchild's ears:

J—!
I—!
N—!
X—!
JINX!
JINX!
JINX!

And the voices bounding and rebounding in the gym as if amplified by the powerful lights, the gleaming hardwood floor, the fact of no shadows and no cracks to seep into.

(There are nine white cheerleaders on the varsity squad, all so pretty, and one high yalla . . . first time in school history that a nonwhite girl has been so honored. Of course she's the cutest thing you ever saw: dentist's daughter, nice clothes, snubbed nose, and smooth glossy brown-black hair bobbing in a ponytail just like the white girls'.)

Iceman isn't interested in what occurs beyond the margins of the court; he's the kind of player, so rare, who can play an entire quarter without glancing at either the scoreboard or the clock. It's the game that has him in its grip, tight as a python . . . or maybe he has the game in his grip. His hands and feet are so fast people say they blur, when you watch. There's that liquidy motion to his body as if it comes to rest only in the spectator's eye but, there, it's deceptive, never comes to any rest at all: you're watching the action, the ball being dribbled; then Jinx Fairchild has stolen the ball and is off running down the other side of the court . . . the home crowd's on its feet . . . how did he do it? *What happened?* The split-second steal is Jinx Fairchild's specialty, executed with such apparently effortless grace the college scouts' eyes mist over. They don't know that, not consciously but by hours of absorption, Jinx Fairchild has committed to memory the uneven hardwood floor of the basketball court at Hammond Central, sensing where the ball will go dead to the bounce . . . where, in the heat and frenzy of the game, he'll instinctively channel any opponent dribbling the ball . . . Iceman steals the beat of their faltering dribble for a second or half second before his long fingers reach out, snaky-quick, to steal the ball.

Then it's a pounding drive to the other basket, the home crowd on its feet, cheering, screaming—no matter that Hammond is ahead by twenty points, or thirty-four, or as much as sixty—Jinx Fairchild's head is up and his eye resolutely off the ball that's magic to his fingertips; he comes at the basket from the side with a leaping shot as if his muscled legs can bear it no longer and must uncoil, spring out, up—you'd swear, watching him, he leaps three feet into the air—and the opposing team plods in his wake, the hapless rawboned boy who is Jinx Fairchild's guard shows his shame and bafflement and rage in his face, he's a white boy, good-looking and sandy-haired, beefy in the torso, sweat gleaming on his body like

169

grease. *Fucker. Could kill that fucker. Stinking nigger, dirty filthy stinking nigger tricks.*

The clapping and cheering like Niagara Falls, you could drown in. Drown in and be washed away.

And her eyes . . . the white girl's level narrowed eyes . . . the eyes he knows are icy gray-green because he has looked into them and shivered.

Except, on the court, during clocked time, Jinx Fairchild is safe.

His white teammates aren't jealous of Jinx Fairchild this season. No point to it. Only makes them look bad. Nor Willis Broadman, who's black. Nor Lonnie Jackson, "Black Lightning" when he's playing his best. The coach, Hank Breuer, no longer addresses Jinx in his nasal reproachful manner, misreading Jinx Fairchild for his insolent older brother Sugar Baby, who'd let the team down at the state quarterfinals two years before. No longer feels obliged to say for the others' benefit, "I'm talking to you too, Jinx," or "You listening, Jinx, or you know all this already?"—his ruddy bald-looking face growing ruddier still. Now Hank Breuer is likely to sling an arm around Jinx when he comes off the floor, his other arm around another player: "Beautiful play! A-One!" Happiness like first youth bubbling in him, Breuer's the coach of a winning-streak team, his name prominent too in the papers, the other coaches frank with envy and the college scouts profuse with praise. He's a Seton Hall graduate himself; he has already directed more than one promising athlete to the school, why not Jinx Fairchild?

He'll note, Hank Breuer will, and speak of it afterward to his friends, how the white kid is drenched with sweat and panting like a dog and the Negro kid is practically dry or at the most cool-damp like the underside of a leaf.

Sugar Baby Fairchild was bad business on the team, strutting his stuff in high-topped black sneakers, yeah, you'd have to say he was uppity, damn uppity nigger, cutting classes and failing his academic subjects just to see, maybe, what Breuer would do, what

Breuer could do; but Jinx takes his subjects almost as seriously as he takes basketball—though nothing so compels him as basketball, of course, that fire blazing bright, and brighter still, into which the boy stares mesmerized; if he isn't playing or practicing he's thinking about it, the court, the hardwood gleaming floor he has memorized, the bounce of the ball, the ball at his fingertips, the ball at chest level, the ball lifted in one graceful hand and thrown—though it looks like *tossed,* airily—into the basket: in his twenty-three years of coaching at Hammond, Hank Breuer has never witnessed anything quite like it.

He seems to remember, though, that Jinx Fairchild wasn't always quite so serious about basketball; this new seriousness began suddenly, over a year ago. Suddenly the kid is practicing by himself after school and even after his summer job: eight hours at Cassadaga Gravel, then home to eat, then out to a playground or to the park to practice more hours, the sign of a sure professional, and if Hank Breuer senses from time to time that there is anything excessive or troubling about the boy's dedication to the sport he isn't going to inquire, isn't that kind of coach, and especially not to the black boys on his teams. What he likes about Jinx Fairchild is Jinx is the kind of natural athlete so good at what he does there's no need for boasting and strutting and hogging the ball; it's a sweet thing Jinx Fairchild will do, shrugging off his teammates' occasional blunders, the way sometimes they'll let him down during a game, clumsy passes, stupid fouls, Jinx will say it's an off night for the team, shrugging, saying, Yah, we all got a lot to learn, we ain't the Harlem Globetrotters. Hank Breuer likes it too that Jinx Fairchild can subordinate himself to the team and to the needs of the team: gifted with eyes in the back of his head and always quick to pass the ball to the open man, no matter if the open man isn't going to handle it the way Jinx Fairchild might but he's generous that way, the other boys respect him for it—so there goes one of the eager white boys leaping for the basket—especially if Hammond is far enough ahead, the game is winding down.

On the court, Jinx Fairchild is safe.

He's safe, on the court. Running with the team. The green and white Hammond uniform. The time clock ticking high overhead and every minute on display.

All things about Jinx Fairchild that are in the public eye he takes pride in. His white sneakers he keeps clean and dazzling-white . . . white socks, a double pair, that never droop down his calves like most of the other boys' . . . shirt straps never twisted or slipping off a shoulder . . . hair trimmed short but those sideburns growing two inches below his ears for a sharp arrowlike look. And the set of his shoulders, and his backbone, and the way he holds his head up high; even dribbling the ball he doesn't look down at the floor or at the ball—the ball is *his* if it's at *his* fingertips—there's a feeling of pride in it, and control, Iceman style, Iceman cool. It's no surprise that the college scouts and recruitment officers are drawn to Jinx Fairchild like a magnet 'cause surely this Negro boy is going to be a credit to his race like Joe Louis, Jackie Robinson, Henry Aaron, Sugar Ray Robinson, someday? Eighteen years old and six feet three inches and still growing, one hundred eighty pounds lean, muscled, loose-limbed, a star who's willing to be a team player, precious as gold. And soft-spoken and gentle off the court, or seeming so.

If Jinx Fairchild takes note that there are never more than two or three Negroes on any Hammond sports team, football, basketball, volleyball, nor, during basketball games, more than four Negroes on the court at a single time, he says nothing to his white teammates or to his coach but wonders is it a written-down rule the Man abides by here in upstate New York or maybe everywhere? Except in the South, where naturally there wouldn't be a single nigger on any team 'cause there wouldn't be a single nigger at most of the schools? A written-down rule or just some belief or custom or superstition or instinct the Man abides by without fail?

He doesn't ask, though. That's not Iceman cool.

Like say some white boys on some opposing team—Lebanon, for instance, or Wrightsville, big hulking farmboy fuckers— they're frustrated seeing Hammond score so they start in taunting *nigger* during the game, say it's an away game and the crowd is restless and hostile, if Jinx Fairchild hears *hey, nigger, hey, shine, hey, coon* he doesn't give a sign, or even if he's getting fouled accidentally-on-purpose, elbowed in the gut or neck, stiff-armed when he jumps to shoot—blocked by some hefty bastard so hard he's knocked to the floor—tries not to show his hurt or pain or worry or fear he's been injured . . . or if he's angry enough to tear out somebody's throat with his teeth. He'll tell the referee his side of it but won't ever raise his voice to argue, that's Mr. Breuer's job; slow and collected-cool he gets to his feet long-legged as a colt, holding his head steady in dignity, shifting his shoulders to loosen the muscles, and takes the ball from the referee and goes to the foul line to take his free shot . . . and maybe at this time, at this moment, like sunshine pricking its way through a worn-out shade, he'll have a thought of Little Red Garlock, whose head he bashed in, Little Red Garlock grinning at him, showing his crazy teeth, and the hair lifting in snaky tufts in the moonlit water, and the eyes, the wide-open dead eyes . . . but if Jinx Fairchild breathes in deep and easy, once, twice, three times, his fingers gripping the ball at mid-chest, his eyes unblinking on the basket, if Jinx Fairchild steps into his own secret space where no one can follow or even perceive him there, seeing merely the outermost husk of his bodily form, understanding he's safe on the court, under the principle of the brightly clocked time, if he directs the ball in his fingers to rise and arc and fall into the basket in a trajectory determined by his eyes . . . he can't fail.

And applause or groans and jeers, he won't hear.

That's Iceman cool.

On the court, Jinx Fairchild is safe.

> I believe we are born with Sin on our head and must labor to cleans ourselves all the days of our life. It is not a matter of Gods punishment but of Conscience, if there is no God nor Jesus Christ there is still Human Conscience.

Jinx Fairchild spends days on the assignment, a five-hundred-word composition for his senior English class on the topic "I Believe," writing it out in large looping letters in blue ink, writing and rewriting in a ferocity of concentration nearly as singleminded as his concentration on basketball. The effort is exhausting. He has never thought of words on paper as expressions of the soul, the voice on paper a silent rendering of his own voice.

When he gets the composition back he sees to his shame that his teacher Mrs. Dunphy has marked it in red: numerous grammatical errors, several run-on sentences, a fatal "lack of clarity." The grade is D+, one of the lowest grades Jinx Fairchild has received in English, in years.

"Ordinarily I would give a paper like this an F," Mrs. Dunphy says, peering up at Jinx over her half-moon glasses with a steely little smile of reproach. "You know the rule, Jinx, don't you? No run-on sentences."

Jinx mumbles, "Yes, ma'am."

"Didn't I write it out on the blackboard? NO RUN-ON SENTENCES."

"Yes, ma'am."

"And is the argument wholly your own?" Mrs. Dunphy asks doubtfully. "It doesn't sound . . . like something you'd be thinking."

Jinx Fairchild stands silent as if confused. Is the white woman accusing him of cheating?

As if reading his thoughts Mrs. Dunphy adds quickly, "The tone of the composition doesn't sound like *you*, Jinx. It sounds like somebody else, a stranger. It isn't *you*. And the thinking is muddled and incoherent." She gives a breathy little laugh, uneasy, annoyed: this tall hooded-eyed Negro boy standing there so unnaturally still.

He's about to turn away so Mrs. Dunphy says, relenting, "If you rewrite it, making corrections, I might raise the grade. I might make an exception, this time."

Jinx mumbles, "Yes, ma'am."

"Will you, then?"

"Ma'am?"

"Rewrite it, make corrections? Hand it back in again, by Monday?"

Jinx slips the composition in his notebook. His heart is beat-

174

ing hard and steady, keeping him cool, Iceman style. He's thinking that once there's blood on your hands, blood cries out for blood, doesn't it? This white bitch on her fat girdled ass, looking up at him with a fond-familiar smile, as if she has the right.

He says, "Yes, ma'am, thank you, ma'am, I sure will."

And he does. And the grade is raised to B+.

It's early winter . . . smelling of snow, sun spilling like acid through the Fairchilds' kitchen window.

The frost on the pane so sparks and glitters, Jinx Fairchild shifts his chair sideways to avoid the strain on his eyes. He pours milk into a bowl of Rice Krispies and begins to eat.

His mother, Minnie, and his little sister, Ceci, are talking over his head but Jinx Fairchild is in an open-eyed dream . . . doesn't hear a word.

The night before, he'd dreamt of it again. Not for months had he dreamt of it, but the night before he'd dreamt of it with such force he awakened sick and faint with terror, seeing the white face floating just beneath the surface of the water: Little Red Garlock's face soft and white as bread dough but the eyes unmistakable, the teeth bared in a grin. And the legs that had dragged so heavy with the weight of deadness came alive suddenly to kick and thrash. And Jinx felt fingers closing hard around his ankle; the dead boy had hold of him and was pulling him into the river. . . .

No! You dead! Can't harm me now!

Minnie lays a hand on Jinx's head, on the green and white woolen cap Jinx is wearing indoors, and chides him as she's been chiding him for days, an edge of jealousy in her voice. "That hat— you got to wear it in my face? Every damn minute? Just 'cause some empty-head high yalla knit it for you?"

Ceci giggles. "Iceman got all the girls, any girl he wants. All the girls—and some old ladies—they hanging on Iceman."

In his open-eyed dream Jinx Fairchild doesn't hear. He eats his cereal without tasting it, slick and numb inside.

Almost, Jinx can see the dead boy's face floating close . . . the jeering eyes. He can feel the fingers closing tight around his ankle.

Lemme go. You dead. Mothafucker, you dead!

"These sideburns is what gets me!" Minnie exclaims. Tickling and tugging at Jinx's hair, pinching his cheek like he's no more than a toddler, this big boy sitting at the kitchen table with legs so long under it, either his knees are nudging Ceci's or his feet are nudging Ceci's feet, every meal interrupted by jostling, complaining, teasing. Most days, Minnie and Ceci vie with each other for Jinx's attention—Jinx Fairchild is a true charmer when he makes the effort—but he's in the habit of hurrying through his meals, eager to get out of the house, on his way to basketball, school, work. Unlike Sugar Baby at that age, Jinx doesn't party much with his friends. Doesn't have time for such trifling matters.

For which Minnie Fairchild thanks God.

Yessir. Thanks God.

She says, still harsh, chiding, "You Verlyn, you going to eat supper at home here or where? Out with one of them college scouts?"

Jinx mumbles something.

"What? Don't know?"

"Yah, guess I am eating out."

"Hear him! Just hear him!" Minnie exclaims. Her eyes, which have a yellowish cast these days, flare up like a cat's. "These white folks stumbling over one another, taking Verlyn Fairchild to Howard Johnson's, to the Pancake House, Lord it'll be the Hotel Franklin next."

"Jinx been there already," Ceci says. "He *told* us, Momma."

Jinx says, "Just the coffee shop."

"Huh! 'Just the coffee shop!' " Minnie cries. "Next thing you know, it's that big room with all the marble. *I* seen the inside of it, lemme tell you it's something. Like some fancy place in a movie, or in a palace. And there's my Verlyn," she says, laughing a little too loudly, "with his big white sneakers and his pretty wool-knit cap pulled down low on his head."

Close under Minnie Fairchild's chattering, like rancid milk beneath a creamy film, there is likely to be hurt or terrible worry or fear; neither Jinx nor Ceci wants to push through to discover what it is.

Minnie Fairchild now works as a maid at the Hotel Franklin, heavy-duty cleaning of a kind she hasn't done in years.

All morning, Minnie has been grumbling 'cause Woodrow Senior slipped away early, before anybody else was awake, to go fishing on the river—ice fishing with his friends—and there are household tasks he'd promised to do. And this new job of Minnie's—not exactly new any longer since she has been working there for five months—this new job is a constant source of anxiety, old-womanish fretting and apprehension her children have never noticed in her before.

Jinx thinks, Soon as I get some money, Momma can stay home.

Jinx thinks, Soon as I get out of here, I can send money home.

When he isn't playing basketball he's thinking about such things in the effort to block thinking about other things.

It's been a long time now. Jinx has lost precise count of the months. He's safe, he isn't going to be caught.

Drinking a tall glass of milk . . . his bones are growing, greedy for milk.

Minnie and Ceci have stopped teasing Jinx since Jinx isn't in a teasing mood. Minnie complains nonstop like it's a sermon, or singing the blues with no music, a whining melodic midnight-blue voice from deep in her throat as she bangs around the kitchen, heavy-hipped in her ugly white uniform, its bulk exaggerated by the white nylon sweater she's wearing under it; the wind these days is so damn cold it'll freeze your ass off, waiting for the bus.

It's no joke, Minnie says, flaring up, as if anybody thought it might be, that damn blizzardy wind coming down from Lake Ontario.

Waiting at the bus stop huddled with your kind like cattle gone mute and mindless with misery. And the white bus drivers treating you like shit if you stumble climbing in, drop a bus token on the floor.

The arthritis in Minnie's hands, swelling in the knuckles,

and throbbing pain that keeps her awake at night . . . that's the true terror. Minnie has about used up the painkillers from Dr. O'Shaughnessy.

Ceci says, on the very edge of sass, "Why you working so far uptown, anyway? Flora's mother, she got a nice job closer by."

" 'Cause they pay higher, uptown!" Minnie nearly shouts. " 'Cause they leave tips sometimes, that nobody's counting in any income tax!"

Minnie Fairchild is angry much of the time now. Angry at Dr. O'Shaughnessy for collapsing as he did, being hauled off to a nursing home in Syracuse, his cold-hearted children, the very worst sort of white folks, coming forward to make their claim . . . just waiting for him to die.

It's the heartbreak of Minnie's life; knowing she'll never see Dr. O'Shaughnessy again.

Minnie was the one who found him. A thousand times she's told the story of how she unlocked the rear door with her key—yes, Minnie Fairchild had her own special key to the white doctor's house—how she went along the corridor saying, Dr. O'Shaughnessy? You here? Dr. O'Shaughnessy? It's Minnie—and found the poor man collapsed in his bedroom in a tangle of bedclothes. One eye open and one eye shut. The eye that was open, Minnie Fairchild would never have known whose it was.

That sight, and the smell of it, Minnie doesn't like to recall.

Yes: Dr. O'Shaughnessy was true to his word like the gentleman Minnie always knew he was, left *my most faithful friend and employee Mrs. Minnie Fairchild* a dozen household items, including a lion's head bronze lamp Minnie used to make a joke of—heavy ugly thing weighed a ton, all curlicues and carvings it was the devil's work to get clean—and $1,200 cash. Which, to Minnie's outrage, the O'Shaughnessy children are contesting.

Imagine! Contesting! These well-to-do white folks, two brothers and a sister, so selfish and so nasty!

But better not get Minnie started on that subject, her breath gets short and raspy, her nerves all the more frazzled. Every joint in her body will start to throb, like electricity.

These days, there's a yellowish sheen to Minnie Fairchild's face, as if something sickly is trying to push through. Minnie hasn't had time or spirit to get her hair pressed for five weeks, so it's matted and heavy with grease—and is she gaining weight, going puffy-fat in the hips and rear? "Don't make the least bit of sense," Minnie says in disgust, "all the work I do. All the *stairs*." But she has had to buy a new girdle and she's out of breath after the least exertion and jumpy and twitchy as if something is buzzing close around her head she can't see to swat.

And the arthritis in her hands.

And the Hotel Franklin. The white staff manager, the white clientele, the way white people cut their eyes at her—not her exactly, not Minnie Fairchild exactly, but her brown-black skin—like all they see, seeing her, *is* her skin. One white lady claimed somebody stole a ring of hers, and was that somebody the cleaning girl, and was that cleaning girl Minnie Fairchild, and thank God the ring came to light: damn thing packed away in a suitcase in some undies. Minnie Fairchild was mortified, though, then ashamed of herself at her own relief, the white bitch managing a smile for her and an apology: "I'm so very, very sorry."

So very, very sorry!

Minnie misses those kindly white lady patients of Dr. O'Shaughnessy who'd looked upon Minnie Fairchild with respect and affection, asking after her health and her family, depending on *her* to make *them* less nervous in the examination room. At the Hotel Franklin it's all different.

Minnie is convinced it's gotten worse, a whole lot worse, how white people regard Negroes, since that trouble back in September, in Little Rock, Arkansas: national troops marching in to help integrate the schools, push back the mobs of angry jeering whites—nasty sight to behold. And so much attention paid to it in the newspapers and on TV, and everybody talking about it, the eyes nervous and jumpy on both sides, worse even than back in 1955 when Martin Luther King led that bus boycott down in Montgomery, Alabama, and some folks was terrified there'd be blood in the streets . . . black blood. "That Reverend King," Minnie complained, "seems to me he's doing more harm than good, preaching 'nonviolence' and 'passive resistance' and 'hate will be returned with love'—making it hot for the rest of us, is all. *I* ain't returning any hate with love 'cause *I* ain't got any love to spare," and her Verlyn fired back so quick and emphatic it stunned her, "Reverend King makes the most sense of any man *I* ever heard." So they quarreled, that day, till Minnie lost her temper and slapped her favorite child around the head, and Verlyn stamped out of the house.

Minnie shouted after him, "You don't know a thing, boy! Ain't lived long enough to know a goddamn thing!"

When Minnie's angry, her accent goes south, down past Pittsburgh and all the way to northeast Georgia, where her folks came from.

Ever after that outburst, Minnie has been careful not to bring certain subjects up in Verlyn's presence. Any one thing that chills her heart, it's her own flesh and blood opposing her on something she knows is right, regarding her with contemptuous eyes.

That too Minnie blames on Martin Luther King, like the New Testament says Jesus warned He would come between parents and children and husbands and wives: I bring not peace but a sword.

"Don't want your goddamn old sword," Minnie fumes.

These days, though, basketball so much on his mind and his name and picture in the newspaper, Verlyn rarely talks about anything else. Basketball, the coach, his teammates. College and scholarship applications for next year.

Thinks Minnie, Thank God.

Thinks Minnie with satisfaction, *He's* on his way.

Now Verlyn has finished his Rice Krispies, drunk down his second glass of milk in thirsty gulping swallows. The green and white knit cap—it *is* a beautiful cap—balled up carelessly under his arm as if to placate Minnie. On his legs, he towers over her.

Sweet-faced boy so handsome the simple sight of him takes Minnie's breath away, sometimes. Lord, she'll forgive her Verlyn anything.

But these near-grown boys, that's the last thing they want—Momma staring at them all melting-eyed with love.

180

Now that Woodrow Junior is turning out such a heartbreak, Verlyn is all the more special.

Verlyn: Jinx. Minnie hates these neighborhood names but lately she's been forced to think of her son that way, the way everyone else thinks of him. Like he doesn't belong just to her any longer.

"G'bye, you, boy!" Minnie growls, giving Jinx a kiss as he's out the door, thrusting his arms into the sleeves of his Hammond school jacket, and Jinx ducks his head, mumbling, "G'bye, Momma." Seeing Minnie's look like she's recalling him as a tiny baby nursing at her breasts or, worse yet, snug in her swollen belly. Schoolday mornings, Jinx leaves the house early, goes straight to the school gym to practice baskets before the first bell rings at 8:45 A.M.

Minnie too will be leaving in a few minutes. Has to catch the 7:50 uptown bus.

Outside it's that mean-spirited damp cold, the worst kind for arthritis. A low sky, clouds soaking up the light like soiled cotton.

This exasperating habit of Minnie's!—waits till Jinx gets out on the street, then calls after him from the doorway, a high-pitched drawling yell more volume than substance. Jinx isn't sure what she's asking: *Is* he eating out that night? What time will he be back?

Jinx laughs and waves. "Be home sometime, Momma!"

Whether Minnie has heard clearly or not she waves energetically back, big happy smile, love in her face so plain it pierces his heart, Jinx Fairchild's black heart . . . like Minnie Fairchild is taking her rightful seat in that special row of the bleachers, where Mr. Breuer saves seats for VIPs, as he calls them, right there in the first row.

That white girl, Iris Courtney.

Now she's at the high school, Jinx Fairchild sees her frequently. And she sees him.

That look in her eyes, so raw in appeal, so without guile or girlish subterfuge . . . or pride. Jinx Fairchild is fearful of it even as he's excited, sexually stirred. She has told him, No one is so close to me as you, no one is so close to us as we are to each other.

Jinx supposes, yes, it's true. But he doesn't want to think why it's true or what he can do about it.

Over five hundred students at Hammond Central High School but somehow it happens that Jinx Fairchild, a senior, and Iris Courtney, a sophomore, are thrown together often, by accident—*is it accident?*—and in any room or field of vision, however vast, they are never unaware of each other.

There's a blindness in their perception of each other. As if, where each stands, the world is too suddenly flooded with light.

On the stairs . . . in the corridors . . . at the bus stop in front of the school. In the school auditorium where, each Friday morning like clockwork, the homerooms file into their respective rows of seats . . . Jinx Fairchild, down front with the other seniors, can't resist glancing over his shoulder to where, at the rear, Iris Courtney will be sitting with her classmates. And in the school cafeteria, that place of clamorous hilarity, romance, hurt feelings, ceaseless melodrama, where, from time to time, Iris Courtney will approach Jinx Fairchild at a table if he happens to be alone or in company hospitable to her, a white. "Do you mind? Is it all right?" Iris asks quietly, not lowering her tray to the table until Jinx gives her permission. "It's a free country, girl!" he says. Baring his teeth in a mirthless smile.

No one is so close to me as you.

No one is so close to us as we are to each other.

At basketball games, this final season of Jinx Fairchild's at the school, 1957–58, Jinx will quickly seek out the white girl before the game begins . . . not to make eye contact with her, still less to wave and grin at her, as his teammates do with their friends and relatives, but simply to locate her, fix her in place. OK, girl. There you are.

Once he'd wanted her dead; now he's worried he's going to fuck her.

In Hammond, the races don't mix much. 'Course they *do* . . . but not in a good way.

White trash, says Minnie. You get you a good decent neighborhood, colored folks owning their own homes, working to keep

182

them up; then it's these hillbillies falling down drunk on the street, beating their wives and children as bad as any niggers, any of the worst cutthroat niggers. White trash moving in 'cause the whites that can afford it won't.

During the basketball game, of course Jinx Fairchild is wholly indifferent to Iris Courtney, never so much as glances in her direction. But then it's this cool black boy's style not to glance in anyone's direction off the court, except Hank Breuer . . . sometimes not even him. Though he's well aware of the eyes riveted to him— the "white" eyes—how he appears through the prismatic lenses of their vision. He understands that whites study him as if he were not even a specimen of sorts but an entire category. They study him, amazed at his athletic gifts, admiring of his personal style, deceiving themselves they are learning something about this category when in fact they aren't even learning anything about Jinx Fairchild the specimen.

Except for Iris Courtney: she's the only white who *sees* him, knows *him*.

There's this mournful jazz song keeps winding through Jinx Fairchild's head, sharp and poignant as actual memory though it's just a song he has heard on the radio, doesn't even remember the Negro singer, a man, he'd heard sing it, *Went down to the St. James Infirmary . . . saw my little baby there*—slow dirgelike lyrics with a clarinet behind—*stretched on a long white table, so sweet, so cold, so bare*. And if he allows the song to continue, a snaky sort of caress that brushes across his very genitals, flooding blood and strength and purpose into them, *Went down to the St. James Infirmary . . . all was still as night. My gal was on the table . . . stretched out so pale, so white*.

"St. James Infirmary" has got to be a Negro song, Jinx Fairchild thinks, doesn't it? Sure sounds like it. And if it isn't, should be.

So pale . . . so white.

So dead.

When he hears this song in his head he finds he's thinking of Iris Courtney without knowing it. Sometimes, watching the girl and her not knowing he's watching, he starts hearing the song in his head.

So too do dreams continue their autonomous narratives beneath the threshold of consciousness, apart from our volition. The dreaming self beneath the thinking *I*.

That *I-I-I* we can't imagine ceasing to exist even as, like Jinx Fairchild on the basketball court, we sense how precariously it's there: how provisional, even nominal, the terms of its existence.

Iris Courtney is saying in a rapid lowered voice, just loud enough so that Jinx Fairchild, beside her, can hear over the rattling bus noises, "a bad dream about it last night, and I woke up so scared, thinking . . . it was all ahead, and going to happen again." She pauses, not looking at Jinx. The two are sitting side by side, stiff as strangers. "Do you think about it, much? I mean . . ."

Jinx Fairchild makes a wincing, shrugging gesture, staring out the window. It's an overcast March afternoon, descending jaggedly toward dusk: not yet five o'clock and already deep in shadow. "Yah. Sure. All the time."

Iris asks shyly, "Do you think there'll ever be a time when . . . we won't?"

Jinx shrugs again.

"If we each leave Hammond, live somewhere else—"

"*I'm* sure as hell gonna live somewhere else."

"You're going to college next year, and after college . . . ?"

Jinx shrugs and doesn't reply. He's sitting with his arms folded awkwardly across his Hammond school jacket, hands gripped beneath his armpits. The green and white knit cap is pulled down low on his forehead, to his eyebrows: makes his long lean face look pushed together. Iris Courtney blows her nose in a crumpled pink Kleenex. Says, as if they'd been arguing, "But we did the right thing, back then. Any other thing would have been a terrible mistake."

Jinx says, almost too loudly, "What 'right thing' you talking about, girl? Not telling anybody what happened, you mean, or killing the fucker himself?"

184

Iris Courtney leans forward suddenly as if she has become lightheaded. There's a small pile of schoolbooks in her lap, a red simulated leather purse, a badly soiled duffel bag of the kind gym clothes are carried in; she leans her elbows on the duffel bag and presses her fingertips hard against her eyes, stretching the skin. It's a gesture Jinx Fairchild has seen before. She says so softly, "Not telling anybody what happened," that Jinx almost doesn't hear.

They're on the East Avenue bus plummeting to Lowertown in a sequence of short, steep hills. Jinx was on the bus first, sitting in a double seat near the rear, directly over the wheels, his cap pulled low on his forehead and his jaws grinding an enormous wad of gum, a cold crinkly steely look of Iceman's that means he isn't in the mood for company. If passengers on the bus recognize him he isn't in the mood for their praise or congratulations or questions about what comes next, now the Hammond team is set for play-offs . . . maybe for a state championship. But Iris Courtney, entering the bus at the front, alone, with no girl companions this afternoon and no boyfriend (Jinx seems to know that Iris has a white boyfriend, he's seen them together at basketball games), made her way to him unerring as a sleepwalker, murmuring, "Can I sit here, is it all right?" even as the bus swerved and pitched her into the seat.

Jinx Fairchild said, as he always says, "It's a free country, girl!"

The first time Iris Courtney sat with Jinx Fairchild on the city bus, as if they were old friends, as if, maybe, they were going out together, pretty white girl and her brown-skinned boyfriend, Jinx was annoyed, upset, embarrassed; in fact he was desperate to escape, wanted nothing more than to jump up, yank the bus cord, get off at the first stop. Wasn't she asking for trouble? Wanting people to see them together and to wonder?

He'd remained where he was, of course. Hot-faced and trembling and resentful.

Feeling the eyes crawl over them. Whites, mainly. But a few blacks too.

Though this is the North, not the South. And it's 1958. All Hammond public schools are declared officially integrated . . . even if most of the residential neighborhoods, de facto, are not.

Jinx Fairchild hadn't guessed he was in the mood for talking, but seems he is. Practically poking his nose in Iris Courtney's bushy hair, breathing warm and damp as a dog in her ear. "*I* did the right thing, *I* didn't have any choice. We talked about this before. Once it got started, only way it was going to end was that peckerhead bastard dead, or me." He's so riled up he nudges the girl, closes his big hard fingers around her elbow; if they weren't in full view of a crowded bus of passengers, he'd sling his arm around her neck and catch her in a vise hold . . . just in play, like you'd throw a hold on a younger brother or sister. Jinx Fairchild is the kind of boy who likes to touch and sometimes to touch hard.

He's saying, "And every hour of every fucking day I'm gonna give thanks it *wasn't* me."

Iris Courtney continues to stretch the skin around her eyes in that old-looking gesture. Like she's thought the same thoughts so many times and can't get free of them. Jinx wants to slap her hands down. He sees the nails are bitten, especially the left thumb. To the quick. She says, "If only . . . I had it to do over again. It was my decision, it was my—"

Jinx says, "Yah, honey, but you did, didn't you. As my daddy says of certain things, 'It is writ.' 'It is writ, Amen.' "

Iris Courtney says, as if suddenly calmed, placated, " 'It is writ. Amen.' "

They sit for some minutes not speaking, a kind of equilibrium between them.

Jinx sees Iris has a tiny cold sore on her upper lip. Her eyes are strange to him: icy, pewter-colored, deep-set beneath her brows. Her skin is pale, smooth, thin, sprinkled with freckles like dirty raindrops. She could be a plain hard-looking girl or she could be beautiful; Jinx can't judge, sitting so close. He's nervous, excited, this close. Smelling the girl's warm, slightly yeasty odor. A stab of desire sharp as pain between his thighs.

No one is so close to me as you.

No one is so close to us as we are to each other.

Since April 1956, Iris Courtney has matured a good deal, has the features of an adult woman set in that girl's face. Jinx can't really remember her, what she'd been like, before the trouble with Little Red Garlock: just a neighborhood girl, very young. Pretty, flirty, reckless-seeming. The kind any intelligent black boy would have sense enough to avoid.

Jinx wonders if she's a little crazy.

Jinx wonders what she wants with him, after the trouble she's already brought him.

These conversations, these breathless improvised meetings, are entirely at Iris Courtney's initiative. Left to himself, Jinx Fairchild wouldn't touch her—to use a frequent expression of Minnie's—with a ten-foot pole.

The previous summer, she'd telephoned him at home. Called three times, the first two times getting Minnie, since Jinx was out. "Who's that girl pestering you? Wouldn't leave her name, like she's ashamed? Did sound like some pissy little white girl to me!" Jinx was astonished by the call and touched: near as he could determine, Iris was in tears because of some unhappiness in her family; she'd told him she didn't deserve to live because she was "fated" . . . just no good. Jinx had talked with her for almost an hour, and when he hung up he'd felt as exhausted as if he'd been working out in the gym for that long.

Next day, and the days following, he'd been on the lookout for her . . . meaning to avoid her.

She's rummaging now in her purse. Says she has something for him.

"How come you always giving me things?" Jinx laughs.

His laughter, with Iris Courtney, sounds to his own ears like wire scraping concrete.

Iris laughs too, as if happily. "Must be," she says, with a sidelong smile, "you're the kind of boy people like to give things to."

Several times in the past year or so Iris has embarrassed Jinx by pressing little gifts on him. He's accustomed to being given things by his mother, and relatives, and certain black girls, and neighbor ladies who think he's sweet . . . but there's an intensity in Iris's behavior that makes him uncomfortable. Is she thinking of him all the time? Plotting things to give him, things with droll little meanings, all the time? Once she gave him a key chain with a thimble-sized brass basketball . . . another time a rhinestone stickpin—Jinx hadn't known what the damn thing was supposed to be—another time a slim gold fountain pen, very elegant. Jinx wonders if he's supposed to remember her sometime, give her something.

He never has and never will.

Nor is he fool enough to touch her; he knows how that would end up.

"Huh! What's this?"

It's a sepia-tinted photograph, very old, measuring about six inches by eight, on stiff cardboard backing . . . a photograph of the Civil War. Stiffly posed across a rural bridge, reflections sharp in the water and sky, in the background massed with junglelike foliage, are a band of Union soldiers, some on horseback, most on foot, and among the foot soldiers are several black men, uniformed like the rest. The caption, in faded ink, reads *Military bridge across the Chickahominy, 1864.*

Jinx Fairchild whistles faintly. "This the real thing? I mean . . . so *old?*"

He's holding the photograph up to the light. The way he stares, it might be he's looking at something hurtful.

It always scares Jinx, stirs him to an emotion he can't name, when he sees the images of people long since dead, considers their strange composure in the face of destiny and dissolution. Contemplating the past, you know there's no Heaven, no place for all those dead to end up. Also, these are Union soldiers, freed slaves among them, in the Man's uniform: just as husky, just as manly, just as composed (though their uniforms are all shabby) as the whites. A photograph is a puzzle, Jinx Fairchild thinks, but what's it a puzzle of? And what's the solution? He's just staring and staring, like a small child.

Iris is saying excitedly, leaning against him, "My uncle, he's a photographer, he has drawers of things like that, things he collects. He goes all around the state, to auctions and junk shops, collecting.

I told him about you and I said . . . and he said, 'Please take it and give it to your friend.' I told him you were my friend. I said . . . I work for my uncle sometimes, if there's enough work to be done. The thing about photography that's so surprising, it's that when a negative is being developed, a print made from a negative, there isn't any true light or color to it except what you make of it. From a single negative you can get a thousand different prints. Not many people know that." Iris is chattering happily, leaning against Jinx's arm, but Jinx isn't paying much attention until she says, "I thought, you know, when I found it . . . one of your actual ancestors might be there. On the bridge."

Jinx looks up sharply. "One of my *what?*"

"Ancestors."

Jinx Fairchild just stares at her. Ancestors?

She says, faltering, "When Lincoln freed the slaves, I mean. And they helped fight the . . ."

Slaves?

Jinx Fairchild stares at the white girl until she looks away, chilled and rebuffed.

He doesn't say another word to her until she gets off the bus at Jewett Street, then only mumbles, "G'bye," and doesn't look after her, as if they were strangers who'd sat together by accident, sure won't peer back to see where she's standing on the sidewalk staring after *him* . . . hurt and lost-looking.

Pissy little white girl, he's thinking. Neck not worth wringing.

Jinx keeps the photograph, however. In fact he must treasure it; his mother will discover it in a mess of old yellowing newspaper clippings and other high school memorabilia, after Jinx's death.

That faded, antique picture, dreamlike in its extraneous detail, of long-dead soldiers, horses. Stiffly yet resolutely poised on a bridge in some part of the world unknown to Jinx Fairchild. (He never learns where the Chickahominy, creek or river, is. Guesses it must be the South.)

Those men living, then. Like me. Alive and walking around in their skins then, like me.

Thinking me, me, me . . . like me.

Jinx Fairchild doesn't feel any kinship with the black soldiers in the photograph. He sees to his surprise that one or two of them look actually younger than he . . . just boys. But he doesn't feel any particular kinship. A black man in uniform troubles his soul, for you got to figure, in North America at least, it's the Man's uniform he's wearing; just one other way for the Man to exploit . . . use up . . . suck dry . . . discard. Jinx doesn't think of ancestors, and he sure doesn't think of freed slaves.

Slaves!

No connection between the long-dead soldiers on the Chickahominy bridge and Jinx Fairchild in Hammond, New York, aged eighteen. No connection between Jinx Fairchild and anybody, whatever the color of their goddamn skin.

Says Jinx aloud, thinking of these things, "Fuckers!"

Though he'd be hard put to say, exactly, what he means or why he's so trembling-angry.

Says Sugar Baby Fairchild with an air of one put-upon, "Ain't nobody said anything about *losin'* any fuckin' game, boy, you readin' me wrong"—his voice both whining and melodic, reproachful and brotherly warm—"you just don't play so cool, is all. A game is won by two points like it's won by twenty. It's the point spread that's the thing, and Iceman surely got his off nights like anybody else. Shit, there's Ernie Banks hisself, he was a rookie with the Cubs . . . I bet you Babe Ruth, Stan Musial, all of 'em. Jinx Fairchild the coolest player these shitheads ever seen, so, comes this night, over at Troy, maybe your team's kind of nerved up, scared, maybe Iceman has got a nasty cough, don't have to do any asshole thing, boy, any actual mistake, you just ain't so cool is all. And nobody's goin' to know 'cause who can read minds?"

Sugar Baby is shooting baskets with Jinx, cigarette in his mouth: if he sinks one, OK; if he misses doesn't give a shit, ain't nothing but a boys' game anyway.

Seeing his brother's face so stiff and his eyes hooded and hurt, Sugar Baby continues, laying a hand on Jinx's shoulder that Jinx shrugs off, "I was watchin' you once, boy, you's just a kid, in the house; you knocked this glass or somethin' off the table with your elbow, then, right in midair, before it crash, you catch it. Jesus, just reach around and catch it! Like it wasn't anything you thought about 'cause can't nobody think that fast, just somethin' you done, like a cat swats a moth. I'm fast too, and I got eyes around the side of my head too, but I ain't like that . . . that's *weird*. So what I'm sayin', boy, is you got reflexes you don't even think about, so any time you start thinkin' about them maybe you're goin' to be slowed up some, which would make you the speed of any other asshole playin' past his capacity, and in the game, that night, seein' it's the semifinals and Troy ain't that bad and all Hammond's got is mainly you and that big clodhopper guard what's-his-name . . . so Iceman naturally goin' to be thinkin' more than just some ordinary game, right? Tryin' real hard to win the championship for all them whiteys, right? Fuck-face Breuer jumpin' up and down like he's comin' in his pants, right? Well, maybe, that night, performin' monkey just ain't so *cool*, is all. It's natural. Ain't nobody goin' to blame you, you do it smooth. And you so smooth anyhow, boy, you can fuck up and look good at the same time. Say there's some asshole gets open, and you know, you pass him the ball, he prob'ly ain't goin' to score, but you pass him the ball anyhow maybe bouncin' it sort of wrong and he loses it . . . or you got a free throw and get coughin' . . . any kind of shit like that. Like I say, two points can win a game like twenty . . . or whatever. Long as you win. Ain't that so, baby?"

It's a cool sunny wind-whisked April morning, Jinx Fairchild bareheaded in soiled work pants and T-shirt, Sugar Baby Fairchild a sight for the eyes in new maroon cord trousers with a wide leather brass-buckled belt (initials SBF in script), antelope-hide jacket, two-inch-heeled square-toed kidskin boots, four-inch-brimmed velour hat pushed to the side back of his head . . . meticulously trimmed sideburns, mustache . . . the whites of his eyes eerily white as he speaks, as if for emphasis. The quieter Jinx Fairchild is, the more Sugar Baby Fairchild talks. It's like singing, his talk, like humming: the same words used again and again till they almost aren't words but just sounds, a comfort to them.

No secret in the neighborhood that Sugar Baby Fairchild is Poppa D.'s newest young man; even Minnie Fairchild must know her boy has got some tight connection with Leo Lyman over in Buffalo . . . Leo Lyman who's so legendary a name among local blacks. And there's the 1956 Eldorado, gleaming pink and gold, chrome like bared grinning teeth, and all the accessories, and the fancy apartment on Genesee Street where he's living with this good-looking high-yalla woman who's an old friend too of Poppa D.'s.

Seem like everybody, in a certain circle, is tight friends of everybody else.

These days, Sugar Baby Fairchild isn't welcome in the house on East Avenue; Minnie won't have him. Won't even accept money from him, or presents. The few times he has offered.

Sugar Baby Fairchild has told his family it's privileged work he does for Poppa D. . . . whole lot better than janitor work or shoveling gravel or cleaning up white folks' shit at the hospital or some hotel uptown or hauling away their garbage, which is what his friends from high school do, mostly. He doesn't see Jinx very often, runs into him on the street sometimes; this is the first time he has actually sought Jinx out, approaching him in the playground where Jinx is practicing baskets, and at first it isn't clear to Jinx what Sugar Baby wants, why he's so friendly, so interested in Jinx's plans for the future . . . this is the brother who hadn't troubled to attend one of Jinx Fairchild's games this year.

And in those clothes, tight pants and high-heeled shoes, and smoking a cigarette, Sugar Baby surely isn't interested in fooling around with a basketball.

Now Jinx knows what it is, Jinx isn't saying anything. His legs stiff like a zombie or robot in a movie and he's missing half his shots . . . and Sugar Baby's getting impatient, working up a little sweat. "Shit, you actin' like some gal thinks her pussy's so special can't nobody touch it. What you care about them white mothas? You think they care about *you?* You think they give a shit about *you?*

All you is, boy, is a performin' monkey for them, same as I was, and if you don't perform, you on your ass . . . and they turn their attention to the next monkey. You think they give a shit about *you?* Truth is, asshole, they don't even know *you:* never heard of *you.*"

He makes a contemptuous spitting gesture.

It happens like this: Sugar Baby's penny-shiny face is screwed up like he's in pain, and with no warning Jinx rushes at him, and easy as the blink of an eye Sugar Baby sidesteps him—raises his right knee so fast, so unerring, and so hard, into Jinx's testicles, the move so exquisitely timed, it's clear the move can't have been performed for the first time.

Could be, there *is* a God.

Could be, He's got punishment on His mind.

Kneeling, Jinx Fairchild prays Help me, God, help me to be good, his mind drifting off even as he prays thinking of pumping himself deep in one of his girls or in Iris Courtney or in that white cunt Mrs. Dunphy who's always smiling at him . . . thinking of bringing that rock down on Little Red Garlock's head. . . . Help me, God, I'm waiting.

Thinking, God, what you going to do about it? I'm waiting.

Slow at first, then fast, like a rock slide gaining momentum as it falls, accelerating as it gets heavier, Jinx Fairchild's life starts to unravel.

So much pressure on the boy with the state tournament games coming up, all the publicity of Hammond Central's first undefeated basketball season in fourteen years, and these scholarships he's being offered—or the rumor is, he's being offered—from Cornell, Syracuse, Penn State, Ohio State, Indiana . . . no wonder Jinx Fairchild is becoming nervous, edgy, short-tempered, strange, not like himself.

If not like himself, then like *who?*

Ceci, who saw the movie with her girlfriends, says, "Jinx gettin' like 'three faces of Eve'—nobody ever know which face is comin' up."

* * *

He's partying, too. Which he'd never had time for, before.

Drinking, trying a little reefer.

A late-night party one weekend, at somebody's house on Peach Tree Street where there's no adult to interfere, music turned up so high you couldn't hardly hear what it is—Jerry Lee Lewis, maybe, singing "Great Balls of Fire," closest thing to black any white music can get—and suddenly Sissy Weaver who's so crazy for Jinx Fairchild, and crazy-drunk tonight, throws herself on Louise Thornton who's been hanging on Jinx, and the two girls fight over him while Jinx stares stricken in embarrassment.

"You get your fuckin' hands off him—cunt!"

"*You* stand off, girl—you crazy!"

Sissy Weaver with her smoky skin and hot eyes and Louise Thornton with the red-haired glamour wig, the black-sequined jersey dress: two good-looking girls fighting over Jinx Fairchild, there's screaming, there's fists, there's kicking . . . the red-haired wig flying! . . . glasses and chairs crashing! . . . the two girls rolling on the floor cursing and punching trying to kill each other while Jinx Fairchild scrambles over them trying to pull them apart but fearful of touching them, not knowing what in hell to do.

Jerry Lee Lewis bawling "Great Balls of Fire" so it's coming out of your ears, not going in.

Next day, and the next, when the story of the Fight Over Jinx Fairchild goes around the neighborhood, it's generally said that Sissy Weaver won. Leastways, she's the girl Jinx Fairchild went home with.

These weeks, the end of basketball season and the start of the state tournament, Minnie Fairchild understands that things are drifting out of her control but doesn't know why or how to stop them.

She's frightened at the change in her boy, the way his natural sweetness is going sour, she hears the neighborhood stories, she knows, but her fearfulness gets twisted around and comes out loud and accusing and mock enraged . . . like she's a TV mother saying her words bright and sassy and exaggerated, hoping to make light of the very fearfulness behind them. Saying to Jinx, storming after him while he shields his head, "Some slutty little gal's going to catch you sure enough, smart-ass," and, "Don't pay your momma any mind, huh? Don't think I know what's going on—can *smell* it on you?" and, "Who you think you are, boy, the King of Siam? King Farouk?"

One day, Minnie traps Jinx in his bedroom, confronting him with things she's heard—things her women friends delight in telling her—and Jinx hunches up like a little boy, his face suddenly crinkling, his eyes wet with tears, and he says, "*You* tell *me*, Momma; you know all the answers," and it isn't even sass as he says it, but straight from the heart.

And Minnie Fairchild just stands there, blinking.

Performing monkey.
  S'pose you decide to stop performing.
  Jinx Fairchild has cut the morning's classes, probably he'll cut the afternoon's too but show up at three-fifteen for practice . . . if Mr. Breuer knows he's been truant, Mr. Breuer won't say a word.

Clapping his hand on Jinx Fairchild's back as he did Friday night after the Lebanon game, giving off his brassy sweaty smell that's the smell of pride.

Take your hand offa me, white mothafucker, Jinx Fairchild doesn't think, 'cause Jinx Fairchild's not the kind of black boy to think such thoughts.

Naw. Jinx Fairchild the kind of black boy, anybody wanted to be integrated they'd want to be integrated with *him*.

Jinx is leaning out over the railing of the Main Street bridge, drops a glob of phlegmy spit twenty feet down into the river. The current's rough, flecked with white; the color of the water is steely . . . thousands of thinnesses of steel wire. There's a harsh metallic smell too, a harshness to the April air that goes directly to the bone and the marrow inside the bone.

He shivers, feels something rough and fiery at the back of his throat. Phlegm in hot coin-sized globs keeps wanting to come up, rack him in coughing.

He's facing east. To his left is the raggedy shore bordering

Diamond Chemicals; to his right, the railroad yards, the warehouses, the wharfs, docked freighters and trucks loading and unloading, and the waterfront saloons and the crazy-steep hills of Gowanda, Pitt.

Coming straight at him, bound for the lake, is a freighter, head on, slicing the choppy waves, appearing foreshortened like a bulldog.

Jinx is just staring out, not thinking. If he were thinking . . . if he goes to the police now, this morning, and confesses his crime, his life will be interrupted yet it will be complete. There's a pleasure in that. There's a satisfaction.

He tries to recall how old he'll be, his next birthday. The date falls on the far side of an abyss wide as the Cassadaga.

At the police station, they'll take him into an interrogation room. They'll ask questions; he'll answer. His voice slow and hollow-sounding as it has been lately, in school. As if his voice isn't inside him but being thrown across a distance. As if he's a ventriloquist's dummy.

But he isn't thinking these things, exactly. His eyes are misting over in the wind. He's flexing and straining his arm muscles, leaning out over the railing. Jinx Fairchild has got good, solid muscles . . . maybe a little tight . . . the kind of muscles that can tear.

Muscles, tendons, bones. He's read that the perfect athlete is a machine made of flesh. Doesn't need to think 'cause his body thinks for him.

Jinx Fairchild has been taping his ankles carelessly these days, preparing for games.

Doesn't like to be touched, these days.

I would like to confess to . . .

That boy who was found in the river, two years ago . . .

My name is Verlyn Fairchild and I am the killer of . . .

Then he won't be playing with the team this Saturday in the semifinal game of the New York State High School Basketball Tournament, won't ever be playing basketball again. Won't hear the cheers and whistles and stamping like a Niagara Falls of happiness washing over *him*. Rising up to drown *him*.

Performing monkey.

Jinx squints at the river. So much winking, glittering, like chips of mica or flashes of thought. More powerfully than Peach Tree Creek this river forces the mind to unmoor itself and rush forward, a sick helpless feeling rising from his toes. *My name is . . . I am the killer of. . . .* Twenty feet below, his reflection is dark and shimmering; beneath it, pushing through, is the face of the other: the broad cheeks, the close-set malicious eyes, the teeth bared in a wide white smile.

Jinx stares in horror: hair lifting from the head in tufts like clumps of baby snakes.

Jinx is paralyzed in horror: feeling the fingers close around his ankle. Tugging down, down, down.

How long he's there, leaning precariously out, his fingers slipping on the rusted railing and his eyes dilated as if the pupils have begun to bleed into the irises, Jinx Fairchild doesn't know. He has very nearly lost his balance. He has forgotten where he is and why. The river is no longer the Cassadaga River but a churning rushing living thing, a region of spirits; the *me, me, me* in Jinx Fairchild's brain has been drowned out by their deafening murmur.

But he doesn't fall. Doesn't drown.

He wakes from his trance to see to his shame that someone has been watching him . . . waiting for him to fall? to jump? It's a pasty-faced man squatting below the bridge on a slab of concrete amid a jagged peninsula of similar slabs of concrete near shore, fishermen's perches, though the man peering up at him, amused, waiting, is not a fisherman. A man Jinx has never seen before, in a railroad cap, soiled trousers. Not young, not old, a stranger, grinning and gaping up at Jinx Fairchild in expectation of seeing him plunge into the river.

Jinx feels his face pound with sudden heat as if he'd been slapped.

The man below isn't embarrassed in the slightest; he cups his hands to his mouth and calls out, "Hey boy, whatcha doin' up there?" in mock solicitude, and Jinx backs off, giving him an obscene gesture: "Go fuck yourself, whitey."

Jinx retreats. The spell is broken. Below the bridge, idiot laughter echoes and reverberates amid the rusted girders.

Hey boy—boy—boy!

There's a single Courtney listed in the Hammond telephone directory (*Courtney, Leslie, photographs*), and when Jinx Fairchild dials that number a man answers, friendly sounding, explains that Iris Courtney is his niece, would Jinx like her number? And Jinx mumbles yes, thanks. And dials that number. And the phone there rings and rings. And he's about to hang up when a man answers, his voice gravelly and intimate, as if lifting from a pillow, and again Jinx asks for Iris, says he's a classmate of hers, and the man says, "OK, kid—hang on," and there's a wait, a considerable wait, during which time Jinx hears muffled voices and music, radio noises; then the phone is taken up again with a thud and again the man's voice is close in Jinx's ear, slurred as if the speaker is mildly drunk. "Looks like the girl isn't here right now . . . and the mother can't come to the phone."

Jinx hangs up. Never tries another time.

Ten minutes into the final quarter of the game against Troy, the Hammond team with a slim, chancy lead, Jinx Fairchild's basketball career ends.

One minute he's leaping straight up into the air . . . then he's falling, falling.

Amid the deafening cheers and screams: *Jinx! Jinx! Jinx!*

Since the start of the game the Troy guard has been hot-breathing in his face. Stepping on his toes. Using elbows, shoulders. He's a white boy with a Polish-sounding name, Baranczak, six feet three inches tall, eyes glaring as new-minted marbles, a fair flushed skin, blond hair trimmed in a brutal crew cut; Baranczak is a strong defensive player, not quite so fast on his feet as Jinx Fairchild, but fast . . . and tricky, and mean. In the first quarter when Jinx spins to throw a hook shot Baranczak is there to surprise him . . . fouls him with an elbow in the ribs that nearly knocks him to the floor.

That look of fanatic hatred! Muttering over the referee's whistle, "Slow down, you black prick, this ain't Harlem."

Not once, though, does Jinx Fairchild look Baranczak in the face. Plays his game so deadpan cool it's like the fucker isn't even there. That drives them wild.

Never lock eyes with your man, only observe him at mid-chest. Seeing is he *there,* and *where* . . . and *where's* his momentum going to take him.

As, at the foul line, feeling the grain of the ball against his fingertips, Jinx Fairchild takes care never to glance to the right or the left, at the crowd. He'll furrow his forehead up like an old man's but his expression is still deadpan; can't nobody in this place guess is he praying *God don't let me miss, please God don't.* . . .

A thousand times he has positioned himself here, at the foul line. Never knowing why. Asshole boys' game, but if you're in it, asshole, got to play it out.

Jinx Fairchild snaps the ball from him . . . sees it arc, strike the rim wrong, and ricochet back out.

So he misses. And the crowd responds as the crowd always does: groans of disappointment, screams of jubilation.

It's an off night for Hammond; maybe they've been anticipating this game for too long. Their team rhythm is off, their rapport is off, it's one of those nights, even championship teams have those nights, who can say why? Jinx Fairchild the star forward is playing harder than he usually plays, isn't able to pass the ball 'cause his teammates are so closely guarded, and his own guard, Baranczak, is always in his face . . . if the big bullish flush-faced kid is intimidated by guarding Jinx Fairchild it comes out not in nervousness but in aggression and rude words.

Smart-ass nigger who won't acknowledge he's *there* . . . he *exists.*

For Jinx Fairchild, though, as the minutes pass, the game is becoming remote, like something seen through the wrong end of a telescope. Hammond is behind by eight points, then by twelve . . . he doesn't glance at the scoreboard or the clock . . . but he knows.

God don't let me fail. Please God don't let me fuck up.

199

He's breathing through his mouth, he's running on leaden legs. There's a raw scraped hurt to his throat and he's been swallowing phlegm . . . and these painkiller pills Sissy Weaver slipped him out of her momma's supply (doctor's prescription pills, from the welfare clinic) make the throbbing in his head weird and muffled like a piston wrapped in yards of gauze.

Caught a bad cold up there on the bridge, just what Jinx Fairchild deserves.

The referee's whistle . . . the shouts of the other players . . . the maniac cries of the crowd . . . Hank Breuer, poor bastard, leaping up from the bench as if he's going to have a heart attack: all have become remote and unreal.

Still, Jinx Fairchild's beautifully conditioned body keeps him in the game. Long legs, quick hands and feet, sharp foxy eyes. Like Joe Louis out on his feet in the first match with Schmeling, but still going through the motions of fighting. That zombie look, that glisten to the eyes. Same principle as the praying mantis Sugar Baby cruelly decapitated in the garden when they were little boys and the thing kept on crawling around and twitching . . . for minutes. *Don't that fucker know he s'pose to be dead?* Sugar Baby protested.

Troy scores, Hammond scores. In the second half of the game Troy begins to lose its momentum. And Jinx is fouled another time by Baranczak . . . that broad-cheeked sweaty face flush in his but the black boy won't *see* . . . and the pain of the fall shoots through his vertebrae but goes remote too, and muffled, as if wrapped in yards and yards of gauze.

One more foul, Baranczak is warned, and he's out of the game.

Jinx Fairchild gets to his feet stiff in dignity. Eyes not quite in focus but he takes the ball, positions himself at the foul line, prepares to shoot. There's a whispery quiet to the gym . . . strange quality to the overhead lights as if suddenly they've become brighter, almost blinding. The hardwood floors glare with wax, and the smell of it underlies the galaxy of other smells.

God don't let me miss Jinx Fairchild is thinking, swallowing down hot coin-sized clots of phlegm, *God what you going to do about it?*

The tall lanky forward for the Hammond team, number 3 uniform soaked in sweat, preparing to shoot . . . glancing neither to the right nor the left nor even at the first row of Hammond VIPs where his own mother Minnie Fairchild sits with the family in a paroxysm of anticipation and dread, her big-knuckled hands folded tight as prayer in her lap.

But he doesn't look, her Verlyn.

Naw: that boy way beyond *her*.

And this time, snapping the ball out from him, Jinx Fairchild sees it fall smoothly through the rim: that ellipsis you know is a circle.

And his second shot goes in too.

So Hammond slips into the lead. Four points . . . six points . . . eight. Who can say why a team regains its rapport, why another team loses its edge? Shortly into the final quarter there's a dazzling pick play and Jinx Fairchild has the ball running the baseline to the farther court . . . leaps three feet into the air and the ball glides outward from his fingers, graceful as an ascending musical note . . . then, coming down, and he comes down awkwardly, and hard, his ankle turns . . . and the *crack!* of the snapping bone sounds through the entire gym.

$\mathscr{8}$

Iris Courtney brings the florist's delivery upstairs to her mother in the kitchen: one dozen blood-red roses and a handwritten note for MISS PERSIA DAICHES.

Persia opens the envelope with an expression of anticipation and worry, reads the note, rereads it, hands it over to Iris.

Commemorating the first official day of our divorce.
SINCERELY I pray for your happiness in this harvest we have yet to reap.

Your former husband
"DUKE"

Iris's laughter is brief, scratchy, and mirthless.

She says, "Why has he put quotation marks around his name? Is he only a *name?*"

She takes the tall blue vase from the cupboard, her favorite vase, fills it partway with water, arranges the roses carefully inside, with as much clinical detachment as a florist's assistant. Covertly, though, she's watching Persia as she stands so very still . . . so stricken and silent.

If she cries, Iris thinks calmly, I won't be able to bear it.

If she cries, Iris thinks, I'll slap her face.

She says, lightly, "I wouldn't think he could afford roses, or would want to. The less we see of him, the more mysterious he's becoming. I'd swear, that note isn't Duke. I don't know who it is but it isn't *Duke*."

Persia is standing on the linoleum floor in her stocking feet, in a lacy black slip, hair haphazardly set in rollers. She has been ironing—her black satin hostess's dress for the Golden Slipper Lounge—and there's a warm, familiar, comforting scent of ironing in the air, an odor both of damp and of the faintest scorch. On the radio, in voices like Kleenex dissolving in water, the Everly Brothers are singing "All I Have to Do Is Dream."

Iris holds the heavy vase at arm's length. Yes, the roses are beautiful, fresh-cut roses always are.

She persists. "Don't you agree, Mother? That note doesn't sound like *Duke*."

But Persia is crying. Soundlessly.

Leaning against the wobbly ironing board as if for support, her damp face exposed, her chest flushed and mottled, breasts prominent. Through the coarse lace of her slip her black brassiere shines with a fierce metallic glitter; since childhood, Iris has shied away from looking at her mother's breasts, as if, so visible, so blatant, they constitute a reproach of a kind to *her*. Iris's own body is tall, lean, tight-muscled, with small hard breasts, a hard flat belly, hard hips, thighs . . . nerves coiled as if to spring. She sees with despairing satisfaction that the flesh of Persia's upper arms is going flaccid and that her shoulder-length coppery-blond hair—dyed, though Persia's euphemism is "rinsed"—has a harsh synthetic sheen, like a mannequin's.

My beautiful mother. No longer beautiful.

And dangling foolishly upside down from the ironing board is the black satin dress, that demeaning costume, short tight skirt, scoop neck, *The Golden Slipper* in yellow stitches on one breast and the cartoon figure of a small yellow slipper on the other. Worn with smoky spangled stockings and three-inch heels, the dress is provocative as a burlesque costume.

Iris cries, exasperated, hurt, childish, "For God's sake, Mother, you wanted the divorce! *You* wanted it! And it was necessary! Why are you such a hypocrite?"

Persia's weeping is so unnaturally silent, her lovely mouth so contorted, Iris is almost frightened.

Isn't there the mimicry of madness in the face of grief?

And Persia, loose as a drunk, is leaning against the ironing board oblivious of the fact that the burning-hot iron is set precariously on end. It wouldn't be the first time in this household that the iron has toppled over, crashing to the linoleum floor. Iris has overturned it, and so has Persia.

Persia is saying, through her sobs, ". . . never love any man the way I loved your father."

Iris says, in a rage, "Shit."

It's as if a radiant flame has illuminated Iris, this rage. She slams out of the kitchen. Runs down the narrow corridor into her bedroom, this cramped stuffy room she has already outgrown. Cheap fleshy-pink chenille bedspread, limp dotted-swiss curtains, a mirror into which she doesn't dare look, somber wallpapered walls . . . photographs, in frames, hung in profusion on the walls . . . *not* photographs of the Courtneys but photographs of strangers long dead, or stark landscapes or seascapes, given to her by her uncle. In the wildness of her dissatisfaction with herself Iris can stare at these photographs, all of them in black and white, taking solace in them as profound and irreducible answers to questions she has never voiced.

Why are we here? What are we to one another?
What is this life: its dimensions, its circumstances?

Duke Courtney has never been invited to the Jewett Street apartment, though he has telephoned many times. (Because of Duke's persistence, Persia has had to get an unlisted number.) And came, once, in the time of Virgil Starling, pushing his way inside the door, so coldly furious it had not seemed at first that he was drunk—in a sharkskin suit, white shirt, bow tie, his eyes yellow-glaring—insisting he had a right to be here, had a right to spend the night . . . and when Persia tried to push him away he'd swung wildly and struck her on the side of the head, knocking her back against the kitchen table . . . and when Iris screamed he'd turned to *her,* seemed for a moment to be about to strike *her.*

"I'm Iris, Daddy!" she'd said. "Don't hit me."

And Duke Courtney hadn't. He'd gone away without touching her at all.

Tonight Iris too is preparing to go out: she'll babysit for a woman friend of Persia's in the neighborhood, for which she'll be paid $5. Iris Courtney's adolescence is a kaleidoscope of small jobs, after school, Saturdays, summers, savings of $5, $10, $20 she puts in the First Bank of Hammond, Persia's own bank uptown on Main Street; one of the sacred possessions of her life is the grainy dark-blue account book in which tellers, over the years, have recorded the steady accumulation of her fortune: $460 by the time of her six-teenth birthday. The saving of money is an end in itself, a satisfaction in itself; the thought of spending it leaves Iris faint with dread. For what material possession, what exchange of the abstraction of money for the concrete fact of experience, might justify such a transaction?

Money might constitute freedom, though, someday. Freedom from Hammond, from the memory of Little Red Garlock, from that woman sobbing in the kitchen as if her heart, broken so many times, has the capacity to break again!

Hypocrite, thinks Iris, listening.

You wanted the divorce . . . *you* must want this life that's ours.

She makes a few rough swipes with the hairbrush at her dense, springy hair, regards herself distrustfully in the mirror: her eyes shadowed from insomnia but oddly bright, teary-bright, though *she* isn't the one who's crying.

She's eager to get out of the apartment before Persia leaves.

205

Eager to get to Mrs. Cupple's house up the street, neutral territory.

Taking with her an armload of books, as usual . . . this is the summer Iris Courtney is reading the novels of Jane Austen, poetry by Keats, Shelley, Robert Frost, nature books, photography books, anthologies of poetry, short fiction, and drama selected at random from the shelves of the Hammond Public Library: an adolescent reading, fevered and directionless, its common principle the attraction of *not-here* and *not-now*.

In the kitchen, Persia is still crying.

Still standing flat-footed in her stocking feet, in her lacy black slip . . . one strap slipped from a shoulder.

Persia has resumed ironing, though her face is wet with tears and her mascara, so methodically applied within the hour, has begun to streak. Rivulets in the pancake makeup mask like discolored rain.

On the ironing board, in plain view, there's a glass of something clear: gin.

Iris says angrily, "Oh, Mother, why? You said you *wouldn't*."

Iris says, "You have to drink at that damned place you work, you said, so you were going to cut down at home . . . you *said*."

The dozen blood-red roses are on the counter beside the sink where Iris left them.

It's a sixteen-year-old's breathy helpless spite: "You *said*. You *said*. Liar!"

Iris Courtney stands in the kitchen doorway of the apartment upstairs at 927 Jewett Street, Hammond, New York, late in the afternoon of a featureless midsummer day in 1958. Her heart is pounding as if she . . . *she* . . . has been insulted. Her hair is fierce and burnished about her head; righteousness shines in her young face; she might be a form of an angel of wrath, a creature in an old painting, one of those medieval or early Renaissance paintings she contemplates in art books at the public library . . . feeling, for all their beauty, no human warmth, but a cold inquisitiveness, an analytical curiosity, wondering at the myriad forms human desire has taken.

But Persia, slatternly looking in her black slip, jiggly pink plastic rollers on her head, refuses to be drawn into one of their exhausting quarrels. She's too smart! She's a woman of thirty-six obliged to conserve every ounce of her energy for the long night ahead; her duties as "cocktail hostess" at the Golden Slipper Lounge (a seminotorious roadhouse three miles north of Hammond, on Route 63) begin at 6 P.M. and end at 2 A.M. . . . at least, 2 A.M. is the Lounge's official closing time. No, Persia won't exchange words with her bratty daughter; Persia takes a large therapeutic swallow of her drink, steadying the glass with both hands. Her pretty rings glitter, on both hands.

Iris wipes roughly at her eyes. "Maybe Daddy *is* right—the things he says about you."

The telephone begins to ring.

On the radio, there's a loud happy advertisement for automobile sales, new and used, a local Hammond dealer: former friend in fact of Persia and Duke Courtney.

Persia takes up the iron again, with more dispatch. She's oddly dignified despite the clownish streaked mascara. Saying, "Your father is right, maybe, about everything. That's what's so terrible."

Iris retreats. The telephone is still ringing, so on her way out she snatches up the receiver, listens a moment, says, "No, she isn't here! Nobody's here! Sorry! Try somewhere else!"

9

Days, he's getting in the habit of prowling the world with his camera, too restless and excited to stay in that sad little studio on North Main Street, the CLOSED sign hanging in the door, no one to answer the telephone. Nights—and the nights are *long*—he sips Scotch and is back to reading St. Augustine, whom he'd first read as a young man, a lifetime ago, beset by lust and idealism and dreams of worldly grandeur.

> What, then, do I love when I love God? Who is this Being who is so far above my soul? If I am to reach him, it must be through my soul. But I must go beyond the power by which I am joined to my body and by which I fill its frame with life.

In middle age Leslie Courtney has become increasingly convinced that, by way of his camera, he can locate God . . . he can at least love God. For is not God evident in all His images, shining forth in splendor in every visible form? Leslie knows better than to speak too casually about such things, however. People think he's crazy enough: lanky, on stork's legs, two-day beard, scuffed moccasins and rumpled trousers and gold-rimmed schoolboy glasses, popping up everywhere in town with his camera, asking May I? Do you mind?

On a given day Leslie Courtney will strike up conversations with as many as twenty or thirty people, most of them strangers. The conversations are preliminary to, often accompanying, his taking of their photographs. But he tries to keep his talk casual, breezy, attuned to the latest news, or sports, or weather . . . local scandals, if any. Like many shy people his shyness can be turned inside out, exploding in bright gouges of talk . . . it's remarkable!

Then he returns to the natural silence of his being.

The big hefty Kodak slung around his neck on a worn leather strap, the solace of its weight.

Yes, but you're a hypocrite, a fool.

You'd surrender God if you could love, and be loved by, Persia Courtney . . . don't deny it!

Now that the divorce is official she isn't Persia Courtney but Persia Daiches, and Leslie makes an effort to think of her as "Daiches" . . . to imagine her restored to a condition not simply of unmarriedness but of virginity.

An absurd sort of gallantry. But he tries.

(Though he knows . . . *must* know . . . about Persia's numerous men friends, knew a good many unwanted details about Virgil Starling, how could he not know? Hammond, New York, is a small town.)

Of course, he calls Persia frequently. Is there anything she needs? Can he be of help? How *is* she? Undiscouraged by the fact that they seem to be forever busy, he invites Persia and Iris out to dinner, to the movies, to the Orleans County Fair (where Leslie Courtney's photograph of ice-locked bodies of water wins a blue ribbon in the Professional Photographers' Competition), to picnics in Cassadaga Park. It seems he's always in the Jewett Street neighborhood; camera on its strap around his neck, he'll ring the door bell at Persia's just in case . . . a risky venture, courting humiliation.

At the end of July, it happens one evening that things work out ideally: when Leslie Courtney drops by at 927 Jewett he has come at a magically opportune time: Persia home, Iris home, mother and daughter in reasonably good moods and unusually considerate of each other . . . which isn't invariably the case now that Iris is growing up.

Seeing him on the doorstep Persia cries, "Just the man! Just the man we were missing!" and he's invited for supper, and afterward he and Persia sit in the living room watching television and sipping the tart California wine Leslie brought, laughing at Red Buttons, Ernie Kovacs, Jack Paar, and then it's 1:30 A.M. and time for Leslie to leave and at the door above the stairs saying good night he squeezes Persia's hand in sudden desperation, begins to speak, smiles the smile of a man about to throw himself into flames . . . but Persia, quick and shrewd, forestalls him.

"Les, no."

This is the season Leslie Courtney's impromptu conversations with strangers, which in the past have given him such pleasure, begin to take on a new, troubling urgency . . . shade sometimes into quarrels. It seems he wants to explain himself, defend himself, hold himself up as an object of curiosity: "Without this damned thing, just holding it in my hands, I don't *see* somehow."

An airless August afternoon in the shabby square facing the Orleans County Courthouse, and he's talking so strangely passionately, holding captive a rheumy-eyed derelict to whom he has given $5 for the privilege of taking his picture. "As if, without it, I wouldn't have the power, somehow," Leslie Courtney says. "Wouldn't have the eyes."

The derelict on the park bench squints grinning up at Leslie Courtney as if he suspects a joke . . . a joke in which he isn't interested. The $5 bill in his hand, there's a powerful sunburst of craving in his throat, chest, belly, for the sweetest Mogen David he can find in the wine and liquor store just across the street.

"Eh?" he says, to be polite. "How's that?"

Leslie Courtney laughs, gripping the Kodak. "If I knew, I'd know!"

In Hammond, though, he's becoming increasingly restless.

Drives to other cities in the state, in Pennsylvania, across the border in Canada . . . no particular destination. Wasting rolls of film. One delirium of a night at Olcott Beach, on Lake Ontario, he gets so drunk in the company of several newfound friends male and female he's incapable of driving back home and spends the night passed out in his car . . . in the morning wakened by two small boys tapping on the car window close beside his head, grinning and giggling.

Hey, mister! You dead or alive?

In Buffalo, in a sleazy strip off Main Street, he "buys" a woman . . . a woman with black-dyed hair, olive skin, nothing at all like the other.

Most of the time, though, he's drawn to Lake Ontario: walking along the bluff, along the pebbly shell-strewn beach, though the water and the vast mountainous overreach of the sky above it cannot provide him with more than commonplace "picturesque" photographs . . . a further waste of film.

But he's happy here, can lose himself for hours. Hours, days, weeks. Sometimes the air has the taste of autumn already: scalpel-sharp winds slicing down from Canada. Other days, it's still summer, a region of torpor and deadly peace, the stench of rotting fish, broken oyster shells, tangled seaweed lifting to his nostrils.

What, then, do I love when I love?

Who is this Being who is so far above my soul?

Whether he pauses to take pictures or not, Leslie Courtney requires his camera. All the time. Without the hefty Kodak slung around his neck on a strap, he'd be blind.

10

And there's the day deep in winter, January 1959, when Iris Courtney writes in her secret journal, *She's an alcoholic.*

As if testing out the words: *alcoholic, alcoholic.* Daring to commit them to the terrible authority of ink on paper, its impersonality. *I despise her: can't wait to escape her!* Gouging the paper with her pen's sharp point as she hears the anguished sounds of her mother emptying out her guts in the bathroom beside Iris's room . . . spasms of helpless vomiting, sobs and vomiting, that go on and on and on. *I love her too OH JESUS WHAT CAN I DO.*

It isn't the first time of course, and it certainly will not be the last, that Iris Courtney is interrupted late at night by her mother stumbling into the apartment, stumbling to the bathroom . . . and the rest.

✳   ✳   ✳

The narrow rectangular journal in which Iris Courtney scrupulously records the side of her life she thinks of as in eclipse—that is, the secret side she doesn't speak of, ever, to anyone—is an old financial ledger with a marbleized cover and crinkling yellowish pages she'd found in a trash can in a neighborhood alley, years ago. The first twenty pages were covered in meticulous penciled notations and these Iris tore out, claiming the remainder of the pages as her own. *Iris Courtney is the most frugal of persons,* Iris Courtney boasts of herself in the journal.

Like most boastful statements, it's an acknowledgment of defeat.

All her life Iris Courtney is going to remember: stooping to remove the overflowing trash bag from beneath the kitchen sink and discovering behind it a tipsy little cache of empty bottles Persia must have been intending to dispose of herself but forgot . . . as, in these final years of her life, she forgets so much.

Three empty gin bottles, two empty bourbon bottles, one empty Scotch bottle, several empty wine bottles.

Their shapes, sizes, labels are wholly familiar to Iris Courtney, of course: she has been seeing them all her life.

The gin bottle, though empty, is still fairly heavy. Gordon's Distilled London Dry Gin. With the eerie drawing on the label of a wild boar, meticulously rendered, with double tusks, small malevolent eyes . . . the orange coloring suggests that the drawing is a cartoon but if you look closely you see that it isn't a cartoon.

Iris jams her knuckles against her mouth, stifles a sob.

"Oh, Momma. Oh, my God. *Why?*"

As for beer: the accumulation of empty Schlitz bottles must not seem to Persia a matter of particular embarrassment or shame, since these numerous bottles Persia doesn't try to hide but keeps in plain view in the kitchen, ranged along the floor in the six-pack cardboard carriers they come in. There's a deposit of three cents on each bottle so Persia takes care to return them, week following week, to Ace's Beer, Wine & Liquor around the corner: returning empties,

213

buying Schlitz six-packs, returning empties, buying Schlitz six-packs . . . week following week. Ace's has many faithful customers and none more faithful than good-looking cheery-smiling Persia.

Why doesn't Persia hide her empty beer bottles? She's so seasoned an alcoholic, Iris realizes, that, to her, *beer doesn't count.*

"How dare you? *You!* Have you nothing better to do with your time than spy on me?" Persia cries, furious when, after days of hesitating, Iris finally brings up the subject of Persia's drinking. "My own daughter spying . . . like every busybody and asshole in this neighborhood. Are *you* so perfect? . . . Little Miss Honor Roll! . . . Little Miss Smart-Ass! . . . I do what I do and what I damn well want to do. . . . I deserve some happiness. . . . *I'm* the one who pays the bills around here—on my feet every night at that damned place required to smile at every son of a bitch who comes in, pinches my rear, sometimes the bastard will squeeze my breasts . . . what you do then is smile, sugar, smile, *smile, SMILE,* 'cause if you don't you're out on your ass—what do *you* know about it? . . . Such disrespect . . . such selfishness . . . Little Miss Perfect! . . . If I hear you're spreading tales of me, to Maddy or Les or any of my friends, or to your goddamned father—*especially him*—I'll slap your mean little face so hard you won't know what hit you. . . . My own daughter . . . spying on me . . . after all I've sacrificed for you . . . *after all I've sacrificed for you you little bitch!*"

So, each time, Iris Courtney is overwhelmed.

Defeated, demoralized, obliged even to apologize.

Momma, I'm sorry. . . .

Momma, you know I didn't mean. . . .

More and more frequently Persia flies into such rages and Iris shrinks before her as before a giant woman . . . as if Persia were no longer her mother, no longer an individual human being but a force of nature, splendid and terrible as a hurricane, storming through the cramped rooms of their life, slamming doors in her wake, churning the very air to madness.

And Iris retreats, hides away in her room, trembling, in tears.

In such circumstances it seems a truly petty matter that Persia pours herself a drink, or two, or three, out in the kitchen . . . lights up cigarettes, tries to relax. As she says, she does what she does and what she damn well wants to do. She deserves some happiness.

11

It's only 12:20 A.M. but it feels later. Not Saturday night any longer but Sunday morning.

Alone for just a few minutes, she's so lonely it *scares*.

She's singing, under her breath. One of Duke Courtney's old habits.

Persia's in the pink-lit powder room of the Golden Slipper Lounge out on Route 63 . . . again . . . taking another five-minute break. A quick Chesterfield, a vodka she's sipping slow as she can, she's freshening her makeup that's caked and creased and primping her stiff-piled hair with fingers there's no sensation in at the tips, unless she's imagining it . . . her mind plays all kinds of tricks on her these days. No customers in the powder room just now so she's singing in her sweet, thin, slightly nasal voice, trying to keep ahead of something she hopes won't happen, " '*Blue skies smiling at me—*' " and in comes Molly McMillan clattering in her spike-heeled shoes, just a girl in Persia's eyes, twelve years younger than Persia. "Hey, *you* sound happy tonight," Molly says with her prissy little smile that can be a sneer too, and Persia says quickly, "Why shouldn't I be happy, I try to be happy . . . it's the least thing you can do not to drag other people down," and Molly laughs, only half hearing, staring at her face in the mirror, her dilated eyes like dime-store jewels glaring out of her face. "Uh-huhhhhhhhhhh. Jesus, *yes.*"

Molly doesn't have a drink but Molly lights up a cigarette so fast her hands fumble. Exhales smoke in a furious cloud. She's one of the cocktail waitresses always angry about something. Tap-tap-tapping on the floor with the toe of her spike-heeled shoe.

Both women are wearing black satin dresses that fit their bodies snugly, with tiny gold-stitched slippers on their right breasts, plunging V necklines, puffy little-girl sleeves; black spike-heeled shoes with sharply pointed toes; black fishnet stockings. There's the beginning of a run in Molly's stocking.

Persia's hair is upswept and lacquered around her head like a crown, an ashy tawny-red; Molly's hair is platinum blond, pale as Marilyn Monroe's.

In the flattering fleshy-pink light of the powder room it isn't immediately evident that Persia is so many years older than Molly McMillan . . . unless you look closely.

Says Persia, bright and edgy, "My ex-husband, he'd go around most days in a good mood too. High-flying. At least so you could see . . . on the surface. Guess I picked it up from him. The habit."

Molly's eyes swerve onto Persia's, in the mirror. "Duke, you're talking about?"

"Actually in a way he always *was* in a good mood . . . in a way."

"Yeah. I know Duke. He's *fun.*"

"Like things never went deep in him, you know?"

"Do I know! They're all that way."

The ventilation's so poor in here, even with the fancy simulated-velvet wallpaper and the giant mirror that glitters as if it's been sprayed with specks of gold, Persia has trouble breathing . . . has a fit of coughing.

She's sick. Going to be violently sick.

She's been sick for months: can't keep anything in her stomach, makes appointments to see the doctor then cancels out at the last minute, the telephone receiver trembling in her hand. . . .

Now Persia is steeling herself, waiting for Molly McMillan with her brash careless mouth to inquire after Duke Courtney who's so much fun. She's standing very still waiting for the question, so still and apprehensive she loses track of what she's waiting for . . . only that she'll have to answer the question . . . an answer that won't shame her, that can be repeated around town. She knows people talk about her, spy on her, have their theories about her. But she has never been one of those embittered divorcées forever whining and complaining with whom people pretend to sympathize . . . then ridicule behind their backs.

Her voice is shaking suddenly. It seems she's angry. "My daughter I'm worried about. How to keep her from harm."

Molly murmurs a vague assent.

"So much harm in the world . . . so much *shit*."

She's so angry suddenly, so incensed, Molly McMillan's eyes swing on her face again in the mirror.

Persia has more to say but somehow it happens that she has begun to vomit: so quickly she can't set her drink down on the ledge in front of the mirror, can't stumble into one of the toilet stalls in time, she's vomiting onto the floor, into one of the sinks . . . her vomit hot and searing, liquidy in part, pure vodka, but in part thick as oatmeal and so abrasive her throat feels scraped and she's sobbing too, she's humiliated and helpless and she knows she's going to die, it's Death she's trying to vomit up, her stomach failing her and her nerves tight-strung as wires, and she hears Molly McMillan exclaiming in disgust, "Oh, shit, oh, *no*," because some of the vomit has splashed on her dress, her fishnet stockings . . . but Molly helps Persia too, feels damned sorry for the woman, steadying her shoulders as you would with a small scared child, murmuring, "Going to be all right, hon, just hold on . . . going to be all right."

Molly McMillan's cigarette slanted at an upward angle between her reddened lips, half her young face screwed up against the smoke and the stink of Persia's vomit.

Persia hopes Molly won't tell tales on her, endanger her job at the Golden Slipper. It's all she has, right now.

I wanted not to be lonely. That's all I ever wanted.

When you were born I thought I'd never be lonely or unhappy again . . . my heart swelled almost to bursting.

It was like God made me a promise: I would never be lonely or unhappy again in my life with my baby girl my sweet little baby Iris.

13

It's a frosty iridescent day in November 1959.

Iris Courtney and a friend are walking on Main Street holding hands.

When Iris isn't in her mother's company and isn't in the apartment on Buena Vista Avenue (they've moved again: shabbier neighborhood, tackier apartment, but at least no freight trains every night), she is capable of going for hours without thinking of Persia . . . her heart *lifts*.

She's seventeen years old. A senior at Hammond Central High School. She'll graduate fourth in her class of one hundred fifty-three, she'll win a full-tuition scholarship to Syracuse University, she's so poised, so coolly mature, adult men sometimes approach her on the street, in stores, in the public library where she works evenings . . . not realizing until they see the alarm in her eyes that she isn't the age she appears. Whatever that age is.

But this afternoon Iris is in the company of a boy who imagines he loves her, a boy avid to one day marry her, and she's feeling hopeful, if not happy precisely (Persia *is* a sick woman, Persia *will not* go to a doctor), and half listening to his conversation . . . and she sees to her astonishment a truck rattling by, ORLEANS CO. MAINTENANCE on its side, several black men in the open rear in thick jackets, wool caps, amid shovels, sandbags, road repair equipment, and one of the black men, the tallest, Jinx Fairchild—*my God, isn't it?*

Iris doesn't call his name, only waves after him. Tries to catch his elusive eye.

Of course, he doesn't see her.

Of course, the truck just barrels along Main Street, carrying its human cargo away.

The several times Iris Courtney has sighted Jinx Fairchild in the past year and a half, by chance on one or another busy Lowertown street, he hasn't seen her. Turns casually away.

Now Iris's friend asks who she's waving at and Iris says quickly, "No one you'd know . . . anyway, it wasn't him."

As if she'd betray Jinx Fairchild in his current diminished state to someone who knows who he is . . . or was.

A blowy January night, temperature around 15 degrees Fahrenheit, so deep a chill it enters the marrow of her bones. Forever.

She's weeping with the insult: sent home dazed and feeble-limbed in a taxi, prepaid.

Like a match that's extinguished . . . you go *out*.

Her public collapse, the first of her life, is not an event Persia witnesses, nor is it an event, strictly speaking, she experiences. It occurs without her volition, participation, or awareness.

You go *out*.

Striking her forehead above the right eye on the porcelain rim of the sink. In the women's lavatory, Covino's Bar & Grill, where she's working the 6 P.M. to 2 A.M. shift.

She falls. Her legs melt away. She's just a body, brainless, falling.

The first time Persia has ever blacked out in public.

Amid the smells, the frank undisguised stinks of the lavatory. Sprawled on the floor, that filthy floor. Dripping blood. Dazed and moaning and bewildered like a cow stunned by a sledgehammer blow. . . . It takes them minutes, long minutes, to revive her.

"I don't want no ambulance, what the fuck it's gonna look like, fucking ambulance at the door . . . people come to have a good time on Friday night, these customers are all my friends, and some stupid cunt it's her own damn fault drinks too much and passes out! I *told* her! I *warned* her! *Get her out of here!*"

Sent home in a taxi like any passed-out drunk.

Prepaid: don't bother coming back.

And it isn't her fault! Under such stress. Run off her feet. That wop manager. All the girls drink if they can. Singling her out. And the others staring at her . . . breasts, belly that's swollen and sore, buttocks starting to sag. Whispering filthy things to her she can't quite hear. Whispering their filthy slanders about her behind her back.

The alternative is taking money from men. Persia refuses to do that.

She has her pride. God knows it's all she has.

The taxi driver's ringing the bell for 16-D. Prolonged ringing like a summons to disaster.

It's 11:20 P.M., Iris Courtney has long been home from her library job, hasn't yet gone to bed. Don't let it be trouble, she prays.

Iris Courtney's prayers are lightweight aluminum; she imagines them skittering, skimming, flying across the surface of a body of water, knows they won't be heeded so she fashions them cheap and disposable.

She runs, though. Downstairs. Three flights of drafty unheated stairs. Buena Vista Arms, 3551 Buena Vista Avenue kittycorner from the Hammond Farmers' Market, there's that advantage at least.

Iris cries, "Oh, Momma!" seeing Persia slumped against the wall, face like putty, eyes blurred, a swelling the size of a hen's egg on her forehead . . . she's being held up by the taxi driver, who's a

223

kindly taciturn oldish man not so embarrassed by his task as one might expect, and he helps Iris maneuver her mother upstairs to the apartment and inside the door murmurs courteously, "Thank you, no, miss," when Iris offers him payment, a tip at least, Iris Courtney biting her lips to keep from crying and fumbling, faltering, like a small child not knowing what she'll do . . . what it is her daughterly task to do.

Next day Iris stays home from school in the morning, brings Persia the only food Persia claims she can stomach, heated milk with pieces of white bread soaked in it, Lipton's tea so weak it's practically colorless, a bowl of sugar cubes if she craves something sweet.

And her pack of Chesterfields.

She's sitting up in bed; she looks a little better. But still her face is battered and scraped, the ugly bruise above her eye lurid as a growth. Without makeup her skin is oddly shiny as if it has been scrubbed with steel wool.

Iris says, gentle, hopeful, *not* that accusatory voice she understands now has been a tactical error these many months, "Now you know you'll have to stop drinking, Momma, now you know that, don't you?" expecting a shrug or a sarcastic rejoinder or at least resistance . . . but Persia astonishes her by immediately agreeing.

"Yes, honey, you're right." She's repentant, guilty, rubbing the swelling on her forehead: "Guess I'd *better*."

She tries to smile, squinting up at Iris. Her eyes are webbed in broken capillaries and appear thick, rubbery, like hard-boiled eggs.

Persia speaks with such sobriety, such chastened sincerity, it's clear she speaks the truth.

And you lied. You lied. You always lied.

"Insurance? Blue Cross—Blue Shield?"

"No."

"Cash, then, or check? If it's check, dear, the hospital requires two kinds of I.D.—"

"Cash."

The blond cashier at ACCOUNTS, Hammond General Hospital, has a blue jay's perky bobbing manner, a crest of stiff-permed hair that lifts almost vertically from her forehead. She's kindly, though, perhaps seeing that Iris Courtney's fingers have gone virtually blue at the tips, the nails a ghoulish purplish-blue with cold, fear, low blood pressure. Iris fumbles a little, removing bills from her wallet, crinkly fresh-minted bills of which she's perversely proud that they are hers . . . even to give away.

Drawn out of her savings account at the First Bank of Hammond that very morning.

The tests, itemized, are: blood, thyroid, chest X rays, barium X rays, urinalysis, two or three others. Payable in advance. Each item includes a penciled-in figure but Iris has been too rattled to add up the column of figures in her head, it's as if she childishly prefers being surprised . . . stunned . . . by the sum the cashier announces as if it were nothing extraordinary: $149.76.

"Is that tax included, or——?"

"Oh, no, dear." The cashier laughs. "There's never any tax here at the *hospital*."

Iris laughs too, though her teeth are chattering. "Well, that's good!"

She passes bills one by one through the window to the cashier, watches them being taken from her as if they were mere pieces of paper. No emotion. No emotion that shows. The Hammond Public Library pays her $1 an hour, 78 cents after taxes and deductions, she works fifteen hours a week for less than $12, but of this melancholy fact she isn't going to allow herself to think.

Momma, it's the least I can do.

The night before, sipping wine to steady her nerves, smoking her endless cigarettes, Persia said, "Damn it, Iris, it should be *me* paying for *you;* this is the wrong way around, I feel like such a . . . failure as a mother," and Iris said, embarrassed, "Oh, Momma, don't be silly, you've done enough for me," and Persia said almost crossly, "Why is it silly to worry about costing my own daughter money? I know how hard you work."

Iris said stiffly, "Momma, it's the least I can do."

Thinking, And why do you lie? Why, always, do you lie?

Not only has Persia been lying about her drinking these past several weeks, since the blackout in Covino's; she has been lying about her lying. In her journal Iris writes, *And what if she can't distinguish any longer between truth and lies, what does that mean about "truth" and "lies"?*

The floor tilting beneath one's feet. No directions fixed.

It has become a game of a kind. In the cupboard, as if on

226

display, are a half-dozen bottles . . . the usual. But they're untouched. Persia's *real* bottles are hidden in the clothes hamper . . . in the grease-encrusted oven . . . in Persia's carelessly made bed where the bedspread's raised, nubby material can be made to appear accidentally bunched. She has even hidden precious bottles of Gordon's gin wrapped in newspapers on the outside stairway where anyone might find them . . . an act, Iris guesses, of flamboyant desperation.

She can stop if she wants to. She must be made to want to.

What matters at the moment is that Persia has at last consented to see a doctor, has acknowledged that, yes, she *is* sick; in fact it was at Aunt Madelyn's urging, and whatever Persia told Dr. McDermott, or failed to tell him, about her drinking and eating and sleeping habits, the frequency of her vomiting spells, her fugues of dizziness and disorientation and forgetfulness and weeping, whatever admixture of truth and lies, lies and truth, the crucial matter at the moment is that she's here at Hammond General Hospital to take a battery of routine tests . . . striding off alone and almost cheerful into the interior of the labyrinthine old building while Iris Courtney, shivering in her coat, sits in the fluorescent-humming reception area adjacent to the outpatients' clinic and waits.

Another day of missed classes, another legitimate excuse: *mother, medical.*

The other day one of Iris Courtney's teachers asked her if it was anything serious, her mother's "medical" situation, and Iris said, No not at all, it's under control.

And it's true, isn't it, once the results of the tests are in, once the facts are known, the nightmare will begin to lift . . . won't it? Surely?

She sits, coat unbuttoned, fingertips pressed against her eyes. Without knowing it Iris has begun her siege of waiting . . . a premonitory mourning. And she's exhausted already!

Hearing a dim fading voice, *I'd cut the child's throat and then my own, to spare her.*

* * *

227

Iris's attention is drawn by voices and movement in the outpatients' clinic . . . a young mother is wearily scolding her two small boys, who are fighting together, her West Virginian voice raised in protest. "Y'all stop that, damn you, ain't I *told* you, do I got to *beg* you?" There is something familiar about the woman's pale, plump, sallow-skinned face, the set of her features, the foxy eyes . . . she's in her early twenties but has the worn look of a much older woman, hair so sadly thin that patches of scalp show through, swollen ankles . . . and she's pregnant, hugely. She's wearing an army surplus jacket, unbuttoned, and a shapeless black skirt, and thick cotton support stockings, and men's boots; she watches with an air of spiteful helplessness as one of her little boys crawls prankishly beneath a row of connected chairs, annoying patients who are sitting in them, while the other boy, whose face is covered in sores, runs beside him trying to kick him, screaming with laughter. The child might be mildly retarded . . . perhaps both boys are retarded . . . it's amazing that he doesn't seem to see the clublike white cast on the foot of a man seated in one of the chairs but trips over it, falls, goes sprawling. The mother calls out plaintively, "Y'all stop that! Danny! *Bud!* Come back here!"

Iris Courtney hurries over to pick up the wailing boy, brings him back to his mother, who seems startled at such kindness and flushes with embarrassment and pleasure. "Oh, thank you, that's real nice of you," seizing the little boy by his shoulder and giving him a violent shake. "Ain't you terrible! You and *him!* Y'know I'm gonna tell your daddy about all this, tonight!" Iris says, "Aren't you Edith Garlock?" and the woman smiles at once, showing damp babyish teeth, "That's right, used to be, now I'm Edith Bonner . . . still Garlock, I guess."

So they chat together for several minutes.

So Iris Courtney, who could never have premeditated such a meeting, who would have laughed in horror at the very possibility, finds herself talking companionably—or almost companionably—with a woman related to Little Red Garlock: a cousin of his, as it turns out. Iris tells Edith that she and her family used to live on Holland Street, near Gowanda . . . she went to school with several

Garlock children . . . and her mother was friendly with Vesta Garlock, sort of.

Edith gives a little cry of pleasure. "Did she! You tell your momma my Aunt Vesta's all improved now . . . she went back home to West Virginia that she never wanted to leave . . . poor woman was just so unhappy up here. And I don't blame her none, the nasty weather we got to put up with, and"—casting a covert glance at the nurse-receptionist close by—"the kinds of people you run into that don't give a damn if you live or die once they get the word on you you ain't *rich*. They see you're on the county, they look at you like you're shit, make you wait long as they damn please. My little Bud here—Bud, you sit *still*—that's got these nasty sores on his face, and near a constant flu, they're telling me he's *allergic,* handed me a list of, I swear, one hundred things the child can't come near let alone *eat*. Like dust, like animal fur, like whole grain, like *milk!* I mean, *milk!* You ever heard of anything so crazy? When I come home with that list, last time, my husband just about . . ."

Iris Courtney's eyes mist over in sympathy.

"I can imagine," she says.

Edith Garlock glances up at her, amused. "Maybe you can and maybe you can't." Not at all sarcastic.

Iris draws a deep breath. "Little Red, he was in school with me . . . it was such a—a shock about him. I guess the police never found who killed him, did they? There was all this talk about motorcyclists, but—"

Edith astonishes Iris by laughing derisively.

"Huh! *That!*"

To quiet her little boy, who has stopped crying and is now fretting and squirming beside her, Edith reaches into a deep, zipped-open side pocket of the army jacket and draws out an orange . . . which, as she talks to Iris, she peels with quick, precise little pluckings of her fingernails, as if she were defeathering a small bird and enjoying the process. "Listen, hon, it was never any secret to some folks, what happened. Who did it."

"It . . . wasn't?"

"Naw."

229

Edith gestures for Iris to step closer, she has something to tell her she doesn't want overheard . . . as if, in this noisy place, with a baby wailing two chairs down and the hospital P.A. system blaring announcements, anyone could overhear. The sweet tart aroma of orange and orange rind lifts to Iris's nostrils mixed with the grimmer odors of damp wool, oily hair, the white-flaking salve on the boy's face. Not quite boastfully, but with an air of pride, Edith says, "We knew. The men, anyway. A quarrel like that is bad blood between folks dating back to home. West Virginia, I mean. It gets settled. It gets put right. Don't matter what the fool police think they know or don't know." She pauses, handing over sections of the orange to her boy and dumping the peelings into an ashtray, not noticing that some of the peelings have fallen onto the floor.

Iris is struck by the simplicity and logic of these remarks. She feels, in a way, subtly rebuked . . . as one whose comprehension of the universe has been mistaken and is now exposed. "So that's how it is! The family settled it."

Edith smiles mysteriously. "The men, *they* did. Like they always do."

By 3:30 P.M., Persia is back.

Iris quickly lays down her book and stands. She looks at her mother searchingly.

"I guess it went a little faster than you expected—?"

"Iris, it went slowly enough. Don't ask."

Persia's bronze-red lipstick is gnawed partly off and there's a glisten of sweat at her hairline; she looks both tired and euphoric with relief. Her hair has been fastened at the nape of her neck with a clip, she's wearing nondescript wool slacks and a shaggy mohair sweater . . . an old sweater she'd fished out of a drawer, wears frequently now because it hides her embarrassing little potbelly as well as the protruding bones of her shoulders and wrists. Still, there's an air of glamour about her. Her dyed hair, her heavy cosmetic mask, her brittle public manner . . . she draws attention from strangers; it never fails.

First thing Persia does is rummage through her purse, locate her cigarettes, light up. Her eyelids tremble with relief; she's been so long without, in the interior of the hospital where smoking is forbidden: an hour and ten minutes.

Persia draws on the cigarette as if it were oxygen itself.

Next, in a pose of indignation, she pulls up her sweater sleeves, shows Iris a half-dozen small circular Band-Aids on her arms. "There was this crude, cruel nurse who kept poking me with a needle, couldn't find a vein and blamed *me*. Jesus, those needles hurt! Duke was scared to death of them, remember he said he'd end up like Al Capone, he'd die rather than have a needle stuck in him? Well, I'm not that bad, thank God, but I couldn't help flinching when that woman came at me, I swear she had it in for me—a woman's worst enemy can be a woman, you know, especially a woman in authority like a nurse. 'You better get used to it,' she warned me, sort of smug and nasty as if she knew something about me I didn't know. Can you imagine!" Seeing people in the vicinity staring at her, Persia hurriedly pulls her sleeves back down, well over the wrists. She stands for a moment swaying on her feet as if she can't remember where she is or what she has been doing.

Iris gives her a gentle half hug. "Momma, I'm sorry," she says guiltily, "but anyway it's over now?"

"Over *for* now."

"And when will the results be in, did they say?"

Persia shrugs, not meeting Iris's eye. "They didn't say."

It is at this precise moment that the thought occurs to Iris Courtney, too swift and too chilling to be absorbed, that maybe, just maybe, Persia walked out without submitting to the rest of the tests . . . no matter that her new doctor McDermott prescribed them and that Iris has paid for them. Iris says, fumbling, "I guess the hospital will telephone your doctor . . . I guess that's the procedure. When the results are back from the laboratory."

Persia murmurs carelessly, "I guess."

She snatches up her coat and Iris helps her slip it on . . . the old fake fur meant to resemble silver fox that Virgil Starling used to bury his face in, clowning in ecstasy, declaring it sure had class . . . just like Persia. The coat is frayed and shabby now and Iris is

231

embarrassed by it, as Iris is embarrassed by her mother's Hollywood-color hair and excessive makeup and a certain tough histrionic manner that comes over her in public. As if she's keenly conscious of being watched: both shrinking from attention and inviting it.

Iris herself wears an imitation camel's-hair coat, a classic style, neat, attractive, schoolgirlish in its covered belt and tortoise-shell buttons . . . camel's-hair coats, the authentic kind, are worn by most of the well-to-do girls at Hammond Central High School.

Outside, it's a blinding winter day. Early February. The wind off the river lifts skeins of dry powdery snow like snakes many yards long. Persia, bundled in her coat, a white angora scarf wound about her head, shivers and says, "I'd never miss this damn weather, that's for sure!"

Iris doesn't quite catch this. Her eyes flood with tears from the cold.

Persia deserves a reward, and Iris is readily talked into the proposition that they see a movie instead of going right home; *Butterfield 8* is playing at the Palace, and Elizabeth Taylor is Persia's favorite actress. "Then we can have dinner at Schrafft's, maybe," Persia says, squeezing Iris's arm as if they were girls together, on an impromptu lark. "I'm sure I'll be able to eat if the food is good and the atmosphere is attractive. That's what I tried to explain to McDermott, but I don't think the man *heard*. You know, a woman can speak directly and lucidly to a man and the man will not *hear*."

Iris quickly shuts her mind against the memory of Persia, the other morning, vomiting up a soft-boiled egg and toast Iris brought to her for breakfast, in her bed, eyes bulging, frantic with the terrible strain. Heaving and heaving as if to turn herself inside out long after there was nothing further to bring up.

Iris had to run for a basin, brought it to her just in time.

Iris, I don't know what comes over me.

Iris doesn't think of that now, it's the prospect of an afternoon movie with Persia that excites her: the two of them, mother and daughter, have not gone to a movie together for years. Iris too is in awe of Elizabeth Taylor, gorgeous Liz with her heartbreak skin, impossibly lavender eyes, sumptuous lips, breasts, hips, palpitating *life;* and there's the tacky-elegant Palace, with plush crimson draperies, deep-cushioned seats, a golden "Egyptian" motif. Suddenly, Iris Courtney wants nothing more passionately than to see *Butterfield 8* with her mother.

"But there's the library," she says, disappointed. "I have to be there by four-thirty, I can't be late again."

Persia links her arm snug through Iris's. She's thinking of Clancy's across the street from the Palace where she'll have a drink to steady her nerves, placate her queasy stomach. "Oh, hell, honey," she says, mischievous as a truant schoolgirl. "Call in sick."

When we are hurt, when we are frightened, befuddled . . . we take up our pens. And in secret.

She has become utterly unpredictable . . . untrustworthy.

She has no soul: all slipping sliding surfaces.

She could stop drinking if she wanted to. She just doesn't want to.

There is not the slightest connection between us.

Late winter 1960. When Iris Courtney is fearful of returning home to the apartment on Buena Vista Avenue: for either Persia is gone, and Iris will be compelled to wait with mounting anxiety for her to return; or Persia *is* there, and Iris will be compelled to confront the person her mother has become.

So begins Iris's season of wandering the streets after the library closes, eating supper alone . . . reading, doing schoolwork, writing furiously in her journal while she eats, in public. At the start she was intensely self-conscious, in terror of being sighted by high school classmates, for how odd it would seem to them, secure in their families, how odd in truth it is, a girl Iris Courtney's age eating supper by herself in the clamorous cafeteria in the Greyhound bus station . . . or at the counter in Rexall's . . . or one or another of the anonymous Main Street restaurants where solitary diners are the rule—but older, and usually male.

By degrees I've come to like it. I do like it. There is nothing that gives perspective to one's life like eating alone in a public place.

Iris's favorite restaurant is Kitty's Korner at the corner of Buena Vista and Fifteenth, a small square stucco building painted canary yellow, a dollhouse look to it: hanging plants in the windows, a single row of booths, and an L-shaped counter kept spotlessly clean by a waitress named Betty. When Iris eats there she sits in one of the booths with her back to the door, and rarely in these surroundings does anyone approach her to ask is she alone? Does she want company? What is she reading? What is her name?

Nor does Betty, smiling good-natured Betty, intrude: seeing from the first that Iris Courtney is not the kind of customer who wants friendly chatter. *Please leave me alone. Yes, I see you are very nice. No, I can't bear it.*

At school too Iris Courtney is rapidly acquiring a reputation for being cool, reserved, distant, "aloof." How much easier, that way.

On the rear wall of Kitty's Korner there is a Girl Scout calendar that invariably draws Iris's eye to it . . . makes her think guiltily of the uniform still in her closet which she hasn't worn in years but hasn't been able to throw out. Strange how quickly she'd lost interest in the Girl Scouts once she joined, and in her friends too who were Scouts, how she'd lost interest in religion and the church choir and Caroline Braverman with whom, now, she scarcely speaks.

Persia once said, You know? You're your father's daughter.
Iris asked what did she mean.
Persia said, Cold as ice.

Tonight in Kitty's Korner, Iris is sitting in the booth farthest from the door, her back to the door . . . never so much as glances around

235

when she hears it open. He's late. He isn't coming. Why should he come? She doesn't expect him really.

A weekday evening, mid-March.

Persia is out with her new boyfriend Rafe, probably a scribbled note for Iris on the kitchen table, *Don't wait up please. Love you! P.*

Or maybe there's no note at all.

Or maybe they aren't out, maybe they're there, drinking . . . or in bed.

How brightly lit Kitty's Korner is, achingly overexposed, like a photograph gone wrong. Iris rubs her eyes; Iris wonders can you always trust your eyes; the process of vision is a sort of photographic process, and photography always lies . . . the one clear truth Leslie Courtney has taught her. *No visual truth, only inventions. No "eye of the camera," only human eyes.*

Here, in this place Iris has come perhaps wrongly to trust, it seems that the edges of things are too sharp, too emphatic. You expect almost to see outlines as in old retouched photographs: the arm and hand of a customer at the counter lifting a cup of coffee to his mouth . . . the bulldog profile of another customer beside him. The problem is: too much reality to be absorbed.

Light ricochets off surfaces. The green Formica-topped counter kept so spotlessly clean, ceaseless motions of the waitress's hand, a chunky sponge in her hand: the counter alone is ablaze with reflected light. And the chrome napkin holders . . . the salt and pepper shakers . . . black plastic menus . . . lozenge-shaped floor tile in green and black like a jigzaw puzzle. Colors too defined, voices too loud. A jukebox, turned up too high, is playing Harry Belafonte's "Water Boy," all honeyed slides and diphthongs.

She sees by the clock it's ten-fifteen. He's late.

Yes, but he probably isn't coming, never intended to come. Yes, you knew that when you hung up the phone, didn't you.

Three postal workers at the counter laughing with Betty the waitress, trading quips, wisecracks, good-natured teasing; Iris takes a kind of pleasure in their ease with one another so long as it doesn't involve her. She's sitting glancing idly through a discarded copy of that morning's Hammond *Chronicle,* headlines, always headlines, "news," the public life so distant from her and from everyone she knows; yet the world *is* real, the world *is* us, no escape.

It's ten-twenty. The restaurant closes at 11 P.M.; at that time Iris Courtney won't have much choice but to go home.

Harry Belafonte continues to sing "Water Boy."

At the Hammond Public Library, Iris Courtney is perceived as a quiet but excellent worker, a librarian's assistant who can be, and frequently is, trusted with librarian's work. The salary is low but the work *is* interesting . . . isn't it? Books, magazines, the solace of shelves and shelves of strangers' inventions, competing versions of the truth. The salary is low, all available salaries are low; why shouldn't I be a cocktail waitress, says Persia defiantly, why the hell not, what am I saving it for, at my age?

At the counter the laughter fades when the door opens, someone pushes in. . . . Betty the waitress and her customers stare almost rudely and Iris Courtney's heart leaps, *He's here.*

It's Jinx Fairchild. Looking very black.

Young, coltish-lanky, but very black and very tall, standing in the doorway of Kitty's Korner but reluctant to come inside, just there to catch Iris Courtney's eye. He's wearing a leather jacket creased and scuffed so it looks white in places, soiled work trousers, a navy blue wool cap on his head . . . the kind of wool cap it seems half the black men in Hammond wear.

There's a thin little mustache on his upper lip Iris Courtney has never seen before.

He catches her eye, nods, no smile, then he's gone again and it's silent in Kitty's Korner as quickly, fumblingly, Iris Courtney gathers up her things, puts on her coat, pays her bill at the register, hurries to join Jinx Fairchild out on the sidewalk . . . not a word as Betty and the others watch her. These white faces, expressionless eyes. What will they say, when she's gone?

Even the jukebox has switched off.

Outside Iris catches up with Jinx, seeing he's impatient, edgy, won't look at her. Not wanting her to touch him either but she does: squeezes his fingers, says, "Thank you for coming, Jinx."

This is embarrassing. This is unexpected.

And the shock of the white girl's hand in his, fingers so frankly gripping his, as if she had a right . . . he laughs, nervous, annoyed, says, "Hell . . . sure. It's no big deal."

Iris says, "Your hands: did you hurt them?"

Some of the scabs are fresh, some healed.

Jinx mumbles words Iris can't hear, walking away.

Jinx's car is a low-slung rust-pocked 1955 Chrysler with a long cruel scrape on its side, must have been in a sideswiping accident. There's an awkward moment when Jinx goes to open the passenger's door for Iris and she's about to open it herself so she draws back, smiling, face very warm, and he opens it, nudges her inside, as if they're old friends with a mysterious grudge between them, something not quite resolved, or brother and sister.

He's kept the motor running. Iris climbs into gusts of hot dry air billowing up from the heater.

She says again, "I didn't think you would come. I . . . it's very nice of—"

Behind the wheel, gunning the motor, Jinx says, neither friendly nor unfriendly, "We better not go anywhere, like for a drink or anything, people gonna see us. Gonna see *me*, ask questions of *me*. Just drive around and you tell me what's what, then I can take you home . . . said you and your mother moved, close by?" He pauses, glancing at her. "*I* got to get home early."

Iris says, "Yes."

Iris is thinking she has no further wish than Jinx Fairchild's presence, the strangeness of his being here with her, out of all of Hammond.

So Jinx drives east on Ontario Street; he doesn't speak and neither does Iris, that white girl always so fixed upon him, crazy white girl with those eyes fixed upon *him*, what's he going to do? *Not* going to touch her, that's for sure.

Like bringing a lit match close to human hair.

Just for the hell of it . . . bringing it close.

The interior of the car smells: hair pomade, spilled food, something tart and ammoniac like baby diapers.

Iris says finally, shyly, "I . . . heard you're married? You and your wife have a little baby?"

"Uh-huh. That's right."

"I wanted to tell you congratulations, when I heard."

"Thanks."

"And where do you work now?"

Jinx shrugs. "Here and there."

"You used to work at that gravel place across the river, didn't you?"

Jinx just shrugs.

"Your wife is Sissy Weaver? I knew her sister, back in grade school."

"Yah. Sissy Weaver."

"Where do you live?"

Jinx glances at her, laughs as if almost annoyed, or maybe he's just amused. "Sure got a lot of questions, Iris, don't you: like my momma. We live down on Tenth Street, got a place there. Upstairs place."

They drive for a while in silence. Iris's face is very warm, her heartbeat painfully fast. They're passing darkened stores . . . banks of gritty snow . . . familiar sights now unfamiliar. At this time of night the intersections are deserted, or nearly: traffic lights a continuous quick-flashing yellow.

"Do you think you'll ever go back to school? To college? You were planning—"

Jinx makes a derisive snorting noise.

Must be, folks have asked him that question many times.

Iris Courtney persists, though. It's that way she has about her, pushy, unrelenting. "You could go back, couldn't you? Sometime?"

"You kidding?"

"No, I'm not kidding."

Jinx looks at her as if she's simple, and he doesn't have much patience with simple.

After his accident playing basketball Jinx Fairchild quit both basketball and school . . . drifted clear away from the white folks' expectations and good wishes for him.

Iris recalls how Hammond school officials and student government officers debated the issue, the then-controversial issue, of
whether Jinx Fairchild should be granted a Hammond Central High
School diploma despite his failure to complete his senior year . . .
this, the traditional token diploma granted to hopeless but tractable
students, often black, sometimes mildly retarded, in place of the
New York State Regents—approved diploma, the real thing. In the
end they voted to grant Jinx Fairchild the diploma, though worrying he'd refuse to turn up for graduation to receive it on stage with
his fellow seniors, which of course he did; they had to mail it to him
at home.

Iris says, not pushy now but tentative, nervous, "Look: *why*
did you do it? That 'accident'? I knew you did it intentionally, I
knew right away." She pauses. Jinx makes no reply as she knew he
wouldn't, behaves as if he's hardly listening. She says, "He deserved
to die. That's the one clear thing. If he was alive and it was that
night again . . . the same thing would happen. I know there's a way
of seeing him, of the person he was, or the thing, the . . . the
circumstances, there's a way of understanding so you couldn't hate
him or want him dead, you'd be a part of him like God is a part of
him seeing things from his perspective, but I don't care, I *don't*
care. I don't want that perspective or that sympathy, I don't want
him in the world."

Jinx Fairchild doesn't speak for some time then, tight-jawed,
he says, "I don't know what in hell you're talking about, girl. You
better shut your foolish mouth."

She touches him, his arm . . . it's all he can do not to flick it
away like an animal flicking off a fly.

They're on North Main Street approaching the bridge. It's one
of the steepest hills in Hammond, Jinx is braking in quick pumping motions; he's a skillful driver set on maintaining control.

Iris says, "You know what I'm talking about. We know each
other. That basketball game . . . you did it deliberately . . . ruined
everything for yourself. And *why?*"

"You crazy? Shut *up.*"

"Nobody knows, but I know. You never fooled me. And it was

a mistake, we didn't do anything wrong. We don't deserve to be punished."

"How'd I ruin everything for myself? I'm happy," Jinx says. "Doing what I want to do; I'm happy, got me a baby boy, two little boys 'cause Sissy has a four-year-old I'm a daddy to, he calls me Daddy and that's who I am. . . . How'd I ruin my life? You don't know shit."

"You even talk different, now," Iris says. "It isn't you, it's like somebody up from Georgia. You *look* different."

"Some damn dumb ignorant nigger, huh?"

"Well, you don't fool me."

"What you know about niggers, you? Smart-mouth white cunt don't know *shit* about *shit*."

Jinx pushes her from him, with his elbow. Not hard . . . just hard enough.

Approaching the ramp to the bridge Jinx is driving just a little too fast; the rear wheels begin to list to the right. Jinx pumps the brakes coaxingly . . . and the wheels hold.

Winters in Hammond, there's rock salt, sand, cinders spread everywhere on the pavement; now, on the bridge, a rapid near-inaudible pattern of *ping! ping! ping!* starts as minute pieces of grit are thrown up against the insides of the Chrysler's fenders.

The car holds, though. They don't swerve into the railing.

Iris wipes her eyes and looks up, out . . . sees they're speeding over the Cassadaga River. Where are they going? At shore the river is locked in ice, great broken wedges of ice; in the middle the ship channel is open . . . dark turbulent fast-flowing water in a snaky stream. On both shores, the lights of human habitation are small and inconsequential.

Iris whispers, teasing, "You don't fool me."

Her eyes are drawn to Jinx's scabby scarred fingers on the steering wheel, his hands gripping the wheel as if he's fearful of losing control. And if they skid and plunge into the water? Is it deserved? Is it their punishment? Iris says, "It's true, I don't know shit about shit. I don't know the first thing about anything." She rests a hand over one of Jinx's hands, closes her fingers about his. He

241

doesn't push her away but there's no warmth in him, no acquiescence.

His face is shut up tight as a fist; his thick, sullen lips, beautiful to her, are shut tight.

Headlights of oncoming cars flash onto them, blind them, and are gone.

Iris says, "I don't want anything from you but the fact of you. I don't even love you, really . . . it isn't that. I know you're married, and . . . it isn't that really, it's just that there's no one but you, for me. And there *isn't* you . . . I know that. Please don't misunderstand me, I know that."

Jinx shakes his head like a dog shaking off water but he doesn't shake her off.

Coming off the bridge, he turns onto a narrow semirural road that leads . . . who knows where it leads? Beyond the several buildings of Diamond Chemicals . . . past open marshy land . . . scattered farms . . . a scrap-metal yard . . . more land, more hills leading away from Hammond.

In the accumulated snowfall of months there's a vast whiteness on all sides.

Jinx? . . . I'm so afraid.
Afraid of what?
Of things.
You mean . . . what happened by the river?
No. Not the past. What's coming.
My momma's got a saying: the future's gonna take care of itself, just like the past.

Her breasts, naked, in his hands, the little nipples hard as peas.

Breasts that fit completely in his curved, cupped hands . . . astonishingly soft, so *white* . . . the skin seems too pale and thin to protect her.

And her bones, her skeleton, so delicate: so breakable.

And her throat, which he can close his fingers around so easily

. . . feel the powerful artery beating, beating. In trust of him! In infinite trust of *him!*

And her strength, melting into him as warmth melts into water, drawn violently away.

(Why, Jinx Fairchild once asked his high school physics teacher, do molecules in water so rapidly drain off heat from molecules in warmer substances in contact with water? And his teacher said, Why? Just *is.*)

All Jinx does is hold Iris, however; that's all she seems to want of him, now, tonight, all she dares want; it's clear she has never made love with anyone and Jinx isn't about to initiate her: *Uh-uh, honey, not that . . . you got plenty of time for that.* She's like a child stricken with a fear or a grief she can't name, nor does Jinx in his shrewd maleness want to hear its name; he's in dread of that intimacy between them. Isn't it enough just to hold the girl, comfort her . . . to stroke her breasts . . . kiss her. The way, almost, he'd kissed girls back in grade school. Just to touch. Just to get close to. *You're gonna be all right, y'know? Gonna be all right.*

Iris Courtney isn't altogether real to Jinx: she's a kind of doll, doll-sister, little white doll-sister, not a woman.

It's the fragility of the bones, the lethal-looking thinness of that etiolated skin . . . how *can* it protect her, or anyone, adequately?

If Jinx made love to her . . . fucked her, as with Sissy . . . the intimacy would be too great, repugnant to him.

It's Sissy he loves, Jesus he's crazy about that woman, her body a true woman's body in which, groveling, shouting, half sobbing, he can bury himself deep, deep . . . his consciousness, so frequently terrible to him, snuffed out like a candle flame. Jinx loves his young wife for her boldness, her brazenness, her appetite for all things . . . her quick bad temper . . . her capriciousness and unfairness and sudden radiant grin and her crazy wild ways that can't be thwarted: tugging and tearing at his clothes, unzipping his pants and seizing his cock in her fingers when she wishes, a woman making her claim. And riding atop him, riding the root of him, a black woman

243

sucking him deep deep into her, always that promise of sweetness and pleasure and oblivion more precious to Jinx than his own life now he's an adult man . . . now he's a father and no longer just a son.

In Sissy, all that's not-Sissy is obliterated.

In that white man's city two or three miles away across the Cassadaga River, a hive tonight of tiny chill winking lights . . . no look of movement to it, though, or life.

But he's with the little white girl Iris, his doll-sister, this strange sweet-breathed weeping girl, beautiful, her eyes brimming with tears and her fair bristly curly hair that's nearly the texture of his sister Ceci's hair, not kinky exactly but neither is it the kind of hair you associate with white people, the hair that's smooth, straight, glossy . . . and he's laughing at the ease with which he can give comfort, like spilling coins from his pocket . . . his long arms wrapped around her, and her arms slung tight around his waist, tight, tight so it almost hurts. He's laughing; it seems funny to him. *Girl, you about squeezing the life out of me! Girl, I better get you home fast!*

In this high-flying mood he doesn't ponder how she's free to be here with him, this time of night, what her home is like, her parents if she has parents; he senses her aloneness that's keener and more painful than his own . . . mixed up too with her sad white skin. The legendary aloneness and coldheartedness of white folks as Jinx's mother has so frequently said these past two years, *Jesus God, how do white folks get so mean!*

How relieved Jinx is, how euphoric now, princely feeling, to know this girl wants nothing of him beyond his power to give.

It's a little less than an hour that Jinx Fairchild and Iris Courtney huddle together in the battered Chrysler parked above the Cassadaga River, a short distance north and east of Hammond . . . car motor running, heater blasting heat, the silent snowy countryside surrounding them on three sides and the river deep below them invisible from their perspective. Yes, it's a situation in which lovers have sometimes drifted off asleep together and died together, heavy-headed from carbon monoxide poisoning, but that isn't going to happen here, not tonight. Jinx Fairchild makes certain of that.

Not at the time, but later, after Persia is hospitalized, Iris Courtney will record in her journal: *How swiftly, once it begins....*

And how irrevocably. In one powerful direction.

In a patch of sunshine on the faded linoleum floor the supple young midnight-black cat Houdini lies watching Iris Courtney overseeing Persia's breakfast . . . a meal served at an odd hour, late afternoon of this windy April day. Scrambled eggs, lavishly buttered whole wheat toast, orange juice, weak Lipton's tea. Persia raises a forkful of egg to her mouth, lowers it to her plate; raises it as if it were something precious, or mysteriously heavy . . . then lowers it again to her plate. Iris is teasing, cajoling, begging, threatening, pleading. "Try. Try. Just *try*. How do you know you can't keep it down if you don't *try*?"

It's one of those howling days of late winter, winds blowing debris on the street, last year's leaves. A sky so blue it hurts.

Houdini, the stray tom who followed Iris home one night a few weeks ago, skeletal thin at the time, one ear shredded and scabbed with coagulated blood, covered in fleas and mites, is now so at ease in Persia's kitchen he rolls on the floor, on his back, kicking in mock fright, his green-tawny eyes opened wide . . . so much life in the beautiful creature, it's as if currents of electricity pulse through him.

He's hungry too. Always alert in the presence of food.

Never never never never will there be enough food, and the guarantee of food, for Houdini the midnight-black cat, whose anxiety is a loud crackling sort of purr that begins as soon as Iris moves to pet him.

Sometimes as soon as Iris appears in a doorway and their eyes lock.

At the kitchen table in apartment 16-D on the fourth floor of the Buena Vista Arms, this wind-rocked April day, Iris sits facing Persia but with her head averted to spare Persia the indignity of being watched.

To spare Persia too the indignity of being seen, in the state she's in, close up.

It's possible, though, that Persia needs help . . . needs someone to close her fingers around Persia's shaky fingers and help her raise her fork, or her glass, or her cup, to her mouth. And the two fingers on Persia's right hand that Rafe Fuller broke a while back (not that they were fighting 'cause they weren't fighting exactly but Rafe just lost his temper, didn't know he was *hurting*) have not properly healed and may never properly heal.

But Iris knows better than to try to feed her mother.

There are some indignities a human being cannot *tolerate* says Persia.

Tiny beads of sweat like pain pushing out on Persia's forehead.

"Mother, if only you'd *try*."

"I did. I am. I *have*."

"You *haven't*."

"I did eat some, a little. . . . I hate eggs."

"The toast, then? The juice?"

"I *did*."

"I've been right here and you *did not*."

"If for Christ's sake you'd only leave me alone, I *could*." Persia lowers her fork to her plate a final time, reaches for her pack of Chesterfields, lights up, sucks in a deep grateful breath as if the smoke is fresh reviving air, life.

Iris furiously waves smoke away.

She could eat if she wants to. Simply doesn't want to.

As if she could deceive me!

As soon as the *click!* of Persia's fork sounds against the plate, Houdini scrambles to his feet as if his name has been called; he's in Iris's lap mewing and purring frantically . . . kneading his sharp claws into Iris's thighs. He's hungry.

He's hungry.

Iris feeds him Persia's rejected eggs straight from the plate, cold eggs, cold toast, anything, Houdini will eat anything—purring loudly even as he eats—his tail twitching, his lithe little body quivering with excitement. Since Iris brought him home one night in her arms and saved him from starvation in the street his stomach has grown tight and round and hard as a pregnant cat's but that seems scarcely to matter: Houdini is hungry.

Another day, Persia is dressing to go out, drinking from a bottle of Schlitz's as she moves from her bedroom to the bathroom and back again, half dressed, in her stocking feet, and she's chattering about something Iris can't quite follow, she's laughing softly, she's on the edge of anger, complaining of people spying on her, people staring at her openly in the street, and there's an "influence" she's been aware of lately . . . like radio waves . . . television interference. In a lowered voice she says, "They're trying to talk through me, I think. Trying, you know, to communicate."

Calmly Iris asks, "Who is trying to communicate?"

247

"I don't know!" Persia says. Her forehead crinkles in sudden perplexity. She smiles wanly. "I don't know their identities and I haven't seen their faces."

A long moment follows.

In the apartment overhead there's a jarring thump, a thud, the sound of a child's running feet. The sounds too of a radio or a television, a ceaseless murmur as of water flowing rapidly over stones.

Iris says, swallowing, "I don't understand, Mother. *Who* is . . . ?"

Persia is in the bathroom, the faucet is turned on full blast. She calls out petulantly, ". . . seem angry with me, or with someone. I mean, that's the general tone of the communication. It exhausts me and I resent it. I mean, what has it to do with *me?* I'm not to blame."

Iris would speak, Iris would confront her mother, but she feels a warning tinge of pain behind her eyes: the onset of a migraine headache, if she isn't cautious.

Lately, increasingly this past year, Iris has been susceptible to these fierce paralyzing headaches. White piercing pain and a hammering inside her skull . . . better to be cautious.

And that night she manages to sleep heavily . . . isn't wakened until five in the morning when she feels something nudging against her thigh and a rhythmic jiggling of the bed: Houdini the midnight-black cat, who sleeps on top of Iris's bed whenever she allows him, awake now and grooming himself with quick deft motions of his tongue, his warm furry weight pressed snug and importunate against the curve of her thigh. When Iris pets him, he's startled at first; then his purr erupts crackling like small mad flames.

Is Persia home?

Clearly not: Iris would have heard her come in.

Still, Iris calls out, "Mother?"

No sound. Only Houdini purring and nudging his sleek bony head against Iris's hand.

Iris falls back to sleep exhausted and in the morning has forgotten much of the previous evening, the exchange with Persia, the words she'd uttered or meant to utter or had not the courage to utter. *If I remember, it's in vague watery patches like any of my dreams.*

May 11, 1960. By chance, Iris Courtney sights her mother on lower Main Street, late afternoon and there's a warm rich sepia cast to the air; yes, it's Persia, unmistakably Persia—though the fiction is, these days, she's given up entirely on men; she's working part-time as a salesgirl in a hosiery shop—there she is, about to enter Lucky's Bar & Grill in the company of a man, a stranger . . . short, thickset, coarse bulldog look to him: *mean.*

Has he got money, though? Is he one of the paying ones?

Listen to Persia's laughter: high soprano laughter like glass being broken.

And she's in her glamorous new raincoat, dark maroon shot with iridescent threads, tight belt; she's teetering in high-heeled shoes, her hair a gaudy tangle.

Twenty feet away, Iris Courtney stands staring, simply staring. She knows she should turn away, in prudence, in shame, in caution for her own emotional well-being, quickly before Persia sees her; but Iris is in an unnatural state, a vindictive small-minded state . . . coldly staring at this woman who is her mother who has betrayed her so many times.

Now Persia has seen her and there's no retreating.

"Iris? Honey? Why are you . . ."

Persia stands with her arm linked tight through the arm of her man friend, as if for support. She's trying to smile, a crooked lipsticked smile.

Iris doesn't reply; Iris stands her ground, smiling too, but bitterly.

Persia, agitated, tries to bring the scene off with something of her old aplomb, stammering, "Roy, this is my daughter, Iris; I've told you about Iris, haven't I? . . . Iris, this is my friend, Roy. *Roy Baker.*" Roy mumbles "H'lo," gives Iris a grudging embarrassed smile. He's a fairly well dressed man in his mid-fifties with an alcoholic's red pulpy nose and close-set liquidy eyes.

Though she is eighteen years old and hardly a child, Iris

behaves like a child. Says nothing. Not a word. Just this look of hers, this Angel of Wrath look, knowing, accusing, brimming with contempt.

Does he pay you, Momma? In cash, or just in drinks?

As if overhearing Iris's thoughts Persia reaches out weakly toward her, makes a vague motherly gesture. "Say! Why don't we all go get a bite to eat together? What time *is* it?" Persia's voice is gay, a party voice. In this public setting, the dull pink-neon sign LUCKY'S BAR & GRILL behind her, city buses careening past issuing clouds of exhaust, this voice sounds a distinctly desperate note.

Iris murmurs coolly, "No, thank you, Mother, I can't."

Roy Baker snuffles loudly and stares at his feet. Persia's suggestion seems to have made him profoundly unhappy.

But Persia is still trying to bring the scene off, half angry, half pleading: she's Doris Day in a Technicolor comedy, an American tale of harmlessly crossed motives, confused identities, protracted but soluble misunderstandings. Seeing that her daughter is about to walk away, she says, "Roy, dear, I think I'd better go with Iris. Do you mind, dear? I'll call you later tonight, I promise." Roy Baker says, "What? *Why?*" The tone of his voice suggests that he's a man accustomed to having his way with women . . . with a certain class of women.

Roy Baker pulls Persia off to the side. They speak sharply together. "Listen," says Roy Baker, and "*You* listen," says Persia, and Roy Baker pulls at Persia's arm, and Persia tries to shove him away, poor Persia staggering in her high heels, wisps of hair in her face. . . . Suddenly before Iris's eyes it's a public scene of a generic sort, a man and a woman, both slightly drunk, quarreling in front of Lucky's Bar & Grill, truculent red-faced little man, shrewish middle-aged woman. Roy Baker is damned angry and so is Persia but it's clear she wants, still, to placate him, to charm him; it's what Persia knows best, her deepest most feminine instinct . . . no matter that the man is gripping her hard by the arm, shaking her, hurting her. Iris stares transfixed. Is this really happening? Is that woman my mother?

She turns blindly away, and Persia calls after her, and Iris calls back over her shoulder, her eyes hot with tears, "Stay with *him!* Of course, stay with *him!* You disgust me!"

Iris begins to run. She hears Persia call after her, "Iris! Iris!" but she doesn't hesitate, just runs, runs.

Iris works from four-thirty until eight-thirty at the Hammond Public Library, then has supper at the restaurant in the Greyhound Bus terminal, sits at the counter and afterward in the waiting room reading . . . underlining passages in her book with brisk motions of her pen as if she were in a place suitable for such schoolgirl activity and not in this place of noise, commotion, the arrivals and departures of strangers. If Iris is aware of the occasional men who approach her, the one or two who seat themselves deliberately beside her, crane their necks to look at her book, she's careful not to give any sign. In the inhospitable light her face looks pale and chiseled, the eyes deep-socketed. Her shoulder-length hair is a fair crisp brown dusted with ashes.

Iris Courtney has never returned to Kitty's Korner since the night she met Jinx Fairchild there. Telephoned him, and asked him to meet her there. Her fantasy that Jinx might return looking for her is continually and scornfully overruled by her knowledge that he would never do such a thing; she doesn't exist for him.

And why should she, for him?

Iris Courtney, for *him?*

And how could he help her with Persia, in any case?

Iris is still sitting in the bus station at eleven-thirty when a policeman approaches her. "Miss? Are you waiting for a bus?"— eyeing her as if she's a runaway or an inexperienced prostitute—and Iris says quickly, "No, I'm just . . . just waiting," gathering up her things, hurrying away, angry and chagrined. Could she be arrested? There's a NO LOITERING sign prominent on the wall.

Main Street is nearly deserted, the storefronts darkened; she's walking in long fast strides hoping the policeman isn't following her. She's only a few blocks, in fact, from Lucky's Bar & Grill. She wonders where Persia is, what Persia's condition is now . . . though the incident six hours ago has blended with the many incidents of weeks and months previous, indistinct as muddy water splashing into muddy water.

Here's the regal-fronted Palace Theater where she and Persia saw *Butterfield 8* that afternoon months ago. Like schoolgirls playing hooky together, like sisters with shared secrets . . . except Persia had lied about the hospital tests and would subsequently lie about her very lying, blaming the hospital for "losing" the laboratory results.

She wants to drive both of us crazy. I will never succumb.

Now playing at the Palace is the biblical epic *Ben-Hur* starring Charlton Heston. At this late hour the ticket window is darkened and a solitary usher stands yawning in the foyer, waiting for the last show to end.

Iris walks all the way home, fueled by desperation and rage: about three miles along dim-lit, near-deserted streets. Much of the distance is steeply downhill and there's pleasure in that, a kind of euphoria.

When she unlocks the door to 16-D of the Buena Vista Arms she sees to her surprise that there's a light burning in the kitchen . . . a light burning in the living room . . . Persia's raincoat has been tossed down on the sofa. Persia is home already; Persia came home before Iris did!

And Roy Baker isn't here with her because there's no sign of him, not a whiff. Iris Courtney can smell her mother's man friends sometimes before she enters the apartment.

Here's Houdini the midnight-black tomcat with the frayed ear and the round little belly, materializing suddenly underfoot, mewing to be petted, or to be fed. He's called Houdini because of his gift for materializing out of nowhere, purring his eager proprietary purr.

Iris stoops to pet him; sees that his food and water bowls are full; whispers to him, "Quiet, Houdini! No noise!" She's feeling a wave of gratitude . . . sheer relief . . . that she's home, safely home, and Persia too is home, in bed. Quietly Iris moves through the rooms switching off lights. She undresses in her bedroom, uses the

252

bathroom, stands by Persia's closed door for some minutes, listening for Persia's breathing (heavy, rasping, arrhythmic), scarcely breathing herself. She's in her floral-print flannel nightgown, bare toes curling on the chill linoleum floor.

She pushes the door open. "Momma?" The familiar smells of soiled laundry, sharp perfume, Persia's chemical hair, Gordon's gin. Persia is in bed asleep or seemingly so, breathing in waves; there's a faint ghostly light filtered through the curtains and Iris shyly whispers, "Momma?" and again Persia makes no response. Iris tiptoes to the bed, trembling, lies down beside her mother, on the outside of the covers. Persia gives off heat. *Is* she asleep, or pretending? As often she'd pretend to be asleep when Iris crept into her parents' bedroom as a little girl, wanting nothing more powerfully than to slide beneath the covers with them, with Persia especially, wanting to hug and cuddle, and it was nicest when Persia wasn't fully awake but would turn to her sleepy, sleepily smiling, and gather her in her arms and not a word. And if Daddy was asleep on Momma's other side, not a word.

Iris settles back on the bed, cautious not to wake her mother. She crosses her arms across her chest, crosses her ankles, lies very still. So grateful to be here she could cry, Jesus she could cry, still shivering but it's with excitement not with cold.

They lie like that, side by side, until morning, Houdini the midnight-black cat curled snug at their feet.

And a week later Persia Courtney is dying.

Tiny red ants in the curly hair under her arms, and in the crinkly hair between her legs. She's weeping and muttering, trying frantically to pick them off. Pick them off! *Pick them off!*

And the shards of broken glass on the bathroom floor, glittering. And on the kitchen floor. Wavy drunk zigzag lines in the linoleum tile so her vision jumps and she can't see . . . walks barefoot whimpering in pain.

She'd lifted the glass of gin in both hands; still it went squirming out of her hands like a live thing.

Iris where are you? Iris can't you help me?

She's screaming. No one to hear but the neighbors. But they won't hear.

She's asleep . . . for hours. Trapped in sleep like sludge. Something holding her head down. Something furry and warm and heavy against her mouth, smothering.

That thing, that beast. The green-tawny eyes flaring up in the dark.

Iris? Can't you help me? Help me—

The black-furred creature runs panicked and skittering on its sharp claws, trying to escape. Specks of froth at its mouth.

Caterpillars in the bedclothes . . . she feels them but can't move away. Asleep but fully conscious, the curse of full consciousness, even in the grave, even in death, this terror. She feels them in her hair, crawling over her face, her breasts, her unprotected belly. *Iris help me! Iris!* Her nipples ache as if she's been nursing.

She has died, they've buried her alive.

Sweating like a pig.

No amount of talcum powder can disguise the smell, nor can face powder disguise the tainted cast of her skin . . . the color of rancid butter.

Is the telephone ringing? It's Duke Courtney come to save her.

Begging her forgiveness but it's too late.

In any case, she won't touch the phone any longer. She has felt it quiver in her hand, heard the tiny mocking whispers inside.

Iris please help me . . . honey where are you?

It's spring. The fragrance of blossoms and death. She's screaming and sobbing and someone begins knocking at the front door and she jams the pillowcase against her mouth to stifle her cries until the danger is past.

It might be the police, come to bury her alive.

Police with grinning faces, leering eyes, standing over her.

How they'd laugh, seeing the infestation of red ants! A frenzy of red ants! In her pubic hair . . . inside her vagina.

Cunt, they'd say, laughing. Filthy cunt.

She's pouring the last of the gin into a glass and the surprise of

254

it, the precious liquid sloshing out, the smell in the bedclothes, soaking into the mattress. So quickly! An old faded lizard-shaped stain of menstrual blood in the mattress . . . years old. Persia has not had a menstrual period in a year, still she's fearful that one of her men friends will see, will smell her, will recoil in disgust.

The ants! Red stinging ants! She runs water in the tub, lowers herself desperately, slipping, losing her balance, knocking the back of her head against the tub, she's partly unconscious but still the hot water splashes frothing into the tub. Her mind is a stained porcelain tub on old-fashioned claw feet splashing with frothing water.

Time pleats. The sun swerves overhead.

She's in the bedroom . . . she's in the kitchen and her mind is clear. Like a windowpane briskly washed, a flood of light shining through.

God help me, please God help me. It isn't too late.

Again, the furry black creature, the bright-eyed beast, skulking in the corners, watching. As soon as she weakens and lies down it will settle itself over her mouth and suck away her breath.

Devil. *Devil!*

Her bare toes and the heel of her right foot are bleeding from fragments of broken glass. Yet there is no glass that she can see . . . the floor has been swept fastidiously clean.

She's a good homemaker. Old Dutch Cleanser, Brillo pads, Oxydol. But she's out of cigarettes and it's a thousand thousand miles to the store.

Here's what she does: fills a three-quart pan with water, sets it on the stove, turns the gas burner on high. Panting, excited. Hair sticking to her sweaty forehead. Calling, Kitty! *Kitty-kitty-kitty!* But the creature is smart, wary, apprehensive. The cunning of the devil. Green-tawny eyes flaring up . . . claws on the linoleum floor . . . stumpy tail erect in arrogance. Persia's enemies sent this creature home with Iris to smother them both in their sleep but Persia has a plan, calling, *Kitty! Here, kitty-kitty-kitty!* She's in her old glamorous negligee, champagne-colored, lace, pleats, tiny bows, a present from her husband, her adoring young husband, many years ago. . . . *Here, kitty! Pretty kitty!*

The water is slow to come to a boil.

Eventually, it comes to a boil, the big pan rattling on the burner.

Hunger lures the black cat out of his hiding place . . . suddenly he's in the kitchen, underfoot, mewing his plaintive hopeful meow. Persia's eyes flare up too. Persia is barefoot too, toenails braced against the floor. *Kitty, here kitty!* she calls in her hoarse voice and as Houdini rubs and preens against her leg Persia reaches for the pan of boiling water, lifts it by both hands, no time for pot holders; she tries to step out of the way as she pours the seething water onto the cat but the cat trips her, the cat is wild, frenzied, the two of them are screaming. . . .

Help me! Help me Iris!

It seems that Persia's negligee is on fire, her very flesh is on fire. She runs to the door, throws open the door, runs out onto the landing, and the stairs are gone, the apartment building below is gone, Buena Vista Street, the city of Hammond, New York, all Persia knows, gone.

Iris Courtney notes in her journal merely: *May 18. Mother was taken to Hammond General Hospital today by ambulance. Uncle Leslie and I followed.*

Not until years have passed will Iris understand that Persia's story is a familiar one: an alcoholic's slow, then rapid, decline; dizzying rapidity at the end. A familiar story but utterly new and strange and terrible to Iris and she will never learn to tell it properly, even to herself: only in pieces, shreds, quick short takes.

Hearing Persia's screams on the stairway landing outside the apartment, a neighbor came and saw and called an ambulance, and now it's through others' eyes that Iris Courtney begins to see her mother.

How had Persia become so emaciated? Nearly skeletal except for her grotesquely swollen belly, astonishing to observe. And astonishing too the breasts collapsed and flaccid as balloons emptied of air . . . Persia's lovely breasts!

And her skin, coarse, a sickly orangish yellow, even the whites of her eyes jaundiced: the hue of urine.

And her breath, rasping, labored, foul. And a grainy white powder at the corners of her mouth.

Iris Courtney sees. Yet somehow cannot *see* . . . cannot *comprehend*.

Recording neatly and succinctly in her journal: *May 19. Mother is in intensive care. The doctor says it will be a while before she'll be well enough to come home.*

Iris's thinking is initially optimistic, and Persia's relatives and friends seem to agree: now that Persia is safely in the hospital she will receive the treatment she needs. No more making appointments with doctors, then breaking them at the last minute . . . as, it turns out, she'd been doing for more than a year.

Says Madelyn Daiches, "Now that Persia is in the hospital she *can't* drink, and she'll be so scared, when she gets out, she *won't* drink."

And when it's explained to Iris that her mother has a condition called "cirrhosis of the liver," among other medical problems of varying degrees of seriousness, Iris's first response is one of childlike relief: It isn't anything serious, then. Like cancer or heart disease.

As for the second-degree burns on her legs and feet, the burns are only external, superficial. They'll heal.

Those days, weeks . . . slate-colored skies streaked with rain . . . accelerating gradually like water approaching a falls. The roaring deepens so slowly you can't hear it.

Persia remains in the intensive care ward, kept alive by IV fluids dripping into her exhausted veins and by a tube sucking bile and body fluids into a clear plastic bag taped to the side of her bed. A somber proposition, the body as a mechanism for taking in and expelling fluids. Persia's few visitors (Madelyn, women friends, a neighbor or two—Persia is conscious enough to forbid all male visitors, including Leslie Courtney) are shocked by her appearance, claim they wouldn't recognize her: the eerily discolored skin, the eyes swollen nearly shut, a look of weariness, fatigue, age. And that puffed-up little belly, the belly of a woman in an advanced state of pregnancy, mysteriously out of proportion to the rest of her body.

The first time Iris Courtney sees her mother in the hospital, in that unnaturally high-cranked bed, she stares uncomprehendingly . . . is that frail, motionless figure *Persia?* A thick rubber tube has been forced through one of Persia's nostrils, with a weight attached, so that the weight will force its way down through her throat, through her chest, into her stomach. Thus one nostril is grotesquely distended, the other pinched shut. Persia's eyes are swollen as if they've been blackened and it isn't possible to determine if they are open, exactly . . . or whether, open, they are in focus.

Iris cries, "Oh, Momma!" in a voice of hurt, shock, accusation. There's no response.

For the next several weeks, Iris Courtney spends her days sitting at her mother's bedside waiting for Persia to emerge from this terribly sick woman . . . she no longer attends, or even thinks of, her classes at Hammond Central High School. Maybe she'll make up papers and exams later in the summer, maybe not at all. She's here at the hospital waiting for Persia to wake, to look at *her* . . . to say she's sorry. Waiting for Persia to begin to recover up to the very hour of Persia's death.

One morning, early in the second week, Persia is conscious enough to speak in a faint, exhausted voice, and Iris grips her hand hard; Iris leans close as possible desperate not to miss a word. "Wanted not to be lonely . . . like God made a promise . . . my baby girl . . . little baby girl . . . I know I failed . . . failed to be a good mother . . . a mother. Honey, I know I . . . failed."

When it seems she isn't going to speak further Iris says quickly, a little loudly, "Momma, you *were* a good mother, you *are*."

Persia tries to look at her. It's remarkable, the strength she must summon just to look; there seems to be a scrim across her eyes, a fever blur. Persia has contracted a hospital infection, her temperature is high.

Iris repeats several times, "Momma, you were a good mother,

you always were a good mother," thinking *Liar, liar, why do you lie,* gripping Persia's hand hard, and how frail, how without strength, that hand, the hand of an elderly woman.

Persia says hoarsely, "I could have been better . . . I *am* better . . . inside. Don't you believe me?" For a moment she seems to be almost angry; there's a flurry of purpose and resistance, the old Persia, flaring up at a word of opposition. Saying, "*I* know . . . could have been better . . . lost control . . . you think I'm not a better person than I . . . showed?"

Iris stares at Persia's bloated, discolored face, at those jaundiced crescents of eyes, and wonders, Are we arguing? Is this an argument? Here? Now? Quickly Iris murmurs yes Momma, yes Momma you're right.

Persia says passionately, "You don't know . . . too young. Shouldn't judge," and Iris says she isn't judging anyone, and Persia says, "Loved *you* . . . my little girl. But it didn't help, did it?" and Iris says yes yes it did help of course it helped, and Persia says impatiently, "Don't lie, damn you, there isn't time, don't try to lie to *me,* just promise . . . promise you won't make the mistake I made."

Iris says, "What mistake, Momma?" and Persia says, her voice beginning to wander, to weaken, "Just like me. Iris. But *don't* be like me," and Iris says desperately, "Momma, what do you mean? What mistake?" and Persia says vaguely, "Knew what goodness was. But I was always . . . bored with it. That kind of . . . man. That kind of life. Don't make that mistake, honey . . . don't turn away from goodness if you can find it. I knew what your father was . . . didn't care, I loved him so . . . I don't care now, I guess . . . it's too late now . . . and other things. . . ."

She's becoming sleepy; it's as if a powerful drug were overcoming her; Iris can feel her mother's consciousness, her strength, life, seemingly ebbing through Iris's own fingers . . . it's unbearable to Iris that she can't stop this draining away.

Persia's final words that day are, "*Promise me.* . . ." and Iris says, "Yes, Momma," without knowing what she says, what she is promising.

* * *

Still, she's faithful to her vision of the real Persia: the healthy Persia: the woman so frequently and so lovingly photographed with her daughter, throughout their lives . . . the two of them even now on display, on seemingly permanent display, in the window of Courtney's Photography Studio on North Main Street.

It's a matter of waiting for this woman to return.

It's a matter of thinking optimistically. Or not thinking.

Leslie Courtney seems to feel the way Iris does. *When Persia leaves the hospital. When Persia gets well.* There are plans for a summer excursion to Crystal Beach, in Ontario; to Lake Placid, in the Adirondack Mountains; plans for a new apartment or duplex in a better neighborhood. Leslie Courtney is hopeful but it seems he's been sufficiently shocked by his sister-in-law's collapse to have stopped drinking himself.

Permanently, Leslie swears. Permanently one day at a time.

Eleven o'clock in the evening of the twenty-first day of Persia's hospitalization and the telephone rings in the apartment in the Buena Vista Arms and it's Duke Courtney, from whom Iris has not heard in more than a year, complaining bitterly that he's being kept from Persia's bedside: "Came at once when I heard . . . it's outrageous . . . at the hospital yesterday, and again today, and *I* said . . . I have a right, I said . . . this woman's husband of sixteen years, I said . . . who has a right if I don't? . . . want to see you both, Iris . . . from the bottom of my heart . . . need to see you both. Tomorrow at the hospital—"

Calmly Iris says, "No."

"I'd have come sooner except I've been out of town . . . I've been traveling. This new business. These are exciting times, Iris, for men who aren't dazzled and intimidated by . . . I feel so distant talking to you, so . . . strange. My own daughter I'm talking to and I feel so . . . Iris? Why don't you say something? I'm desperate to see you and your mother both and make it up to you if you'd see it in your heart to—"

"No."

"If I come up? I'm in the neighborhood. If I—"

"No."

There's a moment of silence. Then Duke Courtney laughs harshly, with an air of surprise. "My God, Iris, you certainly are . . . aren't . . . very friendly, are you? What has happened to *you?* Your own father calls and . . . frankly, I haven't been in ideal health myself . . . Leslie says Persia refuses to see *him* . . . it's clear the woman isn't in her right mind, can't be trusted to make her own decisions. Poor Persia! So self-destructive! I hate to say it but I saw this coming years ago . . . years ago. If you could explain to her, Iris . . . bring her a note from me . . . this Dr. Who's-It, that self-important bastard, cut me off cold . . . and the nurse in charge of intensive care—what a harridan! . . . Look, this is crucial I said, this is a matter of life and death I said, who has a better right to see this patient if I don't? Married to her for sixteen years and *you can't tell me that in her heart we're not still married.* Nobody better try to hand Duke Courtney that kind of bullshit! Your mother isn't in her right mind and she needs me . . . Jesus, don't we all need one another? *I* acknowledge it . . . why can't *she? Why can't you? Who has a right if I don't?"*

Again Iris says, her lips numb, "No."

And hangs up the receiver.

Next morning she's prepared: as she crosses the hospital foyer to the elevators she sees Duke Courtney waiting for her; he takes several quick steps forward, then hesitates. He calls her name in a surprisingly tentative voice, as if he doesn't exactly recognize her.

Duke Courtney is a tall thin man in his mid-forties, with a ravaged handsome face, thin silvery hair, silvery stubble glinting on his chin. His eyes are worried, his smile is faint. His blue pin-striped suit appears to be a size or two too large for him and the trousers have lost their crease, but his black shoes, his expensive shoes, are wonderfully shiny.

Behind him, yet clearly with him, is a woman his age with smudged eyes and a bright lipsticked mouth.

Iris sees them both, Iris looks through them both, impassively, now at the elevator with a small group of other visitors . . .

she doesn't stop for Duke Courtney, who's saying, "Iris? Iris? *Iris?*" in a baffled voice.

I walked past him. I don't know him. By the time I got to the sixth floor I'd forgotten all about him.

Mostly, Persia is unconscious.

Or too exhausted and confused to open her eyes.

Iris Courtney learns that the effort can be heroic . . . simply to open your eyes.

But once, a few days before the end, Persia jerks herself awake and her eyes shift into focus, or seemingly into focus, and she reaches out for Iris's hand, gripping it with a child's quick vehement strength. Her lips are scabby with sores. Her hair, now a dull faded brown, very thin, has been skimmed back severely from her face. She whispers, "Iris? Why are we here?" Iris tells her it's the hospital, she's been here awhile, she's getting medical treatment, she has to rest, lie still, she's going to get better. But Persia is agitated; her eyes darting from side to side, she says wildly, "Help me out of here! This *coffin*—" And Iris says, "I will, Momma," Iris says in a buoyant girlish voice, "I will, Momma, as soon as the doctor says you're well."

Persia's wasted body is nervy, coiled tight. Iris feels the trembling begin deep inside her bones. But the rubber tube, that snake through her nose, holds her fast, traps her. And the IV fluid dripping into a vein on her left forearm. And the tube sucking poisons from her body. And the weight of the crisp bed linen, so white. Within seconds Persia goes limp again . . . a breath quietly exhaled. "No, that's all right, hon," she says, relenting. "It's where they want me. It's their plan. I'm in one place now."

PART THREE

Ceremony

She's fated too. She's ours. She's the bond between us that can't ever be broken—but I have broken it.

Thinks Iris Courtney in triumph, and in defiance.

She's gone away, she has left Hammond, New York . . . intends never to return except as a visitor.

For one thing, she hasn't any home there. Any place, any site, to which anything more substantial than memory might accrue. That makes it easier.

Thus when kindly vague-minded Dr. Savage inquires, late one afternoon in November 1962, "Are you going home for Thanksgiving recess, Miss Corey?" Iris Courtney says with a polite smile, "I *am* at home here in Syracuse, Dr. Savage. And my name isn't 'Corey.' "

* * *

In November 1962 Iris Courtney is twenty years old, twenty years six months old, living alone in a small, minimally furnished, but quite reasonably clean and private room in a rooming house near the shabby end of South Salina Street, Syracuse, New York; she pays a monthly rent of thirty dollars, including all utilities. It's her third year as an undergraduate at Syracuse University and it suits her temperament to live alone, nearly a mile from campus, in a red-brick residence, formerly a private home, populated mainly by graduate students: Iris endured her freshman year in university housing, amid other freshmen women, miserably out of place as an adult might be in such circumstances; now she accepts her fate as one of those marginal not-quite-in-focus students who can afford only to live off campus and who are obliged to supplement their scholarships by working, sometimes at more than one low-paying job. One of those sober industrious self-assured young people who, whatever their ages, never strike the eye as young.

Iris's dense springy hair, cut shorter now, to the nape of her neck, is unevenly streaked with silver; there are faint, near-invisible lines in her forehead; even her freckles are rapidly fading, like childhood memories. Her otherwise smooth face is a chiseled face, high cheekbones, high narrow forehead, but it's a beautiful face . . . or so Iris Courtney supposes since she's been told this, many times.

Not laughing in reply. And what good will beauty do me?

Not twisting her mouth. And what good did beauty do . . . her?

Still, Iris is happy here in Syracuse. Much of the time.

She's happy living by herself in her room on the top floor of the three-story red-brick house on South Salina Street . . . she's happy at this university where her grades are unswervingly high and where, in her junior year, she has a job as student assistant to the highly respected Byron Savage of the Art History Department, editor of *The Journal of Art and Aesthetics* . . . she's happy in a city five times the size and population of Hammond that's no more than a two-hour drive from Hammond yet might, for all its differences, for all the surface busyness and dazzle of its cultural life, be thousands of miles away. She jokes that even the wind off Lake Ontario has a different taste here.

If Iris Courtney's skin has been abraded raw from grief or, more than grief, insult . . . if her response to being touched is one of nervous recoil steely disguised and controlled . . . it's entirely likely that she isn't aware of it, herself. She rarely thinks of Persia's death and never voluntarily speaks of it.

For Iris has learned that to experience a thing is not to know it, or even to have the power to remember it coherently. Still less the power of language to express it.

And what is "fact," that it can be used to explain? It is "fact" that must be explained.

She was thirty-eight when she died.

He disappeared immediately after the funeral, leaving no forwarding address.

There was no insurance. The bills came to just under $8,000: L. took out bank loans but I intend to pay him back.

I am readying myself to fall in love. It's time.

"Miss Courtney," he says in his gentlemanly voice.

"Iris," he says. Enunciating each syllable evenly.

Has Byron Savage lived so long abroad, he speaks English with a faint, exotic accent?

Now he's more keenly aware of Iris and, aware of having offended her, he takes pains to call her by name. He smiles as if smiling were an obligatory part of speaking; his fair, blue, quizzical eyes are alight with solicitude. Iris perceives that her employer is one of those innocently vain but genuinely charitable persons of power who, once he imagines he has been rude, goes to elaborate, unceasing lengths to compensate . . . his self-estimation is so high, he knows the hurt he has caused is considerable.

Iris Courtney sits behind an old high-domed Remington-Royal typewriter in Dr. Savage's outer office, soothed by the staccato surges of her typing, which banish most of her own thoughts. The office with its twelve-foot ceiling and antiquated radiators and drafty leaded windows is a curiously consoling place, and she often works late, past five o'clock, typing up correspondence, university forms, highly detailed readers' reports on articles submitted to the *Journal*. She believes herself privileged to be here and suspects she was hired by accident: Dr. Savage mistook her for a graduate, and not an undergraduate, student; she did very well in his popular undergraduate survey course, thus her name and face were vaguely familiar to him, though not known.

He's a fussy, fastidious man, but fair-minded. In his late fifties, Iris estimates. Medium height, nearly bald, with a fringe of baby-fine brownish hair; thirty pounds overweight, and soft in the torso and belly; rather ponderous in his manner. His habit of perpetual throat-clearing gives him an air both tentative and magisterial . . . it's a maddening habit, in fact. Iris hears him in his inner office, hears him approach her. *Hmmmm! Uh-hmmmm!* then, "Miss Courtney? Iris? May I interrupt?"

Iris thinks, If I am called by my first name, shall I call *him* by *his?*

Unfailingly, Iris calls her employer "Dr. Savage." There's a pleasure in such sounds that's almost tactile.

For all his courtesy, Byron Savage is a strong-willed man: it's known among art history majors, of which Iris Courtney is one, that you dare not oppose him in matters of theory; aesthetics is Dr. Savage's religion and his voice quavers with passion when he discusses what he calls "the great tradition" in Western art . . . the subject of his numerous books and monographs. In the *Journal* office too, Dr. Savage can be fussy and demanding: Iris knows he has dismissed previous assistants for minor errors. Like all persons of power Dr. Savage isn't to be trusted, and Iris doesn't trust him.

But one afternoon when Iris has elected to work late proofreading galleys for the magazine, Dr. Savage asks her almost timidly would she like a ride home? It's already pitch dark; there's a rainy sleet being blown against the windows. Another day, in mid-November, he surprises her by asking would she like to join him and

Mrs. Savage and a few others for Thanksgiving dinner, "Since, as you said, Miss Courtney—*Iris*—you aren't going home?"

To each invitation, Iris hesitates before accepting.

But she accepts, certainly. As if Byron Savage has given her a precious stone and her instinct is not even to look at it but to close her fingers quickly over it.

So, by accident, Iris Courtney is drawn into the Savage family . . . she feels so palpable a sense of excitement and anticipation, it's as if she knows her life must be changed.

3

Of the fourteen tenants in the red-brick house at 2117 South Salina Street, ten are men; all ten men are "older"; seven of the ten are foreign students . . . from Taiwan, India, Nigeria, Jamaica. It's the husky six-foot-four-inch Jamaican, Claude St. Germain, to whom Iris Courtney is most attracted and with whom she's likely to exchange greetings; her eyes linger on him, contemplatively.

It isn't clear from Claude St. Germain's mumbled, heavily accented speech whether he is an advanced student in the mechanical engineering program at the university or an undergraduate; perhaps he doesn't know his own status. He appears to be in his late twenties, has never lived in the North before, is frowning and distrustful of the politely smiling white girl when she says hello or tries to engage him in casual conversation in the vestibule of the rooming house (where tenants get their mail) or in the kitchen at the rear in which tenants have "privileges" . . . for weeks,

St. Germain won't look her in the face. Then by degrees he turns friendlier, though his mood is never predictable. He's a big-bodied man, very black, handsome, with outsized sculpted features like a Rodin bust cast in iron, thick nappy hair, a broad nose, an abrupt wildly ascending laugh that erupts without warning while his eyes remain unmoved.

English is St. Germain's native language but he speaks it less fluently than most of the other foreign students, and even in one of his noisy ebullient moods he seems suspicious . . . fearful he's being laughed at behind his back. One day Iris overhears another tenant ask St. Germain how he is, and St. Germain says with a mocking laugh, "Who is it wants to know, eh? *You? You* give a damn? 'Speck me to believe *that!*'" The sound of his feet on the stairs is hooflike and thunderous.

Still, Iris is keenly aware of Claude St. Germain: listens for his voice, his explosive laughter; watches him, unseen, from her window; even follows him sometimes in the street for a block or two, when he doesn't see her. She feels a viselike sensation around her chest, a sensation intimate as sleep, watching him. When he isn't aware of her.

When he's aware of her, she's likely to feel a stab of apprehension.

Ah, but that walk of his, that rolling gait . . . that bobbing motion to his head: Iris watches as if memorizing. On the streets near campus the Jamaican walks now fast, now slow; now with an angry determination, now with an air of aimlessness, slightly hunched in his overcoat as if to minimize his height; making his way with unerring grace through clusters of strangers, virtually all of them white. For how *white* this world is!

In early November Iris happens to hear from one of the other tenants that Claude St. Germain is having trouble with his courses, and the thought crosses her mind that she might help him. Not with mathematics of course but with English . . . if he needs help with English.

This thought crosses Iris Courtney's mind swift and momentary as a high-scudding cloud and is forgotten. With her courses and the hours she puts in for Dr. Savage, she hasn't any time to spare; even if she weren't doubtful of approaching St. Germain, she hasn't any time to spare. Her chronic sense of herself is that of a figure running just ahead of a wall of flame.

"You like to go out with me sometime, Iris? A drink? Dance? Sometime? No?"

Abruptly it happens that St. Germain begins to be aware of Iris Courtney, and now he's lingering in the corridor outside her room and on the stairs, knocks on her door late at night to invite her for a drink in his room, waits for her to leave the house mornings so that he can fall into stride with her. No matter how stealthily Iris descends to the kitchen in the evening St. Germain is sure to follow, bursting in, rash, noisy, hopeful, belligerent, primed with questions to put to her, quick to erupt into his wild reckless laugh. He persists in inviting her out: "To the movies, maybe? Dance? Just up to Marshall Street for a drink? Eh? Iris? What's the word?" His eyes are cold and mirthless.

Iris says politely, "I'm sorry I can't," and, "I'm really sorry, I *can't,*" trying to meet the black man's gaze directly, not shrinking from his rage; "Look, please, Claude, truly . . . I don't go out much, I haven't time."

" 'Haven't time! Haven't time'!"

Iris overhears St. Germain mocking her in a falsetto voice, to others; overhears him telling smutty jokes when she's certain to pass by; discovers him on the third floor, beltless, his trousers partway unzipped . . . St. Germain's room is on the second floor and he hasn't any business on the third. When Iris says, trembling, "I think you'd better leave me alone," St. Germain says, with a quick glistening smile, "*You* better leave *me* alone, baby . . . ever think of that?"

The week before Thanksgiving, Iris is downstairs in the kitchen at about ten o'clock in the evening—there's another roomer there, making coffee, a mild-mannered white man in economics named Hodler—and in comes the Jamaican smelling of beer and perspiration, blustery, aggressive, all smiles. "Well, hel-*lo* Iris:

275

where you been keeping yourself, baby?" And within seconds, discreet as a cat, Hodler slips out of the room.

St. Germain is jeweled in sweat like an athlete who's been warming up. He's wearing a red Orlon V-neck sweater with no shirt beneath and he's carrying a can of beer, chattering like a drunken parrot. Iris says, interrupting, "You—you're forgetting your pride!"

St. Germain squints at Iris Courtney as if these peculiar words of hers might be in code. But he can't decipher the code, so he shrugs, grins loose-lipped, says, "*You*—wanna dance?"

Iris turns off the stove's gas burner and prepares to leave the kitchen but St. Germain, wriggling his hips Presley style, snapping his fingers above his head, blocks her way. He's bawling a song in a calypso beat. "How 'bout Harry Belafonte, baby? You like *him*, eh? Sure you do! All the white cunts hot for Belafonte . . . that asshole."

Iris tries to force her way past St. Germain but he crowds her back, pushes her against the stove . . . this old-fashioned gas stove, eight burners, enormous . . . wriggling his hips defiantly, not smiling now; and Iris, who has been under the confused impression that maybe Hodler hurried to get the house manager (who is well aware of St. Germain's behavior in recent weeks; has in fact quarreled with him repeatedly), begins to realize that there won't be any help—she's alone with this embittered, disturbed black man—and tries to think what to do. What to do! Yet it's without thinking that she ducks past St. Germain to get to one of the kitchen drawers, he seizes her arm and tries to spin her as if they're dancing a rough giddy dance, and Iris wrenches away, yanks open a drawer, takes out a knife, a paring knife, too small so she discards it and fumbles for another, a carving knife . . . now crouching, she lifts the knife toward the astonished St. Germain, saying, "You touch me another time and I'll kill you," pointing the blade at his throat, speaking calmly and even dispassionately, until, with a shuddery little laugh, both hands uplifted in a parody of surrender, St. Germain backs off.

He makes a long wet whistling noise with his lips . . . bugs his eyes at her.

276

Iris Courtney doesn't move. She continues to hold the knife erect, blade pointed at St. Germain's throat. Her face is dead white, the freckles bleached away; her eyes are dilated but her hand is steady . . . it's remarkable, how steady.

She says, in that same quiet, unhurried voice, "You mistook me for someone else, didn't you—someone I'm not. *Don't ever do that again.*"

St. Germain is sober now, the defiance drained from him.

"OK, baby, you said it . . . *you* got the last word."

To save face he backs out of the kitchen as if it's a calypso step he's executing, clumsily, a glance over his shoulder to see if anyone has witnessed his humiliation; and then he's gone, and it's over; and ever after tonight St. Germain takes pains to avoid Iris Courtney— or, if he can't avoid her, to look, with dignity, through her. And Iris Courtney makes an effort not to look at him . . . not to let her gaze linger on him.

In any case, the Jamaican engineering student disappears over Christmas recess and is never seen again in Syracuse. His room on the second floor remains unoccupied for weeks.

T wo-thirty in the morning of this windy November day, past two-thirty, and Iris Courtney is too excited to sleep; it's the fever excitement that precedes one of her migraine attacks but she can't control it; she dresses hurriedly, slacks pulled up under her flannel nightgown and no underwear, bare feet thrust into boots, winter overcoat, nothing on her head and no gloves—no time for gloves—she runs in the cold sharp air two blocks to a telephone booth near an Esso station, there she drops coins into the telephone, dialing the operator panting as she requests directorial assistance, and even as she's being told the Hammond telephone number of "Verlyn Fairchild" she's forgetting it . . . she's defeated, makes no effort to remember. For how can she call Jinx now, so late at night, now or at any other time; how can she? *She* . . . who is *she?*

She hangs up, the coins fall down into the slot.

She presses her forehead against the cold plastic mechanism and shuts her eyes. This abject posture, preceding pain.

Iris Courtney has neither seen nor spoken with Jinx Fairchild for a very long time. She has no right to him, no right even to think of him really, he's the husband of a woman she doesn't know, he's the father of children, she has no right to telephone him and interfere with the distance between them and his indifference to her, she swears she doesn't even think of him much in her new life: except tonight she took up a knife in revenge for him . . . Jinx Fairchild's pride, honor, manhood debased in another.

Of course I didn't call. I never would. He'd think I was insane. It's impossible.

She feels too weak to leave the telephone booth and return to her room. So rare is it that remnants of her old life protrude into her new life, like shrapnel fragments working their way through flesh, she's shaken, can't quite comprehend what happened, or almost happened; she's thinking bitterly how far away her lover is, how maybe it's that man she hates, the knife so poised and steady in her hand.

Thanksgiving Day dawns cold, clear, frosty, a metallic taste to the air. Even the sky looks frozen . . . like frozen water, rippled and webbed. But Iris Courtney doesn't give it a glance.

This is the day, the holiday, she's been awaiting. With both anticipation and dread.

Undercutting her childish pleasure in the invitation by admonishing herself, It doesn't mean anything; he only feels sorry for you.

And, It's just charity. In his eyes "Iris Courtney" is a stray.

And, in her journal, where, a year later, she'll read the entry with astonishment: *Prediction: a mistake. But a minor mistake.*

If Iris Courtney had brought along to college with her, as relatives urged and common sense directed, a few of Persia's good, not too flamboyant dresses, she'd have something suitable to wear to an occasion special as Thanksgiving dinner at the home of Dr. Byron Savage: but of course, in the stubbornness of grief, she hadn't taken a thing. Couldn't bear even the sight of Persia's clothes, clothes purchased always and forever in the hope of achieving . . . whatever it is women hope to achieve by way of the purchase of pretty clothes.

Beside, Persia was a size ten; Iris is a size seven.

Thus out of desperation, two days before the dinner, Iris is forced to inveigle a friend into offering her the use of a dress: a lovely wool Lanz just slightly too large for her, with long graceful sleeves, a pleated skirt to mid-calf, a row of neat bone buttons. The fabric is heather-colored shot with threads of turquoise and gold, and in it Iris Courtney appears to advantage since the hazel of her eyes is heightened and her skin seems warmer, less translucent.

Regarding herself in the mirror in this dress Iris bites her lip, murmurs aloud, "Who is *that* . . . ?" Smiling with surprised pleasure.

A world of surfaces, many-faceted, infinite. And Iris Courtney one among many.

Yet what is art except surfaces? Works of art, photography, "the great tradition" in all its plenitude?

Surfaces by way of which, and by way of which exclusively, the interior world-soul shines.

If there is a world-soul. If it is capable of shining.

Since Dr. Savage is going to be in the university neighborhood picking up another of the Savages' guests for the holiday dinner, the widow of the late Dean of the Humanities, he picks up Iris Courtney too at her rooming house; no need for her to take a taxi. Arrives at 2117 South Salina promptly at four-thirty in his pearly-gray Lincoln Continental and Iris is waiting in the parlor with her coat on, hurries out to the curb, and climbs into the car's cushioned back seat; breathless she's borne off to the Savages' home in what must be a distant part of the city . . . Springdale Road bordering the golf course of the Onondaga Country Club.

There's a conversation between Dr. Savage and Mrs. Wells, the dean's widow, who is seated beside him in the front seat of the car, and from time to time Iris Courtney is obliged to contribute, or to reply to questions put to her, though she has very little idea of what she says. Dr. Savage is explaining that, over the years, the celebration of Thanksgiving dinner in their household has gradually shifted from early afternoon to early evening; he hopes their guests won't mind, but it seems more civilized somehow; Mrs. Wells reminisces warmly of holiday celebrations sixty years ago when she was a young girl, then turns with a smile to ask Iris Courtney what Iris's earliest memory of Thanksgiving is . . . and Iris hears herself say apologetically, "I'm afraid I really don't remember."

It's a puzzling answer. But neither Mrs. Wells nor Dr. Savage seems to notice; already they're talking about something else.

Then there's the surprise of the Savages' house.

Iris's first thought is, How monstrous.

Iris's second thought is, How beautiful . . . is that a *house?*

Iris had heard that Byron Savage is from a wealthy Syracuse family, that *The Journal of Art and Aesthetics* with its full-color cover and color plates is partly, perhaps wholly, funded by Dr. Savage himself, but she isn't prepared for the Victorian grandeur of the man's house. It's a craggy little mountain of tall peaked towers, Roman arches, massive walls and chimneys and pediments, a nightmare of grinning windows. When Dr. Savage turns up the winding drive Iris says breathlessly, and quite sincerely, "Oh, Dr. Savage is that . . . your *house?* It's like a castle. I've never seen anything like it."

Dr. Savage laughs as if he's both embarrassed and pleased.

He tells Iris that the house was built in the early 1900s by his father, Lawrence Savage; it's in an American architectural style known as "Richardsonian Romanesque," named for the architect Henry Hobson Richardson. The stone of the exterior is pink Missouri granite in certain of the pediments and purple Colorado sandstone elsewhere; all the sculpture detail was done by hand of course, by stone carvers brought from England; each of the gargoyle figures on the downspouts is distinct from the rest. "Some people think Romanesque is appallingly ugly and some think it very beautiful," says Dr. Savage, smiling, "but since I've lived here most of my life I'm not required to see it . . . I don't judge."

White-haired Mrs. Wells tells Iris, "Dr. Savage is being too modest. The Savage House, as it's called, is famous in this area. It's listed with the National Register of Historic Places. And it *is* beautiful, isn't it?"

Says Iris faintly, "Oh, yes."

In the waning November light the Savage House with its highly detailed, ornamental façade looks as if it were made of papier-mâché. It's a dream castle, a movie castle, yet so massive . . . so *weighty* in the eye . . . Iris Courtney wonders if, living in it, people come to resemble it.

"*Please* call me Gwendolyn."

Mrs. Savage takes Iris Courtney's hand in hers, not to shake it briskly but simply, for a moment, to hold it, her fingers warm and dry and assured. "So pleased to meet you, dear, and so delighted you can join us. Byron has said such good things about you . . . about your work on the *Journal* and as a student of his—you're doing a thesis with him, are you . . . and, ah, what else?—your good solid common sense in the office."

To these words, murmured in a rich melodic North Carolinian accent, Iris Courtney has no reply, just smiles sweetly.

Iris isn't doing a thesis with Dr. Savage, she's only an undergraduate. But the point is too minor to correct and, in any case, Dr. Savage hasn't overheard. Aswim in Mrs. Savage's cobalt-blue eyes Iris just smiles.

Gwendolyn Savage is an attractive, intensely feminine woman in her late fifties, with a soft moon-shaped powdered face, silvery-white hair, those striking blue eyes. She's short, inches shorter than Iris Courtney, but holds herself tall; there's something stately, even regal, about her posture, her voice, the assertion of her smile. She is wearing a black jersey dress with a draped satin apron front; her shoes are black suede; on her left breast there is a star-cluster diamond brooch, an antique-looking piece of jewelry, beautiful.

283

Beautiful too her diamond earrings and her rings. One of the rings glitters icy-blue . . . a star sapphire?

Persia's favorite "precious stone," as she called it.

Not that Persia Courtney had ever seen a star sapphire up close. Nor has Iris Courtney until this moment.

Later, noticing Iris standing in a corner of the reception room shy and stiffly smiling, staring at a little mud-colored Corot on the wall, Mrs. Savage reclaims her, introduces her to other guests . . . too many guests . . . their names fly past even as Iris shakes hands and repeats their names. (An old politician's trick, Duke Courtney said, repeating names: nothing is so sweet as the sound of one's name.) But Iris Courtney is too dazed to remember much: a professor of history and his wife, a tall bald gentleman in a cleric's costume who resembles Adlai Stevenson, a young Renaissance scholar known in the department as Dr. Savage's favored protégé. . . . She's even introduced again to Mrs. Wells and is about to shake Mrs. Wells's hand when the older woman says smilingly, "Ah, but we've already met! *Iris,* isn't it—or, no, *Irene?*"

Next, Dr. Savage himself advances upon Iris, intent on introducing her to . . . visiting professor, University of Rochester, specialist in the English neoclassic artist John Flaxman . . . this name too Iris doesn't catch.

Too many guests. The din of voices is alarming.

But a lovely room: a fifteen-foot beamed ceiling, white mahogany woodwork, stenciled wallpaper, Chinese import furnishings, a fire gaily blazing in the fireplace which Dr. Savage, abloom in the midst of his guests, frequently stokes. Above the mantel there's a mirror of old glass and absentmindedly Iris Courtney seeks her reflection in it . . . passes her own face by several times before recognizing it.

In the amiable crowd there's a sudden black face. A strong-boned walnut-stained face. Iris is alert, curious . . . but the black woman is wearing a maid's costume, passing glasses of sherry and tiny shrimp canapés on a silver tray. How she smiles, how happy she appears! A fattish woman, fattish smiling bunched-up cheeks. Smiling as she makes her way clockwise about the reception room presenting the tray to the Savages' guests, smiling as people take what's offered and murmur thanks without looking at her or, caught up in the intensity of their conversations, fail to murmur thanks. Not meaning to be rude of course and in this context not rude, surely?

Iris Courtney too, taking a glass of sherry, mumbles thanks without looking up. She's stricken with embarrassment, an almost physical shame. The senseless words run singsong through her mind *All the white cunts hot for Belafonte . . . all the white cunts hot for . . .*

As the time for dinner approaches it happens that some of the Savages' guests are leaving the house; evidently they were invited only for drinks. Iris's spirits rise tentatively.

The sherry, to which she's unaccustomed, has warmed her throat. There's even a curl of something in the pit of her belly, a tickle of sexual desire . . . this, too, senseless.

Mrs. Savage and an admiring little circle of women are standing around what appears to be a bishop's throne, out in the grand hallway. It's French Gothic, Mrs. Savage explains, stroking the beautifully carved oak with her beringed fingers, thirteenth century, *isn't* it exquisite! Iris Courtney joins the women with an air of schoolgirl interest. Mrs. Savage is saying that her husband's grandfather Ezra Savage became, in his old age, an avid, insatiable collector of good, old, solid things, things with the weight of time behind them: " 'The imprimatur of history,' Byron used to quote him. He died at the age of ninety-four, and they say he never had a day of illness."

Mrs. Savage is asked about Ezra Savage's background, and in an animated voice, as if the story were altogether new to her, Mrs. Savage tells the group how her husband's grandfather began his career in Syracuse as a woodware dealer at the age of fifteen.

Fifteen! Imagine!

So *young!*

Ezra Savage had in fact run away from his home in Liverpool, England, at the age of fourteen, in 1860. He emigrated alone to the United States, knowing no one, was hired by the pioneer dealer in woodware Matthias Goodwin in Albany, loaded a flatboat with woodware (broom handles, bowls, butter churns, ax handles) and started down the Hudson River, making stops at various settlements; by the time he reached Poughkeepsie he was completely sold out. So this enterprising young man returned to Albany, got more supplies, and went into business for himself in Syracuse in 1862 . . . his first store was downtown on State Street in the same block that Sibley's is now.

Says one of the admiring women, with a gesture meant to indicate the entire Savage House, "And the rest is history!"

Says Mrs. Savage, "It *is*."

Seeing that Mrs. Savage is smiling so warmly at her, with an air almost of expectation, Iris Courtney summons up her ingenuity to say thoughtfully, "History can be interpreted, some theorists think, as the story of just a few individuals' destinies . . . a few very special men, geniuses." It's an innocent paraphrase of a remark Dr. Savage is given to make frequently in his lectures; a remark Iris will one day discover is, in fact, a paraphrase of an aphorism of Nietzsche's. But in her ingenuous crystal-clear voice it sounds wholly spontaneous.

At any rate, Gwendolyn Savage doesn't recognize it. Her smile deepens, her lightly rouged cheeks dimple with pleasure. As if her own study of history has led her to this conclusion she says, "Oh, it *is!*"

Hypocrite.

Aren't you the one, though!

To accept Dr. Savage's invitation for Thanksgiving, Iris Courtney was obliged to break a previous engagement. Sorry, she'd said guiltily, but something has come up: I have to go home after all to Hammond.

She'd agreed to go to Cleveland with a friend, to meet his family; the young man is a doctoral candidate in chemistry at the university who imagines he's in love with Iris, and though Iris is not in love with him she'd said yes, thinking at the time yes; but when Dr. Savage tempted her with his invitation how could she resist?

Not that Iris Courtney is in love with Byron Savage as, it

might seem, some of the art history majors are in love with him, female and male; but she admires him very much. Simply to hear the man lecture, to read even cursorily one of his monographs or books, is to admire him.

And while Iris is fond of her friend Tom, who imagines he's in love with her and would like to buy her an engagement ring, she finds his high regard for her disconcerting since she knows it's based upon a misreading of her, a romantic illusion, or delusion, of a kind. Each time he says I love you, Iris must suppress the urge to say, But you don't know me! She foresees a time, and very soon, when she won't be able to bear the young man's groping impassioned kisses and his hesitant hands on her. And those words, those words, those empty words: *I love you, Iris.*

It isn't by design that Iris Courtney seems to have fallen into the practice of cultivating people, or allowing herself to be culti-vated by people, for temporary and expedient purposes . . . then to move on, or break away, or, simply, forget. She means nothing deliberate by her behavior with friends, acquaintances, would-be lovers . . . she's never cruel . . . and always reacts with surprise when others respond with anger. *What did I promise you? What did you imagine I meant?*

Iris knows that only two people in her lifetime have ever known her intimately enough to love her, or not-love her, and these are her mother Persia and Jinx Fairchild; and Persia is dead.

Before accepting Tom's invitation to go with him to Cleveland Iris had been planning vaguely to go to Hammond, to have Thanks-giving there with her uncle Leslie. That good-hearted, lonely man, whom in fact Iris does love—who writes to her often at college, calls her on the phone—thinks of her as his only link (Leslie doesn't say this, but Iris knows) with Persia. But Iris has grown impatient with her bachelor uncle's bachelor ways, and his eccentricities seem less charming to her now—indeed, the profession, or trade, of photog-raphy seems less attractive to her now—since her exposure to the high ground of art history and "the great tradition." Byron Savage doesn't so much as mention photography in his survey course.

But the plans to visit Hammond had been vague. And when

the invitation came from Tom, who imagines he's in love with Iris Courtney, Iris had said yes, yes why not, and canceled her plans with her uncle. Sorry sorry sorry, she'd said, quite sincerely, but something has come up.

Now Iris is thinking of these things, seated at the Savages' lavishly set dining table, listening eagerly to what is being said, staring with such intensity she feels the strain at the tender roots of her eyes.

Iris's cheeks will be permanently dimpled from so much smiling.

How warm, how gracious the company . . . these dozen or so men and women who, seeing Iris Courtney, see a guest of the Savages and accept her, at least for the evening, as someone like themselves.

And how lovely the dining room, which Mrs. Savage declares to the company is her favorite room in the entire house: the French crystal chandelier overhead glittering like ice; the French Empire table and chairs (the table has been opened out to accommodate twelve guests comfortably); the built-in English oak sideboard, elaborate as an altar, in Jacobean style; the Chinese carpet, all crimsons and greens, larger than any carpet Iris Courtney has ever seen in a private residence. From the remarks of others Iris knows that she's eating from Wedgwood china (the Parthenon-frieze design by John Flaxman, in fact), drinking from Waterford crystal; her silverware is Parisian, early nineteenth century; the white lace tablecloth is Portuguese, made by hand of course. And the gold-plated many-branched candelabrum with its tall slender candles . . . and the apple-green French moiré wall covering. . . .

So many courses! So much food!

Iris has difficulty with the first course, a heavily creamed lobster bisque, though it's delicious, she knows it's delicious, but she can swallow only a few mouthfuls and sets her spoon down unobtrusively by her bowl, seeing that Mrs. Savage sees . . . nothing at this table eludes Mrs. Savage's eye.

Then there's the giant turkey: Dr. Savage radiant with pleasure as he carves the turkey, expertly, yet with a good deal of hilarious banter on all sides.

And two kinds of stuffing (mushroom, oyster), and two kinds of cranberry sauce (sweet, tart), and whipped potatoes, and candied yams, and diced carrots, and several kinds of hot breads including cornbread. Never has Iris Courtney had so much food set before her in her lifetime, never has she felt so transfixed, so dazed, so . . . unreal. *Impossible for me to dissociate, since P., the spectacle of eating from the spectacle of vomiting.*

Still, Iris tries. With Mrs. Savage watching her and smiling, Iris tries.

From time to time during the course of the elaborate meal the black woman appears, to help Mrs. Savage serve her guests and to bear away dirtied plates and emptied bowls. Mrs. Savage introduces her to the company as Mercedes: "Mercedes" and no last name.

In her rich melodic North Carolinian accent Mrs. Savage declares she wouldn't know what to do without Mercedes.

Mercedes laughs, shakes her head, makes no audible reply. She's a husky, capable woman, walnut-dark skin, good-natured eyes. In her mid-fifties perhaps. Big drooping breasts, waist sliding into hips, her hairnet slightly askew on her oiled "pressed" hair. Moving behind Iris, resting one end of the heavy platter on the edge of the table, Mercedes exudes a fruity smoky odor.

When Iris hesitates, Mercedes says, half chiding, "Doan you want any more, honey? There's plenty!"

Moving about the long candlelit table with Mercedes and the platters of food, Mrs. Savage is flushed with happiness. She has slipped on a white ruffled apron over her black jersey dress, she's giving all credit for the meal to her mother, grandmother, great-grandmother . . . old recipes handed down through the family . . . dating back to Mary Washington herself: "That's her recipe for oyster stuffing. *Truly.*"

"You mean . . . George Washington's *mother?*"

"His mother. *Truly.*"

Dr. Savage is on his feet, pouring wine in his guests' many glasses as if nothing in the world could give him greater pleasure. Byron Savage, so radiant in his role of host, so seemingly transported . . . he's clearing his throat repeatedly but it's a contented sound, like a cat purring. All his guests adore him, and he adores his guests: "Just a little more, Emma dear? A touch of red? White? And you, Andrew? A little of both? Iris? No? Just a touch? Ah, yes, dear, good, you've hardly drunk any, and this is *special*, I think."

Dr. Savage is wearing a nattily checked suit with a glossy maroon vest, a holiday sort of vest, and a silk necktie affixed with a diamond stickpin.

"A touch more, Julie? And you, Gwendolyn, dear? Yes? Good!"

Flickering candlelight that glitters in the crystal overhead and in the crystal on the table, a small galaxy of winks and sparks.

White roses, baby-bud roses, in beautiful white and blue Wedgwood vases.

Iris Courtney drinks white wine, anxious to please.

She's staring hard. She's listening. And talking too, with surprising quickness, animation. Sitting very straight in her French Empire chair in her borrowed Lanz wool dress that brings out the hazel in her eyes and the faint golden glow of her skin. How is it possible that I am here? That "I" am here?

Dr. Savage is seated again, beaming with pleasure, and Mrs. Savage is seated again, fresh servings of food on everyone's plates, Mercedes unobtrusively in and out of the dining room, in and out of the kitchen through the soundless swinging door, the antique grandfather clock beside the sideboard companionably ticking, and talk resumes: . . . talk of art, talk of politics, talk of the university administration and of the university's football team and of mutual acquaintances not present, talk of the weather, talk of the space program, talk of President Kennedy who is, or is not, trustworthy, since the farce of the Bay of Pigs: "The man is a monster of egoism," says Dr. Sewall the history professor, with a look of distaste; "The man is our only *hope*," says Dr. Savage, throwing his hands into the air. For some minutes there is an intense conversation, very nearly a debate, which most of the company joins in but which is dominated by Dr. Savage, Dr. Sewall, and the Reverend Andrew Reed (the tall bald gentlemanly cleric is an Anglican minister), concerning the proposed Soviet-American nuclear peace pact, the central issue being whether the Soviets can be trusted, whether Marxists "who make no secret of their agenda" can be trusted, and whether in fact America's leaders can be trusted . . . and Iris Courtney sips wine and listens, wondering at the vigor, solemnity, and passion with which these men talk, as if their opinions, so forcibly uttered at the Savages' dinner table, Thanksgiving 1962, Springdale Road, Syracuse, New York, were of profound, lasting significance—were in fact expressions of political power.

As she often does at such times, in such pockets of time, Iris allows her thoughts to drift: there's the perpetual memory, or is it by now sheerly fantasy, of herself in Jinx Fairchild's arms, in his car above the river, Jinx Fairchild kissing her gently but teasingly— there was a playfulness to it, not mockery but playfulness, kissing her—touching and fondling and kissing her breasts, and she'd wanted him to make love to her but had not dared speak though in memory, in fantasy, she makes herself speak, she's brazen, reckless, a little crazy maybe . . . that curl of desire in her loins flaring up, up, up into flame. *I love you, I would die for you. You are the only real thing in my life.*

Now they're talking animatedly of travel: Italy, Greece. Mrs. Wells is reminiscing . . . Mr. Malone is recommending . . . Mrs. Savage is asking advice on . . . Dr. Savage makes everyone roar with laughter by telling an anecdote about. . . . Mrs. Sewall speaks of a recent visit to Amsterdam, and Dr. Reed speaks of a recent visit to London, and there's The Hague, that remarkable museum there, and in Washington the Phillips Collection, and there's Brussels to which Dr. Savage once journeyed solely to see the museum and, there, discovered to his horror . . . isn't that typical of travel: the unforeseen. There's Picasso who simply *continues.* There's Matisse . . . rather like Yeats in his old age. There's El Greco, there's Titian, there's Vermeer, on whom Dr. Savage's son Alan once worked, spending a year in the Netherlands, and he'd come up with some splendid things before, alas, "moving on" into the slovenly twentieth century . . . and there's Constable, with whom Dr. Savage is now engaged . . . and there's Bosch, whom Dr. Savage can bear only in small doses.

Dr. Reed speaks of Bosch's untitled triptych in the Prado Museum in Madrid, what a singularly unpleasant but powerful work, and Dr. Savage agrees; in fact as a young man he'd made a study of sorts of the painting's effect upon visitors to the gallery; he's entirely ambivalent about it himself, he's been puzzling over it for decades and has never felt certain that it is, or is not, a work of surpassing genius but surely it *is* a riddle: *The Garden of Earthly Delights,* so-called. And he jars Iris Courtney out of her hazy erotic trance by asking her what she thinks.

It isn't a cruel professorial tactic to trip up a daydreaming student, it's posed with genuine sincerity, even gallantry, but Iris Courtney is taken aback, feels the blood pound foolishly into her face. She's astonished that Dr. Savage should believe that she thinks anything at all on the subject or that her thoughts, impressionistic and random, should merit articulating, in such company at least. Stumblingly she says, "I . . . feel the same way, I suppose. In class, when you showed the slide, I could hear a collective intake of breath. . . . It *is* a code of some kind, at least on the surface." Dr. Savage questions Iris further, a benign sort of catechism, and by degrees she begins to speak more knowledgeably: not only has she studied the rudiments of Hieronymus Bosch with Dr. Savage but she proofread the galleys of a *Journal* article on an aspect of his iconography not long ago; thus she knows a fair amount, or can give a fair impression of so knowing, enough to acquit her with Dr. Savage and with the company at hand. Recklessly she concludes that the code of the work doesn't matter anyway, the "meaning" doesn't matter, it's the fact of the work, whether, seeing it, you are stopped dead in your tracks . . . nothing else matters.

"Oh, really! Is that so! *Really!*" Dr. Savage says, amused.

Others join in. Iris falls silent. She's embarrassed, chagrined, afterward she'll realize to her horror that she'd spoken disparagingly of the very enterprise of art history and of iconography, Dr. Savage's religion, Dr. Savage's life's blood, it's amazing he should let her off so easily.

Mercedes has been unobtrusively gathering up dirtied plates and cutlery, and as she heads for the swinging door, a weighty stack of china in her strong arms, Mrs. Savage's melodic voice rings out, not sharply, but on the edge of sharpness, "Those bottles, Mercedes—you've forgotten the wine bottles." Mercedes mumbles, "Yes, ma'am, comin' right back to get 'em."

Hearing this exchange Iris Courtney says, *"I'll* take them," jumping up impulsively from her chair before Mrs. Savage can protest. She snatches up the empty wine bottles and bears them off in the black woman's wake . . . brazenly out into the kitchen where no guest is welcome.

Thinking, Why am I doing this?

She sets the wine bottles down on one of the counters where there's space. How disappointing the Savages' kitchen is: old-fashioned fixtures . . . an immensely ugly stove . . . a single overhead light emitting a pitiless glare . . . dishes, pots, pans heaped on all sides . . . twin sinks filled with sudsy water and stacked with china. The air is heavy with the smells of turkey grease, gravy, and percolating coffee.

Mercedes is staring at Iris Courtney, this pushy white girl who is in *her* kitchen, uninvited . . . and Mercedes isn't smiling. The surprised, gruff-growling sound she makes only vaguely sounds like "Thank you."

But almost at once Mrs. Savage has pushed through the swinging door, diamond earrings glittering in alarm, and Mrs. Savage *is* smiling . . . smiling rather hard at Iris Courtney. "No need for you to help clear the table, dear," she says, reaching for Iris's arm. "You're our guest, you know!"

Iris resists the instinct to draw away. She says, "I get restless, just sitting. I don't like being waited on."

Mrs. Savage laughs as if Iris has said something clever.

"But that's what being a guest *is*, dear."

Her arm linked snug through Iris's, leading Iris back to the table.

Penetrating the voices of the company are a series of liquidy reverberating chimes.

Chiming the hour, the half hour, the quarter hour, and the hour again . . . to eternity.

Says Dr. Reed, beside Iris Courtney, showing his gums in a wide smile, "You almost don't mind the passing of time, do you, when it's heralded by such music!"

It's the tall ivory-faced grandfather clock beside the Jacobean sideboard: a Joseph Mills clock, they are told, ca. 1740, London. One of the most prized possessions of the late Lawrence Savage.

Misty-eyed Mrs. Wells fingers her rope of pearls, smiles at Iris Courtney across the width of the table. She says almost vehemently, "There *is* such beauty in the world, isn't there! I always feel, coming here to the Savages', that it compensates for the *other.*"

The remark is the sort of random social observation, uttered spontaneously and lyrically, that no one is obliged to answer.

Iris Courtney quickly smiles.

For dessert there are three delicacies, each from a recipe handed down through Gwendolyn Savage's family, the Makepeaces of Raleigh, North Carolina: a pumpkin pie with whipped cream, an airy prune whip, chocolate puddings in fluted little half-pint cups. Up and down the table Mrs. Savage is lavishly praised, praised most lavishly by Dr. Savage himself, who smiles at her adoringly. He clears his throat and says, "And my dear wife is as good as she is capable."

Mrs. Savage blushes prettily and says, "Oh, with these recipes, anyone could succeed. Truly."

Iris Courtney is no longer hungry but she spoons chocolate into her mouth and feels a powerful rush of sweetness, sweetness raw as pain flooding her mouth. Suddenly she wants to cry, Oh, Jesus, how she wants to cry . . . sitting at this table among strangers.

Two hours have passed. Two hours fifteen minutes. And still

the antique clock ticks on, its finely calibrated mechanism preparing for another outburst of chimes.

But the dinner is concluding, and talk has fragmented into smaller, more casual groups. It seems clear that most of the Savages' guests are intimately acquainted with one another. Iris hears Mrs. Wells inquire of Mrs. Savage in a gentle voice, "And how is Jenny, Gwendolyn?" and sees a flicker of dismay or hurt in Mrs. Savage's face as she says, "Oh, she's generally happier, we think. Sometimes it's hard to gauge. She has a new job . . . she's still living in Manhattan. Of course, as you can see, she isn't here with us today." There is more to be said but Mrs. Savage doesn't continue, and Mrs. Wells discreetly changes the subject: "Did I mention to you, Gwendolyn, Alan was *so* sweet, he remembered my birthday? Imagine! He sent me a lovely card from Paris this summer. How is he?" Mrs. Savage's expression brightens. She says, "Oh, Alan is *fine,* thank you; Alan is *very* fine, working enormously hard to get his book finished. Byron and he disagree about the merit of what he's doing—not the quality but the subject—but Alan did get a Guggenheim fellowship to do the research and Byron was delighted about that . . . you know, it isn't easy to be the son of Byron Savage *and* an art historian, people tend to be envious. But Alan has been doing very well, we think. He's still in Paris, we won't see him until Christmas; he's promised to come home for Christmas."

At this moment Mrs. Savage glances toward Iris Courtney, locks eyes with her, smiles. That lovely radiant smile. Throughout the meal she has drawn Iris into conversations, has asked her questions; now she asks, "Iris, where did you say you're from?" and Iris says, "Hammond, New York," and Mrs. Savage says, "Oh, yes, that's near Lake Ontario, isn't it, and near Rochester?" and Iris says, "Yes," and Mrs. Savage says, "And your family is from Hammond?" and Iris says hesitantly, as if uncertain of the question, "Yes," and Mrs. Savage says with a searching look, "And are your parents . . . ?" and Iris, who has been turning her dessert spoon slowly in her fingers, lays it down on her plate and says, with a slow shake of her head, "My mother died two years ago . . . of a long illness." She pauses. She hears Mrs. Savage and Mrs. Wells make murmurous sympathetic sounds but she doesn't look up. She says, with a slight stammer, "It was a peaceful death. I mean, at the end. I mean, she was at peace . . . at the end." She pauses again. She's breathing quickly and shallowly and her eyes are hot with tears. She says, "It was . . . no one's fault. They operated, but . . . " Her voice trails off; the grandfather clock begins its slow mellifluous chime. Again the older women murmur words of sympathy but Iris doesn't look up and Iris doesn't hear.

Then she's hurrying from the table . . . finds herself in the front hall . . . it's the guest bathroom she's seeking: this black-and-gold-papered little room, interior, windowless, a mirror with wavy glass in which her pale guilty face floats in the instant before the slow-gathering wave of nausea inside her breaks and she vomits out her guts in the toilet.

So it happens that Iris Courtney stays the night at Savage House. Seeing the condition she's in, both the Savages insist.

Iris is too weak, too sick, too frightened to protest. As the Savages help her up the stairs, to one of the guest rooms, she has to lean heavily on them . . . her legs are barely strong enough to support her.

They are murmuring words of consolation, encouragement. But Iris is too confused to hear. And sleepy: can't remember when she has been so sleepy in the presence of others.

Since the death.

Since the funeral when she slept twelve hours.

She's led to the room by Mrs. Savage, and how cavernous a room it is, how chilly, dark silk wallpaper in panels, twelve-foot ceiling, a braided carpet on the polished floorboards, the high canopied bed piled with bedclothes awaiting Iris Courtney's body.

Mrs. Savage is speaking in her kindly concerned voice: Here are towels, Iris, here is one of Jenny's nightgowns, Iris, one of Jenny's bathrobes, the bathroom is through that door, there is soap, there are toiletries in the . . . in the morning you'll feel much much better.

Iris is trying to explain something but the words won't come. Mrs. Savage sits beside her on the bed stroking her hand, squeezing the weak icy unresisting fingers, saying gently, Never do we know why, Iris, never never do we know why, why such things happen and we must bear such grief, such heartbreak for which we're unprepared, why God expects so much of us, what His plan for us is. Iris begins to cry. Iris begins to cry and stops. Forces herself to stop. Otherwise she'll begin to laugh. Talk of God, Duke Courtney used to say, is fancy jargon for "What's the odds?"

Iris manages too to forestall a violent attack of shivering until Mrs. Savage is gone and the door is safely closed. Then she undresses with slow clumsy fingers, she slips into the bed trembling with the need to sleep, the high hard-mattressed bed is like a boat adrift on a dark sea, heavy chilled sheets drawing her body's warmth from her, but Iris lies very still and unmoving *God help me God help me please help me* and eventually her body's warmth returns.

But by then she's asleep.

If I remember, it's in vague watery patches like any of my dreams.

6

"Here, kitty! Here, kitty-kitty-kitty! Here, Houdini! Where the hell are you?"

Leslie Courtney spends a half hour tramping in the stinging cold, coatless, bareheaded, nostrils pinched against the garbagey smell of the alley . . . and today has been one of his busiest days: a long morning session at Precious Blood Church photographing the choir, two portrait sittings after lunch, a week's work backlogged in the darkroom, and financial accounts to balance, and the telephone is probably ringing at this very moment, no one in the shop to answer it. Damn, Leslie is thinking, goddamn, he should have hired someone to help him out; the photography business invariably picks up in the weeks before Christmas and now it's less than a week and there's a barely controlled frenzy in the air you can almost smell, people driving their cars recklessly, customers vague and impatient not knowing what they want or how much they want to spend, Christmas carols blaring on all sides, the bright lurid silly-sentimental strings of lights up and down Main Street and the winking red and green lights Leslie Courtney feels obliged to tape around the border of the front window of Courtney's Photography Studio . . . there's a simpleminded cheerfulness to holiday lights you can't deny, whether you approve or not.

This intoxicated end-of-the-year atmosphere to which in theory Leslie Courtney should be immune (he's familyless, has no crucial presents to buy) but to which he seems to be vulnerable not only as a Hammond merchant but as a citizen of the United States.

Where Christmas isn't just an annual religious celebration, it *is* the religion. Crammed into a hectic week or two, then finished for another year.

He cups his hands to his mouth, bawling, "Houdini! Damn you! Kitty-kitty-*kitty!*"

Houdini the midnight-black cat with the stumpy tail and the frayed ear and the green-tawny eyes has been missing for nearly two days. Leslie Courtney can't bear to think that something might have happened to him, the damn cat is in his trust.

"Houdini? You know who this is! *Kitty*-kitty-kitty!"

Tramping through the snowy trashy alley where, if you stumble out of the rutted tire trails, you're in snow anywhere from six to eighteen inches deep. Past Ricardo's Shoes, past Aiken's Hardware, past the Hosiery Box, past Rexall's, the rear entrances of stores almost as familiar to Leslie Courtney as his own. Tonight, a Thursday, most of the downtown stores are open until nine.

It's pitiful, Leslie thinks, how merchants vie with one another to draw the customer *in*, hope to lure him into *buying*. A society where everything is for sale, all things have their prices. Making of its citizens prostitutes of varying degrees of success and failure.

His voice is becoming raw, despairing: "Houdini? Kitty?"

At the cross street, Sixth Street, Leslie pauses. His breath is steaming. He wonders if he should continue the search, following the alley another block, or should give up temporarily and go back home. The telephone might be ringing. Houdini might have come back in his absence. He's hungry and cold. It's six-thirty and pitch dark: December 20. Tomorrow is the darkest day, longest night, of the calendar year.

There's a steady stream of traffic on Sixth Street, the hissing of tires in slush. Across the street PIZZA STAR flashes in red neon. It's no place for an animal, even hardy street-wise Houdini. Leslie checks the gutters looking for the cat's corpse . . . steeling himself for what he can't believe he might actually find.

A man Leslie knows, by face rather than name, happens by, asks what the hell Leslie is doing, and Leslie says in a bemused voice that doesn't suggest his concern, "Oh, I'm looking for this damned cat that belongs to my niece; it's staying with me while she's at school." He's grateful the other doesn't linger to chat.

Leslie's teeth are chattering, the cold is penetrating his bones. His hair has become so thin in the past year he pointedly feels the cold, if he's hatless, like an eerie breath blowing slyly on his scalp. He decides to give up.

Hurrying back along the alley he calls, "Houdini!" a few more times, purses his lips, and whistles. That sharp piercing whistle sometimes has the power to rouse Houdini from his hiding place inside the house. When he's inside the house.

Leslie doesn't want to acknowledge how fearful he is, how sick he's beginning to feel. For what if, this time, Houdini *is* gone . . . his niece's beloved cat.

Leslie Courtney's living link, as he thinks of Houdini, with Persia Courtney.

Leslie enters his ground-floor apartment through the rear vestibule, a space about the size of a telephone booth, enters the kitchen, takes off his glasses at once to wipe the steam from the lenses. The telephone isn't ringing. The apartment is deathly silent, only the vibrating hum of the aged refrigerator that's as internalized as Leslie Courtney's own heartbeat.

He fits his glasses back on, adjusts the earpieces. The familiar room, the kitchen, leaps back into focus: but to what purpose?

That sick helpless feeling deep in the gut.

That sense of loss, irreparable loss: loss of which, if you want to remain sane, you must never think.

Mechanically, as he's in the habit of doing at least once a day, he opens one of the cupboard doors, checks the bottle of Seagram's high on the shelf. It's the only bottle of liquor. He no longer drinks hard liquor, not even wine, not even beer or ale, but he keeps the unopened bottle of Seagram's on the shelf. In case, some day or some night, he simply can't bear what his life has become . . . can't bear it.

When Persia was first hospitalized Leslie vowed he wouldn't take a single drink until she was well and discharged from the hospital, at which time he would celebrate the occasion with a drink . . . and he hasn't had a drink since.

There's a sense in which he's still waiting.

"Houdini? Are you in *here?*"

He checks the corner of the kitchen floor where the cat's bowls are kept, neatly on a sheet of newspaper: a bowl of water, a bowl of dry cat food. At first it seems to Leslie that some of the cat food has been eaten; then he decides it hasn't.

Misery mounting in him, he wanders through the rooms touching walls, pieces of furniture, like a blind man. He's seen these surroundings so many times he isn't required to see them again.

In the two years in which Iris's cat has been living with Leslie he has wandered away from home twice, but never as long as this. Both times before he'd returned excited and hungry, showing no signs of having been injured. This time, something must have happened to him: a fight with another tomcat, or with a dog, or an accident in the street.

It's one of the ironies of the situation that Leslie has a mild allergy to cat hair. That he often wakes with his sinuses packed and throbbing to discover Houdini snuggled up close beside him in his bed, atop the covers . . . the damned creature can force open Leslie's bedroom door in the night without disturbing him. And, once Leslie discovers him sleeping on the bed, he hasn't the heart to make him leave.

He's become absurdly fond of Houdini though he disapproves of the cat's sly ways, his pose of innocence until Leslie's back is turned, and, God knows, he's appalled sometimes by the animal's *hunger* . . . a nearly metaphysical hunger of the kind that can never be satisfied.

Whenever I see a picture of myself I think, There's proof: I really am here.

But the camera preserves images only. Images of things dying, or dead.

Iris said, tears streaking her face, I can't bear to see them! Take them away! Hide them!

So Leslie has removed most of the photographs of Persia and Persia-and-Iris from the front of the shop and has hung them on the walls of his bedroom. In rows, framed, under glass: the earliest was taken in May 1940, Persia Courtney as a lovely, very young bride in a ruffled white dress and a bridal veil; the last was taken in August 1955, here in the studio, Persia and Iris in their pretty summer dresses, seated side by side on the wicker love seat. In chronological order on Leslie's bedroom walls are images of a wide-browed smiling woman as she ages subtly yet unmistakably from girlhood to maturity: Persia in a strapless chiffon gown with her dashing husband Duke as "The Incomparable Courtneys" (one of a series of publicity photos Leslie volunteered to take); Persia just home from the hospital gazing dewy-eyed at her infant daughter nestled in her arms; Persia in a Rita Hayworth pose, smiling seductively at the camera, in an off-the-shoulder Spanish blouse; Persia with dark-defined lips and upswept hairdo, her little girl resting her head against Persia's shoulder and gazing too into the camera with frank smiling eyes . . . and so on and so forth. How many poses, how many years, now completed. The Persia Courtney Leslie last saw, being carried into the emergency room of Hammond General Hospital, a raving, delirious, jaundice-skinned woman with matted hair, bears no kinship to any of these images . . . none that Leslie can bring himself to acknowledge.

Leslie has hung the many photographs of Persia Courtney in his bedroom to spare Iris distress when Iris visits him, but Iris rarely visits now that she is in college. Iris is rarely in Hammond now that she is in college. Even her summers, if she can, she spends in part or wholly away from Hammond. And now there is a family in Syracuse, it seems, that has befriended her . . . she spoke evasively of them, and with girlish pride, the last time she called. She won't be coming home over the lengthy Christmas recess because she has so much schoolwork to do. And because this family—the Savages—has been kind enough to invite her for Christmas Eve and for other holiday events.

Leslie said, "I'll miss you, Iris, but I certainly understand."

Iris didn't say a word to that.

Leslie said, "As long as you're happy, Iris: that's the main thing."

Iris didn't say a word to that either.

Leslie Courtney is thinking of these things, sadly but not grievingly, for he isn't the kind of man to grieve over what's hopeless, as he develops prints in his darkroom until about nine o'clock when he stops to prepare himself a kind of supper. Leslie Courtney's bachelor meals are expeditious affairs but sometimes inspired: eggs whipped with cottage cheese and chunks of canned pineapple; greasy hamburger crumbled and stirred in the skillet amid sizzling onions, tomatoes, frozen corn kernels, all of it topped with melted Kraft's American cheese and dumped on white Wonder Bread. And it's in the kitchen as he fusses with what he's found in the refrigerator that he hears a furious scratching and muffled meowing close by, and opens the door to the cellar, and out bounds Houdini the midnight-black cat, purring in midair, twining himself around Leslie's legs, and trying to climb up his body with needle-sharp claws. Leslie is so astonished he forgets to be relieved: "Houdini! Where the hell have you been!"

Leslie stoops and pets the frantic cat and feeds him part of his supper—tonight, an old favorite, Spam heated and fork-crumbled in a pan of Campbell's cream of mushroom soup, dumped on white Wonder Bread—trying to figure out how Houdini can have been in the cellar all these hours, undetected. The cellar was one of the first places Leslie searched; and since Leslie has been in and out of the kitchen frequently during the past two days, he would certainly have heard the cat clawing at the door. And can Houdini *claw:* it's as if fresh-sharpened knives have been hacking at the wood.

Finally, unable to contain his curiosity, Leslie goes down into the cellar to investigate . . . finds one of the windows on the alley pushed in. So that's the explanation.

So Leslie Courtney's anxious vigil has a happy ending. And Leslie *is* happy . . . buoyed on waves of relief rising to euphoria. He sits in his cramped little kitchen scarcely minding saccharine-voiced Bing Crosby singing "I'm Dreaming of a White Christmas" over the radio, eating his Spam supper with Houdini at his feet eating and purring simultaneously. Many times in the course of this evening Leslie will murmur to the cat, "Damn you, Houdini, you really had me worried . . . don't ever do that again!"

He's thinking if he weren't an alcoholic, or alcoholic-prone, he'd pour himself some Seagram's, to celebrate.

This much is clear: sometime in the early hours of February 19, 1963, in an apartment on the eighth floor of a slum tenement on Randolph Street, Buffalo, New York, Sugar Baby Fairchild ("Woodrow Fairchild, Jr.," as the newspapers will identify him) meets with an appalling death: he's stabbed superficially a dozen times, pushed naked into a bathtub, covered with gallons of boiling water so that his skin reddens, blisters, bursts, peels away from his flesh, and, while he's still alive, his several killers stand over him jeering and urinating on him.

The incident, partly censored for home news consumption, will be reported in the Buffalo *Evening News* under the headline FIFTH KILLING AS RIVAL DRUG DEALERS FEUD, but the talk on the street in both Buffalo and Hammond is that Sugar Baby Fairchild's own boss Leo Lyman ordered him killed—assassinated in a "special" way—as a warning to other young niggers in his organization like Sugar Baby Fairchild who are possibly cheating him of small change and not paying him the respect he deserves.

When Jinx Fairchild is told the news, it's as if scalding water cascades down his own body: a pain, a horror, an infamy beyond words, that renders him speechless, paralyzed.

For days it lasts. Days and days. A smothering drowning cascading sensation inside his body and out like applause bouncing off the walls of a gym that just goes on and on . . . on and on . . . no end to it. Jinx pushes Sissy away when she tries to comfort him 'cause he doesn't trust that woman any longer (too many times she's tricked him, wheedled him into forgiving her, then tricked him again) and he can't face Minnie and Woodrow for a long time 'cause he can't imagine himself looking them in the eye, the terrible knowledge passing between them of how Sugar Baby died . . . not just the stabbing and the scalding water, so his body was near-unrecognizable, but his killers jeering at him, pissing on him, up to the very moment of his death.

The Buffalo police won't ever find Sugar Baby's killers, his murder is only one of a number of murders; it's the drug trade, heroin trade; it's black men killing one another . . . self-contained for the most part, like sharks in a feeding frenzy turning on themselves, devouring not only their own kind but occasionally, in maddened ecstasy, their own entrails spilling into the ocean.

Mrs. Savage has stopped asking Iris Courtney to call her Gwendolyn. But there is an air of both tenderness and conviction in the way Mrs. Savage calls Iris "Iris."

It seems that the older woman has taken a particular liking to the younger, since she invites Iris frequently to her home or conveys invitations to her by way of Dr. Savage: invitations to receptions for visiting speakers, to large heterogeneous dinners, an occasional smaller luncheon where the guests are all women . . . some of them young women in their twenties, the wives of junior faculty at the university. It becomes Mrs. Savage's custom to telephone Iris mid-week to ask if she might be free to come to the house for a simple family dinner, an early evening, nothing fancy; and Iris always accepts, Iris always accepts with gratitude, saying yes she'd like that very much, yes very much thank you Mrs. Savage, hanging up the phone, thinking, Why am I doing this? I'm never comfortable with these people.

Iris has become familiar with Mrs. Savage's manners and mannerisms: the southern accent, the voice inflections, the quick radiant smile and the slower, more contemplative smile in which, at times, there is an air of wistfulness . . . the frankness of the lovely cobalt-blue eyes, turned searchingly upon Iris *as if there is a question she wants to put to me she can't formulate.* For all Gwendolyn Savage's skill as a hostess, and the pleasure she so clearly takes in that role, she appears at times lonely: rarely alone, but lonely: as Iris Courtney, so frequently by her own design alone, is rarely lonely.

Several times, and never with less than consummate tact, Mrs. Savage has asked after Iris's mother, and Iris has provided a few, very few, details: the portrait that emerges of Persia Courtney is of a woman of unusual warmth, vitality, and strength of character who chose not to remarry after an early divorce and who was determined to support herself and her daughter without asking favors of relatives at a succession of low-paying jobs (sales clerk, typist, librarian's assistant), a woman who displayed not only extraordinary courage in facing her final illness but who tried to the very end to shield her daughter from guessing the extent of her suffering. Mrs. Savage is warmly sympathetic; Mrs. Savage says in a hushed murmur, "Your mother sounds like a remarkable woman, Iris, you were lucky, you know, to have *had* her . . . to have had the blessing of her. There have been such strong, selfless, unfailingly good women in my family too, and Byron's mother, with whom I was very close, was exemplary . . . a sort of model, truly. Your mother was a religious woman?"

Iris says hesitantly, "Mother didn't belong to any congregation but, yes, she was naturally religious . . . she seemed to believe."

Mrs. Savage murmurs, "Ah, then, that's enough! I'm sure that's enough!"

The remark is made in all innocence, merely one of Mrs. Savage's commiserative asides, but Iris Courtney feels a prick of something like anger: Really? Is it "enough"? And "enough" for what, entry into your smug Christian heaven?

On the subject of Iris's problematic father, so long absent from her life, Mrs. Savage has been even more tactful. Iris has suggested that her father is a politician of some kind . . . in one of the western states. She remembers him as a very busy man, a brisk, steely-eyed man; she hasn't seen him since she was five years old but bears him no ill will since her mother bore him no ill will: just said, simply, that the marriage had not worked out and never dwelled upon it. Listening, Mrs. Savage nods gravely; it's clear she is impressed with the pluck, the hardiness, the determination, the extraordinary strength of character of Iris Courtney's mother, Persia.

She says, sighing, "Even her name is so beautiful. . . ."

In turn, Mrs. Savage has confided in Iris . . . always somewhat obliquely.

She has suggested that she and her husband are not altogether happy with the life their twenty-seven-year-old daughter Jenny is leading but she has not said why, specifically, except that Jenny is "indecisive" . . . Jenny has "difficulties" with men . . . Jenny rarely telephones, never writes, and lives a life her parents can't "understand." She shows Iris a number of snapshots of a dark-haired, stocky, rather plain young woman, several of them photographed on a tennis court in stark overhead sunshine. Iris perceives in this daughter of the Savages an obdurate, stony spirit bearing very little resemblance to either parent.

About Alan, the Savages' thirty-one-year-old son, former Rhodes scholar, current Guggenheim fellow, so bright, so industrious, so serious, and so unfailingly sweet, Mrs. Savage is far more optimistic. "I'm truly sorry that Alan didn't get home for Christmas as he'd hoped to," Mrs. Savage says, "but it's a long way from Paris . . . he seems so *involved* there. You'll meet, though, Iris, I'm sure, very soon. And I think you'll like each other immensely."

As if she has been trusted with an artifact both precious and mysterious, Iris studies the slender, boyish, dark-haired young man of the family snapshots, seeing in his narrow, tensely smiling face certain of the distinctive features of his mother: the set of the eyes, the lean Roman nose, something soft and provisional about the mouth. She says thoughtfully, "Yes, Mrs. Savage, I'm sure we will."

Only afterward does she realize her slip of the tongue. But so far as she can recall, Mrs. Savage seemed to notice nothing. She rarely does.

Mrs. Savage has confided in her young friend Iris that Byron Savage is both the most remarkable man she has ever encountered and one of the most exasperating. Yet even Mrs. Savage's complaints turn mild in her mouth, domestic and wifely: "That man is possessed of such energy, such willfulness, I've long ago stopped trying to keep up!" And: "I'd known as a young bride that it would be a true challenge to live with an intellectual genius, but, Lord, I had no idea!"

She has confided too, in more somber moments, often at the end of a social occasion when she and Iris are alone together awaiting the taxi that, prepaid, will bear Iris back to South Salina Street, that her religion is "of paramount significance" in her life. She was born and baptized Presbyterian, made her "decision for Christ" when she was thirteen years old, and has never wavered in her faith . . . despite tribulations, heartaches, betrayals. "I don't simply *believe* in God," Mrs. Savage declares in her exclamatory mid-southern accent, "I *know* there is God. And I know that He lives in us. Truly."

To this, Iris can think of no appropriate reply.

Mrs. Savage continues warmly, "It seems clear to me that God reveals Himself to us when He is needed, but not otherwise. For the sacred presence is so powerful, Iris, it makes the remainder of the world seem shrunken."

"Does it!" Iris murmurs, shivering.

She finds herself staring out the window at the mottled late-winter sky, fearing she'll find it shrunken. It *is* bleached out.

Thinking afterward, borne away by taxi back into the city of Syracuse and the busyness of more ordinary lives, How easy, if you're a Savage, to believe in God! Seeing that, obviously, God believes in *you*.

With the passage of months Iris Courtney gradually draws away from her friends, friends her own age, including the young man who imagines he's in love with her; the Savages, in their undemanding way, demand all her concentration. When she doesn't visit with them she stays in her room on the topmost floor of the shabby redbrick house on South Salina Street, preparing her course work, plotting and dreaming her life. In her imagination Gwendolyn and Byron Savage take on the luminosity of gigantic dream figures whose dimensions can only be sensed, not observed.

Under Dr. Savage's guidance she is becoming more career-minded.

Under Mrs. Savage's guidance she is becoming more self-effacing, more feminine.

Occasionally Iris will challenge a dogmatic remark of Dr. Savage's and the two of them will talk together animatedly, with a heady intellectual passion. Less frequently, Iris will challenge a remark of Mrs. Savage's but the two of them never precisely disagree . . . such head-on confrontations are not Mrs. Savage's style. (When the subject of Martin Luther King comes up, in connection with King's proposed civil rights rally in Washington, D.C., in late August of 1963, Mrs. Savage says, "I do admire Reverend King, it's a blessing from God that the Negroes have such a saintly leader. If it weren't for him there'd be such *anger* everywhere," and Iris says impulsively, "But not to be angry, for some people, is hypocritical," and Mrs. Savage says, "Oh!" in a small, still, quizzical hurt voice . . . and changes the subject.)

Though Mrs. Savage is convinced that she and Byron are poles apart in temperament, let alone intelligence, Iris perceives, as she comes to know them more intimately, that the couple is perfectly matched. Each is in possession of a dazzling amplitude of spirit curiously constrained, finely and sharply focused, like a powerful beacon of light shining into the darkness that illuminates not the darkness but its own trajectory of vision. For all her amusing complaints of busyness Gwendolyn Savage is happily caught up in the cyclical tasks of domestic and social life while showing little awareness of, let alone concern for, much that lies beyond this life; while Byron, though ebullient with talk of the issues of the day, focuses his prodigious analytical mind exclusively upon his field of specialization: yet, within that field (Renaissance, eighteenth- and nineteenth-century European art), upon minor iconographic and historical problems beside which works of art seem sometimes mere illustrations, proof. Iris perceives too that her friends' very magnanimity is granted them by means of an infrastructure that surrounds and protects them yet remains unexamined as the air they breathe: their inherited wealth, their social position, the color of their skin. The Savages' great good fortune is an accident of history they seem to assume is not accidental but natural . . . their God-given birthright.

Impossible, Iris Courtney thinks. These people.

So good, so generous, yet so *smug*.

Still, when the telephone rings downstairs and Iris is called to answer it, her heart leaps at the prospect of an invitation from Mrs. Savage . . . never, never does she say no.

What am I but a sort of mirror or reflector for them, beaming back their happiness to them? Magnifying their happiness to them?

And do I mind?

9

Ah: a luminosity as of liquid fire spilled into her veins and turned her radiant. Where there was the darkness of the mere body, the diseased uterus, there flowed fire.

It entered through a vein, a delicate blue vein on the inside of her left wrist.

She died, her skull opened onto blackness . . . a roaring assailed her . . . there was God in His glory as a beacon of light searing but not blinding speaking not in words yet unmistakable His wisdom: Gwendolyn my daughter your childbearing years are over but others will bear children in your place and these children you will hold in your arms and love as if they were your own babies of your blood and desire and these children in turn will bear children and these children in their turn to the very end of human time thus when she woke from the anesthetic (seemingly within seconds: the two-hour operation performed on her body was swift as a flash of lightning in her brain) she was buoyed upon God's certainty and the unflagging joy of this certainty beneath the terrible pain of which she could not in her weakened state speak, and as she regained her strength in the days following in the hospital, and then at home, she dared not speak except obliquely to her dear young friend Iris.

What do I fear, Iris, that others might think me mad?—a God-struck lunatic of the kind, in my girlhood, my family abhorred?—the Negro sidewalk preacher shouting and wailing Jesus! Jesus! Jesus! and the hill people shrieking in tongues dancing in ecstasy holding poisonous snakes aloft or twining them around their necks, kissing their mouths these creatures of Satan rendered harmless by Jesus's love but in truth she dared not say such things even to her young friend Iris for fear of revealing weakness to her, confiding too impulsively in her (who surely looks to Gwendolyn Savage for strength), spilling her heart's inchoate desire as one must never do, as Gwendolyn Makepeace was counseled never to do, *For once a truth is known it cannot be unknown, it can only be denied,* her mother's own wisdom and that of her mother's mother, *For once a truth is known it cannot be unknown, it can only be denied,* better silence, better muteness, even in delirium muteness, for there was Byron above her gripping her hands in both his hands his strong capable hands as she rose from the anesthetic thick as fog in her brain, her beloved husband Byron calling to her across the distance telling her the operation was successful she was going to be all right telling her he loved her loved her loved her how brave and good a woman she was though confessing to her days afterward, when she was home, no longer an invalid though weak on her feet and still on a regimen of painkilling pills, confessing it had been one of the shocks of his life seeing her in the postoperative room so aged, so worn, so pale, her face like a mask, waxen and white as a death mask; he'd come close to breaking down having denied the seriousness of the impending operation and not having so much as a single time uttered the dread word *tumor* as if it were an obscenity somehow seeded in his beloved wife's body of which no gentleman could speak, confessing, I knew then I could not live without you my beloved Gwendolyn I realize I am a selfish man a self-absorbed man a creature of infinite vanity but I am no one without you my dear, my darling wife, and though dazed with pain and painkilling

314

pills she knew she must comfort him, she must soothe him, perhaps in his childlike way he had blamed her for the obscenity in her womb and now she was obliged to comfort him, poor Byron Savage to whom the most trivial interruption of his daily schedule is a matter of profound grief, the orderliness of the Savage household from the time the children were babies is a phenomenon wholly unexamined, as natural and as unquestioned to him as the laws of Euclidean geometry, and as impersonal in its workings, never to Byron Savage could she speak of her experience under the anesthetic the touch of God's fire in her brain, *For once a truth is known it cannot be unknown, it can only be denied,* and though she was deeply hurt that her own daughter failed to visit her, telephoned only three times, she rejoiced in the company of her young woman friend Iris in whose face that first day in the hospital she saw such raw fright she understood *Yes there's love, there's love that cannot be simulated* though she would certainly never embarrass the girl or herself by speaking in such a way except obliquely perhaps or, as now, by an exchange of glances, a quicksilver exchange of smiles, though it's true that more than once during the course of her convalescence when Iris came to visit, remaining with her for hours, so sweetly solicitous, so cheering, sometimes reading aloud to her (*Pride and Prejudice, Sense and Sensibility, Emma*—these novels Gwendolyn has read and reread since the age of eighteen, never tiring of so much as a single line) and sometimes simply sitting quietly listening to the birds in the garden yes she'd yearned to tell her friend of God's luminosity pouring through her veins and God's promise that children of her blood and desire would be borne not by her (who has been too old in any case to bear children for years) but by way of her and these children in their turn will bear children to the very end of human time yet certainly Gwendolyn Savage didn't say such a thing though thinking *Iris, how is it we lack speech; who has deprived us of speech?* for all that Gwendolyn Savage is so articulate and practiced in speech of another kind, inquiring of her guests who will have coffee? who will have tea? a little honey in your tea? though once boldly and humorously (in July, on an afternoon she was feeling exceptionally fine) she'd remarked to Iris that she didn't at all mind the removal of her uterus any more than she'd minded the cessation of menstruation; indeed, she assured Iris, there are losses in growing older one scarcely misses or even realizes that one should miss, and Iris smiled at her with a look of relief but did not ask of Gwendolyn Savage what those losses are.

Filthy habit, smoking . . . and Carter's strong-smelling parchment-colored Algerian cigarettes make it all the worse.

He's saying reproachfully, exhaling smoke in thin curling tusks, raising his voice to be heard over the din of the café, "*Alan, tu sais que tu es irresponsable . . . perfide. Moi, je—*"

Alan Savage says sharply, "Speak English, for Christ's sake: you aren't French and neither am I."

Carter stares at Alan Savage for a long astonished moment, the outburst is so uncharacteristic. Then, hurt, fumbling with his cigarette: "I thought we'd come here to talk. To understand each other. French, English, what difference does it . . ."

His voice trails off. The men sit silently, not looking at each other. Alan Savage feels his face heat, a vein begin to throb alarmingly in his head. Where is the waiter? A party of Americans enters the café, two couples in expensive sports clothes. Don't sit by us, Alan Savage thinks. The American voices, broad midwestern accents, are jarring to the ear.

It's summer. Paris will shortly be emptying out. But the café in which the two men are sitting, on the place Saint-Sulpice, one of numerous undistinguished neighborhood cafés Alan Savage has frequented in the past year, is companionably crowded, buzzing with voices.

In the near distance the bells of Saint-Sulpice begin. Alan wonders if it's possible to have heard these bells and to have felt one's heart curiously torn by them too many times.

11

It's as if a lighted candle were thrust up close to her face, Iris Courtney smiles so beautifully.

She's wearing a crocheted summer sweater, turquoise threaded with white. And white linen Bermuda shorts . . . given to her by Gwendolyn Savage, who'd bought them for herself earlier in the summer, wore them less than an hour, decided such fashions were no longer for her.

Alan Savage, shaking Iris's hand, staring at her, says, "Iris Courtney! I almost feel we know each other already, my mother has written me so much about you."

The young man's words are either lightly ironic or a simple statement of fact, Iris can't determine. She senses that Alan Savage is one of those persons who speak ambiguously because their reading of the world and of others is ambiguous and ambivalent. But his handshake is forthright and friendly, and here on the lakeside terrace of the Savages' splendid white-shingled summer house in Skaneateles, New York, in late August of 1963, Iris Courtney's happiness is suddenly effervescent as a bottle of sparkling water violently shaken.

All three of the Savages looking on, she says, "Well. Your mother hasn't told me a word about you," and naturally they laugh in delight; Dr. Savage's laughter is always explosive and hearty, wonderfully infectious, and Iris's vision mists over in the warmth and wonder and hope of the moment even as she's calmly calculating: Families like to laugh together: remember that.

And all that long lovely summer Sunday Byron Savage continues to laugh, heartily and infectiously, and Gwendolyn Savage is the most radiantly happy she has been since her surgery the previous spring, and Alan Savage, temperamental Alan who has been since early boyhood edgy and sardonic and as nervously restless in company as a whippet, one of those highly bred dogs that love to run—indeed, live primarily to run, their hearts beating naturally only when they run—is gradually eased into relaxing . . . for Iris Courtney's shining presence amid the Savages is a subtle altering of the old family equation that no one, not even Mrs. Savage, who has been eager for a very long time for her son and her new young woman friend to meet, quite anticipated.

That long lovely summer Sunday: Mrs. Savage whispers in her husband's ear, in quiet triumph, "Aren't they a perfect couple! Aren't they getting along well! Didn't I tell you!" and Dr. Savage, who perceives his wife's maternal solicitude in this as in other instances as a finely calibrated species of female hysteria, simply smiles his enigmatic smile and places a forefinger over his lips and says, "Gwendolyn, love: caution."

Says Mrs. Savage, mildly offended by her husband's obtuseness, "Oh, of course, Byron. I know."

It might be the case that Byron Savage hopes for the union, if there is to be a union, if it isn't entirely female fantasizing, as much as Gwendolyn Savage . . . for he knows a good deal more than she why marriage, and marriage fairly quickly, might be well advised for their son. And this little Iris Courtney, despite her shadowy background, might be ideal: she's an outstanding student, she's a very beautiful young woman, she's clearly yet not cravenly adoring of Byron Savage.

Before dinner, there's a rowdy game of croquet played on the grassy slope above the lake, with Mrs. Savage looking on. This long lovely summer Sunday shading into dusk.

Below, Skaneateles Lake mirrors the flawless sky, bluest of blues.

And there's blue in the Savages' immaculately tended lawn: hydrangeas, Mrs. Savage's favorite flower.

The croquet game, played by the Savages, father and son, and Iris Courtney and three local guests, is alternately serious and slapdash. Sitting in a canvas chair close by, Mrs. Savage is caught up in the action; she's the kind of sympathetic spectator who is always caught up in others' games and never very good at games herself . . . forthright competition wasn't part of Gwendolyn Savage's upbringing. But now she's gaily absorbed in the players' antics: roguish Dr. Savage, who swings his mallet with such gusto the others cringe, and beetle-browed Alan, who plans his moves shrewdly, then swings wildly and misses or scores by default, muttering in comic deadpan, "It's only a game! Only a game!" and Iris Courtney, who has never gripped a croquet mallet in her hands before today yet whose playing is so inspired . . . and so funny. If one of the chipped balls ricochets off a wicket, or flies into the hedge, or rolls drunkenly down the hill, it is invariably Iris Courtney's, and much good-natured hilarity attends the retrieving of these balls . . . old and battered as they are, dating back, in the Savage family's history, to when the children were very young.

From time to time Mrs. Savage calls out breathlessly, "Iris, don't let Byron distract you—take care!" And, "Iris, you're learning! Lord, are you *learning!*" And, "Now, Alan, *you* take care, don't get reckless!"

Since her operation the previous spring (that operation of which, in mixed company in particular, Mrs. Savage is loath to speak), Mrs. Savage has been frequently breathless and tires easily, but today she's clearly the happiest she has been in a very long time.

In another minute she'll go into the house to oversee the preparation of the evening's dinner, but for the moment she's intent upon watching the game: watching Iris Courtney, who's so clumsy and graceful at the same time, and such an attractive girl, the color up in her face, her springy hair laced with silver like frostwork, her young body quivering with life . . . lean, lightly tanned legs spread, as she swings her mallet with an athlete's natural sense of equilibrium. Mrs. Savage sees a gleam of perspiration on Iris's face and hopes the girl won't overheat herself and turn suddenly sullen, like poor Jenny, years ago.

Jennifer Savage, never good at games, always bested by her older brother.

Thinks Iris Courtney, quickly showering and changing her clothes for dinner, This is the happiest day of my life . . . isn't it?

In her delicate, musical voice Gwendolyn Savage calls out, "Will you all please come in? Dinner is ready."

Dinner is served, not in the house but on a screened-in porch at the rear of the house, overlooking the dark-glittering lake; the table is circular, glass-topped, made of wrought iron painted white. There are four guests, including Iris Courtney, who has begun to perceive the advantage of a public domesticity, to alleviate the difficulties of marriage.

"How lovely!"

"The night air . . ."

". . . the lake, can't you?"

". . . a smell of autumn."

A young black woman has been brought out from Syracuse to help Mrs. Savage serve dinner: her name is "Evie" or "Ava," it isn't clear which.

She smiles at everyone and no one. A gold filling prominent between her two front teeth.

Drawn by the glimmering pale heat of the candle flames,

moths and other insects throw themselves repeatedly against the screen, but very few penetrate it, and there are no mosquitoes at all. "Thank God," says Dr. Savage, with a humorous little shudder. "If there's one insect I can't abide, it's the mosquito."

Says Alan Savage slyly, engrossed in cutting his food on his plate, "That's probably because you haven't had much experience with the bedbug, Father."

Iris hears Mrs. Savage's intake of breath. Tactfully, no one pursues the subject.

Instead, there's talk of sailing on Skaneateles Lake, the most beautiful of the Finger Lakes, where motorboats are forbidden; and the local summer stock production of *Porgy and Bess,* which is so moving and authentic-seeming; and the Moscow–Washington, D.C. telephone hot line installed this very day in the hope of preventing an accidental nuclear war ("Which doesn't prevent the possibility of a deliberate nuclear war," Dr. Savage wryly observes); and the wayward manners of a prominent resident's sheepdog; and since Alan Savage is newly returned from Europe there is a good deal of talk—reminiscing, speculative, complaining—of Europe; and there are discreet inquiries into Mrs. Savage's health and Alan Savage's future plans (he'll be dividing his time between Syracuse and New York, completing his research on the Surrealist artist Man Ray primarily, visiting Boston too, and the Rare Book and Manuscript Library at Yale); and Byron Savage's future plans (he'll be on sabbatical from Syracuse University but he will continue to edit *The Journal of Art and Aesthetics* between trips to London for purposes of research and his lectures on Constable at the Courtauld Institute); there is a generalized lament for the passing of summer . . . the fact of cooler nights, the scent of autumn, the approach of winter. Conversation rippling and rhythmic as music, and a celebratory air beneath it—though what, at such times, *is* being celebrated? Iris Courtney wonders.

She's happy, she's hardly listening. Candlelight blazing in her eyes.

Seated beside Dr. Savage on her left and a middle-aged man named Flann or Flynn on her right, almost directly across from

Alan Savage, who in this dreamy muted light more clearly resembles his mother than he had outdoors on the lawn, and many times during the ninety-minute meal Iris feels his eyes shift onto her . . . hook onto her. Though he doesn't in fact address her directly at all.

And she lifts her gaze to his and smiles.

Thinking calmly, You're the one.

Her heart beating calmly against her ribs, You're the one.

She sees that the son lacks the father's spirit, yes, she perceives that at once; very likely he lacks the mother's warmth too, that can't be helped. But he's an attractive man. His hair curling over his shirt collar, his skeptical smile, slender shoulders, preoccupied air, brusque at times, yet kindly . . . yes, Iris is certain that Alan Savage is kindly, in his heart.

Mrs. Savage's word for him is "sweet."

It's a word Mrs. Savage employs as the highest praise: "sweet."

Iris wonders if she, Iris Courtney, has been described to Alan Savage as "sweet."

Thinks Iris, smiling, Am I sweet?

It's memory, or is it fantasy, the way Jinx Fairchild cupped her breasts in his hands, kissed and sucked at the nipples, in play, only in play, Mmmmmmmm, little sweetheart! he'd said. But only in play.

White titties. Black nigger cock.

Only in play.

Iris Courtney has been quiet, though giving every appearance of listening attentively to her elders, listening and laughing and wonderfully absorbed, so like Gwendolyn Savage in this respect, so feminine. She wears crimson lipstick for these occasions, and it suits her. Powders her face with a pale apricot powder, and it suits her. Jewels for eyes. Fragrance behind each ear. A ready smile, intelligent sense of humor. She knows she's approved of, otherwise she would not be a guest at this table to which Persia Courtney in all the beauty and charm of her youth would never never never have been invited.

Seeing that Iris hasn't been actively involved in any conversation, Mrs. Savage adroitly draws her out, as Mrs. Savage never fails to do, and there's talk for a brief while of Iris's course work at the university, and is she going to continue to live in that dreary place on Salina Street (Mrs. Savage has seen the rooming house from the street), and does she like Skaneateles . . . it *is* beautiful, isn't it; the Savages have been coming here for thirty years. Iris agrees that the lake is beautiful. Iris says that the lake is the most beautiful lake she has ever seen. One of the other guests, a stocky middle-aged woman with a braid down her back, a "summer artist" as she calls herself, tells a story of a tragic sailing accident here some summers ago, two young people drowning in a sudden gale, and after a pause Iris Courtney speaks of a tragic boating accident when she was a small child. Her father was involved in local Hammond politics, and the Hammond mayor took a number of his friends and their families out on his yacht, on the Erie Canal, and somehow, Iris isn't quite sure how, it happened that a boy fell over the side and drowned—a red-haired boy she remembers distinctly, about eleven years old—maybe in fact the boy had meant to swim from the side of the yacht; maybe the yacht was docked and most of the adults had gone ashore, Iris can't remember the details. She has no idea why she is telling the Savages and their guests this story but she's speaking rapidly, breathlessly now, sweat breaking out on her forehead and in her armpits . . . a strange quavering to her voice like the quavering of candle flame . . . and it's the reflection of candle flame in the glass-topped table she's staring at, saying she was too young she can't remember her only clear memory of that day is the sight of the red-haired boy's body being lifted from the water, the way the earthen-colored water streamed from him, making his features look for a moment or two almost as if he were alive.

She hears her voice rapid and headlong, unable to stop.

Though she knows these people, these strangers, are staring at her, perplexed.

"You don't forget. Some things you see, you're a witness to, you never forget. Even if there's no . . ."

Her voice wavers and goes out, her mind too seems to have gone blank.

She senses in a panic that Dr. Savage and Mrs. Savage who are so fond of her are exchanging a startled glance, that she has backed herself into a corner, embarrassing her listeners, and, summoning up her ingenuity, she shakes her head as if she too is perplexed, laughs, makes a joke of it, saying, with just the right degree of appeal and helplessness, "Which is why, I think, I never learned to swim. I'm afraid of the water and I never learned to swim."

Both Byron Savage and Alan Savage say, at once, "I'll teach you."

Says Iris Courtney, laying down her napkin and rising quickly from her chair when the black woman appears, "Now, Mrs. Savage, let *me*," and in her role as convalescent Mrs. Savage acquiesces with a weak, pleased smile; by this time Iris Courtney is so much a part of the family it seems quite natural for her to help out with a meal now and then in Mrs. Savage's place.

In the kitchen Iris says to the black woman, "It's always so friendly at the Savages', isn't it?" and the black woman nods emphatically, "Yes'm, sure is," the gold filling winking between her two front teeth, and Iris says uncertainly, "You're from Syracuse?" and the woman says, "Yes'm, I am," as they stack dishes in the sink, set out cups and saucers on a tray, and Iris has something further to say but suddenly can't remember what it is, she's aware of the black woman watching her out of the corner of her eye, a certain tension between them, the black woman is solid, slender, about forty years of age, beautiful purplish-black skin like Jinx Fairchild's and, like his, scintillating with myriad pinpoints of light . . . Iris Courtney has something further to say or to ask but she can't remember and in any case there's no time to waste; the coffeepot is percolating, a rich luscious coffee aroma fills the kitchen.

The candles have burnt to a quarter of their original lengths but the moths continue to throw themselves against the screen, soft *pings!* barely audible against the saw-notched singing of the crickets.

There's a breeze bearing a chill up from the lake. A frank smell of autumn.

Says Alan Savage, who has been asked about his work by the

326

woman with the braid down her back, "Art is art for a specific time and a specific place; 'art for all the ages' is bogus," and as he speaks in his carefully modulated voice in which Iris Courtney can hear, so very subtly, the cadences of North Carolina, Byron Savage begins to clear his throat with more and more force, and drums his fingers on the edge of the glass table with more and more impatience, until, when Alan says, "As Man Ray says, what is art but 'the giving of restlessness a material form,' " Dr. Savage suddenly explodes, saying, "I hope art is more than that! More transcendent, I hope, than that! Mere *nerves!* Mere *twitches!*"

There follow then some minutes of sharp disagreement between father and son, and Mrs. Savage who has been looking very tired now looks very upset, and the woman with the braid down her back tries humorously to intervene but without success, and finally, after a virtual monologue by Dr. Savage the substance of which Iris Courtney has heard many times, in different forms, Alan Savage laughs and says, addressing Iris, "The Surrealists believed that personal history is irrelevant, your family background, childhood, all that's merely personal; they believed you must erase the past and begin at zero, and you can see the logic of it, can't you, Iris? At such times?"

Iris Courtney sits staring, wordless. For the first time since her arrival at Skaneateles Lake she cannot think of a reply.

Iris! Where are you going?

Downstairs in the cavernous foyer the floor is fake marble and polished to a cheap sheen; upstairs the corridors are laid with carpets no-color and ratty with age.

It's all interior. Windowless. A sharp medicinal odor to the air. Rows of office doors stretching out of sight . . . opaque glass in the doors . . . names painted in uniform black letters with the initials M.D. or D.D.S. after them.

And the tremulous fluorescent tubing overhead.

Iris, come back!

Suddenly she's running. For no reason she's running . . . snatches her hand out of Persia's hand . . . runs. Though the dentist's office is on the twelfth floor and the elevator has stopped at the seventh and each previous time she's been brought uptown to this place she's been subdued and docile, a good girl, suddenly she snatches her damp hand out of Persia's and runs breathless and giggling knowing that Persia will chase her . . . except this time Persia doesn't.

She runs partway down the corridor; she stops, looking over her shoulder expecting Persia hot-eyed and furious to be hurrying after her, running awkwardly in her high heels, that grim look to her mother's pretty mouth that can be so hilariously funny though it presages a scolding and maybe a slapping, but this time Persia isn't following after her; Iris stands paralyzed staring in disbelief and horror as her mother remains in the elevator unmoving . . . her face cold and indifferent as a stranger's.

Then the elevator door closes. And the elevator is borne silently away, upward.

Iris screams.

It is the great terror of her life: lost on the seventh floor of the Osborne Building, and Persia borne away somewhere above, and there is nothing but the corridor stretching off, rows of office doors, opaque glass set in the doors, the air smelling of medicine, disinfectant, dust.

She's crying *Mommy, Mommy!* reduced within seconds to anguish; she runs back to the elevator door but the elevator is gone, Persia is gone; she stands there stunned not knowing what to do . . . sobbing helplessly.

Somewhere down the corridor a door opens sharply: a man with a gleaming head peers out . . . peers at her . . . but he withdraws almost immediately, doesn't want any part of Iris Courtney, *bad bad girl how can you be so bad!*

She's four years old. She's going to die.

She blames the navy blue suit with the flared skirt Persia is wearing, the dressy look Persia has for this Saturday-morning visit to the dentist's; most of all she blames Persia's high-heeled shoes, the white and tan leather shoes, the special pair . . . special gift from Daddy. . . . One day they were walking on Main Street and Persia noticed the new spring shoe fashions in a window and pointed at a pair of shoes saying there, that's for me, just joking naturally because these shoes are *expensive* but before she can get her breath Duke Courtney has hustled her inside, before she can figure out what is going on the shoes are hers.

Says Persia, laughing, You know why? The crazy fool just came from his bookie, that's why. He'd won his bet and never even let on.

Says Persia, Sweetie, this is a serious task . . . I mean serious. Handing Iris the little brush, the little shoe polish brush, it's the white polish you apply to the beautiful high-heeled shoes set atop a sheet of newspaper on the kitchen table. Be careful not to splash any white on the tan part, says Persia; if you're going to do this for Mommy you'd better do it right.

Iris's hand trembles just a little.

Iris's hand trembles but she concentrates on the task, she's so careful she forgets to breathe, and the white polish doesn't splash on the tan part of the shoe, and Persia sees what a good job she's done and kisses her on the nose, says, Hey you're smart! My special little sweetie.

By the time Persia pushes through the door marked FIRE EXIT at the end of the corridor Iris is weeping quietly . . . hopelessly. She's standing rooted to the spot in front of the elevator, never looking around until Persia whistles at her, that sharp shrieking comical whistle that's Daddy's whistle too; then she turns, astonished, sees Persia advancing toward her out of nowhere like one of the creatures in the movie cartoons where any surprise is possible, any abrupt change of fortune, any appearance or disappearance, any maiming, any metamorphosis, any transcendent happy ending, any humiliation or nightmare or hilarity, and she rushes head-on at Persia, sobbing violently, and Persia is so guilt-stricken and moved by the child's grief she forgets she'd meant to give her a good hard slap on her bottom; she stoops and hugs her, stoops sighing and hugs her, wipes her tear-streaked snot-streaked face with a Kleenex, *Did you really think your mommy went away and left you?* kissing her, hoisting her up in her arms, *Did you really think that? Did you? Silly little Iris?*

* * *

330

"Momma?"

It's just dawn. It's no day and no season she can name.

Her mother's arms have vanished. Her mother's heated face, her mother's sighing kiss, vanished.

She's an adult woman . . . in an adult woman's body.

She's lying paralyzed in a bed not known to her in a room and a place not known to her, exhausted from her dreaming as if she has fallen from a great height . . . unable to recall where she is or why, except she knows she isn't home.

After some minutes the world rolls back. As the world always does.

Iris Courtney tells herself: she's in Syracuse, New York; she's in her bed in her rented room on South Salina Street; she's safe, she's successful, she's supremely happy; there's a man who imagines he's in love with her though she can't, for a few perplexed seconds, remember his name.

A wet autumn morning, a garbage truck clattering down in the street. The first snowfall of the season, blossom-sized flakes falling languidly and melting on the ground, a premature snowfall delicate as lace, rapidly melting.

13

He says, How beautiful you are, Iris . . . but you must know it.

He says, Your face is a Botticelli face . . . but you must know it.

He says, I'm very attracted to you . . . but you must know it.

He *is* kind; Iris Courtney hasn't been deceived.

And gentle in his touch, not demanding, not in fact very confident, as if, though ten years older than she, he's in a way less experienced, more cautious, choosing his words with care as if fearing that even the most ordinary of words might betray him, or offend her.

He's a gentleman; he respects her virginity.

How happy I am, Iris records in her journal, her now-shabby journal whose early dog-eared pages she'll one day tear out without rereading. *Alan is exactly as Mrs. Savage promised except perhaps sweeter.*

Sometimes when she's too restless to sit at her desk she stoops over to write. *Tonight was a typically lovely evening at the Savages'. Alan was so warm so funny so well-spoken so affectionate.* Where once, and not so very long ago, Iris's handwriting was crabbed and minuscule now it has become gay, capricious, marked by swashes and flourishes. *He says he loves me HOW HAPPY I AM*—sometimes filling the rest of the line or even the page with the squiggly marks with which one fills out the space on a personal check, after the numerals.

At Skaneateles Lake, the morning after they'd first met, Alan Savage proposed to Iris Courtney that, if she was interested, he teach her to sail.

It's sailing, he said, not swimming, that's the true transcendental experience.

They could use the Savages' old twelve-foot sailboat, which Alan had loved so, as a boy. Which he missed, his many summers away from home.

Iris said, after a moment's hesitation, yes she'd like that.

Iris smiled happily and said yes she'd like that.

She chose to ignore how the young man stared at her, smiling but clearly uneasy in her presence . . . not knowing what to think of her or whether he should think of her at all.

But Iris reasoned, She can't have told him anything but good of me: what else but good of me has she seen?

Down at the dock, setting up sail and for nearly two hours afterward on the lake, they exchanged very few words: Alan Savage called out directions; Iris Courtney made every effort to obey. Like children, they did a good deal of scrambling about the deck, and breathless laughing. The wind was up moderately, the sky clear, the sun bright as a heated coin.

Within minutes the Savages' house was hardly more than a white blur on shore.

Iris discovered that she liked sailing, liked it very much; surely it was obvious to Alan Savage how much she liked it, how happily she smiled, their eyes hooking onto each other's sometimes as if by accident. *The tyranny of the sail before the tyranny of the wind: nothing simpler.*

Hair whipping in the wind she cried to Alan Savage, "It *is*—it *is* a transcendental experience, just like you said!"

By the time they brought the sailboat in Alan Savage was enough at ease with Iris Courtney to say, jokingly, with his quick shyly aggressive smile and the habitual downcasting of his eyes that was seemingly a sort of tic with him, "Too damn bad, my mother found you first."

He doesn't mean it, though.

He telephones Iris immediately after Labor Day, when he and his parents have returned to Syracuse, and arranges to meet her: takes her to dinner at a restaurant in the city for an evening quite deliberately not shared with the elder Savages. When Iris inquires after them he says, smiling, an edge of impatience to his voice, "You see my parents often enough, Iris, don't you? It isn't necessary for us to talk about them tonight, or even think about them. Look: we've just met. I've walked in this place, seen you sitting here; I've come over. *Hello!*"

He's grinning like a boy. Reaching over the table to grip her hand in his, hard, and shake it.

Iris thinks, How strange he is.

She says, "What a good idea."

He says, "*I* think it's a good idea."

Though two hours later when they're sitting in his parked car in front of the rooming house on South Salina, talking quietly, not touching (after the impulsive handshake Alan Savage hasn't touched Iris Courtney except to help her with her coat), he does shift to the subject of the elder Savages, as if unable finally to resist. He says, "My parents are very fond of you, as you must know. You're particularly close to my mother, I think?"

Iris says quickly, "Your mother has been very kind to me."

At once, her eyes begin to fill with tears.

Alan Savage watches her closely, perhaps suspiciously. "Has she? Really? In what way?"

"Various ways."

Iris speaks so softly, Alan asks her to repeat what she's said. He says half in protest, "But you've been very kind to *her*. Visiting her in the hospital, and at home; it meant a great deal to her. Especially since my sister . . ." He pauses, reconsidering. Then, in a different tone, his clumsy jocular tone, "*Are* you the sort of person one should be kind to?" he asks. "Somehow you don't give that impression."

Iris says, hurt, "What do you mean?"

"I mean that there are some people, men and women, more often women, who give the impression of not requiring anything from anyone. Who seem impervious, detached. Like works of art that are simply there and don't require anyone to confirm their worth." He pauses. He's breathing audibly, flexing and clenching his fingers. Iris thinks swiftly, He dislikes women. "When I first saw you the other day, after hearing so much about you from my mother, I wasn't prepared for your beauty, I must admit! You have a Botticelli face, the face of Venus or one of the faces of Spring, such strange dreamy detached faces set atop their bodies . . . their incongruous fleshy bodies."

Iris's eyes are brimming with tears but she begins laughing suddenly, and her laughter is harsh. "Is that how I seem to you!" she says.

Alan Savage stares at her in astonishment. A glimmer of oncoming headlights illuminates her contorted face.

* * *

Next day, Iris Courtney is on her way out of the house at 7:55 A.M. when the telephone rings in the front parlor, and the call is for her: Alan Savage calling to apologize.

He's a poor judge of character, he says, his eye is mesmerized by surfaces.

"Iris? Will you give me another chance?"

How happy HOW HAPPY I AM. You didn't think, did you, that I COULD BE SO HAPPY.

He touches her, they're lovers. If not completely.

His touch is caressing, lingering . . . something melancholy in it. In the midst of talk of other, more personal matters, he'll break off to tell her about one of the subjects of his professional research: Marcel Duchamp, for instance, who turned from art to chess and became so obsessed with chess he wanted to transcend mere "winning" in order to comprehend the phenomenon of chess.

Or he tells her of Man Ray, who, when his mistress Lee Miller left him, revenged himself upon her by "breaking her up": that is, fragmenting visual representations of parts of her body and using them in his art. ("Of course," says Alan Savage, seemingly with utter conviction, "the artist's supreme revenge *is* his art.")

Sometimes as if in frustration he grips her head in his hands, frames her face between his spread fingers, kisses her, shyly yet hungrily. It's as if he is kissing a work of art, a work of exquisite beauty, his face so close to hers Iris Courtney can't see it, has no need of seeing it.

One evening Alan says, "I'm very attracted to you, Iris . . . but you must know it." His downcast gaze, his faintly reddened face, throat. Mrs. Savage once chanced to remark that her son had *her* sensitive skin: he's susceptible to hives, rashes, wheals that mysteriously flare up and as mysteriously subside.

It's as if this quick-witted man has been presented with a puzzle, a riddle of sorts, and can't comprehend it. Thus there is an undercurrent of accusation in his voice, subtle yet to Iris Courtney's ear unmistakable as the melodic southern accent beneath the harsher nasal vowels of upstate New York.

Iris smiles; Iris says brightly, "Well. I feel the same way about—"

Alan Savage says, "No, you don't."

What of your mother, what of your father, what was your life before we met? Like any lover, Alan Savage is curious about his beloved's life, the vision of the world from her perspective when it excluded him. He listens avidly, frowning, smiling, often stroking or gripping her hand. As if to say, to urge, yes, yes, and then . . . ?

He doesn't ask if she has been in love before, nor does he volunteer such information about himself.

When she speaks of the past, particularly of her childhood, Iris Courtney's eyes are often damp but her voice is poised and unhesitating as if what she tells him is true, or contiguous with truth; her primary concern, of course, is that the life of Iris Courtney as it is conveyed to the Savages is consistent, seamless. So Alan Savage is told that Persia Courtney died of cancer of the liver at a young age: thirty-eight. That she'd faced death bravely as she'd faced so much in life, shielding her daughter from her own pain and apprehension. That she'd chosen not to remarry after an early divorce because she wanted desperately to be financially and emotionally independent of any man. That she was a loving mother, a remarkable human being, and kind and patient and funny and uncomplaining, never asked favors of relatives, worked at a succession of low-paying jobs: hosiery clerk, typist, librarian's assistant. . . . Iris has an amusing anecdote or two about Persia's stint in the Hammond Public Library, her steadfast refusal to acknowledge the lovelorn glances sent her by a middle-aged bachelor who came virtually every evening to the library to sit in the reference room pretending to read the *Encyclopedia Britannica*.

She liked to sing. By herself, doing household chores, in the shower, on the street. Humming, singing under her breath, *Blue skies smiling at me*, yes and she'd been a wonderful dancer too, before life caught up with her.

Alan Savage says, "She sounds like a remarkable woman. Do you have a photograph of her?"

Iris says, "Not here in Syracuse."

As for Iris's father, still living, apparently in California now, this mysterious man whom Iris hasn't seen since she was five years old: Mr. Courtney was a complex, idealistic person who allowed the insoluble problems of the world to break his spirit, problems of evil, of selfishness, of brutality, of poverty, of injustice and hatred and blindness, a man whose very health was affected by his deep moral disapproval of mankind—yes, and he rejected the practice of law, and his involvement with politics, after being betrayed by associates in Hammond—so Iris tells Alan Savage in a breathless rush of words, so that, though she says otherwise, it's clear that she loves and respects her long-absent father very much.

She says, "I don't take after him in any way, people tell me. I take after my mother."

She says, "One thing I do remember about him: he loved horses. Maybe he still does. He had a true love of horses."

"Really!" says Alan Savage. "Saddle horses, or race horses?"

"I guess I don't know. Just horses."

In her journal she has recorded a remark of Man Ray's quoted to her by Alan Savage: *The tricks of today become the truths of tomorrow.*

He's a reserved, perhaps secretive young man, with the faintly arrogant air of the self-effacing; the facts of his life must be indirectly assembled. In any case, Iris Courtney isn't the sort of person to ask direct questions except as a mode of conversation.

He'll be thirty-two years old in January 1964.

He received his B.A. from Harvard, his Ph.D., in art history, from Yale. He has traveled frequently in Europe, has stayed for extended periods in Rome and Paris, has received postdoctoral awards and fellowships, has been offered teaching positions at Yale, Boston University, Columbia, Cornell. . . . It's Cornell of course that the elder Savages are urging Alan to accept. Only an hour's drive south along I-81 from Syracuse at the southernmost tip of Lake Cayuga.

For too many years, by his own account, he's been "restless."

That is, since the age of nineteen when, between his sopho-more and junior years at Harvard, he traveled alone in Europe for the first time without his parents. And there, in Europe, discover-ing "freedom."

And quite loving it, reveling in it . . . for a while.

Indeed, for more than a decade.

But: "You do get homesick, for your own language especially."

And: "You do come to feel sometimes that you're unraveling, like a loose thread that gets longer and longer."

And: "You glance up one day and see that your contemporaries are all so much *older*."

So he has returned to the United States and is surprised at how happy he is to be here. Of course he misses Paris, he misses his life there, certain of his friends . . . but he can always return for brief visits. (But never again to live there.) He plans to live in America without in the deepest sense living *in* America but in a world of his own work and imagination.

For Alan Savage's work is his true home. His life *is* his work.

So he explains to Iris Courtney: who is quite sincerely inter-ested in the Modernist art in which Alan Savage has specialized; she's enraptured by the several original artworks Alan has acquired (by Man Ray, de Chirico, Magritte) and by his ambitious plans to collect more, much more, once he's settled into a "permanent household."

Art is a world overlaid upon this world with the power to obliterate this world . . . thus its enormous attraction.

So Iris Courtney is coming to see. So Alan Savage explains.

And because his life is so much his work, his work so much his life, he isn't political: doesn't have time.

"What is politics but the folly of the ephemeral, the pursuit of the futile?"

Though of course he's perfectly well aware of contemporary

340

American issues, he's liberal-minded, nearly always votes Democratic when he votes at all. He supports the Kennedy administration's aggressive efforts to reconstruct the racist South, he's sympathetic with the new civil rights bill, and with Martin Luther King, and it was certainly a pity about Medgar Evers, and the four young girls just killed in the church bombing in Alabama; yes, something certainly has to be done, for in a sense you *can* legislate morality, you *can* and you *must*, though it isn't in Alan Savage's nature to quarrel about such things for politics is after all the folly of the ephemeral, the pursuit of the futile.

In Paris, it's true, he had a political-minded friend, quite a close friend, a brilliant freelance writer-historian, and from this man Alan Savage had learned unsettling things about, for instance, the recent escalation of American involvement in Vietnam (the number of "military advisers" has risen from 2,000 to 15,000 in two years!), and the NATO pact, and nuclear weapons testing, but he has no strong opinions of his own; his temperament simply isn't political.

Nor is he religious, though baptized Presbyterian and respectful of the church, of Christianity generally. Never quarrels with religious believers and certainly never with his mother, to whom belief is crucial.

(Of course, when Alan Savage is home, he sometimes attends church services. At Christmas, at Easter, for weddings, funerals, accompanying his parents. A way of honoring his parents. He supposes too he'll be married in a church ceremony one day, should the prospect arise.)

He doesn't believe in God: anthropomorphic self-delusion.

He believes in the human will, in human possibility, human imagination. In principles of certainty, moments of exquisite clarity. Like Cézanne for whom the rock-hard stratum underlying mere impressions was the organizing element in his art. The intractable reality beneath the playful shimmer of light.

And he believes in love. Romantic love.

A belated discovery.

* * *

341

*Do you have any questions about me, about my life before we met, he asked,
and I saw the worry in his face, I saw but didn't see; in any case it was a
casual conversation, nothing intense or profound, I made a joke of it
remarking that his life before we met was virtually his entire life, how could
he be held to account for it?*

*So sweetly so shyly he has asked me several times if many men have
been in love with me, and finally he asked after great difficulty have I ever
been in love with anyone—anyone in the past—and I made a quick joke of
this too; I said, "If nothing came of it, what does it matter?" and a little
later, to tease, to shock him a little (the Savages love to be "shocked":
mildly), I said, "I think, Alan, you're asking in a roundabout way am I a
virgin?" and he blushed crimson and denied it and I poked his arm lightly
and said, "Since I've never loved anyone seriously I guess the answer is
obvious."*

With his enigmatic smile, Alan Savage quotes Magritte to Iris
Courtney: " 'I detest my past. And anyone else's.' "

A night in late October 1963, gusty, rain-lashed, when Alan Savage
drives Iris Courtney home from a semiformal dinner at the Savages'
where there'd been lavish talk of Europe, specifically of Paris, and
Iris says in a neutral voice, "I've never been to Europe," as if this
were a fact Alan might not know. And Alan says, "I'll take you
sometime soon, Iris, shall I?" as casually as if they were already
engaged.

That night Alan accompanies Iris upstairs to her room on the
third floor of the shabby red-brick house at 2117 South Salina Street
instead of saying good night to her in the parlor as he has always
done: Iris Courtney's clean neat sparsely furnished $30-a-month
room. She isn't quite sure if she has invited him but once he's inside,
and the door is shut and locked, she thinks, Yes, it's time.

I do love him. It's time.

Through this young man's nervously quick-darting eyes she
sees that her room, ordinarily invisible to her, is a cozy place, a
secret sort of place, twilit, charmingly feminine, with lumpily

342

wallpapered walls in an old-fashioned floral design of purple tulips and ivy, and a narrow bed with a purple corduroy spread, and white ruffled curtains at the single dormer window overlooking the street. Her small desk is pushed into a corner made cavelike by six-foot bookshelves of synthetic pine; on the battered unpainted floorboards there's a shaggy oval rug in greens and beiges; on one of the walls there are a number of striking photographs, framed, under glass, given to her by her Uncle Leslie: the largest, a constellation of hundreds of children's faces in the shape of a Christmas tree.

Says Alan Savage with a strange smile, "So this is where you live!"

And, staring, "Somehow I didn't expect . . ."

He stands in the center of the room, turning slowly, glancing about as if searching for something. How curious a man he is, how naturally inquisitive: it's the eye of the professional decoder.

Iris wonders with a stab of resentment if her friend is contrasting this modest room, its dimensions, its textures, its diminished signs and symbols, with the rooms of his family's mansion: if he is, perhaps not entirely consciously or voluntarily, assessing the relative powerlessness of one who would inhabit such a room. *And she shares a bathroom with two other tenants on the floor: what of that!* But she dismisses the thought as unworthy of Alan Savage and of herself. He loves and respects me, she thinks. He has become my friend.

Iris Courtney's closest, most reliable friend in all the world.

That evening, at the dinner table, she'd observed Alan in the company of his parents, seeing how, in the weeks since his arrival at Lake Skaneateles, he has become politely deferential to Dr. Savage: wouldn't be drawn into an exchange when Dr. Savage wittily denounced the Abstract Expressionists, murmured only a few words in defense of other artists with whom, in Dr. Savage's eyes, Alan is associated. And of course he's genuinely warm to Mrs. Savage, quite clearly loves, admires, respects her. . . . Watching him, Iris thought, How good he is. How good, how decent, how kind.

Now he's saying, oddly marveling, "It's a lovely little hide-away. Lovely."

"Hideaway? Lovely?"

"The *interiority* of your outer being. Bearing not the slightest relationship to your outer being."

Iris laughs, startled.

Alan had recently described to Iris the way in which Man Ray "designed" his mistress Kiki's face: the artist had shaved the young woman's eyebrows completely off, drew on artificial brows, painted on her a masklike face of stylized beauty, with eerily enlarged eyes and prominent darkly stained lips. Iris thinks at this moment of Man Ray and Kiki.

Alan helps Iris take off her coat, removes his own slowly, distractedly. He's excited. He's nervous. The space in the room is so cramped, such gestures seem outsized and overly intimate.

In the oval mirror above Iris's bureau Alan Savage's face is not one Iris might recognize, it's so intense, so absorbed in *seeing*. In three-quarter profile there's something hawkish about it, but she thinks it attractive.

He's drawn, of course, to the photographs on the wall, examines them with his usual frowning interest. "How odd! How . . . quaint! Wherever did you find these!" he exclaims. He's particularly intrigued by the Christmas tree comprised of hundreds of children's faces with the caption "CHRISTMAS 1946: 'And the Light Shineth in Darkness, and the Darkness Comprehended It Not.' " "It's dated 1946," he says, "but the technique is really quite old. As early as the 1860s photographers were doing things like this: collage, double- and over-exposure, duplication, bizarre things with light. Wherever did you find these?"

At the very peak of the tree is Iris Courtney's tiny face, her four-year-old's face; it's duplicated several times elsewhere. So tiny, scarcely recognizable. Iris says, "Oh, I found them in a secondhand shop. In Hammond." She pauses, her brain for an instant struck blank. "Do you like them, Alan?"

Alan Savage merely laughs. "Of course, Iris. How could I not like anything of yours?"

He goes on to talk of experimental photography, it's a way of erasing the considerable strain between them; he sits on the edge of

344

Iris's bed and pulls her onto his lap, but gently, with a kind of playful formality, for they've never been quite so alone together, never so intimate, or confronted with the prospect of intimacy. The tall milk-glass lamp on Iris's bedside table casts a warm, halolike glow; the fluted shade, beige with an undercurrent of pink, glows too, with a suggestion of radiance suffused in flesh. Alan kisses Iris on the lips for a long tremulous moment.

Then he says in a mock whisper, "*Should* I be here? Aren't there university regulations against men in rooms?" Iris says, "This isn't university housing, this is a private house; I'm what is called an 'upperclassman.' "

"You are, darling! You are!" Alan murmurs, as if making an oblique joke. His arms around her are both tight and tentative, and Iris is thinking, Doesn't he love me? Doesn't he want me? and Iris is thinking, How happy I am, I do love him, and Alan kisses her again, soft probing kisses like questions; they kiss several times and Iris feels his quickly mounting excitement, she has slipped her arms around his shoulders and they're breathless, laughing a little, children caught up in a forbidden sort of play . . . as if they're in this room together in their elders' house, hidden away, door defiantly locked yet still, inescapably, in their elders' house. Too swift to be resisted, the thought of Jinx Fairchild passes through Iris's mind, for all men in their physical presence define Jinx Fairchild in his absence; she thinks, Oh, Jinx, how I love you, but no, she is thinking of Alan Savage; she touches his hair, his fine lank hair, she strokes the nape of his neck, they're whispering and laughing together to forestall a terrible gathering urgency like the wind rising outside lashing the window with rain on the very verge of sleet, and she's thinking too of the ardent young man who'd hoped to marry her, a long time ago it seems, a year ago—in the exigency of this moment she has forgotten his name but she recalls that he too was sweetly patient, gentlemanly, yet affectionate, desiring her— he'd made a tentative sort of love to Iris Courtney in this room, the two of them lying clothed on Iris's narrow bed on top of the corduroy cover, kissing sleepily, whispering to each other whatever words it is that lovers whisper to each other at such times, wistful and insubstantial as smoke, forgotten almost immediately. And that young man had been respectful of Iris Courtney too, as if he believed her fragile, literally fragile-boned, breakable; he'd sensed the resistance in her, not girlish alarm at the violation of her body but womanly disdain for the agent of that violation, as if all that this young man might offer her, all the passion and tenderness and beauty of his maleness, were being rejected beforehand for no reason either of them might name.

Alan Savage whispers, "How lovely you are, how sweet, how . . ."

But he senses too, like his predecessor, the stiffness deep inside her bones, the steely cold behind the soft pliant warmth of her lips.

He says, after a moment, "I suppose I should leave. . . ."

Adding, as if to exonerate them both, "It's late. You're tired. And they're so obviously waiting for me back at the house."

Iris protests, "Oh, don't leave yet, Alan, it's so lonely here."

Alan says, laughing, that laugh that dispels all regret, disappointment, hurt, "Somehow, Iris dear, this doesn't strike me as a lonely place."

"What do you mean? No one ever comes here."

"That's what I mean."

On his feet, Alan Savage prepares to leave, thrusts his arms into the coat sleeves out of which he'd drawn them shortly before; he says he'll telephone Iris tomorrow, early evening, and will Iris be home? "I never go out in the evening except with you," Iris says, "except to eat, on Marshall Street."

Her eyes are heavy-lidded, her hair slightly disheveled but stiff, springy, resilient like the finest of wires. There's a blood-swollen look to her mouth from so much kissing, yes, and her lipstick is worn off too as if in evidence of the utter conventionality, thus rightness, of their courtship.

At the door they kiss another time. "I love you, Iris," Alan Savage murmurs into her hair, and "I love you, Alan," Iris Courtney murmurs into the rough wool of his overcoat.

She accompanies him to the stairs, she kisses him happily on the cheek, waves good night as he descends smiling and squinting up at her, his forehead deeply furrowed as he passes beneath her, his baby-fine brown hair showing its thinness in the cruel overhead light. Iris feels a wave of affection for him. She wonders if that shade of brown, not dark, not light, the hue of damp sand, was the shade of Byron Savage's hair before it turned gray.

How happy HOW HAPPY I AM. You didn't think, did you, that I COULD BE SO HAPPY.

Iᴛ's a white November sky, all
rags and tatters.

Saturday morning, all these things he's supposed to be doing,
still Jinx Fairchild finds himself standing at the wire mesh fence
watching neighborhood kids shooting baskets—it's the schoolyard
behind the Bank Street Junior High, five black boys thirteen,
fourteen years old, skinny, fast, loud-laughing—but it's Sugar
Baby Fairchild he sees among them, not Jinx Fairchild, the snaky-
quick black boy who's a showoff dribbler on the cracked asphalt then
turns serious, whirling around suddenly and leaping straight up
into the air and sinking the ball through the netless rim with a
perfect hook shot, all one fluid motion.

Jinx Fairchild links his fingers through the wire mesh, leans
there, dreamy-eyed, staring . . . can see Sugar Baby as if it had been
just last week, not years ago—man, he wouldn't want to calculate
how many years ago—his brother in the smart Hammond uniform,

green and white, that silky look to it, the graceful white 8 on his jersey. He'd be hardly sweating, the other boys panting like dogs. And the white sneakers that's the sign of pride, flawless white, the slightest blemish you touch it up with polish, and white ribbed socks to mid calf you make sure don't slide down. *Hey Sugar Baby! Hey Sugahhhh! You the sweetest, baby! Doan you know it, man, you the SWEEEEEETEST!*

Strange how it's Sugar Baby he sees in the schoolyard, never Jinx Fairchild. Never Iceman. Like there hadn't ever been, even in the newspaper photographs, any Iceman Fairchild.

Bobo Ritchie's in, didn't wait to be drafted.

Packey Tice: him and his brother both, joined up with the navy.

And Hector Chatwin who was on the football team at school, fullback, crazy-mean, a year behind Jinx Fairchild, big square-jawed black Hector, half his teeth knocked out so he'd grin sly and weird like a Halloween pumpkin . . . his momma waylays Jinx Fairchild outside the grocery store, telling him Hector's in the U.S. Army which is why nobody's been seeing him on the street, she's steamy-breathed, so proud, yakking away showing Jinx snapshots from out of her wallet, big black Hector Chatwin you'd hardly recognize in his dress uniform, visored hat, gloves, smiling, show-ing gold-gleaming teeth, smart and composed and damn good-looking like Sidney Poitier in *Lilies of the Field*. Says Mrs. Chatwin, he's shipped out to this Veet-nam where the fighting is and where he'd been wanting to go; you know Hector. That's over somewhere by Japan. Mr. Kennedy says ain't going to last much more'n a year, the war, so Hector all riled up, you know Hector. Says Mrs. Chatwin proudly, See them teeth? *They* paid for 'em.

Jinx examines the snapshots out of politeness, but he *is* im-pressed . . . can't help but be, seeing that asshole Chatwin looking so good. Like he'd been made to grow up overnight and it suits him.

Seems Jinx Fairchild is always seeing that damn billboard poster upside the East Avenue post office, Uncle Sam in his cartoon red-white-and-blue uniform pointing his crooked finger I WANT YOU, and Jinx knows it's bullshit but his eye is drawn to the giant poster and the pointing finger like your eye is drawn to a water stain in the ceiling in the shape of something you can't figure out but it's something you know you know. Taking the crosstown bus to work so he's facing the billboard every morning, lunch bucket on his lap like back in elementary school, his eyes lift, startled, hopeful. Jinx Fairchild is a married man and a father now, won't be drafted unless there's total war, but I WANT YOU makes you think *somebody* wants you at least, and like Bobo Ritchie said, It's *something,* ain't it? Not just fucking *nothing?*

One day he wakes up, Jinx Fairchild is twenty-four years old.

Now Sugar Baby is dead, he's the oldest boy in the Fairchild family. *He's* the boy.

Except he isn't a boy, he's a married man, always slow to sink in when he wakes in the morning, he's a father three times over, unbelievable as that seems to him (two little boys of his own, one boy Sissy had with another man, when she was sixteen), no matter if he and Sissy aren't always living together like man and wife he's the legal father of those kids and he sure does love those kids like he never thought he had it in him and there's Sissy, he can't quite get into focus in his thoughts does he love the woman or just ache with missing her when she's gone off and he's left bitter and jealous and bewildered and shamefaced or maybe is it just fucking that binds them together . . . Sissy Weaver is Sissy Weaver that any man would go through a whole lot of shit for no matter she's had three babies and drinks too much and pops those nasty little "diet" pills . . . or maybe Jinx truly hates Sissy, the bitch, the lying lying bitch, secretly relieved when she went off with her old boyfriend Meldrick leaving the kids with her mother, except Jinx Fairchild *was* shamed in the neighborhood, drunk and talking loud of ways he'd murder them both, and Minnie says, You know they ain't worth it, honey, them nigger trash ain't worth it, and Jinx screams he knows, he knows, but what's he going to *do?*

350

Fucking Hammond so fucking small, everybody in everybody else's face, what's a man going to *do*?

One of Jinx Fairchild's most desperate drunks, he got it into his head he'd join the Peace Corps, maybe his high school diploma would be enough, and certain of his grades—used to be, Jinx Fairchild *did* get high grades—and he'd be sent to some African country, Nigeria let's say, Ethiopia, where he'd devote himself to teaching and helping people worse off than himself, Jesus those poor Africans are a whole lot worse off than himself so they'd be certain to admire a young black American like Jinx Fairchild, never guessing who he is or where he comes from . . . the shamefulness of his own life. And if he got one of those terrible African sicknesses like malaria, leprosy, maybe he'd die over there, like Medgar Evers he'd be the center of some TV footage and Minnie would take pride in him again and Sissy would be brokenhearted regretting her deceitful ways. Man, you got to figure now's the time! Now's the time! John F. Kennedy opening the White House to Martin Luther King and the Southern Christian Leadership Conference, photographed shaking Reverend King's hand, united with the black man to change the cruel face of the United States forever! In the Blue Moon Lounge Jinx Fairchild was acting the fool, carrying on: I got a dream too! I got a dream too! I got my rights and I got a dream too! and the winos hooted and laughed and pounded on the bar: You tell 'em, Iceman! Yah, you tell 'em, Iceman, you the one!

Except a week later Sissy comes trailing back, and they work things out, and Jinx Fairchild acknowledges, yes he's hard to live with especially since Sugar Baby, and that humiliation last year about "Negroes" finally being let in the UAW local, then getting laid off almost as soon as they started work, nasty mood half the time says Sissy and heavy-hearted the rest of the time says Sissy, ain't no goddamn fun any longer says Sissy, cutting her bronzy-black eyes at him, and you *young* yet, honey, what you gonna be by the time you ma daddy's age? *dead?*

And it's just the two of them. Stone cold sober staring at each other at three in the morning so it chills Jinx like the touch of death, the truth of what the woman is saying, and the scared look in her eyes like maybe she does love him only just doesn't know what to do about him . . . driving her off because he can't love her.

Twenty-four: how you get so old, so fast?

Naw, he knows he isn't old, but neither is he young.

Gets winded like he'd never done playing basketball, like say he's been running. And when he's worn out or has lost the thin tight thread of his concentration, like at work, at McKenzie's, the machine shop banging and clattering inside his head, he'll walk with a slight limp, favoring his right ankle where it was broken so bad.

As long as he's mindful of it, though, he never walks with the slightest sign of any weakness.

He hasn't touched a basketball since that night.

Jesus Gawd how'd my boy hurt himself so bad! Jinx Fairchild's father grieved for weeks.

And Minnie . . . never mind about Minnie.

Sugar Baby kept his distance, never asked questions. Sugar Baby let his brother alone forever after that.

April 1958, the state semifinal game against Troy, and Jinx Fairchild lost his balance falling, nobody's fault but his own; the Hammond people tried to fix the blame on one of the Troy players elbowing Jinx in the ribs after he sank his shot but Jinx says it wasn't anybody's fault, he came down wrong, hit his ankle at the wrong angle so his full weight crashed down on it, on those breakable bones.

He'd tried not to scream when they lifted him. Coming off the court he fainted.

Weeks and weeks with his foot and ankle in that heavy cast, slamming around on crutches, into hot weather, and finally when the cast was removed he'd wake at night sweating, feeling it still on his leg, the clammy weight of it like somebody's fingers closed over him pulling him down, down.

Folks in Lowertown who know him or know of him continue to say to this day, Oh, Jinx, oh, Iceman, weren't that a shame, that

352

was the saddest saddest thing, and Jinx makes an effort to be polite or maybe laughs, saying, naw, he never thinks about it none any more; basketball's for kids and you got to grow up sometime.

But you was going to college too, wasn't you, Jinx?

Like I say, you got to grow up sometime.

And when Minnie brings the hurtful subject up as Minnie invariably does, moaning as if the loss were fresh, not years old, and her boy still her boy not another woman's husband, Jinx points out in a reasonable voice that neither Frankie nor Dwight would be born if he hadn't broken his ankle, if he'd gone off to college . . . and Minnie is crazy about her grandsons, isn't she?

So that quiets his mother down. For a while at least.

About Minnie Fairchild: since Sugar Baby's death she seems to be drinking more than she used to, drinking and hiding the beer bottles like she's ashamed, surely she *is* ashamed, and she's gaining weight so she's now quite a stout lady and her old nice clothes don't fit but she doesn't want to get new nice clothes, reasoning that she'll slim down some and won't have any use for the new large-size clothes so in the mean time she's wearing old baggy slacks and blouses and sweaters and tentlike dresses one or another of her neighbor friends have given her. Ceci, who's married now, lives a few blocks away, shakes her head disapprovingly when she sees her mother in the street, complaining to everyone that Momma's turning into the very kind of black woman she'd always been so scornful of, all bloated up from eating starches and drinking beer . . . and her arthritis is so very painful . . . and she's got female problems too embarrassing to explain to the clinic doctor, this white man who doesn't take any time with his black patients, maybe not with his white patients either for all Minnie knows, acting like there's a bad smell in the air when he's examining her, and his face, my God d'you know who he looks like, he looks exactly like Pruneface in the Dick Tracy comic strip, that's who! Minnie throws back her head, roaring with laughter, breasts shaking . . . but Lord, she's having a streak of bad luck with her finicky white ladies—seems you just can't please them no matter how hard you work, scrubbing their floors and tubs and nasty-stained toilets and say you leave a square inch of kitchen tile unpolished or a single dustball under a bed or forget to do some laundry and they're right down on your ass—and Minnie Fairchild's of an age now she answers back sometimes, mumbling under her breath *Hell with you white bitch* or *Who you mouthin' off to white bitch* or *French kiss ma ass white bitch,* and even if the white ladies don't pick up every syllable of Minnie's words they surely register Minnie's intention so she doesn't work as frequently or as regularly as she once did, it's a despairing thing she's about ready to apply for welfare aid like she swore she'd never never do but she isn't going to take money from her children 'cause they don't have any to spare but at least not working she isn't miserable hustling herself on and off those endless Hammond city buses where the drivers sometimes call her Grandma—that fat-lipped nappy-headed nigger driving the 8 A.M. uptown is the worst, making unfunny jokes at Minnie Fairchild's expense—so staying home she's better off, she can nurse her ailments, and there's day-long TV, and she's on the telephone complaining to whoever's there—her married daughters, her girlfriends—sometimes, speech slurred so he hardly recognizes who it is, she'll call up Jinx in the evening just to talk, talk, talk: worried sick she says about the future of him and Sissy Weaver (never does Minnie call her daughter-in-law anything but "Sissy Weaver," as if Jinx never married Sissy, only took up living with her and could move out again any time he wants) and those innocent little boys . . . yes and she's worried sick about Woodrow too, that bad hacking cough of his and stomach problems he refuses to discuss nor will he go to the clinic with her just puts his trust in the Lord he says. . . . Sunday mornings and Wednesday evenings at the Second Coming African Church of Christ the Redeemer that man is happy, face lit up and eyes shining when he comes home . . . rest of the time he's off in his head though he'll laugh some with Minnie watching her favorite TV program *Beverly Hillbillies* . . . but mainly it's church the old fool lives for. . . . Minnie wishes *she* was that simple . . . yes, black folks are just too craven and eager to believe anything promising, lay themselves down for white folks to walk over or hose down or beat with billy clubs or sic police dogs on, which is why Minnie distrusts Reverend King though granting the man *is* a saint and she acknowledges he *is* accomplishing something for the colored people if not maybe for Minnie Fairchild. . . . What's wrong with imitating Jesus Christ, turning the other cheek and all that, is that Jesus Christ knew he was the Son of God, or was supposed to be, but nobody else *is* . . . that's a disadvantage! And please Jinx you got to drop by the house for sure this week to fix the back steps where they're rotted almost through and insulation strips have got to be put in around the window frames and you know your father can't hustle his black ass to do anything useful . . . and I'm lonely Jinx I miss my children Jinx all grown up and moved out or worse like Sugar Baby but I won't get onto that subject it's just that I'm lonely and thinking if only you hadn't gone for that one basket—that one basket that one minute: that *once!*—you wouldn't had that accident and you'd gone to college and by now you'd be a teacher or a sports coach right here in Hammond or, Jesus, maybe a doctor or a lawyer or stockbroker or something fancy and not married to *that woman* who took advantage of your ignorance when you weren't but a boy—*don't interrupt: I'm telling you what's what*— and your daddy and me wouldn't be living here in this house that's needing paint and repairs surrounded by neighbors getting trashier and more shiftless every year. Oh honey why did that happen to your brother like it did? Why did you that's my smartest child do to yourself how you did? Can't nothing be changed once it starts its course going wrong?

(Jinx notes how, since high school, Minnie Fairchild never calls him anything but "Jinx" . . . no more "Verlyn." Must be Momma figures everybody else calls him that, so why keep up the pretense? Or maybe she'd been calling him that, in secret, all along?)

Like hundreds of other workers in Hammond, Jinx Fairchild has filed his application at National Lead of Hammond across the river. There's a new plant opening up December 1, 1963, it's said that wages will be higher than wages at any other factory in the region, National Lead has a government contract so that means money—

big money for Hammond—some kind of metal or chemical or gas operation processing fuel for "government reactors" is what the work is but nobody in Hammond, let alone Lowertown, has the slightest idea what that is and no questions asked.

In the Hammond *Chronicle* it's stated that the company is reorganizing its operations under the National Security Act but what that is nobody knows either.

Least not Jinx Fairchild, an unskilled factory worker in his early twenties, just fourteen months on the assembly line at McKenzie Radiator ("A Division of General Motors" as the big sign boasts) and a dues-paying member of the United Auto Workers of America, local 483 . . . one of fewer than twenty black men in the four-hundred-man local and lucky, damned lucky, to be in. No matter the din of the machine shop, and the smells, and the summer heat all through September, and the banging clattering hammering in Jinx Fairchild's head repetitive and crazy as his own thoughts could he hear what those thoughts are.

Yah, you better believe you're lucky, man, some white foreman smiling on you 'cause you used to play basketball at the high school, hard not to know how lucky you are every morning at 8 A.M. marching into the machine shop with all the white faces, especially those pasty-pale hillbilly faces with eyes like ice picks going right through you.

A dozen times Sissy says, "You heard anything about that new job, Jinx? That place across the river?" And a dozen times Jinx says, "Not yet," though the truth is: word's out early on before the new processing plant at National Lead even posts its openings that management isn't hiring blacks except for janitorial work.

But he doesn't tell Sissy, it's one of those cautious-peaceful pockets of time when he's hoping to please her by showing how future-minded he is, holding out to her the vague prospect of making a little more money that, multiplied, might constitute the down payment on a car, or a new TV, or clothes for the kids or Sissy herself. At least it's a subject for the two of them to talk about instead of their old worn-out subjects or outright fighting; then

356

they fall into bed thrashing and loving, and Sissy's the kind of hot-skinned woman can be real nice when she wants to be, real nice, so it's *something*, Jinx tells himself, not just *nothing*.

Goddamn, Jinx, what in hell you doing making that nasty old noise, you waking me up every goddamn night grinding your teeth—Sissy's nudging him not fully awake herself and Jinx is confused half asleep and half awake, convinced there's a kind of machine right inside his head revved up and working grinding grinding grinding so he's covered in sweat and his skin stretched tight on his long skinny bones and the big molars in his jaw are aching and hot.

Keeping the U.S. Army in mind, that's Jinx Fairchild's trump card.

There's no quarrel between the two men but when Jinx Fairchild pushes into the lavatory and sees Mort Garlock at one of the sinks, and Mort Garlock's startled eyes lock with Jinx Fairchild's in the mirror, both men freeze . . . for a just perceptible beat. Garlock is a pasty-pale white man in his mid-thirties with a narrow ferret face, damp lashless eyes; he's been on the assembly line at McKenzie Radiator for years and has seniority over the oldest of the black workers; he's one of a loose group of friends at the center of which is Bill Hudkins (lately "Bull" to his buddies in honor of his resemblance, physical and otherwise, to Bull Connor, the much-publicized police commissioner of Birmingham, Alabama: both of them real white men's white men) . . . then Mort Garlock yanks a paper towel out of the dispenser and dries his hands roughly and tosses the wadded towel in the direction of the trash can, not minding that it falls short, falls to the already littered floor; he's on the move, eyes averted, eager to get out of these close confines. Though there's no quarrel between the two men.

Looming up tall and very dark-skinned in the fluorescent-lit space Jinx Fairchild uses the lavatory, smiling to himself . . . thinking how, in the merest flicker of an instant, he'd seen fear in the white man's eyes.

357

Mort Garlock. A relative of Little Red.

Could even be a brother, Jinx wouldn't know.

All the rest of that day, Jinx Fairchild feels good. Humming and singing Big Bill Broonzy under his breath—*Got me a new suit of clothes, got me a big new car, got me a sweet li'l gal thinks the world of me mmmmmmmmmmmmm!*—but inside the humming and singing and the deafening crash of the assembly line he's thinking, Might be I killed one of you once and might be I can do it again any time.

He doesn't mean it, though.

Naw: Jinx Fairchild is a polite-mannered young man, still boyish in manner, tall and long-limbed as if his bones grew too weedy-fast for the rest of him, his eyes are sometimes hooded and glazed over from so many hours in the factory and his deep rich brown-black skin isn't as healthy-appearing as it once was, and his big strong teeth are turning yellowish like old ivory but so slow and gradual you almost don't notice . . . almost don't notice. Sissy runs her red-polished nails teasing through his woolly hair murmuring *Here's the one, here's ma man* in the cadence of a popular song and say they're dressed in their best clothes, Sissy in her electric-bright turquoise taffeta dress, spike-heeled shoes with the skinny straps, wide soft crimson lips made up for her cousin Mimi's wedding, and Jinx is in his good suit too, his only suit, fawn-colored, skinny lapels, tight-fitting in the shoulders but still looking good, so he's smiling and frowning at his face in the mirror thinking things aren't so bad, there's Sissy crazy for him, he's got his sons Frankie and Dwight, and Sissy's little boy Vaughan looking up to him; why should it matter that, when he leaves the neighborhood, he isn't "Jinx Fairchild" in anyone's eyes but a black man, a man defined by his skin and by his facial features and by his voice and by that look in his eyes, how to be something other than what another sees and, seeing, defines, defines without knowing or caring in actual resistance to knowing or caring; why should it matter that, at work, at this work which (if he's lucky) he'll be doing for the rest of his life, the white men surrounding him resent him for his very presence on the floor with them as if he's not only presenting himself as an equal of theirs but is in fact an equal of theirs; why should it matter that that bastard Bull Hudkins and his friends cut their eyes at him, jive-talk with one another in his and other blacks' earshot; why should it matter that, if they had the power, they would extinguish him with a snap of their fingers, make extinct the entire "race" of which in his innocence and impotence he's the exemplar in their eyes; why should it matter? Jinx Fairchild is just biding his time in Hammond, New York.

Contemplating his hands: the basketball hands, the murderer hands.

Long elastic-seeming fingers with which he could still get a firm grip on a basketball, he's sure, send it spinning in an arc to drop through the metal rim lightly fluffing out the net, he's sure, outwitting his guard and the other players and running right up to the backboard and leaping and sinking the ball and the crowd delirious with applause, he's sure, only there's a heaviness in him, a coldness in his guts: Man I done all that already, tried all that.

Hurts to think, though, except for basketball Jinx Fairchild would have been nobody much, those years in school: nobody in his teachers' or his classmates' eyes. Just the family, Minnie primarily: his momma cherishing him because she's his momma not because he's anything special. Why are you behaving like some ordinary shiftless nigger? Why are you cutting your own throat and cutting mine? Minnie had raged. Years ago.

His murderer hands: he's shamefaced in the eyes of God could he be sure there *is* a God, but in the eyes of man, the white man, men like Bull Hudkins and Mort Garlock and the others, and the Hammond city police, and the criminal justice system of the United States, naw, can't say Jinx Fairchild feels any shame or even much regret. Wishes he hadn't done it, Jesus yes, but doesn't feel regret for the fact that his victim is dead, long dead, and nearly forgotten. Like the white girl Iris Courtney said, Garlock was so crazy and so mean, someone would surely have killed him someday.

Bad luck it had to be Jinx Fairchild.

* * *

359

She'd argued with him, Why trade your life for his? when it seemed, maybe, he might weaken and turn himself in.

And, It was self-defense but no one would believe you.

What to make of Iris Courtney? So fixed upon Jinx Fairchild, and so convinced they were special to each other? Saying I don't want anything from you but the fact of you, which is a statement Jinx understands by instinct but not in any more rational way just as he knows things about Sissy, and Sissy about him, by instinct, that could never be explained.

Saying too in her fierce fixed way, No one is so close to us as we are to each other.

In the days back in high school when they'd seen a good deal of each other, Jinx had always thought something would happen between them . . . not that he'd wanted it to happen, but that he'd felt it would come about apart from his volition, as so many things seemed to happen apart from his volition. But when she'd called him that night and asked him please to meet her so they could talk and they'd parked above the river whispering and touching and kissing and finally he'd said, It's late, I better get you home, he'd been proud of himself for the fact that nothing extreme or irrevocable had happened between them after all. He knew she wanted him to make love to her, and Jesus he'd been ready, but he had not done it, just told himself no no no so they were free and clear of each other and could forget each other maybe, if only she'd let him go.

He'd worried some, that she wouldn't let him go.

And if she hadn't . . . what could he have done?

How to explain Iris Courtney to Sissy, for instance? Simply to speak the girl's name would be to violate a secret and to begin a confession that could only end with Jinx Fairchild saying he'd killed a boy once, years ago, self-defense maybe but, yes, he'd done it. This is a strange story, the strangest story of any story I know, and it happened to me.

Iris Courtney respected his distance and never telephoned him again but in the years since she's been away to college in Syracuse she has sent him several odd little letters: single sheets of paper covered in careful schoolgirl handwriting, envelopes addressed to "Verlyn Fairchild" in care of "Mrs. Fairchild" at the old East Avenue address. Skimming these letters, embarrassed, impatient, apprehensive, Jinx believed he could hear the girl's cool pleading voice: *How are you? I would like so much to hear from you. Just tell me anything, for instance where you are while you're reading this? If you look up what will you see? For instance. . . .* Of course, Jinx hadn't answered a single letter.

Sometimes in weak melancholy moods he thinks of her.

Sometimes he fantasizes making love to her . . . the way she'd wanted him to.

He knows she's gone from Hammond more or less permanently but from time to time he sees her, or someone who resembles her. A head of springy pale-bronze hair and the white skin, a slender nerved-up body, a girl walking or standing by herself. And his heart kicks, and he wants it to be Iris Courtney and wants it to not be Iris Courtney.

This summer I was up at Cassadaga Park one day with Frankie and he got sleepy from messing around in the wading pool and the hot sun so I'm carrying him in the crook of my arm and we go in this big dark old building where the girls' and boys' rooms are and there's ice cream and candy and soda pop you can buy and I'm at the counter going to buy Frankie and me both something and there's this girl behind the counter staring at me but my eyes are sort of dim yet from stepping in out of the sun so I can't see her clear and think for a minute it's you . . . this long strange minute the two of us are staring at each other until finally the girl smiles and asks what do I want, and I tell her, and she isn't you but there's a special feeling between us, this girl with pale frizzy hair, big wide innocent-seeming eyes, halter top, bare shoulders and arms and she's young, maybe fifteen, but mature for her age . . . the kind of girl it's obvious likes black boys at least as well as white boys or maybe it's men she likes of any color so I walk out with Frankie hoisted up in the crook of my arm both of us sucking popsicles and feeling pretty good—but this Jinx Fairchild wouldn't write to Iris Courtney, nor even consider it.

He never will write, he'll provide a photo instead.

* * *

361

A long, long day . . . can't hardly remember how long.

Now it's supper time, pitch black outside but Minnie Fairchild hasn't gotten around to starting any meal, she's sitting in the Formica-topped breakfast nook, puffy-faced, nursing a beer, addressing her son Jinx in a voice heavy with sarcasm. "You comparing yourself to—who? Bobo *Ritchie?* That trash? He ain't *nothing,* and you know it. He don't even belong in the U.S. Army except the fool police never caught up with him and arrested him like they should of."

Jinx laughs harshly, says, "Like they never caught up with me, Momma?"

Minnie stares at him for a blank moment, then brings her Schlitz bottle down hard on the table; there's a *crack!* like gunfire but the bottle doesn't break. "Damn you, boy, I don't like you *teasing,"* she says, suddenly furious. "You know it wears me out, you damn kids *teasing."*

She rants for some minutes complaining not only of Jinx but of Ceci, Ceci and her fresh mouth, and then it's Bea, Bea over at Sunday dinner with her in-laws and never having time for Minnie because *why?* Could be, that girl's embarrassed of her daddy. And her daddy's a damn good man, a fine man for all his faults, and not well these days, and, Lord, who knows what's going to—

From out of the bedroom at the rear of the little house comes Woodrow's snoring, a patient, rhythmic drone like the sound of wasps in a giant hive.

Jinx says, mumbling, "Sorry, Momma. Don't mean to vex you."

Minnie says hotly, "You don't vex me, honey, you *worry* me. That's worse." Adding in a low voice, "If I thought you were halfway serious I wouldn't let you out of this house."

Jinx laughs, startled. Says with his old squirmy twist of his shoulders, "Oh, you know I'm not, Momma. Serious."

They fall silent, drinking their beers. Jinx Fairchild is thinking he's never, never done anything like this . . . sitting in his momma's kitchen drinking beer with her. Jesus, never! Never in his life! Minnie Fairchild just isn't the type, or wasn't, all those years she'd been his and her other children's stern chiding momma; now she's drinking Schlitz from the bottle, fastidious little sips, but frequent sips. Jinx throws back his head and drinks in quick gulping mouthfuls, then wipes his lips with his fist, suppresses a beery belch.

It's a windy late-autumn night, a smell of snow in the air and dried leaves. Past seven-thirty and Jinx should get on home . . . but he just sits. He's tired. A tight band around his head, a threat of squeezing pain, from the goggles he'd been wearing most of the day. And a faint roaring in his right ear.

He says in his offhand voice, "Bobo says he signed up for radio and electronics repair, that's a useful trade, huh? And they're teaching him to read and write . . . seems like Bobo went all the way through ninth grade never learning. They damn sure didn't bother teaching him in school, just passed him along."

Minnie says, flaring her nostrils, "That simple fool! If anybody did teach him C-A-T or D-O-G he'd forget the next day." She pauses, breathing hard. The old cardigan sweater buttoned over her heavy breasts seems barely to contain her emotion. "Why are you comparing yourself to such trash, Jinx? You know you're *superior*. You're aggravating me!"

Jinx says, "Why am I superior to Bobo? Only just a little smarter, maybe. In school."

"Smarter *is* superior."

"Yah? You think so?"

"I know so."

"What kind of 'smart' we talking about, Momma?"

"Damn you, shut your *mouth*."

It's at that moment that Minnie erupts in one of her little temper spasms: shrieking and cursing, without rising from her seat she lashes out, cuffs Jinx hard on the shoulder, turns in her fury and frustration to dislodge a stack of old newspapers and magazines on the window ledge, kicking at them as they go flying. Jinx cringes, laughing. Waits it out.

This long long day. Begun so long ago, in the dark, can't remember if it *is* the same day.

In the machine shop at McKenzie Radiator, just inside the main entrance, there's a prominent calendar of the kind that displays just the date, the single date, in large black letters. Early on when Jinx Fairchild began working there he grasped the logic of the calendar, said to one of the other, older black men, You know why they have that there? The date like that? and the black man said, Why? and Jinx laughed and said, So we know we're going forward somewhere, not just stuck in the same day. He meant it to be a joke, but the other man just frowned at him as if he was some kind of fool.

Truth is, Jinx Fairchild doesn't have much to say to the other black men at McKenzie. Doesn't have much to say to anyone.

There's a tiredness leaking out of Jinx Fairchild's bones.

Minnie's talking a blue streak, panting and puffing and complaining—if she thought he was serious damn what she'd do! and there's Sissy Weaver! *her!* and Minnie's own daughters Bea and Ceci! and poor Dr. O'Shaughnessy, who was the kindest most decent most generous man Minnie Fairchild has ever known! and Dr. O'Shaughnessy's cruel cruel children!—and Jinx Fairchild has rested his arms on the table and cradled his head on his arms, he's listening to his momma, to her aggrieved voice rising and falling like music, mixed in with a tremulous zigzag pattern of light, and the roaring of machinery or is it a falls in a river, he's listening—Yes yes yes Momma nobody's serious Momma—and then he's slipping off the margin as if off the edge of the table but it isn't the edge of the table he slips off of, he's just asleep.

"That you, Sissy? Who's that? *You . . . ?*"

He's stumbling in his underwear, barefoot and dazed, out of the darkened bedroom, blinking, not seeming to know where he is or what's the hour. Heart knocking like crazy against his ribs as if he's in danger, as if he's been cornered in the lavatory at work by Bull Hudkins and Mort Garlock and their friends and he's going to be beaten and made to crawl; it's the time of reckoning at last, it's the time Jinx Fairchild has surely known is coming, all these years . . . but no: it's just Sissy coming home: in that shiny synthetic maroon-colored wig that Jinx hates, mincing and sniffing like

Eartha Kitt, Sissy his wife, caramel-colored good-looking Sissy he'd married, swaying-drunk, past 3:30 A.M. and when Jinx asks her where the hell she's been she says, upturning her chin Eartha Kitt style, "With ma girlfriends, smart-ass, where *you* been?" pushing past her husband like he's hardly there, of no more significance than a piece of furniture or her own boy Vaughan, cowering in the doorway of his and Frankie's room, thumb in his mouth: "Lemme *past,* damn you, what you think you are, po-lice?" Sissy's crimson lipstick is smeared not only across her face but onto her mauve jersey blouse and the blouse is buttoned crookedly in back and she's smelling of something stronger than beer, an almost medicinal odor, and there's a large damp stain on her skirt soaked into the tight-clinging black Orlon; Jinx is staring at her as if he has never seen her before, he's going to let her go it seems, slamming into the bathroom where maybe like other times she'll have sense enough to poke a forefinger down her throat and bring up hot gushing splashes of vomit to empty her stomach and help clear her head . . . but, no, he isn't going to let her off so easy, he's fully awake suddenly and yelling, "Whore! Bitch! Dirty cunt!" into her face, his fingers digging into her shoulders meaning to hurt, and Sissy is squealing in pain like a little girl and slapping at him and her wig's askew and the sight of it pisses Jinx off more so he's pounding her against the wall, his lips laid back from his teeth and his eyes bulging so everything in the dim-lit room is shaking and vibrating and the baby has begun to cry in his crib and that makes Jinx angrier and Sissy knees him in the groin just hard enough to throw him into a greater fury so he hits her in the mouth with his elbow and she's spitting blood and laughing, "You prick! You! Who in hell're *you!*" managing to get loose and seizing a brass lamp one of her relatives gave them for a wedding present and if Jinx hadn't seen the bitch lifting it to bring down on his skull he'd be knocked cold but he's got her, he's got her, he's got the bitch, walking her backward into the bedroom crying, "Whore! Cunt! Dirty cunt!" into her face as she's crying, "Fucker! Shithead! Why don't you *die!*" into his and they're wrestling together, Sissy's fancy clothes are being torn, the maroon wig knocked off, Jinx is saying, "You no fit mother, I'm

365

gonna take my boys from you," and Sissy screams, "Anybody tries to take my children from me gonna have to kill me first, and them too!" and on the bed amid the rumpled sheets and blanket Jinx is straddling Sissy's fleshy hips, Sissy is tearing at his undershirt, her long nails drawing blood from his nipples so suddenly his sweaty near-hairless chest is gleaming blood and he knees her thighs apart, kneels between her thighs so swollen and primed to fuck it's as if his penis is hauling him down into her, grunting and pushing him down, down into her, her spread lips and the scratchy pubic hair she'd shaved off when they first were lovers so it's grown in uneven and she's clutching at him murmuring, "Uhhhhhhh— uhhhhhhh—" like she does, her spike-heeled shoes now hanging from her ankles by their straps, her ankles locked behind his thrusting hips, and suddenly without knowing what he does Jinx is pumping his life into the woman, his fury into her, his hatred, his need to hurt, wormlike veins are standing out in his forehead, his lips bared from his teeth in a silent scream and Jesus how he'd like to draw blood from her how he'd like to kill her but all that will come of it is Sissy's wild rhythmic screams in another few seconds and her violent thrashing and pummeling and Jinx will go limp inside her, lost deep inside her, dead suddenly, collapsed on top of her heated body, limp and discarded . . . his breath whistling thinly as he sinks into something like sleep.

Jinx you crazy asshole you know I love you, huh, hon? You know you ma man—her eyes purplish-bruised but soft and damp and acquiescent—You know I'm not serious, don't you, any crazy old thing I say? and Jinx Fairchild laughs saying, Nobody's serious, girl, naw, nobody.

It's a much-folded, badly creased, yellowing document, this birth certificate: VERLYN RAYBURN FAIRCHILD born August 18, 1939, Hammond General Hospital, Hammond, New York. Contemplating it, Jinx Fairchild rubs his thumb repeatedly against the cheap embossed seal of the State of New York.

Strange: you expect your birth certificate to be a large docu-

366

ment, the size of a diploma at least. But Jinx Fairchild's is small, the size of an ordinary sheet of tablet paper.

A pale-glowering windy day, snowflakes blowing like tiny chips of mica.

Birth certificate carefully folded in his inside jacket pocket, Jinx Fairchild takes the bus uptown on this Saturday morning in November 1963 to the United States Army recruiting station on South Main Street and first thing he sees, shyly entering the office, is that the smartly uniformed man behind the counter, seated at a desk, is black . . . which he hadn't envisioned.

At once he's flooded with relief.

Then the second amazing thing: this man Jinx Fairchild doesn't know, could swear he has never laid eyes on before, strong-boned handsome face, skin dark as Jinx's own, a man in his mid-thirties at least, is evidently from Hammond, for it seems he knows Jinx, or recognizes him: rising quickly to his feet, reaching across the counter to shake Jinx's hand, smiling, happy, deep booming voice: *"Iceman*—isn't it?"

Something is wrong, something is happening.

Iris Courtney's one o'clock American literature class, held in a third-floor lecture hall in the antiquated Hall of Languages, Syracuse University, a Gothic structure of fifteen-foot cracked ceilings and falling plaster and violently clanking radiators, isn't dismissed so much as abandoned, shortly before 1:50 P.M. of this Friday in November: an undercurrent of mysterious unrest beyond the room, stray lifting voices, isolated shouts, running feet both in the corridor outside and down in the quadrangle below have by degrees so distracted the gentlemanly professor at the lectern that he gives up on his commentary on Walt Whitman, goes to the door, opens it, turns back a moment later to announce to the fifty-odd staring students in the room, "It's an emergency—the President has been shot."

After this, confusion.

In a crowd of others Iris Courtney makes her way downstairs and out of the building, unwisely taking the spiral staircase in the center of the building, a nightmare structure, narrow, creaking, vertiginous. "President? Which president?" Iris and a companion are wondering. "The president of the university?"

Then from all sides comes the news, disjointed and semi-hysterical: it's Kennedy who has been shot.

President Kennedy, in Dallas, Texas.

In a motorcade. By a sniper. An assassin.

And others have been shot: the Governor of Texas? . . . Vice-President Lyndon Johnson? . . . Jackie Kennedy?

Has Jackie Kennedy been shot?

Are they all dying? Dead?

An armed uprising in Dallas, Texas: the John Birch Society . . . no it's a Communist uprising . . . Cuban attack . . . terrorists . . . Castro's revenge for the Bay of Pigs.

Breathless and strangely exhilarated, Iris is drawn with a stream of people, many of them from her American literature class, into one of the dining halls off Walnut Avenue where the public address system is tuned in to network news, news from Dallas, deafeningly loud. Her quick-darting eyes take in the fact, in itself alarming because unprecedented, that the university's rigid self-contained world has been shaken: there are undergraduates jammed in beside their professors, professors jammed in beside their students; there are secretaries, maintenance workers, kitchen help in their white uniforms . . . a sprinkling of black faces, workers' faces, amid the sea of Caucasians. And how stiff and silent and expressionless everyone is, like frightened children, like people crowded into the cabin of a sinking ship, and Iris breathless among them, wondering why she is here, who all these people are, listening as the radio broadcaster keeps up a continual stream of words in which certain key terms recur: "Emergency operation . . . Parkland Hospital . . . critically wounded . . . neck wound . . . head wound . . . lone sniper . . . not yet apprehended . . . motorcade . . . Dealy Plaza . . . Governor of Texas John Connolly . . . wounded . . . assassin . . . not yet apprehended."

A girl beside Iris says, in a whisper, "Oh, God, I just can't believe this, can you?"

Iris says, "No. Oh, no."

Though instructing herself carefully: It's nothing to you really, you're here with all these others the way, the other night, you were with the Savages and their relatives, but it's nothing to you really, if Kennedy lives, if Kennedy dies, if any stranger lives or dies.

Still, she waits out the news with the others, in dread.

Seeming to know that Kennedy must die: the phenomenon of such an event, so public an occasion, can only mean disaster.

She only hopes the "lone sniper" will not turn out to be black.

"The President of the United States is dead. I repeat, President of the United States John F. Kennedy is—"

Immediately, Iris Courtney turns to push her way out of the dining hall, out of this press of people, desperate to escape. Suddenly she *must* escape. The collective stunned silence, the downcast teary-bright eyes, the first sobs and cries of, "No, oh, *no!*" She can't bear it, simply has to escape.

Out into the fresh cold November air where she can breathe.

As others are pushing in, frightened, excited, near-hysterical, trying to gauge from Iris Courtney's face what has happened.

A girl whose name Iris knows but could not, at this confused moment, have said, cries, clutching at her arm, "Oh, Iris, is he . . . ? *Is* he . . . ?"

Iris draws away. She says, scarcely moving her lips, "He's dead."

Stepping quickly out into the lightly drizzling rain, resisting the instinct to run.

Her eyes have filled with tears.

Angry tears: Hypocrite, liar, what has any of this to do with you!

She's climbing the steep hill up from University Place past the Hall of Languages with its tall narrow gaunt windows now back-lit against the dimming afternoon light, past the Administration

Building whose windows too are lit, past Maxwell Hall where, on the wide-fanning stone steps, several students, young men, stand talking quietly together, their accents foreign. She breathes in the sweet-brackish air of late autumn, an odor of rot, of wet, of earth, of damp foliage and bark, heart pounding hard, senses keenly alert. So often, walking alone on this campus in the early morning or at dusk, she feels herself on the brink, the quivering brink of a revelation: but of what?

There's a needle-fine cold rain falling on her uncovered head, soaking into her cloth coat. It's a handsome coat, a deep winey-red, with black buttons, a stylish collar, but it's a cheap fabric and the lining has begun to rip, the relentless wind off Lake Ontario easily penetrates its seams. Alan Savage has said, gazing at Iris Courtney with his kindly, wondering eyes, How lovely you are, Iris, how flattering that color is to your skin.

Yes? Really?

How lovely. My love.

Really?

In Strouse Hall, where the Art History Department is located, Iris runs up the stairs to the third floor, to Dr. Savage's office, to the *Journal* office, with the vague intention of speaking with Dr. Savage—not about Kennedy's death, not that, that's too immediate, too raw, too public, too impersonal, but about . . . it isn't clear to her yet . . . but she believes that when she sees him and he grasps her hand in his, in both his hands, as he does, saying, smiling, in that voice of absolutely genuine pleasure, Why, Iris! How good to see you, and how well you're looking! she'll know then what she wants to talk with him about, what issue must be decided.

I don't love your son but I love you.

I don't love Alan Savage but I love . . . Savages.

Yes, I love Alan Savage, he is one of you.

And I love, I love, I love . . . *you.*

Mrs. Savage will embrace her, Mrs. Savage is a soft melting lovely woman, she'll be grieving for Kennedy and for his widow and when she and Iris are together (soon: tomorrow evening) she'll certainly want to embrace Iris Courtney, her son's "young woman

371

friend," her own "dear young friend," and, yes, they'll very likely weep together over this national tragedy.

(Though, as Alan Savage has several times pointed out, Mrs. Savage is after all a Makepeace from North Carolina: there's a deep conservatism bred in her bones regarding "liberals," "Negroes," "government interference in private lives.")

The door to Byron Savage's office is shut, however, and locked, of course it's locked; Byron Savage is away in London, lecturing at the Courtauld Institute.

As Iris Courtney must know, since she'd helped him prepare for the trip, assembled and annotated his numerous slides.

As Iris Courtney must know, since only the other evening at the Savages' Byron Savage's absence was conspicuous, and Mrs. Savage said, "Don't we all miss Byron? This house is so *placid* without him."

And the door to the office of *The Journal of Art and Aesthetics* is locked too, a disappointment to Iris; she'd hoped perhaps to begin work a little earlier that afternoon now that classes are canceled for the day, now that time seems to have pleated in a way that frightens and exhilarates her, as in a protracted eclipse of the sun. She's eager, it might be she's desperate, to get inside the office to sit at her familiar little table to resume proofreading galleys for the next issue of the *Journal*—the previous afternoon she'd been forced to break off in the middle of a difficult and much-footnoted article on Caravaggio's *The Last Supper at Emmaus*—this past year she's become nervously irritated if forced to break off any task before its satisfactory completion. Sometimes she discovers an actual eruption on her skin, thin weltlike rashes on her forearms, on the soft skin of her wrists. Her skin is becoming as sensitive as Alan Savage's.

So you're a perfectionist, Iris! Mrs. Savage has observed, with her chiding, affectionate smile. Just like Byron and Alan. I wish you would all keep in mind, "perfection" can lacerate the heart.

Can it?

For some minutes Iris Courtney simply stands with her hand on the doorknob of the door to the office of *The Journal of Art and Aesthetics*,

Room 346, Strouse Hall. She is not thinking of anything, not even of the "assassination," not even of the practical fact that she might go home to her room on South Salina Street and crawl into bed with the covers over her and wait out this strange and inexplicable arousal of her soul . . . this sense of loss and of lostness, true terror.

She might do that. She might give herself up to tears.

And: Alan Savage will be coming to see her that evening, at least that was their plan; he'll take her out to dinner, he wants to discuss something serious with her, his "future plans," her "future plans," too long nebulous. . . . But the prospect of returning to that room fills Iris with dread.

She notes that Strouse Hall is nearly deserted.

She notes that there is no purpose to her remaining where she is, foolishly gripping a doorknob to a locked door.

So she descends the stairs, slowly, as if reluctantly, and on the second floor encounters a shaggy-haired graduate student pushing his way out of a men's lavatory; he's a young man Iris knows only slightly, a young man rumored to be enormously bright, his field of specialization the baroque; and this young man and Iris Courtney on the afternoon of November 22, 1963, exchange swift apprehensive glances—Don't talk to me, don't say a word about what has happened, the assassination, the public death; I don't have time for it, I am not like the rest of you—but there's no danger: neither speaks except to murmur hello, they pass each other quickly.

There follows now a confused period of time, for what use is there to make of time when time is infinite, and where to go when there's nowhere? As she won't be able to explain afterward to Alan Savage. As she won't make much effort to explain afterward to Alan Savage.

He'll telephone her in the late afternoon and no answer, he'll arrive at the rooming house at seven as they'd planned but of course she isn't there, nor any message, nor has the house manager seen Iris Courtney since that morning. It isn't like Iris to forget, Alan Savage will say, it isn't like her . . . but Iris isn't thinking of what it is, or isn't, like her to do or to fail to do; she's forgotten Alan Savage altogether, or nearly, she's simply walking . . . swiftly walking . . .

the steeply hilly streets and sidewalks of the university area, on Comstock, on Waverly, on Marshall, in the fine chill insidious rain, in the waning afternoon light.

Too agitated to remain in one place for more than a few minutes at a time.

Thinking, Why do you care? You don't care!

Squinting at the sky with a sensation of slow-gathering horror, seeing its look of crude, burgeoning life, unicellular life.

Seeing how, just at dusk, the sun appears briefly, watery yet luminous . . . a floating eye. Why do you care?

She's as upset, incensed, as a pauper approached for a handout.

She's as upset as, at the first, those terrible hours at the first, she'd been at Persia's death.

When they came to tell her, Your mother is dead.

Waking Iris Courtney the patient's daughter in the plastic bucket chair in which she'd fallen uncomfortably asleep, neck cricked, mouth slackly open as a dying fish's, those words she had truly not expected she must hear: Your mother is dead.

She'd murmured, Oh.

Hadn't cried. With an air more of surprise than shock, Oh.

And now this public death, this public expenditure of emotion, every face glimpsed on every street, every moment heavy with the news, the latest bulletin, Kennedy's death at the hands of a "lone sniper," why should she care, she does not love John F. Kennedy, though, yes, she has admired him, as naturally she would admire a young vigorous unmistakably intelligent President, his courage in pressing for civil rights legislation in the face of racist opposition; certainly she admires him but she's skeptical, she's inherited Duke Courtney's cynicism about all human motives, thus it's absurd, this sense of loss, of childish grief. Who is the man to you, why shouldn't he die, doesn't everyone die, why not him, why not all of them, why such hypocrisy, why?

In a secondhand bookstore on Marshall Street she's jammed in with a dozen others watching a television news broadcast, standing on tiptoe to catch a glimpse of the suspected sniper Lee Harvey

374

Oswald as he's marched quickly past the camera by Dallas policemen; Iris sees that he's young, slight-bodied, defiant, white.

Iris says, "His name is so American-sounding, isn't it? Like a name in a ballad."

Her voice is strange and wondering, and no one directly replies.

Iris says, "A terrorist has to be willing to trade his life for his victim's."

Again, no one replies.

On the television there is newsreel footage: Vice-President Lyndon Johnson being sworn in as President of the United States.

And where are John F. Kennedy's "remains"?

En route to Washington, D.C. Airborne.

All so unreal.

On University Avenue in front of the popular student tavern the Orange she's stopped by a bull-necked young man named Jake who invites her to come have a few beers with him and his buddies (he's a fraternity man, the cryptic insignia of his house reproduced in imitation satin on his corduroy jacket)—"We're having an Irish wake," says Jake heartily, "just like that s.o.b. would like"—and Iris declines but smiles, trying to bypass this young man with whom she is slightly though not warmly acquainted; there's a history of his increasingly aggressive pursuit of her and her increasingly adamant rejection of him but it isn't a matter of which she thinks much except at such times when she sees him she's forced to think, to realize herself as a figure of some significance in another's life, an annoyance, an insult, an insoluble problem, yes, and his fraternity brothers know too, yes, and he's already a little drunk and thinking well of himself and Iris is thinking, yes, that's the attitude, it's a holiday of a kind, why not simply get drunk, if drunk is what you're happiest in; but Iris is walking away and the bull-necked young man calls crudely after her, "You and everybody else making such a goddamned big deal out of that asshole getting shot, well somebody needed to do it, somebody had the guts to do it, and the next to go's gonna be Martin Luther King"—enunciating the name as if it were a bad taste in his mouth—and Iris calls over her shoulder angrily, "But *you* didn't have the guts to do it, did you," neither knowing nor caring what she's saying but walking swiftly down the hilly street as the fraternity men yell after her, hooting and whistling, sounds she'd rather not hear.

It's dark now. Streetlights have come on, car headlights, lights in homes . . . there's a glimmery insubstantial look to the world, she's walking undersea, deeper and deeper undersea down the long hill out of the university neighborhood as the shapes of things blur and dissolve around her.

And who are you? And why do you care? And why do you imagine it means anything, that you care? What power has your caring to keep another alive?

Hours have passed, it's nearly nine o'clock unless the clock is wrong, a plump moon-faced glowing clock in the darkened window of a branch of the First Bank of Syracuse, and she's crossing Pearce Boulevard into a rundown neighborhood somewhere on the far side of downtown beyond the illuminated buildings of Niagara Mohawk Power, beyond the railroad and warehouse district where a century ago that pioneering genius Ezra Savage built his original warehouses, all the buildings long since razed like the original store on Clinton Street, but the original Savage home on East Genesee still remains and is designated by a plaque from the New York State Historical Society . . . on one of their romantic autumn-afternoon drives Alan Savage took Iris Courtney to see it.

Crossing the Onondaga River on the Erie Street bridge and the river is a wide dark featureless stream from which gusts of cold seem to rise . . . on the far side there's a cobbled street glistening in blinding patches of reflected light, and running across it in the wake of a city bus (brightly lit within like a Hopper painting, only the driver and two passengers) Iris discovers that her feet are wet, her cheap woolen coat soaked through, hair straggling in limp tendrils in her face. *I wrote him three times, he never answered. When my mother died, he never called.*

The harsh brackish smell of the river. Drizzling rain, rising mist, an undersea world miles from the university, on lower ground.

At least, here, you can breathe.

Some of the intervening hills are steep, others more subtle. But always the descent.

You feel these hills most acutely in the calves of your legs.

Iris hesitates but decides to enter a tunnel-like underpass below a railroad embankment, for otherwise where's she to go? Back? Back up the hills? Back to her room so snug so cozy to await deliverance? She's fearless, humming loudly to herself, "Blue Skies" is a witty sort of pop tune to hum on a night of such wet and dark and oblivion and there's a sound of dripping and a sudden shocking stench of stale urine . . . old newspapers and leaves rotted together underfoot . . . darkness. She's fearless and defiant, humming in the shadows but half running up the steps to escape.

I knew how he wanted me, I could feel his blood-swollen penis.

But it was only his body, between the legs. Not him.

She isn't crying, she isn't that kind of young woman and never will be that kind of woman; icy-hearted, harder than nails, her husband will one day say in hurt in outrage in simple bewilderment, Why did you marry me if, why do you insist you love me if? Yes but I do love, yes but I—I do, I will, I'll make the effort, I won't be cheated. She isn't crying but she's tired and everything seems by degrees to have gone soft as in a watercolor wash: the infrequent headlights of passing cars, the street lights, TULA'S BAR-B-Q in red neon and MONTY'S (a tavern) in tawny-gold neon through which white incandescent tubing has begun to show in patches.

And the warm-lit interiors of rooms in this neighborhood of ramshackle houses, shabby row houses, brownstone tenements jammed up against one another where families are watching television together . . . footage of Dallas, reruns of newsreels, interviews, up-to-the-minute bulletins . . . Jackie and the children and Lee Harvey Oswald and Lyndon B. Johnson and the limousine, the motorcade, the rest.

A national mourning, a luxury of grief, in which Iris Courtney isn't going to share.

At an intersection there's a flashing yellow light and a car cruises through, windows down, rock music blasting, a carload of what appear to be young black men or boys but Iris doesn't notice, she's suddenly so tired . . . light-headed. Minuscule drops of rain have collected jewel-like on her eyelashes.

Everything has begun to turn soft, to blur, time too has become soft; you blink and blink to bring your vision into focus but this *is* focus, this *is* the world . . . not evil but madness.

Objects, and we among them, objects in others' eyes, losing their shapes, definitions, names: the boundaries separating them gone, their very skins torn off or peeled deliberately away as in that deathly painting at which Iris Courtney stared for a very long time one day in Dr. Savage's library at his home, turning the pages of an enormous Italian-produced book of Titian plates—a late oil of Titian's titled *Marsyas Flayed by Apollo*. The skinning alive of a satyr who's in fact a human being. Not evil but madness.

No: she's in a municipal building, not in Dr. Savage's home, saying in a strong, clear voice, *He never meant to kill, it was my fault*.

She's light-headed, faint . . . has to go to the bathroom.

Passing open doorways, windows close by the sidewalk, passing children playing in the rain, raised voices inside rooms only a few yards away, curious eyes observing her . . . she pushes into a little café advertising barbecue and Coca-Cola and to the black woman behind the counter she explains her need, the sudden distress of her need, in a low shamed voice, and the black woman blinks at Iris Courtney in turn in surprise at seeing a young white woman in here, this hour, this weather, this day of all days, but she says, "Why sure, honey," though with an air of hesitation, she's a woman of about fifty, thick-bodied, short, with a sad, lined, jowled face, smoky skin, bifocals riding the bridge of her nose, eyeing Iris with an air somewhere between concern and pity, "Sure honey you're welcome to use it, lemme show you where," and once the plywood door is latched shut or nearly shut and Iris Courtney is seated on the cracked toilet seat, no paper tissue to arrange on the seat for protection and no time for such fastidiousness in any case, urine gushing out of her, she's nearly weeping in relief or is it perhaps sympathy with her body, its expulsion of fluid poison. And not minding for a moment the filthy floor of the lavatory, the overpowering odor, the nearness of voices.

There's no toilet paper so she searches her pockets for a Kleenex. Finds a single wadded Kleenex for which she's enormously grateful.

And the toilet flushes . . . for which she's enormously grateful.

When she returns to the front where the black woman and her customers await her, quite frankly looking at her, several men, one or two other women, she smiles stricken with embarrassment at everyone and at no one, running her fingers nervous as small birds through her damp hair. There was no mirror in the little lavatory, thus she's spared a nightmare vision of herself, her appearance in these strangers' eyes. Her shoes are soaked through.

Says the black woman proprietress with a motherly frown, "Anything wrong, honey? You're looking a little—"

Iris says quickly, shyly, "Oh thank you, I'm fine. Thank you." She pauses. Tries to smile. The name stitched on the collar of the black woman's snug-fitting dress is *Mandy*. Gold letters on pale yellow cotton.

She says, "I . . . I'm maybe a little hungry."

Mandy says, "Y'awl sure do *look* hungry, that's for sure!" She slaps her hand down flat on the counter meaning sit down, sit and I'll feed you, no more nonsense.

Iris sits. Iris unbuttons her damp coat but doesn't take it off.

The café is just a storefront, a counter and a single row of stools, several small tables, a mouth-watering aroma of barbecue, grease, French fries, catsup, and the air's thick with cigarette smoke and a scent of hair oil. Iris hasn't wanted to look directly at anyone except squat kindly Mandy, who seems to have taken a liking to her.

That morning Iris had gone out to classes without her purse or wallet as she often does but, good luck, she has some loose change in her coat pocket, enough for a cup of hot black coffee and a thick slab of pie, Mandy's proud to say her home-baked pie for that day is

379

boysenberry and it's *good*, and Iris sits at the counter of the Ninth Street Café trembling with hunger eating boysenberry pie so delicious its taste sears her mouth, drinking coffee sweetened with milk, as, by degrees, the voices of the other customers resume, their low earnest talk resumes, as if she isn't there.

So white-skinned, so provisional . . . maybe in fact she isn't there.

Mandy stares at Iris Courtney, concerned. "You out walkin', or what? You from the university up there?" and Iris nods mutely, mouth filled with pie, and Mandy still staring, says, "How're you gonna get back, then? It's a long way back and it's late." Adding, when Iris doesn't respond, "I was you, I'd take a taxi. Want me to call you a taxi?"

Iris says quickly, "I don't have any money for a taxi."

"Can't you pay the man when you get where you're going? Get some money from somebody where you live?"

Mandy is mildly incredulous, impatient. What's this white girl doing *here*, tonight of all nights?

There's a red plastic radio on a shelf above the grill tuned to NBC News . . . unavoidable news. Iris has walked into a scene of emotion and jangled nerves in this café, it's unavoidable, nowhere to hide tonight in America, nowhere to escape. The latest from Washington, D.C., the latest from Dallas, Texas . . . a rushed interview with an "eyewitness" Secret Service man . . . further information concerning Lee Harvey Oswald, "the lone assassin."

Then music: "Will You Love Me Tomorrow?" by the Shirelles.

Mandy and her customers discuss the news in voices that range from thoughtful to vehement, angry to aggrieved. Iris listens, thinking, Why do you care that a white man has died? Why do you put your faith in any of us? What she most wants to do isn't cry but cradle her head in her arms on the counter, shut her eyes, vanish.

Mandy appears to be the most agitated. She's been crying, that's why her face is so puffy, lined, her big breasts rising and falling with feeling, the lenses of her glasses misting over. Oh Gawd, she's saying, ain't it the terriblest terriblest shame, that poor man, poor Mrs. Kennedy left with those little children, how's she gonna tell those children what a cruel thing happened to their daddy out in plain daylight, and Iris realizes that it's she whom Mandy is addressing, she says, "Yes, it's terrible," but her voice is faint and unconvincing, as if she's thinking of something else or has something to ask of Mandy in turn—*Why put your faith in any of us?*—but thinks better of asking. Just bites her lip, keeps her mouth shut.

The boysenberry pie costs forty-five cents, the coffee ten cents, Iris carefully counts out seventy cents from the change in her pocket, adds another nickel, some pennies—her last penny, in fact—as if she's suddenly eager to get rid of all her money, meager as it is.

While Mandy is elsewhere, back to Iris, Iris leaves her little pile of coins by her plate, hurries out of the café before Mandy returns to see how much she's left and call her back.

" 'Bye!" Iris calls.

She hears Mandy call something after her. As she leaves, the Shirelles are still singing "Will You Love Me Tomorrow?"

Not to police, not to the doctor in charge of the Syracuse Memorial Hospital emergency room or any of the nurses there, not to Alan Savage, not to any of the Savages will Iris Courtney make any attempt to explain why . . . what logic, what purpose, walking alone at night in a neighborhood so far from her own, a part of her mind not numbed with fatigue but brightly alert, even hopeful, imagining she's in Hammond somehow . . . in Hammond, in Lowertown . . . the slow-smiling eyes, the bared teeth glistening, *Mmmmmmmmmm! hey girl!* but you must never look, it's dangerous.

She'll say, I didn't see their faces.

She'll say, Yes they were black but I didn't see their faces.

Walking at the curb on Tenth Street to avoid the doorways, the mouths of alleys. Now the rain has stopped it's cold. Her breath is steaming. There's a tavern brimming with noise and warmth blinking MOLSON'S in the window where black men stand at the bar in a haze of smoke and someone calls, whistles, dances after her . . . but she doesn't look . . . it's dangerous. Iris Courtney's studied, slightly swaying walk and her loose arms suggest she's drunk or drugged but her eyes are fully open, bright, intelligent—don't talk to me, don't approach me, don't touch me—and for several blocks she makes her way unimpeded like a dreamer in a charmed landscape until at Oswego Street and West Avenue a car with a noisy muffler cruises through the intersection, skids to a stop, backs up like a comically agitated insect . . . its rear hiked, its back tires luridly exposed. A black boy's head emerges from the driver's window and there's a soft-sliding call, "Hey: you looking for a ride?"

Iris stares at the pavement before her. Murmurs, "No . . . no, thanks."

"Say what, honey? Huhhhhhhh?" And, louder: "You looking for a *ride?*"

The car, filled with young black men in their late teens, early twenties, is noisily idling in the street, spewing out clouds of exhaust. It's a holiday! You can feel it! From the car radio rock music blasts and all the boys are talking at once, there's a car door flung open, long long legs springing out, black-sneakered feet enormous as clubs. Iris Courtney turns quickly to walk in the opposite direction but somehow it happens (she blinks: he's there) one of them is on the sidewalk grinning, blocking her way basketball-style . . . and when she turns like a trapped animal there's another, gangly limbed and antic, reefer-happy, blocking her way . . . so she's transfixed, thinking, Don't struggle, don't resist, then they won't kill you—but when the playful black boys grab her and drag her into the back seat of the already moving car she loses control, she's weeping and hysterical suddenly, screaming, kicking, pummeling with her fists . . . sprawled helplessly and gracelessly across their laps, three of them jammed in the back as the car guns off, tires squealing, and there's wild laughter as their hands run over her in amazed delight, fingers deft and hard, there's a smell of sweet-acrid smoke and cheap wine and they're grabbing her breasts, squeezing, sticking their fingers into her, into her crotch, she's panicked, squirming like a maddened eel, screaming and sobbing . . . even as her consciousness detaches itself from her struggling body floating and suspended voiceless above it as if she has already died.

But she hasn't.

382

Epilogue

Here is the wedding dress Iris Courtney will be wearing at her wedding to Alan Savage in the First Presbyterian Church of Syracuse, New York: an Empire-style gown sewed for Gwendolyn Savage's mother in 1904, lovely flawlessly white Chinese silk, a bodice of tight, tiny pleats, a many-layered skirt with an illusion of floating, and a long graceful train, and a bridal veil of Brussels lace: an extraordinary costume the bride-to-be has contemplated many times in the past six months and now contemplates in silence another time, holding it at arm's length, reverently, before, with the deft assistance of Mrs. Savage and the seamstress Mrs. Vitale, she tries it on again. (This is the final, or nearly final fitting: the nuptial ceremony is scheduled for 11 A.M., September 12, 1964, scarcely forty-eight hours from now.) The tailor's mirror is positioned to contain Iris's full height, top of head to hemline, and as the feathery parachutelike skirt, then the snug-fitting torso, are eased downward Iris stares into the mirror in wonderment that it is her head—her familiar head, hair, face—that emerges from so much white silk . . . and not a stranger's.

The first time Iris Courtney was urged to try on this heirloom dress, back in June, she'd felt a wave of apprehension sweep over her palpable as a draft of cold air, but laughed to disguise her nervousness, saying, "This is a work of art, Mrs. Savage, it seems wrong for someone to actually wear it," and Mrs. Savage said briskly, "*I* think it's high time it *is* worn . . . what's a wedding dress if it only hangs in a closet?"

Now Mrs. Savage is all business, conferring with Mrs. Vitale quite literally behind Iris's back as, cautiously, Iris lowers her arms . . . the women are rapidly buttoning up the long row of mother-of-pearl buttons in back that's in mimicry of her spine's vertebrae; they puff out the dress's sleeves, straighten the skirt, far more brusquely than Iris would dare. For what if a fingernail snags in the dazzling silk, what if a seam rips? Silk is a strong, durable fabric, Iris knows, has been told, but doesn't believe it.

It was a disappointment to Gwendolyn Savage that her mother's wedding dress, this Empire style, simply didn't suit her, so she married Byron Savage in a very pretty but very ordinary dress . . . she wants something finer for her lovely daughter-in-law, and this is it.

Softly exclaiming as she pinches the bodice, "Oh, damn . . . *is* this loose? Again?"

And Mrs. Vitale says, sighing, "It's loose."

Evidently, since the last fitting, the bride-to-be has lost more weight. Another pleat or two will have to be taken in, another judicious tuck.

The bride-to-be is a tall, slender, high-waisted young woman, inches taller than Gwendolyn Savage's mother back in 1904, her bust is inches smaller, extensive alterations have already been made in the dress. But Mrs. Vitale can certainly take in the bodice a little more and they'll try the dress again after lunch for a final time before the wedding. Then, says Mrs. Savage, it's over to the church for the rehearsal . . . including the Bach organ solo, and the soprano singing Schumann . . . and a reasonably early dinner, just family

386

(though "family" in this instance includes six Makepeaces already north for the wedding) . . . and, Mrs. Savage is going to insist, a reasonably early bedtime.

"When all this is over, and you and Alan are off on your honeymoon, I am going to collapse," Mrs. Savage says, sighing, "collapse," but her jewellike blue eyes light onto Iris's eyes in the mirror, she's flush-cheeked as a young girl and it's clear she doesn't mean a syllable of complaint or reproach, Gwendolyn Savage never does.

Mrs. Savage and Mrs. Vitale help Iris out of the dress, lifting it from her in slow, careful stages . . . over her head, her slender arms out of the sleeves . . . then she's standing bare-armed, shivering in her lacy slip, suddenly exposed. Her face without makeup looks shiny as if scrubbed, the scattering of freckles across her cheeks and forehead has long since faded.

She turns quickly from the mirror, now the dress has been taken from her.

The lovely Chinese silk dress is an heirloom, and so is the antique engagement ring on Iris Courtney's finger. A square-cut diamond edged with smaller diamonds, in a finely wrought silver setting, not raised but recessed, so the tiny prongs rarely catch in clothing or on gloves.

This ring has come down through the Savage family; Byron's mother willed it to Gwendolyn shortly before her death.

Now Iris and Alan have been engaged seven months, she has never taken it off her finger. Not once.

It's a perfect fit.

When, after graduation in May, Iris returned to Hammond for a brief visit and showed this ring to Leslie Courtney, her uncle pursed his lips and whistled . . . but the sound emerged breathy and melancholy.

He said, though, what was foremost in both their thoughts: "Wouldn't Persia be proud!"

Later, Iris visited with her father and her father's new wife Jenny Lou Guthrie. Spoke of her fiancé, Alan Savage, and of the

Savages of Syracuse, New York, passed around snapshots, as if describing a remote tribe of human beings in no way contiguous with the residents of Hammond, New York. Duke Courtney did not question this but when Iris showed him the engagement ring he too whistled, snatched up her hand in his, and brought it to the lamplight; he'd been drinking (and so had Jenny Lou: a brassy-haired good-looking woman in her late forties, former widow of a Buffalo racehorse owner), and he clowned about pretending to be examining the ring like a jeweler, through his encircled thumb and forefinger, "Honey, this is the genuine article, the real goods, are you *aware?*"

Stiffly, with dignity, Iris Courtney withdrew her hand from her father's.

She said, "The ring is priceless. It can't be replaced."

Duke Courtney laughed, his tawny-golden eyes flaring up.

He said, winking, "Not without a lot of money, it can't."

Afterward, Iris wondered why she'd sought him out: her father and his "new" wife.

Her laughing charming silver-haired alcoholic father, his big-breasted big-hipped showgirl-looking wife Jenny Lou, with her half-moons of bright lipstick smudged on glasses, cigarettes, Iris's left cheek. A gay easy-laughing couple clearly fond of each other and determined not to acknowledge, not even to suggest, what possible link there might be between Duke Courtney and the twenty-two-year-old woman who came to visit, what third party, not present, linked them.

They energetically matched Iris's talk and snapshots with talk and snapshots of their own, for in marrying a racehorse owner's widow Duke Courtney had married a stable of seven horses of which two or three were consistent winners, in low-stakes races at least: Here's Princess Meg, here's Will-o'-the-Wisp, here's Iron Heel, if you have time, Iris, let's all drive out to Oldwick to the farm; I'd love you to see Orion, our new trotter, the first yearling I bought myself at auction last August, he's being trained by one of the best

388

in the business and here's the list of stakes he's entered in already and if things go as Jenny Lou and I hope. . . .

Iris Courtney was sitting on an overstuffed sofa smiling and admiring and exclaiming over photographs of horses, and after the two-hour visit she came away amazed and vengeful thinking that not once had Duke so much as alluded to the fact of Persia, the fact that there had ever been a Persia, and she thought, But I won't invite them to the wedding, and then she thought, a while later, more calmly, returning to Syracuse and to her life there, that the new Courtneys hadn't asked about the wedding, hadn't shown the slightest interest, for at the very least it would mean a wedding present, wouldn't it.

Duke Courtney's parting words to his daughter were, "Love ya, honey! Keep in touch!"

Iris intends to invite Leslie Courtney to her wedding—of course. As for Aunt Madelyn, she hasn't decided.

Not because she's ashamed (*is* she?) of her beautician aunt with her cheap colorful clothes and orangish-dyed permed hair, but yes perhaps she's worried of how the Savages will respond to her and interpret her, a woman bearing so little resemblance to Iris Courtney and to the Persia Courtney whom Iris has described, an "aunt" who isn't in fact an aunt but a more distant relative, of ambiguous stature. Iris tells herself nervously, I must invite someone, they will think I am an orphan, or an outcast.

This is the problem, however: in recent years Madelyn Daiches has become passionately religious, an "evangelical" convert, sending off $5 and $10 bills out of her meager salary to Christian causes, speaking of her Redeemer Jesus Christ in familiar, emotional terms, a glisten to her eyes suggesting a true inner light, or madness. Iris had heard of Madelyn's conversion from Leslie but did not know, quite, what it meant, wasn't prepared for the shock of meeting her. According to Leslie, shortly after Persia's death (which upset her greatly), Madelyn went with several women friends to hear the Reverend Billy Graham preaching in Batavia, New York, at a

Christian Revival Festival and has never been the same since. When Iris visited her the first thing she told Iris was that Jesus Christ was the most important person in her life now and "the most important person in your life, Iris, if only you would realize."

And she'd hugged Iris, hard. And kissed her. Eyes shut tight.

It was a strange visit, with Aunt Madelyn. Whenever Iris tries to recall it, in bits and pieces, it seems stranger still.

"You see, Iris dear, people like Persia aren't really 'dead,' they're with Jesus . . . and the Father. Persia is with her loved ones who have crossed over, all of them, your grandparents and your great-grandparents and, oh! all of them, looking down upon us and feeling pity for us in our blindness," Madelyn said. She spoke in spurts, both slowly and eagerly, as if a great pressure were building up inside her that must be contained. Seeing that Iris sat silent, eyes downcast, hands clasped in her lap, and thinking that silence is consent, Madelyn continued speaking in this vein for some minutes, and in her voice Iris believed she could detect cadences not Madelyn Daiches's own but those of a stranger, an inspired and aggressive stranger. Not Jesus Christ perhaps but one of His earthly emissaries?

"Oh," said Iris. "I see."

"*I* commune with Persia every day, sometimes twice a day," Madelyn said. Her eyes were soft, her mouth tremulous. "Persia is there for you too, Iris, if you'd give your heart to Jesus Christ. If you'd *try*."

How do you know I haven't tried? Iris thought.

Aloud Iris said, "Well."

"As *I* want you to, dear."

Iris could not think of an intelligent reply, let alone an adequate rejoinder. Religious fanaticism frightened her less because it was fanatic than because it suggested a reality, however interior, however problematic, inaccessible to her; it was a food that, in her mouth, had no taste . . . gave no nourishment. In Aunt Madelyn's living room she sat for an hour, murmuring "Yes" and "No" and "Thank you" as Madelyn spoke, even read to Iris from her Bible as, oddly, yet in an entirely different context, Gwendolyn Savage had

390

once read to Iris, newly home from the hospital: "*And he said unto them, Ye are from beneath; I am from above: ye are of this world; I am not of this world. I said therefore unto you, that ye shall die in your sins: for if ye believe not that I am he—*"

Iris could not help saying, with a child's futile obstinacy, "Jesus is always threatening us, isn't he? Always saying, If you don't do this, then this will happen to you. If you don't believe in me you're doomed to hell."

Madelyn blinked at Iris as if Iris had spoken unintelligible words. She said, "Why, of course, dear. That's how it *is*."

Outside on the street children were playing, calling to one another. An airplane passed high overhead. Iris felt something tug at her, anger, despair, grief; no, she was wholly in control of herself as always, saying, with a smile, "And Persia isn't gone, as if she'd never lived—she's only watching us."

"Watching *over* us."

"Waiting for us."

"Waiting for you especially, Iris . . . seeing as how she loved you more than anyone else on earth."

Saying goodbye, Iris and Madelyn had embraced again, and this time they'd both cried. As if knowing they might not see each other for a long, long time.

Iris has decided not to invite Madelyn to the wedding . . . and not to examine her conscience about the decision.

Which means she'll have only one relative, Leslie Courtney, as a guest; Leslie, whom she believes she can trust.

In any case, it seems to suit the Savages, the elder Savages in particular, to think of Iris Courtney as an orphan.

But do you really love me?

Of course I "really" love you, how could I not?

But do you . . . forgive me?

You were a victim of circumstances, Iris. You were the victim.

Alan Savage wants to marry Iris Courtney, gave her his mother's heirloom ring, because he loves her . . . loves her more than he has ever loved anyone in his life . . . and is not going to be deterred in loving her. Somehow, Iris thinks, I hadn't counted on that.

Now that the wedding is imminent, less than forty-eight hours away, all family conversations are about *how* a thing should be done, not *why*. Of course. Life is practicality; life is planning and scheduling; life is a sequence of pleasant tasks. No one ever brings up, or even alludes to, Iris's "accident" on that terrible day in November 1963.

That terrible, terrible day.

Iris had expected to see in Alan Savage's eyes, when he first came to visit her in the hospital (alone: the elder Savages had not yet been informed of the assault), a look of distaste, perhaps even revulsion . . . but Alan's eyes brimmed simply with tears; it was as if Iris's hurt were his own: he'd gripped her hands in his and laid his head against her; they'd wept together in mutual commiseration.

Iris thought, disbelieving, Does he love me, then?

Blackened eyes . . . a bloodied nose . . . a cracked rib . . . bruises and bumps and lacerations (particularly of her knees and the palms of her hands; she'd been dragged resisting across pavement) . . . clumps of hair torn from her head, and a chipped front tooth . . . kicks to her lower belly, and between the legs—the assault was "sexual" obviously though not in the most technical sense "rape" since there had been no actual penetration of the vagina. In her early delirium the patient said she didn't think they'd meant to hurt her as much as they had; it was because she'd fought them, resisted.

Eventually Mrs. Savage would say, You must pray for them, dear, you mustn't harbor bitterness.

Oh, yes. Oh, no.

It's the only way. The Christian way. The way of health, forgiveness.

Iris could tell Syracuse police only that her assailants were young black men. She wasn't sure if there had been four or five, hadn't seen their faces clearly, hadn't heard any of them call any other by name, could not identify the car, even its color. Nor was she certain of the location in which she'd been picked up except to know it was somewhere west of the river.

Someone has predicted bad dreams for months, years.

A lifetime of flinching when she sees black skin.

Iris Courtney doesn't think much about it, never speaks of it with Alan any longer, nor does Alan speak of it with her, so many other things to concentrate upon with the wedding Saturday morning and the honeymoon trip by Pullman to New York City where they will stay for six days in a suite at the Plaza Hotel, then return briefly to Syracuse in preparation for their move to a handsome eighteenth-century brownstone on Delancey Street, Philadelphia . . . for Alan Savage has surprised everyone by accepting a position as assistant curator at the Philadelphia Museum of Art instead of an academic position, and Iris Courtney may one day enroll in graduate studies at Penn, in art history, or so it's their plan, once things get settled. Moving into the Delancey Street brownstone, properly furnishing it, taking on the responsibilities of a young curator's wife . . . she'll have a good deal to do.

Please don't laugh when I say I want to be a good wife to you: I want to be worthy.

Alan Savage frames his bride-to-be's lovely face in his hands, nudges her forehead gently with his, kisses the tip of her nose and then, lightly, her lips . . . she's a tall straight-backed young woman but he's several inches taller and friends of the Savages have been commenting for months on the change in him, his new air of maturity, self-assurance, yet playfulness too, he's quick to smile and rarely does he flare up any longer in annoyance at a goading remark of Byron's; yes, perhaps he has begun to see the wisdom of his father's perspective, and at the Philadelphia Museum of Art he'll be in charge of the extensive Duchamp and Modernist holdings in a context (he plans) of classic European art . . . for Alan Savage's agenda is to relate Surrealist experimentation to the tradition and not isolate it, as its practitioners demanded, as if it were sui generis.

My Botticelli: how could you not be "worthy"?

Kissing her gently, questioningly . . . they're hidden away in

393

the guest room on the second floor, rear, overlooking Mrs. Savage's rose garden, in which Iris has stayed since the family moved back to town from Skaneateles at the end of August; Iris Courtney has left forever that shabby rooming house on South Salina Street and within weeks all memory of it will have faded from her mind or perhaps has already faded in this fragrant chintz-furnished room with the graceful white louver shutters (closed now against the humid September sunshine) and her trembling bridegroom embraces her, kissing lips, eyes . . . his mothlike kisses . . . bending to press his warm face against her hard little breasts like a child's fists inside her cotton shirt, stooping, finally kneeling, to kiss the pit of her belly, gently between the legs . . . as she stiffens, just slightly . . . but doesn't close her fingers in his hair and, as if in play, urge him away as she's done many times, so this time he remains kneeling, hugging her around the hips, his warm face pressed against her, his eyes shut.

If it excites Alan Savage to think of Iris Courtney having been the victim of a "sexual assault" . . . by young black men, faceless and nameless . . . it isn't a fact, or even a possibility, he'll articulate.

It's I who must be worthy of you.

Lunchtime but no one wants to sit down and there's the telephone again, it has been ringing ringing ringing for days, and Mrs. Savage's voice lifts another time: *Hello? Oh, hel-lo!*

Twice daily the delivery truck marked UNITED PARCEL SERVICE turns up the looping gravel drive of Savage House, the Chinese-import reception room has become a treasure trove of wedding gifts through which Alan Savage and Iris Courtney move, fingers linked, like staring children . . . in awe, in gratitude, on the verge of mirth. Iris says with a laughing little shudder that she'll be spending the first month of her married life writing thank-you notes; Alan runs a hand through his hair confessing with a smile that he had no idea he had so many relatives: a veritable subgalaxy of Savages, Makepeaces, and blood-related others.

"How will I ever repay them?"

Tugging at his fingers his bride-to-be amends, "*We.*"

They flee from such dazzling sights, the silver alone enough to stagger the eye, wander for a few minutes in Mrs. Savage's rose garden, fingers still linked, and Alan Savage is quiet as if brooding, then says, with that air of sudden perception Iris Courtney so admires in him, like a match suddenly flaring into flame, "Freud believed that only the delayed gratification of an infantile wish can bring adult happiness; that's why money, material things, rarely bring happiness . . . they aren't infantile wishes."

Iris Courtney laughs, murmuring, "What remains, then?"

Someone calls them from the house; it's lunchtime: cold shrimp and scallop salad, green salad, fruit on the table but no one wants to sit down and there's the telephone again and though Mercedes answers it Mrs. Savage can't resist taking any call for it's the caterer with a crucial question, or the photographer with a crucial question, or Dr. Niemann's secretary, or Dr. Niemann himself, or one of Gwendolyn's sisters, or one of Byron's aged aunts, or the society editor of the Syracuse *Journal* wanting to know the exact number of wedding guests expected, the exact number of nights the newlyweds will spend at the Plaza Hotel, the exact title of Alan Savage's new appointment at the Philadelphia Museum of Art.

These many callers, Mrs. Savage is happy to oblige.

(Confiding in the society editor of the *Journal,* an old acquaintance, that she and Dr. Savage will miss their son and new daughter-in-law enormously away off in Philadelphia but the family will be vacationing together in January, in Barbados, two lovely weeks at the resort hotel to which she and Dr. Savage have been returning faithfully for the past seventeen years.)

There's an old favorite song of Mrs. Savage's running through her mind these days, a Cole Porter dance tune; sometimes it surfaces and she finds herself humming or singing under her breath: ". . . *you are the one.*"

But where is Dr. Savage; why hasn't he come to lunch?

His library is empty: he seems to have left the house.

The doorbell rings briskly at the rear of the house; it's the champagne delivery: cases and cases of French champagne.

Lunch is prepared, plates laid on the dining room table, but no one sits down except Mrs. Vitale, who's a special guest today, and hungry, in a grim-smiling mood which only discreet praise from Mrs. Savage can placate, and a glass or two of tart red wine, and food. For it isn't only the bride's dress that requires last-minute alteration but Mrs. Savage's pink silk sheath, which Mrs. Vitale sewed especially for the occasion: the skirt, Mrs. Savage abruptly decided, is a full inch too long and makes her look "dowdy."

Amid the lovely bridesmaids and the yet lovelier bride, she, the matron of honor, the groom's mother, has a horror of appearing "dowdy" . . . it isn't vanity but familial pride.

Alan and Iris, the one in khaki sports clothes, the other in shirt and jeans, appear in the dining room but only to take away plates of melon and grapefruit, and coffee, and sections of that morning's *New York Times* which Dr. Savage left scattered about . . . not that they don't like Mrs. Vitale with her busy monologue and immense appetite but, yes, these precious days, they prefer to be alone.

These languorous September days, a lovesick fragrance to the air.

Even as the Savage household is in a perpetual state of expectation—ah, there: the telephone *again*.

Alan and Iris drift out into the sun porch, this place of white wicker, potted ferns, plump chintz cushions; Iris cuts them both slices of melon and pries apart segments of grapefruit; Alan spreads the *New York Times* out on a table, sighs, mutters, it's Vietnam again, more Vietnam in the headlines, what *is* Vietnam?

A year ago, wasn't it, the prediction was made by President Kennedy that we'd be out of Vietnam within a year, yet it looks as if things are steadily worsening: since the torpedo attack on U.S. destroyers in the Gulf of Tonkin in early August and the Congressional resolution authorizing President Johnson to take all necessary measures "to maintain peace in the free world," it seems that more American troops are continually being ordered in, more military advisers: Where is it going to end, Alan Savage says, another Korea? Another war?

Iris says, "Isn't it a war already?"

396

She's frowning, leaning on Alan's shoulder, quickly skimming the front page, eating grapefruit with her fingers.

Featured on the page is a photograph of a black infantryman, First Battalion, Fourteenth Infantry, Second Brigade, Third Infantry Division, Camp Warrior, Pleiku Province, in eerie juxtaposition with a skull just behind him, hoisted on a tent pole.

Iris says stubbornly, "If people are dying, it's a war," and Alan says, unconsciously echoing a remark Dr. Savage made the other evening at dinner, "If the madmen don't start dropping nuclear bombs on one another it isn't somehow a *real* war. Not in 1964."

Iris turns away.

"News" makes her nervous; it tells us how powerless we are, she has said, shows us how we're only tiny figures in an immense constellation.

Especially war news. Especially news of Vietnam.

Mrs. Savage pokes her head through the doorway of the sun porch, flashes them her lovely loving smile. Though in her own words run off her feet these days, Mrs. Savage has never looked healthier, in better spirits. "There you are, you two! I was beginning to wonder."

Alan lets the newspaper fall, pushes it aside, says teasingly, "Did you think we'd eloped, Mother?"

Mrs. Savage says, "Oh, it's too late for that!"

In another room, the telephone begins ringing.

Where *is* Dr. Savage? Has he driven over to the university?

On Iris's plate two slender crescent moons of honeydew melon remain, one for Alan, one for Iris. "Delicious," Alan says, licking his lips.

That morning, Iris woke long before dawn. Lay there in her canopied bed, on a mattress that sighed beneath her weight. Lay there listening as sparrows began to stir in the English ivy outside the window, small wings thrashing, sweet liquid cries.

Each cry a question? Lifting in a sort of question?

A lifetime of flinching at black skin and, yes, it's true, to a degree it's true, though when she smiles, and she smiles often, her smile is white-glistening and flawless, you'd never know.

A punch in the mouth, knuckles hard as rock.

A kick between the legs. No, kicks.

White cunt. White pussy. Uhhhh-huhhhhh.

You think we don't know you, cunt? We know you.

The chipped tooth, discreetly capped, cosmetic dentistry and no expense spared by the Savages, is indistinguishable from Iris Courtney's other front teeth. Though sometimes, believing herself unwatched, she touches it, pries a little at it. Just to see.

"Delicious," says Alan. "I guess I *am* hungry."

In another room Mrs. Savage is laughing delightedly over the telephone, it must be a relative or a dear friend, there are so many. A constellation, complete in itself. Each figure named and cherished and it *is* wisest to forgive, it's the only Christian strategy, and forget too if you can.

After lunch Mrs. Vitale returns to her sewing, the doorbell rings and it's the United Parcel Service man for the second time that day: an armload of wedding presents hidden inside plain brown wrapping paper.

Where's Iris? Two of Mrs. Savage's friends have dropped by for a brief visit, not more than five minutes, Gwendolyn, they insist, we know how busy you are. But have some coffee at least, says Mrs. Savage, and here's Alan to shake hands, blushing and boyish and yes they've seen this young man grow up, amazing! Isn't it always amazing! The fact of time, time passing, time *passed* and never to be *retrieved* . . . but you do get used to it.

Do you?

Don't you?

Don't you . . . what?

Get used to it.

Used to . . . ?

Time passing.

Oh, no! Oh, yes, I suppose.

Where *is* Dr. Savage, has he driven over to the university?

Today is a day off, he'd promised to stay home and give me a hand but you know Byron, any disruption in his schedule frightens him, and he can't stay away from that office of his, you know Byron!

Where's Iris? Alan is playing a record of the beautiful Schumann song that Matilde Ferri the soprano (a friend of the Savages for twenty-odd years) will sing at their wedding; Iris has heard the song already more than once and agrees it's ideal for the occasion but where *is* she? upstairs in her room? the hi-fi volume turned up and everyone listening attentively to an English soprano singing Schumann's "Help Me My Sisters": *Help me, my sisters . . . help me to prepare for my wedding day . . .* A scratchy recording, made in 1952, but the singer's voice is crystalline, so beautiful Mrs. Savage sits weakly on a chair arm, a gesture unlike her, touches her fingertips to her eyes, saying, "I only hope, Alan, that Matilde can sing half so well on Saturday."

Alan too is brushing his eyes. But he looks up smiling, says teasingly, "Surely Matilde can do a little better by us than *half.*"

When Iris returned to Hammond in May, primarily to visit Leslie Courtney, she was astonished by two things: the first, that her uncle had only the previous week moved both his studio and his living quarters to another downtown location, a nicer neighborhood, on a side street called Chippewa, where COURTNEY'S PHOTOGRAPHY STUDIO is one of a row of small shops, antiques, upholstery, secondhand books, but the major difference is that now, at long last, Leslie is facing the sunny side of the street! After twenty years in the shade.

As he told Iris excitedly, it wasn't just that 591 North Main Street was a shoddy building in a depressed neighborhood, nor even that he'd settled into a sort of permanent rut there, but, one January day, no customers and he'd been staring out the front window observing sunshine on facing buildings bright as Vermeer yellow, and somehow suddenly the words of one of Persia's songs came to him in a sort of waking dream: that bouncy jivey tune "Sunny Side of the Street" which Persia used to sing in one of her characteristically cheery moods. "It seemed to me almost as if I were hearing the song, hearing her voice," Leslie said, "those silly but somehow endearing and inspiring words. You know: *Life can be so sweet . . . on the sunny side of the street!* It was as if your mother had nudged me, Iris, the way she'd sometimes do, a nudge or a pinch, to wake me up—and I did wake up, and thought, Why not? Why not move to the sunny side of the street? What have I to lose? Next year I'll be fifty years old."

So Leslie arranged to borrow money from friends (new friends, Iris gathered: he'd begun teaching photography courses at the local YMCA, and the director and his wife have become quite fond of him, were happy to lend him money), scouted about for a new location in the downtown area, a small studio with living quarters close by, his primary requirement being that the shop face the southeast, thus the morning sun, so precious in winter mornings in upstate New York. "And here it is, 43 West Chippewa," he said, "and here I intend to stay. What do you think of my new place, Iris?"

Iris was thinking that the new shop, apart from the neighborhood, and the building, which was newer and cleaner than the old, very much resembled the old; Leslie seemed to have moved everything intact, including the framed photographs on the walls and the jumble of frames and cartons and paraphernalia at the rear. All his furnishings were the same, and in the same general arrangement. And there was Houdini the midnight-black cat, plumper and more impetuous than Iris recalled, but the same creature still: clambering about on her lap, regarding her with tawny-golden eyes and purring loudly. She said, moved, "It's lovely, Uncle Leslie! It's . . . perfect."

"It *is* perfect," Leslie said, his eyeglasses winking with pleasure. "I sleep better here. I work more efficiently. More customers come in. I'll never be wealthy but at least I'm not in debt . . . I don't want to sound superstitious or mystical, but it truly does seem that Persia had everything to do with it. Her influence, just at that crucial moment! God knows, living as I was, I might have wound up lonely and mad, or even dead, instead of, as I feel now, supremely alive." He was smiling, not at Iris but toward a corner of the room, no doubt a corner of the room in which Persia's (and Iris's) photographs were hanging on the wall. Though his hair was graying to the point nearly of iridescence, and thinner than Iris recalled, he

400

looked scarcely older than he had a decade ago. Iris perceived that her uncle, with his angular boyish face, his eager expression, his sweet smile, was one of those persons middle-aged in youth and, in middle age, youthful; for an enchanted number of years, while their contemporaries age relentlessly, they seem hardly to age at all.

When Persia died, that part of him died too, Iris thought. So he's untouched now, in his soul. He can't be further harmed.

During her three-day visit Iris learned that the photography course at the YMCA wasn't the only new thing in her uncle's life: he was also doing occasional freelance work for the Hammond *Chronicle* as their "arts feature" man; he was shortly to begin a new photography project on the "postwar industrial landscape" of western New York State; he had acquired a small circle of friends who shared cultural interests; and there was even the possibility of an exhibit of his work being held next winter in the George Eastman House in Rochester. "But of course I don't really expect anything to come of it," Leslie said, embarrassed. "I am, after all, the quintessential amateur."

"But that's wonderful, Uncle Leslie!" Iris said. She did not know, however, if she was excited or, rather, stunned by the possibility that the man so long dismissed as an eccentric by everyone who knew him, an affable lifelong failure, might yet be revealed as exceptional after all. This, not even Persia could have anticipated. . . .

The second surprise of the visit was even more unexpected.

Leslie told her that, in early April, a former high school classmate of Iris's, a young black man, now a Private First Class in the United States Army, came to the studio to have his photograph taken, and that he'd left a wallet-sized print for her.

For a long moment Iris could not speak.

"For me?" she asked faintly.

And then, quickly, "Was his name Jinx? Jinx Fairchild?"

"Fairchild, yes," Leslie said, rummaging through a drawer, "but I seem to remember another name." Leslie searched through a much-worn accordion file, frowning, saying, "He wanted, he said, to give his mother a formal picture of himself as a birthday present;

401

he was being shipped to Vietnam . . . a soft-spoken young man, *very* polite . . . a little guarded, I suppose. Were you good friends? I don't remember your ever having mentioned . . . but of course I wouldn't know. Ah, here it is! Why did I file it under I? For Iris, I suppose."

Iris stared at the envelope for a moment before opening it. Her heart was pounding painfully and the tips of her fingers had gone icy. *Iris C.*, he'd written on the envelope in a large looping hand; she was thinking she'd never seen Jinx Fairchild's handwriting and here, and now, with so strange an intimacy, her own name, *Iris C.*, in that hand.

Iris opened the envelope, drew out the wallet-sized print, stared, stared for a long moment in absolute silence, while her uncle chattered casually: "When he came back to pick up the prints he asked if I was related to you, said he was a friend of yours from high school, he was much more relaxed and friendly now that the photographing was over so we got to talking, he said he'd heard you were in college at Syracuse, asked after you, and I told him all your good news, I didn't want to sound boastful, but . . . your high grades, and graduating summa cum laude, and your engagement to a young art historian . . . and he seemed interested though he didn't ask anything more; before he left he said, 'Will you give her one of these next time you see her, Mr. Courtney?' and left that print . . . struck me as an unusually intelligent young man and I thought what a pity it is, a damned pity, his being a soldier in this war no one seems to be able to make sense of." He paused, watching Iris. "You're not upset, Iris, are you? Did you know him well?"

The young black man in the photograph, formally, even a bit stiffly posed, in his dress uniform, hands clasped against his knees, hat smartly set on his head, was certainly Jinx Fairchild: the shock of seeing him after so long, of seeming empowered to look, in an instant, into his eyes, ran through Iris and left her weak . . . weakened. Her eyes began to sting with tears she wiped impatiently away.

Jinx Fairchild sat ramrod straight, gazing calmly, perhaps ironically into the camera, his jaws forcibly set, his eyes large, fully open, the whites distinctly white. Though the photograph was for his mother he was not smiling. The sides of his head had been shaved warrior-style with brutal efficiency, his skin looked very dark, his lips pursed, swollen—but it was his posture, on the basketball court so much a matter of fluidity, sloping shoulders, elastic spine, sly head cocked to one side, that seemed most unnatural: unlike Jinx Fairchild.

Iris thought, All that's missing is his rifle.

On the reverse of the print Jinx had written in that large looping lazy-seeming hand, *Honey—Think I'll "pass"?*

Iris read, reread these words; she was standing with both hands pressed against a glass-topped counter, leaning forward, eyelids fluttering . . . it wasn't tears she beat back but a sensation of starkest horror, a certitude beyond grief. She was aware of her uncle's voice, his words, the movement of his mouth, aware too of Houdini the midnight-black cat nudging and rubbing with persistent affection against her legs, purring loudly, yet she heard nothing, comprehended nothing, simply stood there in a place not known to her on a warm May afternoon leaning her weight on a glass-topped counter, a weight heavy against the palms of her sweating hands.

Leslie touched her shoulder, asked gently, "*Are* you upset, Iris? Is he a close friend?"

Iris said, "I loved him."

And burst into uncontrollable tears.

Memory is a transcendental function. But it attaches itself only to bodies.

That long headache-racked afternoon of walking through the lower streets of Hammond, to the foot of Pitt Street—where, to Iris's surprise, a Sunoco gas station had been built on the vacant lot where Little Red Garlock died—and she'd walked too past the old houses, Java Street where the duplex her parents had once rented looked so narrow, so cheaply "improved" in its beige aluminum siding, and the mustard-yellow stucco apartment house at 372 Holland as shabby and rain-streaked as ever, where she made her way bold and undetected through the hallway to the rear entrance, let herself out into the weedy dizzily familiar yard to contemplate in

403

harsh sunshine that outdoor stairway that had cast her room, "her" room there beyond the meager half-window, into shade: the stairway unchanged these many years though surely it had been painted and its sagging steps repaired, and she'd thought angrily, Why are you here, what is this place to you? It isn't your home any longer.

She's here, now. In the Savages' house.

Slipping the photograph of Jinx Fairchild back into the envelope with *Iris C.* written on it, replacing the envelope neatly in her drawer . . . and her journal, that place of secrets her husband will never share . . . her journal in which she has written just now, *Memory attaches itself to bodies. I must learn to forget.*

In fact Iris rarely writes in the old battered journal any longer, her journal that's nearly filled in any case, only a few dog-eared pages remaining; then perhaps (it's the merest glimmer of an urging, like a dream incompletely recalled) she'll throw it all away. *I must learn to forget, I am learning to forget. I live in the present tense and have never been so happy.*

Alan Savage once kept a diary too, he'd told her, since the age of nineteen, a diary primarily of living abroad, "American Non-American" he'd rather pretentiously called it, but this diary he'd thrown away without so much as rereading when, last summer, he decided to come back home.

Alan said, You have to grow up sometime.

Iris was wakened early that morning, in this bed unfamiliar to her, in a body she knows is hers. *White cunt. Bitch. We know you.* It was the birds fluttering and thrashing in the English ivy outside the window—damned plague of sparrows, Dr. Savage called them—and in the near distance raucous crows, quite a flock of crows, settling only briefly in the wooded area to the rear of the house, always at dawn, then moving on. What a noise! For all its rowdiness and jeering, a happy sort of noise!

Iris perceives that life is a matter of waking in successive beds, each bed erasing the bed that precedes.

"This is the last, the absolutely final fitting," Mrs. Savage says.

"And then I have some telephone calls to make, and then we can leave for the church, I hope I have time to talk with you."

She links her arm through Iris's, says in a whisper, "Isn't Mrs. Vitale cross with me! But it's worth it, I believe, to insist upon doing things right. And her work is really lovely, lovely. . . ."

Iris says, "Oh, yes."

". . . worth every penny. Absolutely."

"Oh, yes."

In the sun-filled room with the organdy curtains Mrs. Vitale has been using Iris Courtney glances shyly, or is it fearfully, at her mirrored reflection; since last year her hair has so rapidly grayed, glinting with silver like hoarfrost, it's as if her very life is speeding before her. But the chipped tooth is perfectly disguised, the bruised eyes have long since healed, the blood-encrusted nostrils. *I never saw your faces, I never heard your names.* "Lift your arms, dear," Mrs. Vitale murmurs, "and just stand still." For this final fitting Iris has changed her underclothes another time: white strapless brassiere, long white taffeta slip with a lace overskirt, seamless nylon stockings. And she's wearing the shoes she will wear on Saturday, white satin pumps decorated with tiny pearl-like beads.

As Iris stands obediently still Mrs. Vitale and Mrs. Savage deftly lower the dress over her head . . . the skirt, the torso . . . a good snug fit in the shoulders and arms, the exquisite pleated bodice now snug too as the dress is buttoned up, not tight but comfortably snug, a perfect fit for Iris's small high breasts. And the waist, and the hips, and the long skirt that must be arranged as if sculpted . . . perfect. Mrs. Savage arranges too the bridal veil, the subtly yellowed Brussels lace, how lovely, how angelic, the women murmur, and Iris is smiling, seeing only her bride's costume in the mirror, silken luminous white, dazzling white; her heart lifts with a kind of anxious pleasure. It's of both older women she asks her question: "*Do* you think I'll look the part?"

405

Joyce Carol Oates
American Appetites £5.99

Affluent American suburbia – a world in which Ian and Glynnis
McCullough are both admired and entirely at home; regarded, after twenty-
six years of marriage, as the embodiment of the American Dream. But,
beneath the surface, there are cracks in the marriage. And it takes only one
moment of irrevocable violence to shatter their idyllic community and turn
the Dream into a nightmare.

'Written with enormous force and freedom . . . a wonderful book about
marriage and friendship, love and loyalty, and how a single act of madness
can change an essentially happy life into tragedy' THE TIMES

'*American Appetites* unreels with as much relentless intelligence and
narrative energy as any thriller . . . she continues to be one of America's
best working novelists' THE INDEPENDENT

'Outstanding . . . Oates manages to be at once sensational and intellectual:
she is brilliant at detecting the fear of death behind luxurious domesticity'
EVENING STANDARD

'This is Oates at her best . . . an intellectual exploration of free will,
predestination and philosophy in the face of grief' TIME OUT

'Her writing has a mesmerising clarity and she uses it to brilliant effect'
THE DAILY TELEGRAPH

All Pan books are available at your local bookshop or newsagent, or can be ordered direct from the publisher. Indicate the number of copies required and fill in the form below.

Send to: Pan C. S. Dept
            Macmillan Distribution Ltd
            Houndmills Basingstoke RG21 2XS
or phone: 0256 29242, quoting title, author and Credit Card number.

Please enclose a remittance* to the value of the cover price plus: £1.00 for the first book plus 50p per copy for each additional book ordered.

*Payment may be made in sterling by UK personal cheque, postal order, sterling draft or international money order, made payable to Pan Books Ltd.

Alternatively by Barclaycard/Access/Amex/Diners

Card No. ⬚⬚⬚⬚⬚⬚⬚⬚⬚⬚⬚⬚⬚⬚⬚⬚⬚⬚⬚

Expiry Date ⬚⬚⬚⬚⬚⬚

Signature:

Applicable only in the UK and BFPO addresses

While every effort is made to keep prices low, it is sometimes necessary to increase prices at short notice. Pan Books reserve the right to show on covers and charge new retail prices which may differ from those advertised in the text or elsewhere.

NAME AND ADDRESS IN BLOCK LETTERS PLEASE:

....

Name_____

Address_____

_____

_____

_____

6/92